# The Deer Stone

## Rebecca Holbrook

Dancing Heron Publishing

This is a work of fiction. Names, characters, and places are figments of the author's imagination. Some incidents portrayed in this production are inspired by family stories, but are fictional.

Book Cover by Emma Mitchell, Sierra Gaelan and Gary Davies

Edited by Gary Nelson

Printed in the United States

Dancing Heron Publishing  Hoodsport, Washington

dancingheronpub@gmail.com

ISBN  979-8-218-90649-8

# Acknowledgements

I am so grateful to all who have contributed to this second book. A special thanks to my mentor, Ilana Lehman from Write On of Lacey, who has taught and encouraged me from the beginning of my writing journey. Thanks also to Strong Paulson, who passed recently. Your guidance is deeply missed. As always, I owe so much to my editor and partner in this life, Gary Nelson. You help make these books the best they can be. Love to my step-daughter Emma Mitchell and fellow author Sierra Gaelan for the front cover photo and your many efforts in behalf of this book. Gary Davies is the graphics wizard who formatted the cover designs. I'm grateful to be able to share these stories with my family. These are their legacies too. To my poetry group, the Laurels, to all my beta readers and fans, you are the inspiration that keeps me writing.

# Also by
# Rebecca Holbrook

For Mark

Kate Lee~Frank Lee
I
Nate Silar~Omie Lee     Emmie Lee~Caleb Decker
I                              I
Ada Kate Silar~James Dillon     Bitsy Decker
I
Tess  Jacob  Cyrus  Olivia  Naomi     Danny Decker

Bartie Silar~Shadrack Cane     Aaron Decker
I
Lilly

Frank Thomas Silar~Jewel O'Dell

Ezra Silar~Polly Miller

Georgia Rose Silar

Grace Silar

# At The Well

Kate held Omie close a moment, and said, "Go on outside and find some peaceful place to sit in the sun. Just empty your mind and listen. Sometimes that's when you'll hear His voice tellin' you what to do."

Omie breathed deeply, trying to clear her mind. It did no good. Standing, she turned and slid back the well's cover, resting it on the bench. Coolness bathed her face, and the smell of damp moss brought up memories of the years this was their only source of water. She'd been a young girl then, unaware of the troubles ahead. The heartbreaks love brought with it.

In the still surface, she saw only reflections. Trees. Clouds framing her face with its sorrowful expression. *Why can't you show me something to ease my soul?*

The deer stone felt warm in her hand in contrast to the coolness rising from the well. She closed her eyes and tried to imagine its comfort flowing into her aching heart.

A twig snapped behind her. "Mamma."

# Chapter 1
## 1921

The first rays of morning reached across the Georgia fields, unfurling opalescent blooms of morning glories as far as the eye could see. Vines cascaded over fences, dressing posts like maypoles, resisting only the hard-packed clay road as a canvas.

Omie Silar was on her way to town early, to purchase more seed. Additional supplies were needed to feed the hungry workers a noon-day meal, as well. She thought how the beauty and bareness of the fields went hand in hand. What had once been productive farms now fell prey to whatever nature intended. Virginia creeper vine and the new intruder, kudzu, vied for possession of barns, outbuildings, even wagons and farm implements. The war and rapid spread of Spanish Influenza had left no one to tend these lands. Even before the war, boll weevils had ravaged the cotton, wasting the plants, ruthless as wildfire.

In 1918, Omie and her friend Phoebee had been fortunate to discover the ease and profit of growing peanuts in place of cotton. Phoebee's daddy raised peanuts back in Stone Mountain, Georgia, and her experience had saved the Silar's farm. Their success resulted in requests to teach other local women. Women who'd been left alone, as their men went off to the other side of the world. Many of their family members, who would have helped in the fields, now slept beneath the clay.

Mrs. O'Dell, the storekeeper in town, had relayed the message: "These women will surely lose their farms if somethin' isn't done for them. The bank is trying to go easy on mortgages, but they have their limits. I don't know who would buy these farms anyhow!"

Thus, a cooperative of women began to help each other plant, weed and harvest their peanut crops. The children worked, as well. Along with vegetable gardens, folks at least had food, if little else. After several years passed, most were able to buy livestock again.

Today, the women were gathered at the Silar's farm.

Omie's husband Nate had been one of the fortunate men to return from the war. He stayed out of the women's way, taking care of the tobacco and corn with the help of their two boys, Frank Thomas and Ezra. However, coming home to a farm that had fared just fine without him apparently stuck in his craw a bit.

Returning shortly after mid-morning, Omie took in the scene of women working the rows in colorful dresses made from flour-sack prints. The bigger children followed at their heels, carrying water to douse the seeds. Little ones were in the care of one of the older girls, making toys from corn shucks. Babies new to the world nestled in slings at their mamma's bosoms. Those babies old enough to sit were propped up and given a feather to pass back and forth between their honey-daubed hands, a common child-minding trick.

Omie pulled the wagon into the yard. "Mamma, would you find the boys and ask them to come unload the wagon?"

Kate waved her response, then went out back to find Frank Thomas and Ezra. She returned to stand beside her daughter, looking out toward the fields. "A much purtier sight than men in dirty overalls, wouldn't you say? Like a field of flowers."

Omie laughed and kissed her mamma's soft, wrinkled cheek. She thought of the cropless fields full of morning glories she'd seen on the way to town.

"I better get this flour to Ada Kate or we won't have any biscuits to *feed* those flowers later."

Omie smiled at the sight of her oldest daughter, Ada Kate, standing at the cookstove in her mamma's apron.

"Everything is ready but the biscuits. Won't be but a minute."

"Thank you, darlin' girl. I 'preciate you."

The boys had set up planks on sawhorses for tables, and Kate covered them with oilcloth. Ada walked out of the hot kitchen and rang the big iron bell on the porch when dinner was ready. Workers stood and stretched, moaning gratefully. As the group approached the pump to wash, some took a moment to remove their hats and soak the head scarves they wore beneath them. Cold water running down hot, grimy necks was a delicious relief.

"Mmmm! Fried chicken!" one little boy cried out. His mamma could barely get his hands washed before he ran to get in line.

Kate, and her namesake, Ada Kate, had fried the chicken the day before and set it in the well house to keep cool for this long, hot day. With the help of their neighbor Phoebee's daughter, Polly, Ada had managed to prepare potato salad from small potatoes missed in last year's harvest. She'd picked the first early peas and opened jars of pickled onions. Biscuits were served with freshly made butter, Phoebee's honey, and various jams the women brought. Cool jugs of tea, flavored with rose hips and mint, sweated on a side table.

Omie walked back outside and put an arm around her mamma. "Ada has learned so much from helping you in the kitchen."

Kate smiled. "That girl is a wonder. Her sister, now, *that one* could scorch water."

They laughed as Bartie brought out the last of the cornbread, asking, "What's so dang funny?"

"Nothin', honey!" Omie gave her daughter a playful swat on the backside and left to wash up.

"What?" Bartie asked her grandmamma, but Kate just smiled.

Omie looked around for Nate, wanting to call him to dinner. He wasn't in the tobacco field so she headed for the barn. No sign of him there either.

Bartie met her mamma outside the house and said, "He's already eaten, Mamma. I carried him out a plate a while ago and he left as soon as he was done. Said there was some business to attend to."

"What kind of business?"

"I don't know. Tell the truth, I think he doesn't much like being in the company of all these women. I think Daddy feels like we don't need him anymore."

"Is that so? He knows these women come to help at planting time and we go help them. Been doing this for years now. Don't mean he doesn't have important work of his own to do."

"Yeah, but y'all grow the biggest crop. Make the most money. I reckon he has his pride."

"His *pride.*" Omie shook her head. "There's much you don't know, Bartie, so don't be judging me about your daddy. He's got no business telling his troubles to his eleven-year-old daughter anyway. He needs to talk to me."

She walked away with an angry swish of her skirts.

"I'm nearly twelve," Bartie mumbled under her breath.

When her mamma had gone inside the house, Bartie skipped down the path toward the river.

"Hey Daddy, how you doin'?"

"I'm fine as frog's hair, darlin'. What say we go see if we can catch Big Jack?"

He handed her two fishing poles to carry while he dug up a can's worth of worms. They headed for their favorite spot.

"You sure there's a fish named Big Jack? You're not just funnin' me, are ya?"

"Naw, I saw him myself once, years ago. Mouth as big as my head! Prob'ly weighs as much as me by now, too. Why I brung the log hook. They's not a line that can hold him if he bites. We'll have to grab him with it quick to get him on the bank!"

Bartie gave him a sideways look and they both grinned.

"Mamma, Bartie's gone again!" Ada Kate had come out to the field after dishes were done.

Omie put her hands on her hips and looked around.

"I suspect she's with her daddy. They'll both come back with their tails tucked soon enough. I'll talk to her then."

"It ain't fair," Ada Kate muttered, bending to cover peanuts as her mamma dropped them in rows.

"*Isn't* fair," Omie corrected. "Don't let Miss Sarah catch you saying 'ain't." Sarah was the schoolteacher who rented a room from Phoebee.

"Ada, I know it's not right that you shoulder much of her share of work. I intend to see to that."

Ada Kate cast a doubtful look toward her mamma but said nothing else.

Shortly before supper, Nate and Bartie walked up from the river road, grins splitting their faces. Each held a string of fish as long as their arms.

Omie stepped outside and called, "You catch 'em, you clean 'em."

The pair carried their catch to a table out back under the oak tree, laughing like fools. Ada stood on the back porch, glowering. Omie came to her side and said, "Ada Kate, take them a couple of buckets of water. We'll have fried fish this evenin'!"

"But Mamma, ain't—aren't you gonna say anything to her for shirking her work?"

"I was working!" Bartie cried out, showing off a big catfish. "Groceries is groceries."

"Get your own water." Ada jutted her chin out and went inside.

Omie watched the easy camaraderie between her husband and daughter as they nailed catfish to the tree and skinned them.

*I know girls need their daddies so they don't go lookin' for somebody to take his place. I just hope she has the sense not to marry a man that fills the same ragged shoes.*


Even Ada had to grudgingly admit that the fried catfish and hushpuppies had been delicious. When the dishes were done and children readied for bed, Omie stepped out onto the porch. The last of a red sun was sliding behind the trees.

Nate sat in a rocker listening to the cicadas when he heard the screen door open. Omie put a cup of coffee on the railing beside him and sat in the other rocker. He picked up his coffee with a nod of thanks.

"You know you're creating hard feelings between the girls, letting Bartie get out of her chores like that." Omie took a sip from her cup.

"I cain't help it if she prefers my company," he responded. "Seems to me she put food on the table as much as anybody."

"Oh Nate, that's not the point. The other children do what needs to be done here. You don't see them slipping off to go fishing. Which is not, I might add, work." Omie turned to him and smiled.

Nate grinned in spite of himself.

"Besides," Omie continued, "I think they feel left out. You do favor that girl."

"I s'pose I do. She understands her daddy. She even likes me."

Omie gave him a knowing look. "Be careful what you tell her, Nate. She doesn't need to be privy to our troubles."

"We have troubles, Omie?" He set down his cup without looking at her, and stepped off the porch into the darkness.

*Dammit! That war took a part of him that I can't reach anymore. I don't claim to understand what he went through, but what can I do?*

Omie stood, stretched her aching back, gathered their coffee cups and glared out at the night. She walked into the kitchen, mumbling to herself. "Prickly as nettles with me, more and more lately."

Kate turned from the sink, taking in Omie's expression. "What's the matter, hon?"

"Nate." Omie set the cups in the wash pan. "Got a burr up his butt 'cause he's not runnin' the farm any more. Well, I'll not give up what Phoebee and I have built here just to soothe his pride. I might've forgiven him, but I won't forget the bind he put us in before he left."


Nate watched Omie through the window from the corner of the barn where he leaned, having a cigarette. He continued to wrestle with bad dreams. Not as often as when he'd just returned from France, but their intensity had not lessened. Omie learned not to try and stop his thrashing after an elbow caught her in the ribs.

The times when he was plagued several nights in a row by them, Nate would disappear for a couple of days and return with whiskey on his breath. He'd sleep in the barn until he felt whole enough to join the family at the dinner table. Bartie was often the first to encounter him on his return. She'd wait until she saw the smoke from his morning cigarette before going to the barn.

This morning, he was slow to stir.

"Does your head hurt really bad, Daddy?"

Nate looked up with bleary eyes. "Oh, I been worse. Come sit by me, Bart. Tell me something good."

She thought a moment and reported, "I got good marks in school this year. And not because Sarah, I mean Miss Gadsden, is my teacher neither."

"Well, that sounds fine, just fine. I'm proud of ya! Now, you think you could do your old man a favor and make me some of that willow bark tea without your mamma knowin'?"

"Why, 'course I can. When did you eat last? I could bring you a plate of something."

"Sure, sure, I'd appreciate that too. But the tea first, if you don't mind?"

Bartie planted a kiss on his scruffy cheek and went to her mamma's store of herbs in the room off the back porch. She looked carefully to see that no one was watching and slipped in the door, trying not to let the hinges squeak. Herbs hung from the rafters to dry, and on shelves, jars of every kind were filled with various potions. She found the willow bark she needed, quickly ground it in a wooden bowl with a pestle, and carried it toward the kitchen. Through the screen, the kitchen appeared empty, so she went inside and put the kettle on. In the warming oven, a few biscuits remained from breakfast, along with some salt pork. Bartie stuffed the meat inside the biscuits and the biscuits into her pocket. As she was pouring water over the tea to steep, her mamma came in the front door.

Omie peered into the mug and said, "You in pain, daughter?"

It didn't really seem like a question though, as her mamma turned away before Bartie could answer. Instead, Omie went out to the porch and brought back a handful of other herbs that she tossed into the tea. With a meaningful look at the barn, Omie turned around and walked out again.

Bartie brought her daddy a pail of fresh water and a bar of soap as well. After he'd had his tea and biscuits, he went out back to clean up. When he returned, she asked, "Better?"

"Whew, I'll say! I feel a whole lot more like I do now than I did a while ago!"

"Oh Daddy, that makes no sense a'tall!"

Nate laughed and hugged her close.


Omie's admonition seemed to have taken, because the children began to go on adventures with their daddy, sometimes singly, sometimes in groups. Nate enjoyed teaching them about the land the way he had with the Higgins boys, who had worked with him on the farm years ago. He figured Omie and Kate could show them all they ever needed to know of plants, so they went hunting for arrowheads instead or learned to call in turkeys.

"If y'all make sounds like owls, you'll lure turkeys in. They don't like sharin' their trees with owls. Not one bit."

He showed them how to snare rabbits and gig frogs. Only Bartie and the boys could stomach this task, but they all loved to eat the legs. They caught snapping turtles by waving a stick in the creature's face until it latched on tight.

"A turtle won't let go until it hears thunder, so keep your fingers clear! Hit'll bite 'em clean off."

Turtle soup became a favorite dish—seasoned with danger as it was.

One Sunday after church, Nate led the children down the river road, cane poles and buckets in their hands. Ada Kate agreed to come on this fishing trip 'to make sure the little ones don't drown', but Nate could tell she was excited as well. He and Bartie made a pact not to ever show anyone their special fishin' hole beneath the big willow, so he took them further downriver.

Bartie and her brothers went to find crickets and grasshoppers for bait. Ada Kate said she and Georgia Rose, their littlest sister, would dig worms. Finally, all had a line in the water.

Frank Thomas was the first to land a fish of eating size, a largemouth bass.

"Whoohoo, looky here!"

Georgia squealed and danced around on the bank. Bartie laughed so hard at her sister's antics that she nearly dropped her pole.

Next, Polly and Ezra found a spot favored by crappie, and filled a stringer full.

"Now, that's some good eatin' right there!" Nate exclaimed.

The children made their way home, bare feet dragging and satisfied grins on their dirty faces. All had caught at least a few fish apiece, and Bartie shared in their delight, knowing she and her daddy kept the best spot for themselves.

Omie and Kate had the batter ready and the oil heating up as the passel of fisher-folk stepped onto the back porch with their prizes.

"Y'all clean those quick. We're hungry!"

Omie smiled at Nate thankfully. He did a little jig as he left the porch, and whistling while he worked, showed the children how to clean their bounty.

Phoebee and Sarah had made coleslaw, potato salad and a honey cake. A make-shift table was set up in the yard for the food, and quilts spread about under the trees for the picnic. Georgia Rose, the youngest of Omie's brood, wound between the legs of the adults.

"You're just like a happy puppy!" Kate exclaimed, watching her family enjoy each other in a way they had not for a long time. *This is a good day.* She could see the lines that connected them, wavering streams of light which reached back to her.

The *Sight* came to Kate less and less these days. It had been some time since she gazed into a teacup to divine the future for another. She read the auguries of nature as they presented themselves to her, but did not look for them. Along with her old friend Aunt Julia, Kate still delivered babies for local women, but it was clear that they both were slowing down.

*Can you still see us, husband? I reckon it won't be so long until we're looking down from heaven together.*

The loss of her beloved Frank was the only regret in this life. Otherwise, she felt fulfilled with her family and healing work. Now it seemed change was an ever-present, touchable thing. The modern world was calling young people to leave home as fast as those automobiles could carry them. Kate understood that her era was ending as the grandchildren grew into their own time. This was the nature of life.


In the evening after dishes were washed, Omie walked out on the back porch with the dish pan and threw the water into the yard. Looking up, she saw the moon rising in the direction of Thistle Town. Its face was covered with a clay-colored caul.

"Mamma!"

Kate hurried outside at the tone of her daughter's voice. Both women stood still for a moment in silence.

"It's not Aunt Julia, I don't feel any trouble around her spirit."

"Me neither," Omie replied.

"Somethin' though."

"Yes, ma'am. Somethin'."

# Chapter 2

Aunt Julia watched from the porch as her great-grandson Willie played with a wooden wagon a neighbor had whittled for him. His small hands pulled the toy through sand beside the lane, and he talked to himself the way small children do who are used to solitude. His grandmamma's thoughts went to the time when Willie's mamma, Missy, was carried in a similar wagon to the old cemetery on the Silar's land, her life sacrificed for his. The love between this young white girl and Aunt Julia's grandson had been the kind forbidden in this world, punishable by death for his black skin. Maybe a worse fate would have waited for a poor white girl with a family of lowlifes like hers, had she lived. They were brutal men. They would have lynched Isaiah. The few whites who did not participate in such vile acts would still likely turn their heads away, afraid of incurring the anger of Night Riders. Sheriff Turner was not of that sort, but he was only one man against many.

"Gramma, watch this!" Willie tied a string from the wagon to his yellow dog's tail. "Go, Ol' Joe." The dog patiently dragged the toy down the lane as his boy yelled, "Gee! Haw!"

*That's his daddy's laugh, for sure.*

The old woman remembered Isaiah's face as he left Thistle Town and all he knew, riding in the back of another wagon taking him to the train station. It broke her heart, but they both knew there was no other choice.

*Best no one knows this sweet child survived.*

She imagined the undertaker, Mr. Obermeyer, opening the bloody bundle of rags Aunt Julia pretended was the baby, before tucking it in the pine box beside the child's mamma. But Mr. Obermeyer, too, had suffered curses and humiliation at the hands of people like Missy's father and brothers, for the simple fact of being a Jew. She figured he would keep her secret, if he knew. The old cemetery on Nate and Omie Silar's land probably held many secrets.

Aunt Julia hoped Isaiah's life in Pennsylvania with the Quaker folk was as good as hers had been. It seemed the best choice to send him there until he was in a position to have Willie brought to him. The education Isaiah could receive up north would ensure them both a better life. His parents would have agreed, if they had survived the fever that carried them both away when Isaiah was about Willie's age.

Closing her eyes in prayer, Aunt Julia turned her face up to the sun.

*Forgive me, Lord, for the sin of my lies. I know you understand the need. I'm grateful for the kindness of Kate Lee and Omie Silar.*

It spoke to the depths of Omie's friendship with Aunt Julia, that she allowed people to think the pale-skinned boy might be the result of her husband Nate's transgression with Minnie, Aunt Julia's neighbor. Minnie had agreed to the charade, taking the boy with her to town where they'd be seen, for a price. It was Aunt Julia's older granddaughter, Alberta, who loved and raised the child as part of her own family.

Aunt Julia looked up from watching Willie play as Alberta came walking along the lane to take him home for supper.

"Alberta, you seen Minnie today?"

"Now, why would I be lookin' out for Minnie?"

"Don't give me any sass. She was going to take the boy to town with her this morning. I didn't see her come home last night."

"Prob'ly out whorin' with one of her white men. I seen her take Willie with her to town sometimes, acting like that Mr. Mason was the boys' daddy, walking real close to him and his wife on the street. She's trouble, that one. I know his driver been bringin' Minnie money an' goods from the store. She better watch walkin' too close to that fire, though. His wife don't look like a stupid woman to me."

The day before, Mr. Mason's driver had brought a message to Minnie, telling her that his boss wanted to meet her that night behind the store.

Minnie smiled like a well-fed cat.

*He been missin' him some Minnie. Maybe he wants to git a little place for the boy and me where we won't be found out.*

She figured she could put up with the child in return for some easy living. Something she'd never known. Minnie would never admit to a fondness for Willie, but felt some possessiveness toward him.

She put on her finest dress, sewn from the satin and lace she'd bought with money intended for the child. Aunt Julia saw her slip out into the moon-cast shadows as night birds began to call.

In the alleyway behind the store, Minnie saw the driver waiting for her.

"He send you to take me someplace special?" She gave him a sultry smile.

"Oh, yes ma'am," he replied, helping Minnie up into the wagon.

As they pulled onto the dusty road leading out from town, a rising moon lit the feed sacks and other remnants from his day's labor. It gleamed off the freshly sharpened edge of a shovel blade.

Over the days that followed, Aunt Julia wondered at Minnie's absence. She'd waited to see if the wanton woman came back with her tail between her legs, but no sign or news of Minnie turned up. Her instincts told her

Minnie was gone for good. Aunt Julia approached Alberta, wondering what the best course of action might be for her great-grandson.

Alberta stood on her porch considering the question. "You know I love this boy, we all do. He's welcome to stay with me, but what are his chances here? Can Isaiah send for him? Seems like he'd have a better chance up north."

"Isaiah is still getting his schooling. I don't think he can manage both a child and an education. I'll ask Omie Silar if she's willing to still let folks think he belongs to Nate. Maybe they would take him in. He could be some help around the place and the other children would be company for him."

"You goin' let a white family raise him? What are you thinkin'? I won't see him bein' no dog to be kicked around. You know how them people is!"

"Now Alberta, I won't have you talking about Omie and Kate that way. You been around them, you know they're different. True Christian women who walk their talk. If Nate thinks that child is his, he'll treat him fairly. The women will see to it that he does. Willie can learn to make his way in the world there until he's older and Isaiah is ready to take him."

Grudgingly, Alberta agreed to drive her grandmother out to the Silar's farm.


Kate heard a wagon pull up and was surprised to see Aunt Julia's smiling face. Beside her sat Alberta, who was not smiling and would not look at Kate.

"Mornin' ladies. What a nice surprise! Come sit and have a cool drink."

Alberta stepped down and helped Aunt Julia to the ground. She took the older woman's elbow, meaning to guide her to the porch, but Aunt Julia pulled away.

"I'm all right, Alberta. The Lord's not ready to take me yet."

Kate smiled at the tenacity of her old friend. Alberta turned on her heel, muttering, and went back to the wagon, pulling it up near the water trough. She sat in the shade of a live oak with her back to the house.

"Stubborn. Proud and stubborn as the day is long." Aunt Julia chuckled.

"I can't imagine where she got that from," Kate commented, wrapping her arm around Aunt Julia's bird-like shoulders. "Have a seat, it's much cooler out here on the porch. Omie and I are canning tomatoes."

Omie came out and stooped to kiss the woman's weathered brown cheek.

"It's been ages! How's your family doing?"

"Oh, fair enough, hon. It was just too hot to walk here today." The older woman sighed. "Been a bunch of babies to deliver lately. I may have to train up one of the grandchildren to help me."

"Amen," Kate replied. "Omie has had to take on most of the birthings around here too. I make the poultices and such, send Ada out for plants. She's been a real help. Seems to have a talent for the healin' arts."

After catching up on the doings of their lives, Aunt Julia got to the reason for her visit.

"You remember the girl, Missy, we buried over yonder?" She motioned to the old cemetery down the hill. "Her baby, my great-grandson Willie, is five now."

"Has it truly been that long?" Kate marveled.

"It has." Aunt Julia nodded. "We've all taken part in raising him, pretending that she- devil Minnie was his mamma. Now, she's disappeared."

"What do you suppose happened to her?" Kate wondered.

"Don't know for sure. All the *Sight* shows me is darkness around her spirit."

"Good riddance," Omie muttered.

"Now, it's time to think about that child's future. Isaiah is not ready to take responsibility for the boy quite yet, though he wants to as soon as his schooling is done and he's found work up there. Alberta has a full house, and there is still the matter of the child's mixed blood. He can't go to the white school and he'll be made fun of at the colored school. Y'all know how children are."

Aunt Julia turned to Omie with a serious expression on her face. "Do you recall on the day of his mamma's burying, you said it would be tolerable if folks thought Nate might be his daddy?"

"And you'd like for us to take him in here, as if he was Nate's."

Aunt Julia looked into Omie's eyes, nodded, then waited patiently for what the young woman's answer might be.

Omie stood and walked to the railing. She was silent for a time, still looking toward the cemetery. A breeze moved through the trees down there, carrying a sense of longing to Omie. The vision of a small boy appeared before her. Pale, with dark, somber eyes.

Omie blinked the vision away, turning toward Aunt Julia with a gentle smile on her face. "Of course. We're always here for you and your family. I mean that. When would you like him to come?"

Aunt Julia looked up at the sky with teary eyes. "Soon. Thank you, ladies. Thank you." After a moment she asked, "Do you think the schoolteacher that rooms with Phoebee would be willing to teach him a little? We'd pay her something for her time."

Omie nodded and placed her hand on Aunt Julia's shoulder. "I'm sure Miss Sarah would be glad to. We'll all help him, no need to pay a thing."

Kate and Omie each took one of the old woman's hands and the conversation turned to day-to-day news. Omie told her how they were teaching other women to grow peanuts for themselves and what a wonderful time they were having doing it.

Seeing Alberta fidgeting, Aunt Julia rose to take her leave. "I'll have a talk with Willie and get him settled with the idea of coming here. I expect this Sunday will do, if y'all are agreeable."

"We know parting with him will be hard." Kate laid a hand on her old friend's arm.

Aunt Julia looked out at the wagon. "I'll have Alberta's husband Rubin come get him on Sundays to visit us."

On the ride back to Thistle Town, Alberta's broad face was lined with tears. Aunt Julia knew her granddaughter rarely showed emotions so openly, and chose not to speak.

# 1939

## JUNE 20

"Morning, Mamma." Bartie carried a cup of coffee to the table and sat.

"My head feels so heavy this morning, child."

Omie's red-rimmed eyes told Bartie the reason why. Tears had consumed a good deal of her own sleep; Daddy's funeral had been emotionally draining. It had also been busy with folks coming and going to offer condolences, leaving little time for her mamma to give herself over to sorrow. The day after was filled with family distractions, but the reality of daily life without her husband Nate was something Mamma now had to face.

"Is there more of that coffee for me?" Omie's sister Emmie asked, tying her robe and sitting down. "I guess I better empty it and make another pot. The boys will be coming in with heavy heads too this morning. I heard them snoring out in the barn like they were just outside my window!"

"Sit a minute, sister. They won't be up for a while yet."

Lilly, Omie's granddaughter, came into the kitchen and plopped onto her mamma's lap. Omie could tell this pleased Bartie greatly.

*I reckon they haven't been this comfortable with each other for some time.*

"Can I have some milky coffee?"

"Of course, honey. Help yourself."

Lilly returned with a well-sugared cup of cream, colored by a dash of coffee.

"It was good to see Willie again, Mamma." Bartie smiled and began braiding Lilly's hair.

"It surely was," Omie agreed.

"Grandma, tell me about Willie? He seems like family. Did he go with the uncles last night? He was really nice to me yesterday. I wanted to ask him about Old Joe. Mamma told me stories about Willie and his dog."

"No more coffee for you, chatterbox!" Bartie tickled her girl's sides. "I guess we thought Old Joe belonged to us all, but he came with Willie."

"Why did he come to live with y'all, Grandma? What happened to his mamma and daddy?"

Bartie visibly stiffened but didn't move from the table.

"Well honey, he's Aunt Julia's great-grandson. Willie's daddy, Isaiah, went to get more schooling up north and the boy stayed with his granny until she couldn't care for him anymore. His mamma died at childbirth."

"Oh. That's so sad."

"Willie's grown into a fine young man though, came all this way to pay his respects. He's become a lawyer, up there in Pennsylvania."

Bartie eased back against the chair. "He took the train home last night, Lilly. You know how it is in the south. He would not have been welcome at the places your uncles go."

# Chapter 3

## 1921

"Hey, Little Man!" Aunt Julia watched Willie drag a stick along the dirt lane, followed closely by his dog. She supposed this was a good time to have a talk with the child and guessed Alberta had something to do with the opportunity.

"Hi, G'mamma." Willie's short legs climbed the steps, and he walked over to her chair. The dog sat with tongue lolling, happy to be in the company of his boy.

"Miss Alberta needs to know if you have some vanilla she can use."

*Baking this child a cake to soften the news, I much imagine.*

"Sit with me a spell first, then I'll get you some."

He clambered up into the next rocker, saying, "Watch your tail, Old Joe."

"You remember how we talked about your daddy being up north, going to school?"

"Yes'm. He's goin' ta send for me when I'm this tall!" Willie reached as high as he could.

"That's right, Little Man. But there's something I need you to do first, something your daddy needs you to do." She looked away up the lane while getting her voice under control.

"There are good schools for you up there too, but first you need to learn reading and writing and your numbers."

"Like Toby and the others? I can go to school with them this year, cain't I?"

"Now see, right there is what I'm talking about. Toby and his brother and sisters go to school, but they still say words like cain't and that will not do. I have found you your very own teacher, Miss Sarah. She teaches at the white children's school, but she's agreed to teach you too, all by yourself."

Willie looked at her with confusion. "Why would she come here to teach just me?"

"Well, baby boy, here's the thing. You will need to go live with her and the Silar family for this to happen. If you help with chores around the farm, you can earn enough money for your train fare north one day."

Willie took all the information in. "Move away from here?"

"Yes, but you'd come back to see us every Sunday and even more in the summertime! It's a nice farm with lots of other children and animals to play with. You could grow your own garden. Wouldn't that be fun?"

He slipped down from his chair and came to lay his head on her lap. "But G'mamma, I don't want to move away. Do I have to?"

She stroked his head, wondering how in the world to make this easier for them both.

"You want to be with your daddy as soon as you can, don't you?"

A muffled 'yes ma'am' rose from her apron. She felt his tears seeping through.

Raising his face, he asked, "But what about Old Joe?"

"I'll see what I can do, so he goes with you."

"Yes'm." He dried his tears on her apron.

"You are my big boy, my Little Man, and I love you more than anything in this world. Now, don't you go telling anybody else I said that!" She cupped his chin and raised his face, looking deeply into his dark eyes. "I just want you to have the best life you can, understand? Now, wait here a minute while I get that vanilla."

Inside, the old woman leaned against the sink and put a hand across her face.

*Lord, I knew this would be hard, but it tears at my heart so!*

A muted sob escaped from her trembling lips.

*Please give me strength. Give all of us the strength to do what's best for this child.*

Taking a deep breath, Aunt Julia looked out the window at the small form standing beside his dog. She whispered softly, "Comfort him too, Lord. He's such a good boy."

She wiped her face on her apron and brought the bottle of vanilla out to him.

"Tell Miss Alberta to send you back later with a piece of that cake for me, hear?"

Willie made his way down the steps and slowly walked back up the lane with his hand on Old Joe's back, his stick forgotten.

Omie rounded up the children, as well as Phoebee and Sarah, telling them to come to the house for watermelon. She'd put one down in the well bucket earlier in the day for a cool treat that afternoon.

"I have some news. Y'all gather 'round now and listen."

The children figured it couldn't be bad if it involved watermelon. They each grabbed a piece and sat on the porch steps with juice running down their chins.

Omie explained about Aunt Julia's request.

Ada sat at her mamma's feet. "Is he the little light-skinned boy I see in town with her sometimes? There's another lady walks with them too. Was that his mamma?"

"How come he's light skinned?" Frank Thomas wanted to know. "Who's his daddy?"

"All y'all need to know, children, is that he belongs to Aunt Julia and he needs a home for a while. His daddy lives up north. When Willie is old enough, he'll go to join him."

The children soon went out into the yard for a seed spitting contest, so Omie was able to talk openly with Phoebee and Sarah.

"Aunt Julia would like to know if you could spend a little time teaching Willie the basic things he needs to know, Sarah. We would all pitch in."

"I'd be happy to. When is he arriving?"

"We'll go get him Sunday."

Phoebee looked out at the target the children had drawn in the dirt. She stood and spit a seed that landed right in the middle. Then another, and another. The children looked at her with open mouths.

Sarah stood and tried her luck.

"Not even close!" Phoebee laughed, slapping her leg. "City slicker."


After church the following week, the Silar family and Polly piled into the wagon and headed toward Thistle Town. Omie pulled up in front of Aunt Julia's house, and the children jumped down.

"Y'all come sit, and let me get us some tea," Aunt Julia called out to the women.

A small, fair-skinned boy came out onto the porch.

Bartie called out, "Hey, Willie! I'm Bartie."

He tucked himself behind Aunt Julia's skirts as she came back out with a tray of glasses.

"Careful, Little Man. You'll make your old grandmamma spill our drinks. No need to be afraid."

The children took turns coming up on the porch and introducing themselves. Finally, after looking up at Aunt Julia for reassurance, the little boy went down into the yard.

Omie, Kate and Aunt Julia passed the time talking and watching the children. As the young ones chattered, Omie's thoughts went to the presence she'd felt recently at the cemetery's edge. Missy's child would be as close to her as possible now. Perhaps knowing he was cared for would be enough to allow her spirit to follow that embracing light home.

The day deepened into late afternoon and soon, it was time to return to the farm.

"Mamma, can he bring the dog too? Old Joe won't be any trouble, we'll all take care of him!"

Omie looked from Ada Kate to Willie. In his small hands, he clutched a length of rope attached to a short-haired yellow dog of uncertain ancestry.

*I swear that dog is smiling at me.* Omie considered him for a moment. *The child hasn't got much in this world. It couldn't hurt to let him bring Old Joe.*

"As long as he doesn't go after the chickens or make trouble, I reckon he can come too."

"Oh no, ma'am. He won't be no trouble a'tall."

Omie had to smile at the earnest expression on Willie's face.

"Everyone load up in the wagon, then. You too, Old Joe."

The dog leaped into the wagon, tail dancing.

*Doesn't look very old to me.*

People in the community began arriving to say their goodbyes.

Alberta got down on one knee to look Willie in the face. "Now you do us proud, hear? Get all the learning you can, but don't forget where you come from. Look at all these 'mammas' here to say goodbye! We love you Little Man, and we're just a few miles away, never far. Remember that." She pressed a bag of sweets into his hand. "We'll see you next Sunday, all right?"

Alberta stood, rested her hand on his head, then walked away without looking back.

Omie and Kate returned to the porch with Aunt Julia, as the folks in the community hugged Willie one by one. Each gave him some small gift and told him to come back to visit often. Even the children who had been most cruel, taunting him about his pale skin, gave him a favorite marble, a wooden whistle or some cherished object. Family was family.

"I know he'll be fine with you all," Aunt Julia said. "He's a good boy, he'll mind. That's a good dog too, Omie. Don't worry."

"Why did he name the dog *Old* Joe?" Omie asked.

"No idea," Aunt Julia said, shaking her head. She looked at the little boy climbing into the wagon, assisted by Ada Kate. Tears coursed down her wrinkled cheeks.

"Just bring my great-grandbaby by when you can, and we'll fetch him Sundays. I'll miss him."

Omie hugged the old woman, then Kate wrapped her arms around her friend.

*She's light as a thistle seed. One of these days she's just going to float up to heaven.*

On the ride home, the children chattered to Willie as he took in the new surroundings with big wide eyes, holding his dog close.

Omie turned and smiled at the scene in the back of the wagon. *Probably never been farther from Thistle Town than to the store.*

Earlier in the week, the women had considered where the child would sleep. Once home, Omie looked around the small house. "You and the girls take up all the space in your room, Mamma, and the boys are stuffed up in the attic like a couple of bats."

Kate had sown new ticking for a small mattress and Omie stuffed it with dry corn shucks. They made a pallet close to the stove where he'd be warm, come cold weather. Beside it, they placed the quilts given him by the women of Thistle Town.

"Old Joe needs to sleep outside though, Willie. He'll be fine in the barn with the other animals."

"Yes'm," he answered, with his head down.

The small boy went outside, and Ada Kate asked quietly, "What's Daddy gonna say when he comes home?"

"I don't much care, Ada. If he was around more, he'd have some say so. Don't worry about it."

The other children were in the back yard, laughing and tussling with the dog. Willie sat on the porch steps and watched quietly. Old Joe ran up to check on him from time to time, licking his salty cheeks. Everything was different now. Except for his dog, who had Frank Thomas' hat and would not give it back. Omie and Ada Kate heard a giggle from the child and smiled at each other.


Lying on his pallet after everyone had gone to bed, Willie allowed tears to flow freely down his face onto the pillow. "G'mamma," the boy whimpered quietly, as the sounds in the house settled. He could hear the wind rattling around the door, and thought of Old Joe out with the mules.

*He's likely scared as me. I better go see.*

In the morning, Willie was found curled up with his dog in the barn. Omie relented and let the dog sleep inside. Soon, Old Joe ran in and out with the children like one of them. Omie supposed he was one of the family now.

September arrived with the scent of autumn tucked in its pockets. Willie and Georgia Rose watched as the other children trekked to school behind Miss Sarah on their first day back.

Seeing the sad little faces pressed to the window, Omie decided to make dried apple pies. She rolled out small rounds of crust and folded apples in the center, then fried them with butter in the iron skillet. Kate sprinkled the tops with cinnamon sugar and set one before each child.

Omie winked at her mamma. "I sure am glad *I* don't have to go off to school today. Too bad they're missing out on these pies."

Omie pretended not to notice the "crumbs" that fell in front of Old Joe's nose.

"Me too!" Kate declared. "Anybody else need a cold cup of milk?"

"Yes ma'am," the children responded.

The next week, Sarah mentioned to Phoebee that some of the school children were talking about the Silar family having a colored boy living with them. Right in their house.

"The cruel things the children said don't need to be repeated, but you see the problem. Frank Thomas and Ezra are going to end up getting into fights. Bartie too, for that matter." They both smiled at the mention of Bartie's fiery temper, when it came to defending another child against bullies. More than once she had proved her punches to be as good as any of the boys'.

"I propose that Willie come stay with us," Sarah said.

"Old Joe, too!" Polly piped up.

"Yep, Old Joe too." Phoebee stroked her daughter's hair and grinned.

The next day, Omie and her neighbor decided to share their washing chores, talking as they stoked fires under the big pots.

Phoebee brought the subject of Willie up. "Are you all right with Willie staying at our house? We have a bunch more room. Sarah can give him lessons while I make supper. Polly will help too, as long as the dog is part of the deal!"

Omie sighed with relief. "That's a fine idea. Thank you both. I don't like having him sleep in the front room by himself."

At Old Joe's warning, the women looked up from their washing. Nate walked into the yard with a couple of rabbits hanging from his belt, as if he'd just been out hunting for a few days instead of curled up on the riverbank with a bottle. A yellow haired mongrel was barking at him from the porch.

"Whose dog is that?" He turned toward the children. "Y'all didn't ask me if you could have a dog!" He turned to glare at Omie. "Is this your doin'?"

Polly piped up, "He's Willie's dog, but we all get to play with him. That's Old Joe."

"Willie?" He looked over and noticed a small boy clinging to Phoebee's skirt. The child was light-skinned, but obviously colored.

Nate looked at Omie.

"Aunt Julia asked if we could let the boy stay with us for a while. She's gotten too old to care for him and needs a hand until she knows what to do."

"Why does she have him? Where are his parents?"

"All I know is, his mamma has run off and left Willie with Aunt Julia."

"Who'd do that?"

"Minnie."

Omie went for more wood, giving Phoebee a wicked smile as she passed.

Nate stood with a stunned look on his face, doing the arithmetic.

Kate rocked on the porch, trying to hide her own smile.

*Willie seems settled in with the other children, and they with him.*

Watching the small boy running back out into the yard, she considered what his future might bring.

*Maybe with a child, it's best not to know. Just hope that he will have more than his people did.*

# Chapter 4
## 1922

As Kate dried the dishes, Omie watched her limp from drainboard to cupboard. Her mamma's hip had begun troubling her in the mornings and didn't seem to ease up until later in the day. She never complained, though, and laughed at herself for waddling like a duck.

Mamma seemed more tired of late. These trips to visit the sick wore her out to the point where Omie wasn't sure it was worth the toll it took. By the time they arrived home, Kate's legs were often swollen and she had to lie down.

*I reckon I could take on these clients by myself, now that the young'uns are old enough to do most of the chores.*

When Omie begged her to sit, Kate always said, "Just got a hitch in my git-along. It'll be better soon, don't worry." Still, Omie found more things for her mamma to do seated at the table, and Kate pretended not to notice.

Ada Kate sat in the kitchen on a quilt with Georgia, plaiting a doll's hair. The bright autumn sun reached through the window, creating a halo around her grandmamma's head.

*She looks just like the angel she is!*

They were all half-listening as Georgia Rose told stories. The child's imagination took in everything and everybody around her, weaving them into tales that made them all shake their heads in wonder.

Omie was tidying up, making her case about taking over the care of distant customers, when she heard the clang of a bowl and potatoes thumping on the floor. She whirled around to see her mamma looking wild-eyed, mouth drooping lopsided and her left arm hanging limply at her side. Omie rushed over in time to catch Kate's slumping body.

"Mamma! Mamma, what's wrong?"

Both women slid to the floor as Ada Kate ran over to them.

"Find your daddy and have him go for the doctor! Tell Phoebee to come quick. Run!"

Ada found Nate outside the barn by the wagon and told him of the situation. She took a moment to catch her breath, then charged up the hill.

"Phoebee, it's Grandmamma!" Phoebee took her hand and they hurried back to the house.

Nate had rushed in the door after Ada's news and was helping Omie lift Kate onto her bed.

"Oh God, Nate! Mamma has had some kind of fit. She can't talk and can't move her arm." Omie sobbed. "Go tell Doc Pritchard to come, and send a telegram to Emmie and Caleb." As he went out, Omie yelled, "Oh, and please pick up Aunt Julia on your way back. She'll want to know."

He nodded. *Likely she'll beat me here.*

The doctor was seeing a patient when Nate arrived. His wife said she would pass on the message as quickly as possible. A phone had been installed in the clinic that very week, and she would call Caleb herself.

She put a hand on Nate's arm. "I sure am glad you have such a skilled doctor for a brother-in-law, son. Emmie did good finding him."

Nate just nodded and climbed back on the wagon. He hurried toward the lane into Thistle Town. Sure enough, a woman informed him that Aunt Julia had already been taken to the farm.

When he returned home, Doc Pritchard's black car was in the yard. Through the window, Nate could see the man seated at the table along with the children. They'd just come home from school and looked at him with frightened expressions. Georgia Rose had her face tucked against Bartie's shoulder, sniffling. Phoebee jumped up and wrapped her arms around Nate, wetting his shirt with tears. He patted her on the back, not really knowing what to say. At his questioning look, she nodded toward the bedroom.

His mother-in-law was laid crosswise on the bed. Aunt Julia sat with Kate's head cradled in her hands, tears running down her dark face. Omie was at her mamma's feet, holding a foot in each hand. He felt, rather than saw, something passing from the women to Kate's body. Quickly, Nate backed out of the room and closed the door.

The doctor shook his head at Nate's puzzled expression. "Cain't say I understand this layin' on of hands, but if it makes the ladies feel useful, I suppose it can't hurt. I can't do much for her, sorry to say. I recommend Kate go to Savannah with Dr. Decker as soon as possible. They'll have better facilities to deal with this. She may have a good chance of surviving, if given proper care."

At the sound of the Decker's automobile, Doc Pritchard rose to confer with them. Emmie rushed past him through the door to the bedroom and knelt at her mamma's side.

On the porch, the older man laid a hand on Caleb's arm and informed him of the situation.

"It seems Mrs. Lee has had an attack of apoplexy. I could do little to help her. She's in your hands now, Dr. Decker. I would appreciate hearing how she fares. I've known Mrs. Lee a long time and respect her healing skills very much."

"Thank you, sir," Caleb replied. "I'll be in touch."

Kate opened her eyes and turned to look at her weeping daughter. She tried feebly to reach out with her good hand.

"Mamma!" was all Emmie could manage, as she took the trembling hand into her own.

Aunt Julia refused to leave Kate's side. Quietly, Omie asked, "Why didn't the *Sight* tell me this was coming, Aunt Julia?"

"Now hon, you know it's hardest to sense things about the ones closest to us. I didn't have any warnings about your mamma either." The old woman shook her head. "Some questions won't be answered in this life, we have to trust that God has His own reasons. But she is still with us. Let us give thanks for that."

Emmie later found Omie in the herb room crying silent tears. She wrapped her sister in her arms and they took comfort from one another for a few moments.

"What good is the *Sight* if I can't help the ones I love most with it?"

"You do the best you can, sister. Please don't blame yourself. Caleb says this probably would have happened, no matter what we had known before."

Within a couple of days, Caleb pronounced Kate stable enough to travel. Omie cried openly as the men eased Kate into the back seat of the vehicle. She covered her mouth with her hand, looking around wildly.

"Mamma! No! I have to go."

Nate folded her in his arms, saying, "Pack a bag. I reckon we can handle the hellions."

Ada Kate nodded her agreement.

He held her tight, then stepped back. "Go be with your mamma. Just let us know if there's anything we can do."

Omie looked up into his eyes, seeing something of the man she'd known before all their troubles. She kissed him soundly, then went to grab a few things for the trip.

Emmie hugged the children, telling them to take care of each other. Caleb shook hands with Nate and the boys, then returned to the Ford.

Getting into the backseat, Omie pillowed Kate's head on her lap. She waved goodbye, gazing at the family through the back window until they were out of sight.

Letters came every few days, giving updates on Kate's progress. One page for the family, and one for Nate.

*Hello my dear ones,*

*I miss you so much! Mamma seems to be gaining ground at a good pace. Caleb and Dr. Campbell are checking on her often. It is hard for her to speak, but the doctors feel that in time, she will be able to. They do not know when your grandmamma can come back home.*

*I am sorry to be gone so long children, but I trust you are listening to your daddy and behaving. I love you all more than you know. I will send word as soon as I am able to come home.*

*Love, Mamma*

*My Darling Nate,*

*I wish the news was better. There is nothing I can say to describe how hard it is watching Mamma try to find her words and fail. The fear in her eyes breaks my heart, it truly does. Her mouth is slack, her left arm lifeless. Emmie and I take turns at being strong, planting bright smiles on our faces in between bouts of crying.*

*I miss your arms around me, giving me the strength to do what needs to be done. I never say that to you enough. In spite of all our hard times, Nate Silar, you are always there when it counts most.*

*Thank you for taking care of the children. I will write again soon.*

*Your Loving Wife, Omie*


Emmie and Caleb's children gathered around their grandmamma like a clutch of chicks. Each day, Aaron was allowed to sit on the bed beside her and play with his wooden trucks, entertaining Kate for hours. She loved when sunlight came through the window, making a golden halo of the little boy's curls. He somehow intuitively knew to be gentle as he traced roads around and over her arms and legs, sensing when she was tired and needed sleep. He would then quietly slip off the bed, taking his toys with him.

When Bitsy and Danny came home from school, the first thing they did was unbuckle their book straps and bring books to her bed. Bitsy would sit Aaron on her lap as she read from one of their 'Baby Ray' primers.

"This one is called *Baby Ray and His Pets,* Grandmamma."


*One little dog he had*
*to keep, keep, keep,*
*Two cunning little kitty cats*
*creep, creep, creep,*
*Three white rabbits*
*with a leap, leap, leap,*
*Four yellow ducks from the pond*
*deep, deep, deep*
*Five pretty little chicks*
*crying peep, peep, peep*
*All saw that Baby Ray*
*was asleep,*
*sleep,*
*sleep.*

"Tha  wa so goo, Bi-ee," Kate would manage.

Danny also opened his primer to show what he had learned. "I can read Baby Ray too, Grandma!"

It was their daily ritual until Omie called the children for supper, leaving Kate with a crooked smile on her face. As Emmie helped her mamma to the table, she smiled also at the sweetness of the scene. This was the longest period of time the children had spent with their grandmamma. Her progress made them all happy, but Emmie understood that her mamma's recovery would soon lead to the sad day she would leave them and go back home.

# Chapter 5

Everyone at the farm had begun fall chores to prepare for winter, missing Omie's guidance. At first freeze, hogs were killed and hung in the smokehouse to cure. Wood was cut and stacked to be split. Most of the canning had already been done before Omie left, so they spent time making cider and stringing apple slices to hang behind the woodstove for drying.

On a mild day, Nate took the children once again on a fishing trip.

"We got to try our luck before it gets too cold and the fish head into deeper waters. They get too lazy to bite then."

On approaching the first turn in the river, they heard a deep bellow.

"Stop!" Nate hissed. The children came to a halt and looked around with wide eyes.

"Ada, you keep everybody back, I'm goin' to get a look at that gator. Sounds like a big bull. Willie, don't let that dog follow me."

"You be careful, Daddy!" Ada answered, gathering the youngest ones close to her.

Nate dropped to his belly and slid to the edge of the embankment. Peering over at the water, he looked into the eyes of the biggest gator he had ever seen. It slowly sank beneath the surface.

*Shit. I'll have to kill it. Cain't have that thing around where the young'uns are likely to meet up with it.*

He quickly and quietly slid backwards until he was far enough from the river not to be seen, then jumped up and herded the children back up the lane a bit.

"Whew, that's a big one! Frank Thomas, I want you to go get my shotgun and that box of shells. DO NOT load it, just carry it back like I showed you. Bartie, harness up one of the mules and bring her down here along with some rope and the bale hook. Go!"

Ada Kate headed back toward the house with Georgia, not wanting to see what came next. Ezra held Polly's hand and she grabbed Willie's, all three terrified and thrilled at the same time. When Frank Thomas returned with the gun, Nate took it and instructed them to stay put. He loaded the weapon and dropped to the ground again, easing the gun in front of him.

After a while, Frank Thomas whispered, "What's takin' so long?"

Bartie rode up on the mule and from her higher perch said, "I can see it getting out of the water on the other side. Must be ten feet long!"

A few more minutes passed, and suddenly the shotgun let out a loud boom. The children looked at one another in anticipation.

Nate stayed in position a moment more to be sure he had hit his target, then jumped up with a war cry as the big gator slid back down the bank and into the water. All the children ran to see, as Nate dropped to the river's edge.

"Daddy, it's gonna float away!" Bartie cried.

"Hand me that rope," he said. Their daddy scuttled down river along the bank to an overhanging tree. He began to crawl out on it, attempting to reach the animal, but was too heavy for the small trunk.

"Let me do it, Mr. Nate!" Willie cried out. The boy grabbed the rope and climbed out as far as he could. The slow-moving current was in their favor as the gator came closer and tangled itself in the low branches. Willie leaned over and looped the rope around one of the gator's legs.

"Careful, Willie. He might be playin' possum." Nate took up slack in the rope and started walking back upriver.

"He's snagged on that branch!" Willie called out, and before Nate knew it, the child slipped into the water, attempting to push the gator free. Whether the movement came from the current, or if the animal was still alive, the tail came around and smacked into Willie, knocking him further into the river. The child screamed and began panicking, trying to swim back to shore.

Frank Thomas dove in and grabbed Willie, hauling him out by his pants. Once they were close enough to the bank, Frank Thomas pushed him up into the mud and swam back out.

"Toss that bale hook down here!" he yelled at Bartie. When he was within reach with the hook but far enough to avoid the tail, he snagged a front leg at the elbow. Between him and his daddy, they managed to pull the animal free. It took what seemed like forever, but the gator was finally motionless on the muddy bank.

Nate prodded its dark head a few times to be certain the creature was dead before he approached the thing.

"Bartie, take the end of the rope and tie it to the mule. We're gonna drag this big ole lizard home!"

It took several tries for the mule to pull the heavy gator up the bank. Once on flat ground, they all gathered around to look at the beast. The glazed eyes still gave them chills and they each touched the slick, cold skin tentatively. Bartie sat on its back, whooping like a bull rider, and all trepidation was gone.

"He's ten feet or more, Daddy! Biggest I ever seen," Frank Thomas exclaimed.

"Yep, he's been around a long time, children. Now, let's get 'im home.

The mule didn't seem to cotton to the smell of what she was dragging, but Bartie kept up a soothing chatter as she led the reluctant animal toward the house.

As the rowdy bunch walked along, Nate picked Willie up and put him on his shoulders.

"You are one brave boy!"

The rest of the children whooped and cheered for Willie, except for Frank Thomas. He hung back with a scowl on his face and kicked at the dirt.

Ezra clapped him on the back. "Good job! You're a gator wrestler now." This made his brother grin.

Polly chimed in, "That's right, Frank Thomas. A real live gator wrestler!"

Both Phoebee and Sarah came down the road with Ada Kate and Georgia to see the excitement.  Sarah asked, "What do you intend to do with *that*, Mr. Silar?"

"Why, we're gonna eat him!" Nate replied. "You won't taste anything in this world better than gator tail, cut up, battered and fried. Just like chicken. The ribs is good too, we'll hang them in the smokehouse."

Georgia stood on the gator, grinning.

"Danger chicken!" Bartie yelled. "This beats a snappin' turtle any day!

Sarah pondered the creature for a moment and said, "Can I try to preserve the head?"

"Why, sure." Nate grinned as the children danced around them.

"My father did some taxidermy—that means stuffing an animal, children—when I was young. I believe I learned enough from him to do this."

Willie tugged at Nate's shirt. "Can I have a claw, Mr. Nate?"

The others cried out for one too.

"After we drag the carcass out back and butcher it," Nate promised.

"Lordy, they look like a bunch of wild heathens!" Phoebee laughed. "He better get them good and cleaned up before their mamma comes home, or Omie will be skinnin' and stuffin' him."

# Chapter 6

Finally, the promised day arrived, and they heard a motorcar coming up the road.

"Mamma! It's Mamma!" Frank Thomas called out, and all the children ran into the yard to greet her. Nate walked out onto the porch in time to see Omie riding in Caleb's vehicle with Marion Decker at the wheel.

The excited group of youngsters crowded around their mamma as she got out, and escorted her to the house. She gave Nate a quick hug and kiss as she was pressed through the door into the kitchen.

"Mamma, Daddy's a terrible cook!" Ezra said. "If it wadn't for Ada Kate, we might'a starved. Would you make us some biscuits?"

Omie laughed and said, "It's good to be appreciated. I missed you too."

Nate turned to see Marion retrieving Omie's things from the boot of the car. He wandered over and took them from Caleb's brother, noticing how thin the man had become. Nate had not seen Marion since the day of his return from the war, accompanied by their younger brother's body. There was an awkward exchange of greetings.

"Thank you for bringin' my wife home. I'm sorry about your mamma. Mrs. Decker seemed like a real good woman. I had to see to things on the farm while everyone else went to the funeral."

Marion nodded his head. "I think my brother Cyrus' death finally did her heart in, weak as it was."

"Come on in," Omie called out the door, but Marion turned away.

"I'm not much good in crowds," he confessed to Nate. "Tell them all I had to get back, would you?"

"Sure," Nate answered.

Marion climbed into the car and was quickly gone.

"Why didn't he come in?" Omie asked.

"Didn't want to," Nate said.

Over supper, Omie told them all the news of Kate's progress, describing the work she and Emmie had done with their mamma to help her learn to use the left side of her body again. Emmie was good at working with their mamma's speech, she said, and it was becoming easier for Kate to talk.

The children politely waited until she finished with her news, then began telling the tale of their adventure with the alligator. She narrowed her eyes at Nate.

"Had to be killed," he stated. "Might'a got one of the young'uns later."

She turned back to face the children.

"I jumped in to grab hold of the gator!" Willie declared, and the children cheered for him.

"Yeah, and I had to jump in to grab you!" Frank Thomas said, then told his version of the story, casting a scowl his daddy's way.

"Well, it sounds to me like Willie is a very brave boy." She turned to smile at Frank Thomas. "You are a hero, young man!"

They all cheered for him, as well.

After the meal, Nate went out to check on the animals and close up the barn. The children were still laughing and chattering about their adventures. While Bartie was drying the dishes, she remarked, "Mamma, Daddy knows everything there is to know about critters."

"Is that so?" Omie rolled her eyes. "Well, just remember children, your daddy thinks frogs and lizards fall from the sky when it rains."

In the sudden silence, she turned to see all eyes on her. "Oh, for heaven's sake. They don't!"

The children looked at each other and shrugged.


The evening grew quiet after everyone had gone to bed. Nate and Omie finally had some time alone, snuggling close under the blankets. Omie laid her head on Nate's shoulder after their lovemaking and stroked his cheek.

"I really did miss you. Missed our closeness, Nate. Sometimes I feel like you've gone away from me."

"It's nuthin' to do with you, darlin'." Nate turned his head to look at her. "They's just things I cain't talk about. If you knew what I done over there . . ."

"You did what you had to do, Nate. I know that."

"Still don't make it right." He turned on his side, ending the conversation.

She looked out the window at the full moon, noticing, in its light, the new silver-gray hairs on her husband's head.

In the deep of night, Omie woke with a start, gasping. She'd been dreaming of gunfire, men running and screaming. A body stuck on the end of a bayonet, her hands grasping the gun. She turned quickly to reach for Nate, but he was not beside her.

Heart racing, she grabbed her shawl from the hook and went looking for him. In the darkness near the barn, Omie saw the red glow from a cigarette. She hurried out the door and wrapped her arms around her husband.

"Are you all right, Nate?"

"I'm fine. Just couldn't sleep. You ok?"

"I am now."

A few days after her return, Omie rode with Nate to town for supplies. Christmas was drawing close and she wanted to look for small gifts to give the children. There had been no time to make them anything while caring for her mamma in Savannah. Emmie sent her back home with lovely packages for them all, but Omie wanted to put a little something under the tree from her and Nate.

This was the first time the two of them had ever shopped together. They nearly felt like children themselves, picking just the right gift to delight each member of the family. Omie thought this closeness to be the best Christmas present she could wish for.

There was a letter from Emmie waiting at the store. She saved it until they were done with their business to read on the ride back home. All in all, the news was good. She just missed her sister and mamma so, that tears flowed down her cheeks.

"Emmie says that Marion has decided to study law. The poor man needs something to give his life purpose. Losing his brother and mother in less than a year took a terrible toll on him."

"I reckon that's a big price to pay for having them medals on your chest."

"What do you mean?"

"Well, maybe bein' a big hero ain't as great as he thought it would be."

"Nate, they didn't join to become heroes, they just wanted to do their duty."

"Not like me, then."

"I don't know why you are acting like this. You did your duty too. None of us wanted you to go. Marion is a good man. He was a comfort to me when Mamma was first brought to Savannah. I didn't know what was going to happen to her, whether she'd live or die or ever get better. He taught me to take it one day at a time, something he learned at a very great price."

"A comfort, huh?" Nate muttered.

"Now don't make it into somethin' it ain't!" she retorted. "You know what I mean."

Nate said nothing more for the rest of the trip, pulling into himself, to Omie's frustration.

Suppertime was quiet, and the children wondered at the tension between their mamma and daddy. All had seemed well before they headed out for school that morning. As soon as he'd eaten, Nate went out to the barn and did not come to bed. Omie assumed he'd curled up on the hay with a bottle. The next morning, there was still no sign of him. By evening, Omie wondered where he'd gone.

"Bartie, have you seen your daddy?"

The girl shook her head and Omie noticed the tears in her eyes.

"What's wrong, honey?"

"Daddy said he needed to get away for a few days and I was not to follow him."

*Oh, Good Lord! Hard headed, jealous, silly man!*

With the weather too cold to be outside, all the children were bored and cranky. Especially Bartie, who moped around for days. She spent most of her time with her chin resting on the windowsill looking for her daddy to return.

Ada Kate frequently cut her eyes in Bartie's direction, then gave her mamma a meaningful look.

Finally, Omie grew frustrated and pulled a chair up beside the girl.

"Bartie, now you listen to me. You have chores like everyone else. You can't just shirk your responsibilities and spend all day sitting here waiting …"

Bartie sat up suddenly and gasped, "Daddy!"

She ran outside without a coat, Omie yelling after her, but it was no use. The girl had followed her daddy into the barn, out of hearing. Omie wrapped herself in her shawl and told the others to stay put in the warmth. By the scowl on her face, they knew this was not a suggestion.

"Bartie, go back to the house."

Her daughter opened her mouth to object, but Omie said, "NOW!"

When she heard the door slam, Omie asked, "Where the hell have you been?"

"Maybe I needed a little 'comfort' of my own," he growled, and pushed past her.

Besides the smells of whiskey and tobacco smoke that usually clung to him after these disappearances, she sensed something else. A softer smell. A woman's smell.

After school the following day, the children gathered at Phoebee's house.

"Can we stay here with you awhile?" Ada Kate asked.

Phoebee and Willie were sitting at the table. "Why shur. What's goin' on, y'all?"

"We can hear pots and pans crashin', doors and drawers slammin' all the way from your porch." Frank Thomas said.

Phoebee opened her door, then quickly closed it.

"Yep, not somewhere I'd wanna be right now neither. Y'all take your coats off and sit a spell. I'll make us some cocoa."

"I'm learnin' to read!" Willie announced proudly. "Miz Phoebee and Miz Sarah are teachin' me!"

Polly plopped into the chair beside him. "What about me, Little Man? Aren't I teaching you too?"

"Miz Phoebee says you're teachin' me to be a ring-tailed-tooter, like you."

# Chapter 7

## 1923

By spring, Kate was pronounced able to go back home. Although she had not fully recovered the use of her left arm, she was walking better and able to speak well enough not to be frustrated. She had been growing restless in the city, wanting fresh air and her own bed.

Homecoming was a joyful occasion. The children had made cards for their grandmamma in school. Omie and the other women, including Ada, now a young woman of nearly fifteen, had sewn a new quilt for Kate. It was done in the bright colors of spring, pieced from material Emmie sent them. Plain squares were mixed in, embroidered with the flowering plants Kate used in her healing potions.

Kate sat rocking on the porch wrapped in her quilt, observing new life springing up everywhere. The air smelled of promise, God's reward for making it through the dark days of winter.

Up at her old house, the dogwood tree Frank planted for her was in full bloom, snowy white. Omie had planted one like it beside Kate's bedroom window when she moved her mamma into the house with them, but it wasn't the same.

*We didn't have a penny to spare in those days, did we, Frank? But that sapling from the woods meant more to me than a diamond ring.*

Biddies followed hens around, scratching at the ground off the porch. A new litter of piglets ran and wheeled in circles, caught up in the pure joy of being. *Mamma always called it 'havin' a fit of delicious'.*

"Grandmamma, look!" Ezra gently placed a young kitten on Kate's lap. The small ball of fur climbed up to nestle itself against her neck and began to purr.

"T'ank you Eza." Kate lifted her face as he bent to kiss her.

"Mabel had eight of them Grandmamma! You can have your pick if you want to keep one."

Polly leaned over to kiss her as well, then the two youngsters ran to catch up with the others headed for school.

An old tune rose up from Kate's memory, something she had sung every spring since her childhood. She began to hum while the words played out in her mind.

*I will twine, I will mingle my raven black hair*
*With the roses so red and the lilies so fair*
*And the myrtle so bright with its emerald hue*
*The pale emanita and the hyssop so blue*

Omie stood behind the screen door. listening. She had been out gathering plants and came through the back, looking for her mamma. Setting down the basket, she picked up her harmonica from the sideboard. On the porch, she took a seat beside Kate and softly played along.

Omie sang the last verse, looking out toward the cornfield where Nate was plowing.

*Well, he told me he loved me and called me his flower*
*That was blooming to cheer him through life's dreary hour*

*I'll live yet to see him regret the dark hour*
*When he won, then neglected this pale wildwood flower*


Omie shook her head and stood up. *Such silliness. Like a lovesick school-girl.* She went to retrieve the basket and show her mamma what she'd found.

"Nettles. I found a big patch of them and couldn't resist. They are a torment though!"

As Omie continued on about her finds, the trace of sorrow in her daughter's eyes did not escape Kate's notice.

*Lord, help me to know when to reach out a hand and when to keep my own counsel. I do sorely wish theirs was a happy marriage.*

She watched Nate for a bit, remembering his sudden appearance in their lives.

*The portents I felt when he first came here have come true. Given Nate's circumstances, plain common sense would have predicted things just as well.*

Kate stroked the sleeping kitten's fur. The beauty of this day was a reminder that there was enough in this life yet to keep her here until she set it aside, like a quilt finally finished, and reached toward heaven for her husband's outstretched hand.

"Grandmamma, I'm about to gather some plants for drying. Do you want to go to the herb room with me?"

Kate looked up at Ada with a lopsided smile. " 'Course."

Ada took the kitten down to the yard where its mamma sat patiently waiting with the others, then returned to the porch.

"Let me help you up, then. Put your arm over my shoulder." Looping her right arm around Ada's neck, Kate stood and they made their way to the back porch.

" 'm good. Go."

She opened the herb room door and went inside. Kate was met with the familiar fragrance of drying plants. All the years of rendering these gifts from the earth into medicines wrapped around her. Memories gathered, playing out scenes of her own mamma and Grandmamma Ida sitting at a table much like this one. The old book of recipes for potions sat on a shelf, greeting her like a dear friend.

Kate turned as Ada brought in a basket of plants to make into spring tonics. She smiled at her granddaughter as the bright spill of yellow dandelions, blue violets and white flowered chickweed covered the table.

"Tha's spring!" Kate declared. The first flowers to bloom always gladdened her heart so. "T'ank you."

Now finished with school, the girl was becoming adept at the healing arts, to the delight of her grandmamma.

"I'm goin' to fetch more." Ada Kate picked up the basket and headed out the door.

Omie came in and took a seat. They worked from the two chairs where Kate and her customers used to sit. Omie still provided remedies for folks, but the readings her mamma had given were a thing of the past. This saddened them both. There was naught to do, however, but accept things as they were.

Omie stood and placed a hand on Kate's shoulder. "When the children get home, I'll have the girls help us finish bundling these, Mamma. Ada Kate can help me mix potions and such. Don't tire yourself out."

"Need sumpin to do," Kate replied. "Ol an in da way."

"Mamma, you are neither old, nor in the way. Silly." Omie kissed the top of her mamma's head and went in the house to bring them more tea.

At supper time, Nate came up on the porch to wash. He and Omie had tried to carry on some semblance of normal life since Kate had come home, but the tension was obvious. Beneath the prickly lights dancing between them, Kate still saw the soft glow of love connecting the two.

The children carried on as if they didn't notice anything amiss. Kate supposed they had become used to things being this way.

"Boys, after school tomorrow I need you to harness one of the mules and get to plowing the peanut fields," Omie announced.

Nate kept his head down and concentrated on eating.

Frank Thomas piped up, "Mamma, I was thinkin' about planting a little tobacco patch of my own, for some extra money. Could I have a corner of the field?"

"Why are you askin' your mamma, son?" Nate asked, looking sternly at Frank Thomas. "You can help me more with what we've got, that's what you can do."

"Just wanted somethin' of my own, is all," he muttered.

"And what are you going to spend *your* money on?" his daddy replied curtly.

"Never mind." Frank Thomas pushed his chair back and went outside.

Nate looked at Omie, but she just shrugged.

"Don't say I told you, but there's a girl he likes," Ezra whispered. "He wants to buy her something."

Nate grunted, and Omie smiled at her mamma.

After supper, Ezra found his brother in the tobacco barn.

"What are you doin'?" he asked.

"Nuthin', why?" Frank Thomas grunted.

"Don't be angry with Daddy. You know how it is between him and Mamma. He does the tobacco. You shoulda asked him."

"I don't wanna ask him nothin'," he replied stubbornly. "He doesn't treat her or any of us like he should. He's a drunk. He stinks. If he wants to act like the man of our house, he ought to act like a man first."

Ezra stood looking at his brother in bewilderment.

"I just know things you don't, Ezra. You feel the way you want to feel about him, but I'm done listening to him."

Frank Thomas walked out, leaving Ezra standing there.

He turned to the ghosts around him. "Wonder what he means by that?"

On a mild summer evening, Omie decided to gather everyone together on the porch for some music. She and the children had played so little together in the last few years. It was time to change that.

After supper dishes were washed, Omie said, "Ada Kate, fetch your autoharp. Boys, bring your instruments. Let's play some tunes for your grandmamma."

Kate gave them a lopsided smile. "Wunerful!"

Sarah had gifted Ada Kate with her own grandmother's instrument, brought back from a trip home to Virginia. The autoharp and piano had enough in common that Ada mastered it quickly.

Frank Thomas got his mandolin. Ezra pulled his harmonica from his pocket, and Ada Kate tuned up her autoharp. They settled around Kate in a half circle in the kitchen chairs Nate brought to the porch.

Omie pulled her own harmonica out of her apron. She and Ada Kate started up with *She'll Be Comin' Round the Mountain*. Ezra found a harmony to blend with his mamma and Frank Thomas joined in. Kate sat tapping the toes of her good foot and Bartie began singing.

*She'll be comin' round the mountain when she comes*
*She'll be comin' round the mountain when she comes*
*She'll be comin' round the mountain*

*She'll be comin' round the mountain*

*She'll be comin' round the mountain when she comes*


The voices of Phoebee, Sarah and Polly were heard coming down the hill. Even Nate got caught up in the merriment. They began making up verses about what *She* would be bringing *round the mountain* until everyone was out of breath from laughing.

As everyone began to put away the instruments and chairs, Omie made them all promise to make time for playing regularly. Time for each other. Where words sometimes fell short, music was a language they all understood.

# 1939

## June 20

Bartie was considering staying another day. This time with her daughter was proving to be a balm for them both. She imagined Shad could do without her a bit longer. He'd understand—he always did.

After breakfast was cleared away and the kitchen cleaned, Bartie asked Lilly if she could re-braid the girl's hair. There was the same careless tomboy look about her daughter that Bartie remembered seeing in the mirror at that age.

"Let's go out on the back porch where it's cooler, sweetie. Mamma, y'all call us if you need us."

Bartie unbraided Lilly's hair and began to brush it out.

"Ouch! You always try to scalp me."

"Sorry," Bartie said, and kissed the top of her head.

"Mamma, you really got to catch an alligator?"

Bartie laughed. "I got to eat it, for sure."

"You did though, didn't you? I'm gonna tell everybody my mamma was an alligator wrestler," Lilly declared.

"Just boys who want to court you."

It was nice having a little quiet time for just the two of them. Their trip to the farm for the funeral had been spent in a silence charged with emotions. Now they seemed to be wrapped in an easy peace, like the softness of this day. A small breeze lifted the Spanish moss on the old oak and played with loose curls around Lilly's face.

Bartie said softly, "I was thinking I might stay until tomorrow. Would you like that?"

Lilly replied, "That would be great, Mamma! You still all right with me staying here the rest of the summer?"

Bartie nodded.

They watched Omie at the pump taking a drink, then letting the cold water spill over the top of her head.

"I've seen Grandmamma pour water on her head like that a bunch of times."

"Yes hon, she's done that for most of my life. She has a place that burns all the time from when the lightning hit her."

Lilly jerked around. "She got hit by lightning? How come she didn't tell me that story?"

"Stop moving so much unless you want this braid to look like the hind end of a horse!"

Bartie was quiet for a moment, and replied in a tight voice. "That was a hard time for Mamma, she hardly remembers any of it. Seemed like we lost her for over a year."

"When did it happen?"

"The same year she got pregnant with Grace."

"But Grace is not that much older than me. I always wondered how she could be your sister."

Bartie looked out at her mamma for a moment.

Lilly's hand went to her head. "Ouch!"

"Sorry." Bartie handed over the brush. "We're done."

The set of her mamma's shoulders as she walked away told Lilly that this story had something to do with Grandaddy, a subject which was off limits.

Lilly went in search of her cousins, padding barefoot down the dirt road.

# Chapter 8
## 1923

Summer passed in a familiar routine of planting, harvesting, and preserving food from the garden. There was comfort in the hard work, knowing they would be well fed come winter. When the children started back to school, there was more time to tend the small chores that had been put off.

Though the days were still warm and humid, the evenings brought a hint of fall. Omie decided it was time to start building up a stack of split wood. She made sure her mamma was comfortable in a chair by the window where she could watch, then called to Willie for help.

"That's it, Willie. Roll those rounds over here and I'll split 'em. When we get enough done, I'll show you how to stack the firewood so it won't fall."

Omie smiled at the boy's willingness to push the logs toward her. He sometimes had to put his back to them, but he was determined. Aunt Julia's grandson was small for seven, not surprising for his early birth. He was not much taller than his best friend. Old Joe followed Willie everywhere he went, game for whatever the next adventure might be. As long as the dog got a nap now and then.

The smell of a late season storm was in the air. A rising breeze tugged at the tree limbs and in the distance, thunder rumbled. The dark line of clouds was still aways off from the river, but Omie judged she might have less than half an hour to get some wood ready for the cookstove.

"Go ahead and put some of these pieces on the porch." she instructed.

*That breeze feels wonderful. It'll cool things down considerable when the rain hits.*

Omie lined up a large piece on the splitting block and took aim, raising the axe high overhead. A bolt of lightning cracked the sky and traveled down the handle of the axe, arcing to Omie's head and knocking her backwards nearly to the porch.

"Miz Omie! Miz Omie!" Willie cried, running to her side.

She was unconscious. Old Joe began barking frantically as the boy tried to raise the limp body up, but she was dead weight for his small arms. He ran into the house where Kate was struggling to get from her chair to the door to see what the commotion was about.

"I think Miz Omie is killed!" he sobbed.

Kate saw Omie's still body on the ground and said, "He'p me, Willie." She waved her good hand toward the barn. "Nate."

He helped Kate down the porch steps and to her daughter's side. She eased to the ground, then put her fingers to Omie's neck. A weak pulse pushed back.

Willie found Nate putting the mules up in the barn.

"Mr. Nate. Hurry." The boy was panting so hard he could barely speak.

"What is it, Willie?"

"Miz Omie."

He picked up the child and ran. When he found Kate out back beside Omie's still form, he cried, "Is she dead?"

"No. Weak."

Nate scooped his wife off the ground and carried her to their bed. He ran back out and, between him and Willie, they got Kate inside as fat raindrops began to hit the tin roof. They got her settled in a chair at Omie's side.

The noise was deafening, causing Willie and his dog to cower beneath the table.

Kate rested a hand on her daughter's chest. It rose and fell, but Omie had still not regained consciousness.

"What can I do?" Nate asked his mother-in-law.

"Wet cloths."

Nate went into the kitchen where he saw the frightened child hiding. Trying to keep his voice calm, he said, "Willie, stop cryin' now. The rain's eased up and I need you to go get Phoebee. She's in the milk barn with Ada." Willie nodded and eased out from under the table with Old Joe at his heels.

"That's a good boy. Thank you."

Ada Kate and Phoebee were in the middle of helping deliver a calf. The mother was Kate's old milk cow, Dinah, and the birth was proving difficult for her. As thunder shook the timbers in the old barn, the cow bawled and rolled her eyes back in her head. All this noise and stress was keeping her from relaxing between contractions.

"Easy girl," Ada crooned. She covered her arms with lard to allow herself to reach inside and help the mother get the baby out.

"All right now, Aunt Phoebee, would you hold her down while I see what I can do?"

"Me?" Phoebee reckoned the cow was triple her weight. "I'll try, but this might turn into a rodeo if I cain't."

They thought they heard a commotion down at the house, but couldn't be sure. Finally, as the thunder eased, little legs emerged and Ada was able to pull the tiny calf into the world. Dinah looked down as if surprised, then began to lick her baby.

Sitting back on her knees, the girl smiled at Phoebee. "They just know what to do when the hard part's done, don't they?"

"Well, Miss Ada, you did a fine job! Ever think you'd be a cow midwife?"

Ada laughed and said, "Let's call this little one Daisy."

Suddenly, they heard Willie's voice.

"Miz Ada, Miz Phoebee, you gotta come."

Kate cradled Omie's head in her lap, gently exploring her daughter's head for injuries. There was a faint smell of burnt hair on top of her head and when Kate touched it, Omie jerked.

Nate filled a pan with water from the well. He found the bundle of clean cloths the women kept for drying dishes and brought it all to the bed. Kate asked him to get scissors to clip the hair away. Omie groaned.

"Lord, that's got to hurt," Nate said, wincing. "I reckon that's where she was struck."

Kate took the scissors from him and slowly snipped around the wound. "Not bad. Cool her head."

Cold water seemed to feel soothing to Omie after the initial shock of touch subsided. When Ada arrived with Phoebee, Kate told her to fetch the burn ointment from the herb room. Phoebee sat on the other side of Omie's bed, crying and shaking her head in disbelief.

"I never in my life, Miz Kate! Can the doctor fix her?"

Kate reached across the bed to pat the young woman's hand. "Hope so, hon."

As the children came in from school, Phoebee took them to her house, explaining what had happened. Frank Thomas ran to the barn and saddled the horse, then rode to get Doc Pritchard. Ada Kate busied herself making supper, tears running down her cheeks.

Doc Pritchard answered the door to Frank Thomas' insistent pounding. "What is it, son? Come in, you're soaked."

"No time! My mamma. Omie Silar." Frank Thomas tried to calm his breathing. "She got lightnin' struck, sir. Can you come?"

"Give me a moment to get my things. Come in and dry off or I'll be treating you for pneumonia." The doctor handed Frank Thomas a blanket, then went to tell his wife he was going to the Silar's farm.

"Martha, Mrs. Silar's son is here. She's been struck by lightning." He kissed her cheek. "I don't know when I'll be back."

"Oh my!" Mrs. Pritchard exclaimed. "I'll be praying for her. Be careful please, this is a nasty storm."

As the two went out, the boy started toward his horse.

"Ride with me, Frank Thomas. You can come back later for the mare. My wife will find someone to tend her."

They arrived in his automobile as the storm began to subside. Frank Thomas jumped out before they came to a stop and ran into the house. Doc Pritchard came puffing in behind him.

Kneeling at Omie's side, he listened to her heart, then nodded to himself. He examined the burned spot, concern apparent on his face. She moaned and opened her eyes slightly as he moved her head to examine it further.

"She's going to take some watching, Kate. Looks as though you have done all you can for the burn. I don't know what the effects of this lightning strike may be. Only time will tell us. The fact that it didn't kill her is a wonder! I'll call Dr. Decker to inform him about her condition as soon as I can."

Frank Thomas refused to eat or leave his mamma's side. He'd go back and get the horse later. Nate felt that somehow the boy blamed him for the accident, though he could not imagine why.

Sarah and Phoebee kept a vigil by Omie's bedside all night to be certain she was still breathing. The next day, the children were exhausted with worry, so Sarah said they were allowed to stay home from school.

The morning sun shone bright through the rain-washed window, striking Omie's face. She cried, "Mamma?" Kate caught her hand before she touched the wound.

"Head hurts so bad!"

"I know. Laud'num. Be still."

Ada Kate was quickly by the bed with a bottle and spoon.

"Lil' bit. Caleb needs . . . talk to her."

Ada could see that the effort to speak was wearing her grandmamma down. Worry and little sleep had made her speech more difficult.

"Let me sit with her awhile, Grandmamma. You'll need to be rested for when Caleb and Emmie come. Here, lay down beside Mamma."

Kate did as she was told, feeling sleep envelope her quickly.

This was the second time in less than a year Emmie and Caleb rushed to the farm. This time, Emmie's prayers were for her sister.

She could not believe such a thing could happen. "I swear, Caleb, it *would* take an act of God to knock my sister down. She's such a strong woman. I believe she could wrestle a bear if necessary. What will this mean for her?"

"I haven't had any experience with lightning strikes, Emmie. I just don't know. Dr. Campbell is going to find out everything he can about it though, darling. For now, we just need to get there and see the extent of her injuries. Then we'll know more how to address them."

As soon as they arrived, Emmie jumped out of the car and went to her sister's side. Caleb followed, medical bag in hand.

The rest of the family, except for Kate and Nate, gathered in the kitchen, making more room for the doctor to do his examination. Caleb looked into Omie's eyes, asking her questions as he checked for responses. She was aware of who he was, but could not answer him coherently. She only repeated that her head hurt.

Nate watched his half-brother closely, still reluctant to pin his hopes on the man, but desperate for help. He wanted to believe Emmie had done well for herself by marrying this 'Doctor Decker', but it was still a hard pill to swallow.

Caleb removed his stethoscope and looked at them all.

"This is a situation where I don't have many answers for you." He checked Omie's pulse. "Her heartbeat is strong. There doesn't seem to be any damage, but it's hard to say what the long-term effects will be."

The young doctor looked imploringly at Nate. "She needs to go to the hospital. We have equipment there that will help diagnose her condition better. You're welcome to stay with Emmie and me while we run tests to see what's to be done for Omie."

"I want to go." Frank Thomas stood in the doorway.

"You have school, son." Nate replied.

"I won't go to school. I want to be with Mamma."

Emmie rose and went to him. "Frank Thomas, the hospital won't allow someone your age to stay with her. Tell you what, how about I come back for you in a few days when we have her settled into a room where you can visit."

He looked up at her with red eyes. "You promise?"

"Cross my heart," Emmie said, and gathered him into her arms.

Sarah and Phoebee stood with the children, watching as the other adults got into the car. This time, it was Nate in the backseat holding Omie's head cradled in his lap. Kate sat up front with Caleb and Emmie. Conversation was quiet, with Emmie turning from time to time to look at Omie's pale face. Nate only looked out the window as he stroked his wife's cheek.

Fields along the roadside were deep green with corn and beans. The rains had come when needed. Temperatures were reasonable for September.

Nate thought of all the work Omie and Phoebee had put into the peanut crop, how proud she was of what they'd accomplished.

*I been nuthin' but a horse's ass about all that. She should be proud and I oughta be proud for her.* Looking down at Omie's limp form, he closed his eyes. *None of it matters now.*

During the time Caleb and Emmie were gone, Dr. Campbell had gathered all the information he could. He met them at the hospital, where Omie was put on a gurney and taken into the laboratory for x-rays. Nate was asked to stay behind in the waiting room with his mother-in-law and sister-in-law.

"I should check on the children," Emmie told him. "I'll be back in a very short while. Mamma, would you like to come with me and get some rest? You look exhausted."

"No. Stay with Nate," Kate replied, knowing how uncomfortable he was with the situation.

Hours later, Caleb came into the waiting room. After assuring Kate and Emmie that Omie was stable, he put a hand on Nate's shoulder and said, "Come with me."

Nervously, Nate followed. All around, bright lights glared at him. Strange machines sounded as if they were alive. He felt as if he had been dropped onto the moon. Omie was lying on a bed in a small room, looking out the window. A pair of doves was nesting on the deep ledge, cooing softly. She turned her head slowly as Nate entered.

"Omie!" he cried and sank down in the chair beside her. She gazed dully back at him, but lifted a hand to touch his. Nate looked at Dr. Campbell standing at the foot of the bed.

"We are giving her morphine for the head pain, so she won't be very responsive for a few days. We'll back down on the dosage slowly until she can tolerate the pain on her own. Her mother will no doubt have knowledge of ways to treat it then."

"Will she be all right?" Nate asked.

Caleb stood quietly at Omie's side as Dr. Campbell replied, "The x-rays showed no swelling on the brain or bleeding. Her heart seems stable, and we see no signs of nerve problems. Time is the only thing that will truly tell us." The doctor reached out to shake Nate's hand. "I apologize, but I must go check on my other patients."

"Nate, you know how tough she is." Caleb rested a hand on Nate's shoulder once more. "Have faith. Dr. Campbell has taken charge of her case and you couldn't ask for better. I'll be doing everything possible too, I promise."

He searched for a way to reassure his brother-in-law. "In a few days we'll have a better idea when she can be released." Caleb turned to leave. "I'll give you a few more moments alone before I bring Kate and Emmie in."

Nate nodded, and said quietly, "Thanks."

He raised Omie's hand to his lips. They gazed into each other's eyes for a long moment. Nate wasn't sure what Omie was thinking, only knew that the light he used to see shining from deep inside her was not there. She touched the tracks of tears on his face, then slowly closed her lids and slept.

In the days following, it was apparent that the lightning strike had affected many things. Her memory, her ability to focus, her recognition of people. She seemed drained of energy and slept a lot.

Omie was settled in a room at the Decker's house where Kate and Emmie could care for her a while longer. Emmie knew the confines of the city were becoming unbearable for Nate, who constantly fretted about getting the crops in. There was really no reason for him to stay.

"Why don't you go back with me when I get Frank Thomas?" Emmie asked. "I promise we'll let you know if Omie's condition worsens."

He looked at his wife's sleeping form and nodded. Then he dropped his head into his hands and cried softly.

Emmie silently left the room.

The ride back to the farm was a quiet one for Nate and Emmie. She couldn't help but be struck by the undeniable beauty that surrounded them, despite being enveloped in their worry and sorrow. Against a palette of greens, purple thistles by the roadside reached for the sun. The breeze from the auto's passing stirred a flurry of monarch butterflies feeding on the blooms.

A few flew in and lit on Nate, but he paid them no mind. "Do you think God is punishin' me, Emmie?"

She turned to look at him. "Punishing you, Nate? How?"

He looked out his window, replying in a low voice, "Striking Omie down like that."

"I don't think God makes another person pay for our sins, no matter what they are. Life just happens. Lightning is an act of God for certain, but it could just as easily be a tree or the barn or one of the children that got in its way."

Nate shrugged. "Maybe."


Arriving at the farm, Nate headed straight for the fields, as if he needed the land like a deep drink of water. Emmie stayed only long enough to report back the news of Omie's progress and to fetch Frank Thomas as she'd promised.

Bartie was eager to go back to Savannah with her brother and aunt. Miss Sarah voiced concerns over the child missing school though. "You could be doing better in your studies, young lady." The teacher affectionately ran a hand over Bartie's messy hair.

"And Ada Kate could use some help," Phoebee added. The girl's protests and promises did no good.

She walked out to the barn in search of her daddy, head hanging.

"What is it, Snake?" He'd given her the nickname after teaching her to swim, swearing that she wriggled through the water fast as a moccasin.

"Please tell them I can go, Daddy. I want to see Mamma and Grandmamma. Frank Thomas needs me too."

"I don't know as I can go up against that passel of women." He thought for a moment. "But what they don't know..."

Nate looked out the barn doors to see if the coast was clear, then waved for Bartie to follow him. They ducked around the back of the automobile.

"Looks like there's room in the boot. Hop in and I'll close it up."

Bartie giggled as she squeezed onto the floorboard below the rumble seat.

"Shush! You got enough room in there?"

She opened the boot slightly. "Yes, Daddy. Thank you!"

"I'll tell them later that I let you go," Nate whispered, and whistled as he sauntered back to the barn.

He grinned at the image of Bartie under the rumble seat, having an adventure. It was worth the hell he would pay later.

*Sometimes actions speak louder than words. I am still the daddy.*

On the trip back to Savannah, Emmie spoke more of Omie's condition to Frank Thomas. He was listening quietly, then suddenly looked back and yelled, "What the...Hades?"

Bartie had popped up like a jack-in-the-box, looking around and grinning from ear to ear.

Emmie nearly drove off the road. She pulled over and walked to the back of the car. "Oh, my goodness! You scared us to death! Young lady, what in the world do you think you're doing?"

"Daddy said I could come."

"Well, we're not turning back now. Get in."

Bartie leaned back and declared, "I like it here just fine!"

Emmie stood speechless for a moment, then got in the car. Frank Thomas was trying very hard not to laugh. Arms outstretched, the girl serenaded crows, scarecrows, and curious livestock along the way to Savannah.

"Hope she doesn't choke on a bug," Frank Thomas commented.

Bartie became quiet as they entered their aunt and uncle's home. Kate met them at the door of Omie's room, putting an arm around each child. She looked questioningly at Emmie, but her daughter just answered with a wry smile.

Omie looked pale against the sheets, her eyes closed. She opened them when she heard voices, smiling as Frank Thomas and Bartie entered. The children went to either side of the bed, each giving her a hug. It felt strange when she did not hug back. She looked so different, so fragile, that neither could speak for a moment.

"Hey, Mamma." Bartie found her voice, and began stroking Omie's long hair, freed from its braid.

Frank Thomas took his mamma's hand from beneath the covers, cradling it in his own. "How you doing?" he asked.

Omie said nothing for a moment, then replied, "Are y'all hungry? There's some biscuits left on the stove. Ask Ada to slice you some ham."

The children looked at Kate in bewilderment. Giving them a reassuring smile, she said, "We'll feed 'em. Rest."

Omie patted Frank Thomas' hand. "Good. Good." She leaned back against the pillows, closing her eyes again.

Kate motioned for the two to follow her out into the hallway. Bartie threw her arms around her grandmamma's waist and began to cry. Frank Thomas turned his back and put the heels of his hands against his eyes.

Caleb walked over, turning the boy to face him and squatted down to be at eye level with his niece and nephew. "I know it's frightening to see her like this, but I promise she will get better. Your mamma got a nasty shock from that lightning. She's strong, though, you know that. You'll have to be patient and help her remember things. I'm counting on you two to make sure the others understand, as well." He held them close, letting his own tears fall.

Bartie wiped her nose on a sleeve and looked at her uncle. "When can she come home?"

"Very soon, I believe. We'll keep you informed about how she's doing, and when your mamma is well enough, we'll bring her back. She'll need to take it easy for a while at home, too."

"I won't let her lift a finger," Frank Thomas promised.

The children were allowed to see their mamma anytime they liked, as long as they didn't disturb her when she slept. Often, Emmie stood in the doorway, watching Omie as she interacted with Bartie and Frank Thomas.

One morning, Caleb stood behind his wife and rested his chin on top of her head. "Perhaps having them near will help with her memory."

"A mother's love is powerful medicine," she agreed. "I know these two should be in school, but I can't bring myself to pull them away. Not just yet."

"Let's see what time brings us. Speaking of time..." he kissed her, picked up his medical bag and headed toward the door.

"See you at lunch," Emmie called, then turned back to watch as Bartie re-plaited Omie's hair. Each day, different flowers went missing from the garden and ended up in Omie's braid. Today's palette consisted of red, orange and yellow chrysanthemums. Omie stroked the soft petals with a contented smile on her face.

Mid-day, she became agitated for the first time, when a thunder storm darkened the windows and she could not see Georgia Rose.

"Get the baby inside!" Omie kept crying, "It'll get her! Willie! Where's Willie?"

Kate put her hands on top of Omie's head as she whispered softly, "It's all right, darlin'. Georgia Rose is asleep and Willie is with Phoebee up at the old house. We're all here. We're all safe."

Caleb was just hanging his hat on the rack when he heard the commotion. He ran to the bedroom and watched in fascination as a soft light poured from Kate's hands into her daughter's head. Both were surrounded by a luminous glow, though the only light in the room was from a candle by the bedside. No one else, including Maizie, who'd dropped by, seemed to find this unusual.

Omie finally rested back against the pillows again and closed her eyes.

# Chapter 9

Elizabeth Campbell closed the dress shop early. She had been trying to finish Emmie's dress orders as well as her own, but was distracted from her sewing by concern for Kate. The older women had developed a friendship during the times Emmie's mother came to Savannah.  Kate seemed to need a woman of her own age to talk to, especially now with Omie's condition. For Elizabeth, there was a softness to Emmie's mother that invited confidences she would not share with women of Savannah.

*Perhaps an outing would be good for Mrs. Lee. It's a lovely day for a carriage ride. I'll ask Maizie to watch over Omie's children for the afternoon.*

Elizabeth parked the Ford and gathered her parcels. She called for Maizie as she entered the house. After sharing her idea, they went out to the carriage house to find Thomas.

"Hello, Thomas. Would you mind taking Mrs. Lee and myself for an outing in the carriage? I believe it would do her good."

"Yes ma'am, won't take me but a minute to harness the horses. I'll see y'all 'round front."

Kate hesitated at Elizabeth's suggestion, but Emmie assured her all would be well in her absence. "Maizie and I can both be here Mamma. Get out for a while. We'll be fine, won't we children?"

Emmie's three circled their arms around their grandmamma, joined by Bartie and Frank Thomas.

"Bring us back some sweets, Grandmamma?" Bartie asked.

Kate nodded. "*After* supper."

She fetched her shawl and linked arms with Elizabeth as they walked down the porch steps.

Emmie and Maizie watched out the window as Thomas assisted the ladies into the carriage.

"Look like two school girls, don't they?" Maizie remarked.

Emmie chuckled. "They do."

As the carriage slowly made its way around the squares and down to River Street, Elizabeth pointed out sites of interest. The gentle *clop, clop* of the horses' feet was calming after the constant chatter of children, and Kate felt herself relaxing for the first time since she'd come to Savannah.

"May I treat you to afternoon tea?" Elizabeth asked. "I know of a lovely tea house nearby that serves the finest little pastries."

"Don't know... I'm dressed right," Kate said quietly.

"You, my dear, are just fine. Let me show you one of Savannah's most enjoyable traditions."

Inside the plush rooms of Mrs. Bascomb's Tea House, the two friends found a small table by a window. Kate took in the fresco-adorned walls and ornate ceilings. Soft light lingered on white tablecloths topped with vases of cut flowers. A steaming pot of Oolong tea was brought to them, along with a tiered silver tray of delightful indulgences.

"All for us?" Kate whispered.

Elizabeth nodded and Kate allowed as she had never seen the likes of it.

Tiny pastries stuffed with crab salad, shrimp salad and pimento cheese lined the bottom tray. Teacakes filled with currants adorned the next, and ornately decorated petit fours topped them all off.

Several of Elizabeth's customers stopped by the table to say hello, and Kate was introduced as her dear friend. They welcomed her like she was just as much a lady as the rest of them.

Before returning to the Decker's home, Elizabeth had Thomas take them to her shop.

Kate looked around in wonder when they entered. "Haven't been here... since Emmie came."

Tears filled Kate's eyes. She felt such gratitude for this wonderful woman. Words would not come. Elizabeth pressed a lovely embroidered handkerchief into Kate's hands.

"Well, it's high time I had you here to visit. I have something else for you as well."

The shop keeper disappeared behind a partition and returned with a gray cloak trimmed in fur. She removed Kate's shawl and draped the beautiful garment over her shoulders.

"Oh, my lands," Kate whispered as she fingered the soft wool and collar. Looking in the mirror, she struggled to speak. "Goat in sheep's clothing!"

"Nonsense," Elizabeth replied. "It's chilly out. You'll wear it in the cool months when you come to visit me, then I'll store it here where no moths dare to enter. You don't need to wait for a wedding or a baby or some tragedy to return. I'll send Thomas for you as often as you'll come. Promise me you will?"

Kate was obviously distressed at her inability to say the things she wanted to say.

Elizabeth took her hands. "I don't know if I've ever properly thanked you for letting your daughter be a part of our lives. She and Caleb and the children . . . they've become the family that we couldn't have. We feel that same way about you and Omie and her family."

Watching through the window, Thomas smiled as the women embraced.

*They both deserves this, they surely do.*

When the women were ready to return home, Thomas helped them back into the carriage. He could see the lines of worry had softened around Kate's eyes, and her smile was relaxed.

Elizabeth asked, "Thomas, would you take us through Forsythe Park on the way?"

"Yes, ma'am. Be happy to."

Frank Thomas had brought his mamma's harmonica, knowing how music was a balm to her. One day, as he tried to find his way around its scales, Omie reached out for it, saying, "Let me show you, son."

She played a few notes, then broke into *Down to the River to Pray*. Stopping about half-way through, she looked at the instrument as if wondering how it had come to be in her hands, and gave it back to Frank Thomas.

Bitsy stood in the doorway smiling at her cousins. "That's a start, right?"

Omie turned her head and in the dim light, she thought this was her sister as a young girl. Slight and pretty, dark haired like their father. She returned the smile, then sank back into her pillow to sleep.

"C'mon," Bitsy said, motioning for Bartie and Frank Thomas to follow her. "The boys and I have something to show you." Walking towards the parlor she called out, "Mamma, we're going for a walk."

"Shhhh!" Emmie put her arms around Bitsy and pulled her close. "Don't wake your Aunt Omie. Where are you children going?"

Danny slid his eyes toward his sister and back. "Oh, just around. We figure the cousins haven't really seen much here."

"Take something in case it gets cooler. Be home before dark. Promise?"

They all said, "We promise," and scooted out the front door.

Danny led them down a couple of alleys, then turned a corner and stood in front of a wrought iron fence dwarfed by dense camellia shrubs and tangled with fragrant Carolina jasmine.

"What is this place?" Frank Thomas asked.

"You'll see," Bitsy answered. "Danny found it a few weeks ago. We haven't shown anyone else, you're the first!"

Bitsy let Danny lead the way, since this was his mystery.

"I know Mamma and Daddy would not approve of us sneaking in here. But I think it's a fairy garden!" Danny proclaimed.

Bartie was already on her knees looking for a way in.

"Follow me!" Danny pulled out a couple of loose spires which had been jammed in place, and a hole opened in the fence, large enough for them all to crawl through. He had broken through the hedge and made a tunnel to the other side which could not be seen from the road.

As each child crawled out of the passageway, they stood in stunned silence.

"We think there used to be a mansion here," Bitsy whispered.

A series of winding paved canals led to a round pool with a lichen-covered stone lion at its center. An orange stain below the carved chin identified the statue as once having been a fountain. The water's surface was choked with lily pads. This once formal garden now ran rampant with overgrown azaleas, lush ferns and wide-leaved hostas.

Noise from the street was silenced in this timeless place, allowing the children to feel as if they had stepped into another world. They spent the afternoon exploring the garden and searching for remnants of the home which had once been beyond it.

Bitsy realized they had been there longer than she thought as shadows crept across the pool. "We'd best get going!" she called to the others, "We'll be late for supper."

Bartie and Bitsy took Aaron's hands, swinging him as they hurried to the tunnel beneath the hedge. Frank Thomas noticed Danny was no longer beside him and turned back to see his cousin talking to something in the gloom beneath the trees. He began to walk toward the younger boy but stopped when he saw what Danny was looking at.

Soft globes of light were moving in the trees. Much too large to be fireflies.

Frank Thomas took his cousin's arm, pulling him away from the darkening garden.

"What in the world...? Were those ghosts?"

Danny thought a moment, and replied, "Don't think so. I think they're spirits that didn't want to be people. Maybe that's what fairies really are. Boy, you can see them a whole lot better when it's dark!"

"You seen 'em before?"

"Oh yeah," Danny replied, "They're always here. They don't mean any harm, I think they just like the garden, same as us."

"Can everybody see 'em?"

"Bitsy and Aaron never have. I guess they like you, Frank Thomas."

In the days that followed, Frank Thomas pondered on the existence of fairies, or whatever those balls of light had been. He held back from sharing this secret with anyone. Ezra's ghosts were something he'd grown up around, like his mamma and grandmamma's *Sight*. This was a whole new kettle of fish, and he wasn't sure what he should make of it.

*Why do they care about me?*

Caleb sat at the kitchen table with Emmie after everyone else had gone to bed. He admired the soft red highlights in her dark hair. And the few strands of silver caught in the lamplight's glow. At thirty-three, she was more lovely than when they married. He imagined she would be one of those women time is kind to, even when her hair was a halo of silver.

She held a sleeping Aaron on her lap, stroking his back, reluctant to put him in his bed. Touching her nose to his sweet-smelling head, she asked, "Do you really think Omie's ready to go home?"

"I think she would fare as well there as she will here. Maybe better, with more familiar surroundings and routines. We'll keep in close touch in case she takes a turn for the worse. Don't worry."

Emmie considered his words, then nodded. "Since it's still mild out, let's make ice cream on the porch after supper tomorrow night. Make it an occasion for Mamma and the children before they leave."

In the morning, Emmie enlisted the help of Maizie and Elizabeth to plan a festive dinner for that evening. Dr. Campbell volunteered to procure the ice and churn the cream. Maizie offered to contribute some of her canned peaches. Though the circumstances were less than ideal, the Campbells had enjoyed visiting with Emmie's family in Savannah for the past few weeks.

Elizabeth had been tutoring Frank Thomas and Bartie on the lessons Miss Sarah sent them. It was a price they were willing to pay to stay by their mamma's side. Their temporary teacher made lessons fun, including visiting sites mentioned in their history books. At dinner, the two children talked about their adventures, seeming reluctant to return to the small schoolhouse near New Abercorn.

It was a lovely farewell supper. Frank Thomas and Bartie were also aware of the difference in this feast and the simple farm fare they'd return to at home. When plates were cleared, Dr. Campbell made good on his promise and soon all were sitting on the porch, enjoying peach ice cream. Omie even felt strong enough to join them for a small dish. The children made short work of theirs and ran around in the yard, capturing the last of the season's fireflies in jars. Omie sat beside Kate, smiling at the scene below until her gaze focused on something in the trees. She called out, "Danny!"

Everyone looked around for the boy, but he had disappeared. Omie started coughing and pointed to the trees. Frank Thomas looked up, seeing a handful of orbs shining in the branches. He took off running toward the secret garden, Bartie at his heels.

"What in the world?" Caleb asked.

"Get a lantern and come with me, Daddy!" Bitsy grabbed his hand, and they ran to catch up.

She led him through the alleys to the iron fence. The spires had been removed, and she dropped down, starting to wiggle through.

"Bitsy!"

"There's a hole through the hedge too. Just come, Daddy. I'll explain later!"

Caleb managed to squeeze through both. When he stood up, he saw Frank Thomas hauling a soaked and crying Danny from a dark pool.

"He couldn't get out 'cause the sides are slimy."

Caleb ran over to his son. He rolled the boy onto his side, slapping his small back. Danny coughed up the rest of the water he'd swallowed and clung to Caleb, sobbing. When Danny calmed down, Caleb asked, "What is this place?" He looked around, trying to make some sense of his surroundings in the lantern light. Shadowy figures loomed among heavy branches and pale blooms.

"It's Danny's secret garden, Pappa. He found it and brought us here." Bitsy started crying, frightened that she'd nearly lost her little brother.

Danny sniffled, "I just wanted to see the lights again in the dark, but I tripped and fell in."

"What lights?" Caleb asked.

Frank Thomas pointed up into the higher branches where a cluster of glowing orbs moved about.

Caleb's eyes widened. He picked Danny up and hurried the children toward the tunnel they'd come through. He had no words for what he'd seen. The boys seemed to have no fear of these odd lights. For now, though, he needed to concern himself with taking care of the shivering body in his arms. Questions could come later.

Frank Thomas turned to wave before crawling through the branches.

As Caleb returned home and hurried up the porch steps with Danny in his arms, Emmie cried out, "What's happened? Is he all right?"

"Yes, just a bit soggy and shaken. We should get him in a warm bath."

Bitsy followed her parents, explaining the situation. Bartie helped Kate put Omie back to bed. She was still frightened for Danny until he came to her after his bath, assuring his aunt that he was fine. When Omie finally fell asleep, Kate and Bartie went back out to clean up the porch.

Frank Thomas sat quietly in a rocker.

"You OK?" Bartie asked.

"Yeah, I'm a'right," he answered. "I just don't know what to make of them lights, though."

Bartie frowned. "How come I didn't see them?"

"I don't know." Frank Thomas turned to his grandmamma. "Did you see 'em?"

Kate sat in the chair beside him and nodded. "Saw 'em as a girl. Thought they were... big lightnin' bugs. Told daddy. He said...was swamp gas. Will-o'-the-wisp."

Kate paused and took a deep breath.

"Wadn't near  swamp. Old cemetery down hill."

"Why do you 'spose only some folks see 'em, Grandmamma?"

"Don't know." Kate ran a hand through his hair. "You're lucky." She rose and went inside to check on Danny.

Bartie plopped in the chair and turned to Frank Thomas.

"Oh, I don't know as I'd call it luck, brother. Most likely they was hopin' you'd fall in too. Two fools for the price of one."

He reached to tweak her braid, but Bartie jumped up and hopped down the steps. Frank Thomas gave chase, and their laughter rang out in the warm night.

# Chapter 10

The morning Omie was allowed to return home was bitter sweet. Frank Thomas and Bartie needed to get back to school and resume their own lives. Caleb felt sure Kate and Ada could manage Omie's care. He knew Emmie would still worry about her sister, though.

They left the next Saturday when the Decker children could be home to say their goodbyes. Maizie and Mrs. Campbell stood in the doorway with Bitsy, Danny and Aaron in front of them. Aaron cried as the cousins left, but his brother and sister grinned, waving until the Ford was out of sight.

Caleb drove them himself, with Emmie and Kate beside him. Frank Thomas and Bartie sat on either side of their mamma in the back, pointing out the changes that had come since they'd all been gone.

"The corn stalks are startin' to go from green to gold. Purty soon the cobs will need shuckin' for feed, the fields plowed, all that fun stuff." Frank Thomas sighed. "Maybe the city life is more for me."

"Mamma, look at the scarecrows!" Bartie pointed to a row of whimsical characters mounted on poles in a cornfield. They seemed to be there for entertainment as much as a deterrent to the greedy birds. A group of children waved as the automobile drove past, and Omie waved back.

A vague memory came to her. She and Nate building a scarecrow. They'd dressed it in Emmie's bloomers and laughed at them flapping in the wind. When was that? They'd shown it to Mamma and Daddy. Tears filled

Omie's eyes at the vision of her daddy. She turned her face away from the window.

"You all right, Mamma?" Frank Thomas asked softly.

She nodded and closed her eyes for the rest of the trip.


Phoebee found things for the children to do as they waited for Omie's arrival. Chickens needed to be fed, eggs collected, goats brushed free of burrs. Just as they were running out of things to occupy them, the Decker's Ford came up the road.

The yard was full of excited faces as Caleb pulled in. Nate opened Kate's door, helping her out. Bartie took her grandmamma's hand, and they walked together to the house. Frank Thomas pushed open his door, then turned to offer a hand to his mamma.

"I'll take it from here, son," Nate told him, reaching for Omie from the other side. They locked eyes for a moment, Frank Thomas struggling with the idea of relinquishing her to *him*.

*Where were you all this time when I was the one helpin' her?*

Finally, the boy got out and walked away. Ezra tackled him, playfully punching Frank Thomas to break the tension showing in the set of his shoulders.

As Omie stepped into the house, Ada Kate gently hugged her, then led her to the sideboard. There sat a lovely cake, decorated with pink frosting and camelia buds.

"I made it for you, Mamma."

Omie's eyes glistened as she took her daughter's hand.

"So pretty," she whispered.

"All right," Emmie announced. "Let her sit at the table and everybody can take turns welcoming her home. Georgia Rose, come sit in my lap right next to your mamma."

Ezra and Polly gave her cards they'd made in school, and seeing Omie struggle to read them, Polly did it for her. "We all missed you, Aunt Omie," she said, planting a kiss on Omie's cheek.

Willie hung back shyly, surprised at the changes in Omie since their experience.

Sarah waited to come down the hill until the family had time to get Omie settled. She brought with her a soft wool scarf she'd knitted and draped it around the woman's thin shoulders. Omie smiled and patted Sarah's hand, though she looked as if she might not recognize her.

In the months following, the family came to accept Omie's lapses in memory. When she called them by each other's names, they made a game of it.

"No Mamma, Ezra's the ugly one. I'm the handsome one."

"Handsome like a monkey's butt," Ezra would reply, making Georgia Rose giggle.

Their little sister drew funny pictures of each member of the family, as well as Phoebee, Sarah, Polly, Willie and Old Joe.

At breakfast one morning she showed Bartie her latest batch, and asked if she would label them for her so Mamma could tell who was who.

"Pretty darn good," Frank Thomas commented. "But Georgia Rose, you forgot the wart on Bartie's nose!"

Bartie rewarded him with a handful of grits on top of his head.

"Children, children," Omie said, smiling.

Sometimes Omie would leave the house and forget where she was going, ending up at the barn with some critter or other in her arms. Or, they would find her 'resting' by the well under the old live oak tree. Old Joe would often seek her out and curl up at her feet until someone found them. The dog would cock his ears to listen as she talked to him. Omie had become familiar to a mockingbird nesting in the oak, and she began to teach it a few notes. Eventually, the two began whistling back and forth in harmony.

Emmie drove down from Savannah often with the children. These visits worked like a tonic for Omie. Emmie would talk about childhood stories, jostling her sister's memory, drawing her into conversations.

At Thanksgiving and Christmas that year, Caleb and Emmie came to the farm with their family, loaded with food and gifts sent by folks in Savannah. Omie was, by turns, engaged and distant with everyone but seemed content to have them nearby.

Gradually, the cloud of confusion that enveloped Omie lifted slightly, but not enough to give them hope of its completely leaving. The children accompanied her on walks when days were not too chilly, helping her build strength again. Willie held her hand, doing his best to keep her steady. The girls picked up twigs and moss to fashion into dolls. Georgia made up stories for each one, doing her best to pull a laugh from Mamma.

Sometimes the boys left them to hunt rabbits and squirrels, running ahead with Old Joe. The dog always had something to lay at Omie's feet, sitting back with his tongue lolling, looking very pleased with himself.

Hoar frost glazed the kitchen window, looking like lace in the pale February sunlight.

"Mamma, what are you doing?" Ada Kate went to stand by her mamma at the stove.

"I'm making biscuits for breakfast, hon. All those workers need feeding."

Ada looked out at the frosty brown fields. She did not have the heart to tell her mamma that planting time was still months away.

"But we just finished eating an hour ago. Don't you remember?"

Omie stood a moment trying to gather her thoughts. She turned to Ada Kate and said, "I guess I forgot, daughter."

She seemed so lost that Ada Kate said, "Well, they're all mixed up and ready for rolling out now. We'll have a head start on dinner!"

Kate entered the kitchen and exchanged a look of concern with her granddaughter. Both worried that cooking at the woodstove might prove dangerous for Omie.

A trip into town with Nate after this incident did not turn out well. He left Omie sitting on the wagon with instructions to stay there. Returning from the store, he found his wife wandering down Main Street, mumbling to herself. A group of boys mocked her, laughing as they followed.

Mrs. O'Dell saw this from her window and ran out, gathering her skirts as she chased the boys away. "I know your mammas and daddies, you wait 'til I tell them what you been up to! Little heathens!" She walked over and took Omie's arm. "Don't pay them no mind, hon. It's good to see you back home."

Soon, word of her condition spread through town. Mrs. O'Dell toned down the gossip as best she could.

"Mrs. Silar is just a little confused and thin as a rail. Not at all surprising with what the poor woman has been through."

Friends dropped by with food and words of encouragement. Some town boys still *happened* to walk by the farm, calling her crazy when they saw her in the yard. Both Ezra and Frank Thomas sported black eyes from time to time, but the taunting happened less often.

Nate began drinking again. It was February, so there were few chores that needed his attention. His state worried Bartie and disgusted Frank Thomas. The rest of the family took his drinking in stride, not surprised that he would turn to moonshine in his grief and frustration. Omie's distance from him, in spite of his care, had been too much to bear.

# Chapter 11

## 1924

Spring unfurled the fiddleheads of ferns and the ground warmed beneath the sun. The local women returned to help Phoebee plant the peanut fields, paying gentle attention to Omie as she greeted them. Those who had not seen her since the lightning strike were taken aback by her appearance. They'd known Omie to be a hard worker, nearly as strong as a man. Omie felt their pity and chose to stay more often with Ada Kate in the kitchen. There, she was able to do tasks that her hands seemed to know of their own accord. She would hum bits of songs and Ada would sing, pretending to forget the words, hoping to draw them from her mamma's memory.

*Oh Susanna! Oh, don't you cry for me*
*I come from Alabama*
*With my banjo on my knee*
*It rained all night the day I left*
*The weather it was dry*
*Sun so hot I froze myself*
*Susanna don't you cry*

The morning air often carried the sounds of Ada Kate's sweet voice, sometimes joined by her mamma's harmonies. After folks were fed their dinner and dishes cleaned, lively melodies from Omie's harmonica helped carry the workers through the afternoon.

One summer evening, Nate turned to look at his wife's sleeping form. Her face had the softness of the girl he had married before life, particularly life with him, took its toll. Gently, he traced the fading flowers embroidered on her nightdress, remembering the first time he'd seen it on their wedding night. Whisps of hair had escaped from her braid and he tucked them behind her ear, then stroked the curve of her cheek to her mouth.

Omie woke with a start. She opened her eyes, at first not seeming to know who he was in the dim light. Her body relaxed, as he whispered soothingly and began to raise her gown. She did not resist him, but neither did she meet him in the urgent way they had enjoyed their lovemaking in the past. Instead, she turned her face toward the window and stared at the rising moon.

"Omie, come back to me!" he cried, as he lay spent, holding her unresponsive body.

There was a change in Nate afterwards that all the family felt. He worked the land, clearing new patches along the sides of fields after the crops were in until there was no more to be done. He stopped coming in for meals, accepting a plate from Bartie in the barn instead. They thought perhaps he had given up on Omie, letting hard toil sweat the grief from his body. Nate knew, however, that it was guilt he was trying to purge.

November began the busy time of caring for colds and other winter ailments folks caught. Ada had her hands full, taking over her mamma's patients. She became concerned when Omie started having bouts of nausea regularly. The girl hoped this was temporary, and not a result of damage from the lightning strike presenting itself.

"Grandmamma, do you think Mamma has the Influenza? Weak as she is, I'm afraid she wouldn't survive something like that."

"No child, she'd be feverish. Maybe just a stomach ailment. Let's give it a bit longer before we tell Caleb and Emmie. Make sure she drinks the teas. Add a few drops of slippery elm to it."

Kate felt a tingle on the back of her neck.

"Omie Darlin', would you come here for a minute?"

Omie came out of her room and sat at the table.

"I just want to check your belly. See what's makin' you so ill."

Resting a hand on Omie's abdomen, Kate closed her eyes and prayed for an answer. After a few moments, her eyelids fluttered and she took her hand back.

Smiling so as not to frighten her daughter and granddaughter, she said, "Thanks honey. Want some tea?"

Omie nodded and Kate rose to put on the kettle. She put a hand on Ada's arm before she could head for the herb room and said, "Hold off on the slippery elm 'til I can talk to Caleb. Just until we hear his opinion, ok? Thanksgiving is just a few days away. We can wait 'til then."

Kate was sure she knew what the problem was, but didn't want to be the bearer of this news.

Ada searched her grandmamma's face for any signs of trouble, but seeing none there, she nodded and went to fetch chamomile for tea.


The house was filled with smells of roasting turkey and ham when the Decker family walked in. Bitsy and Danny went outside with their cousins to play tag in the crisp sunshine and Georgia took Aaron by the hand to show him a new batch of kittens in the barn.

After greetings and hugs had gone around, Kate pulled Caleb aside and asked if he might check Omie over before the meal.

He looked at her questioningly and caught the slight shake of her head, taking her meaning. There was something she didn't want to share with the others.

"Well, certainly. No time like the present."

Walking over to Omie at the stove, he gave her a hug and asked, "Might I have a moment with you? Doctor to patient?"

Omie smiled at him. "I'm fine, Caleb. No need to worry."

"I'm sure you are, but just let me listen to your heart. Would that be all right?"

Kate led them to her room and Omie sat down on the bed.

Kate described the nausea that had been plaguing her daughter for the past few weeks.

After asking a few questions about any other symptoms she might have, he said, "Lay back for me, please ma'am."

Omie settled herself against the pillows as Caleb put his stethoscope on. He listened to her heart, then lightly palpated her abdomen, looking for pain. What he found instead, was a rounded bump contrasting sharply with her slight frame.

He looked into Kate's eyes.

She said, "About four months, I believe."

Looking at them both, Omie asked, "Everything all right?"

Caleb and Kate each took one of her hands.

"Daughter, you're gonna have another li'l one."

"Perhaps we should save this surprise until after Thanksgiving. Just to be sure," he advised.

As Omie's pregnancy became more apparent, Kate informed the family of the new member to come.

When Frank Thomas learned of his mamma's condition, he went into a rage.

"How could he do that to her!" he yelled. "Sonofabitch!"

Phoebee hurried to find Nate splitting wood behind the barn and confronted him, "You bastard! We just found out you got Omie pregnant. Couldn't just do your business with those whores at the roadhouse? I come to warn you, your son aims to kill you. If he don't, I might. You better hightail it before he's got your gun loaded!"

Nate looked up in shock. "Pregnant?" he asked.

Hearing the screen door slam, he dropped the axe and ran into the back field, headed for the river. Frank Thomas pointed the gun and fired, noting with satisfaction his daddy had a limp to his run now.

"Frank Thomas! I cain't believe you actually shot your daddy! What do you have to say for yourself?" Phoebee cried.

"Shoulda aimed higher?" he replied, throwing the gun down.

Caleb checked on his sister-in-law often, doing all he could to help Omie with her pregnancy. Often in her confusion, she called the coming baby by one of her current children's names. She began to wear Nate's old coat over her protruding belly, plopping his hat on her head when going outdoors. Older boys from town went out of their way to come by the farm and tease her, laughing, and running if they saw Ezra and Frank Thomas.

Alone in the house one afternoon, Omie heard the boys' taunts and took Nate's shotgun down from its rack. She went to the sideboard for shells and came face to face with a stranger in the mirror. She stood, feeling the world shift around her.

A familiar voice sounded in her head. *Granddaughter, come home. Your family needs you.*

Ada Kate came in with an armload of kindling and found her mamma standing there.

"Mamma?"

The other children heard the concern in their sister's voice and hurried into the kitchen.

Mesmerized by her reflection, Omie said softly, "Children, I've been gone a long time, haven't I?"

Bartie fell to her knees and began to cry, which made Georgia Rose cry also. Frank Thomas took the gun from her. Ezra wrapped their mamma in an embrace, tears sliding down his cheeks as well.

Kate sent word to Emmie, and the Deckers arrived the next day.

"She's had a breakthrough, it seems." Caleb announced to the family at the kitchen table as Omie rested in her room. They could hear the soft murmur of Emmie and Omie's voices in conversation.

"She's more aware of her surroundings, able to answer questions clearly. I don't know how this happened, but it surely is miraculous. By the time the baby is due, perhaps she'll be fully recovered. Emmie and I will come as often as we're able, but please get word to me if anything concerns you and we'll be here directly."

Emmie emerged from her sister's room with tears in her eyes and a soft smile for the ones gathered at the table. The children clustered around her, laughing and hugging their aunt. At the sound of all the commotion, Old Joe jumped up to put his paws on Willie's small shoulders and they danced around the room. Kate's tears turned to laughter as well.

# Chapter 12
## 1925

There was a morning in late March when Omie woke to a fine fur of ice covering every twig, every blade of dried grass. Even the backs of the cows had a glisten to them. A late frost was not a welcome occurrence. Recent mild temperatures had tricked the apple and peach trees into forming the tiny promise of blooms.

She stood in the doorway taking in the fresh, cold air.

*If this turn of the weather don't last but a day, I expect everything will be all right.*

Taking a seat on the porch and lifting her face toward the rising sun, Omie smiled. This would be a good day. She felt it in her bones. Maybe the worry would leave the faces of her children for a time.

*Please Lord, help steady me. I don't want to be a burden.*

Omie knew there were times when she lapsed into forgetfulness. It was plain to see in the way everyone treated her like one of Kate's china cups brought out for special occasions. She would sometimes fetch a basket of eggs and set it down to hold an old favorite hen, then forget to pick it up again. Or fail to put the milk in the springhouse, having been distracted by a new calf's soft muzzle.

She returned to the well at her mamma's old house time and again, moving aside the cover to gaze at her reflection in its calm water. What she hoped to see there, she wasn't sure, but the face looking back became more familiar, giving her strength.

As the sun spread its warmth across her belly, Omie rubbed the solid curves and felt the baby stir.

*Tell me, little one. Who will you be? The best of your daddy and me, I pray.*

Nate had kept his distance from the farm through the winter. No one but Bartie knew or was much interested in where he stayed. As the weather warmed, Omie began to see the red glow from a cigarette at the edge of the barn, gradually making out his form standing there. She wasn't sure how to feel about their situation. Did not remember having made this child.

There were days when she felt she hardly knew the man she'd loved so long. Frank Thomas bristled any time Nate was mentioned in his presence. Omie didn't remember why, but for once, she was listening to her family's advice to let him be. At least until the confusion that lingered in her mind cleared.

Emmie and Caleb arrived a few days before the baby was due, wanting to be present if there were complications.

Ezra built a new cradle to replace the worn one they had all been rocked in. Omie had passed it on to a new mother in need, not expecting to have use of it again. His handiwork received high praise from Caleb and Emmie, causing him to blush with pleasure.

Bartie collected shed rabbit fur from warrens found on her outings. Kate used it to stuff small cloth animals sewn on her Singer machine.

It seemed there was more leisure time for anticipation with the coming of this baby. More sense of excitement. Perhaps because the previous year had offered so little joy.

"Mamma, look at the pictures I drew for baby!" Georgia exclaimed, eager for the adults to see.

"Oh my, darlin'. Those are beautiful!" Omie spread them across her expanded belly.

Caleb leaned down to look. "Georgia Rose, is that a camel?"

"No, it ain't. You know better, Uncle Caleb. Here's you!"

She pulled out a drawing of a man with a large mustache and a stethoscope hanging around his neck.

"See, there's your stepincope."

"My stethoscope."

"Yep."


Omie felt surrounded by love. Each of her family took part in preparing for the baby's birth. Phoebee and the boys made sure the fields and garden were ready for planting so she would not fret about them. Ada Kate made food ahead that could be eaten cold by those helping with the delivery. Clean cloths were set beside the bed and pots of water filled, ready to be boiled.

She was being physically and emotionally cared for in a way she had never allowed before. When Aunt Julia showed up at the door, they knew the time had come. Omie's water broke within the hour.

Phoebee and Sarah herded the children out to Kate's old house for supper. Good smells wafted down the hill, and Kate told Caleb and Emmie to go get some food for themselves, the baby was still getting into position.

Omie prepared herself for what was to come. *Don't feel right not havin' your daddy here, little one.*

The contractions came surprisingly fast. Aunt Julia and Kate were sitting at the foot of Omie's bed, peering beneath the sheet draped over her knees. Omie groaned.

"Not long now!" Aunt Julia cackled.

"Thank the Lord this child is behaving so well," Kate agreed. "Can't wait to see your family, can you little one?"

Emmie and Caleb returned to the house just in time. The young doctor smiled at the two midwives as Emmie took her place, glad to be allowed in their company.

"All right, daughter. Push!" Kate came around to press on Omie's belly if needed.

As soon as the words were out, a tiny little girl slid into Aunt Julia's hands. The old woman crooned, "Ain't you a fine one!"

There was a moment of silence as Kate and Aunt Julia looked at each other, then removed the filmy caul across the baby's face. Immediately, a healthy wail filled the room.

Omie tried to sit up. "Is something wrong?"

"No, Hon. She had the caul across her face like my mamma did."

"Marks her as special!" Aunt Julia announced.

Emmie tenderly settled the baby against her sister's breast. Omie stroked the baby's cheek as she began nursing. Looking back up at Emmie, she said, "Grace. I want to name her Grace."

"That seems a very fitting name." Emmie brushed the damp hair away from Omie's face.

Aunt Julia's smile was salted with tears. "I believe this will be my last baby."

Omie looked at her with concern.

"It's just these old hands of mine have gotten so shaky."

"And I only have one good hand," Kate declared.

The two old friends smiled at each other.

"Better get Ada Kate trained up then!" Caleb said. "Y'all put me to shame."

"No offense, Doctor Decker, but you are a man." Aunt Julia laughed.

"Amen to that!" Emmie said, and kissed him.


The fullness of spring found its voice in the sounds of gentle rain hitting the tin roof, hoot owls calling and frogs digging out from the mud to sing. Harmonies coming from the pond persuaded Omie to bring out her harmonica, accompanying them from the porch as she rocked baby Grace.

Nate could not resist the call of his fields, working the tobacco seedlings and planting corn. Ezra began to join his daddy in the work, saying little, but much was said in their silent acceptance of one another. Frank Thomas avoided the two of them, helping Phoebee with the peanut crop instead, while his mamma got her strength back.

When he saw Ada Kate outside with the baby on her hip, Nate watched longingly but made no move toward them. One morning, Omie took pity on him and lifted Grace out of Ada's arms. She carried the baby out to the field to meet her daddy. Ezra hung back, wanting to give them some privacy for what needed to be said.

Nate cried unashamedly as he held tiny Grace up toward the sky, then laughed when she rewarded him with a smile. Holding her close, he smelled her sweet baby scent and kissed the downy hair on top of her head.

"Thank you, Omie. I am so sorry."

"Never be sorry for a new life, Nate. She is a blessing."

He began showing up at the supper table. Frank Thomas refused to sit with them and took his food to the porch.

At first, Nate would eat quietly, then go out to the barn to sleep. One evening, Omie heard a soft tapping at her door. Thinking it was one of the children, she said, "Come on in, darlin'." To her surprise, Nate opened it slowly, and stood there with a lantern in his hand. They looked at each other quietly. Holding the coverlet up, she whispered, "Well, get in here, then. Don't wake the baby."

Bartie woke before dawn and spied him leaving the bedroom. She wrapped her arms around his neck and said, "I'm so glad you're back, Daddy."

"Reckon we could sneak in a little fishin' this morning, Snake?"

She beamed up at him, then the two slipped out to grab their poles.

The rest of the family woke up later to the smell of fried fish and grits for breakfast. When Frank Thomas came downstairs, he understood at once that his daddy was back staying in the house. He walked out, slamming the front door. As the kitchen was being cleaned, Omie put the baby on her hip and went to find him.

"Frank Thomas!"

The young man was feverishly chopping weeds between the peanut rows.

"Stop."

Reluctantly, he straightened up and turned to face his mamma.

"I know you're angry at your daddy, but there's things you don't understand."

"What more do I need to understand, Mamma? He don't treat you right. He don't pull his share of work. Then he went and got you with this one," Frank Thomas pointed the handle of the hoe at the baby, "when you was still sick. What kinda man does that?"

Omie felt her temper rise and took a deep breath. She walked over to the boy and put Grace in his arms.

"You think this baby coming into the world is a bad thing?" she asked softly.

"It's not her being here that troubles me, Mamma. It's how she got here. I just don't understand how you can put up with him, why you took him back!" After kissing Grace's head, he handed her back.

Omie looked into Frank Thomas' blue eyes. "I know you're nearly grown, son. But there are many things you need to learn. I made a promise to God and family that I would stand by your daddy through sickness and health, richer or poorer, for all our lives. He doesn't always act right. I know that. There's a sickness in him passed from his own daddy, makes him the way he is. Don't let that happen to you." She paused to gather herself. "Please, son. Try to accept him. For my sake."

Frank Thomas looked away from her gaze and let out a deep sigh.

"I'll do my best to tolerate him, Mamma, but don't expect *me* to 'honor and obey'."

With those words, he turned back to chopping weeds. Omie stood a moment longer, then nodded her head and started back toward the house.

# Chapter 13

In the three years since Ada Kate finished school, she'd been studying with Kate and Omie full time. Little Grace seemed attached to her sister's hip, sometimes riding in a sling across her chest when Ada was working in the herb room. The child was a joy to them all, a healing potion for the struggles of the last year.

When the baby was set on a quilt spread across the floor, Old Joe stood guard, never minding how she pulled at his ears or tail. The day came when she figured out how to grab onto the fur of his back and pull herself up. He became her walking partner until she was able to toddle about by herself, though the dog never let her far from him.

Ada Kate came into the kitchen one morning to find the stove still cold. Old Joe was scratching at her mamma's bedroom door and whining. She flung the door open and saw Omie on her back in bed, staring up at the ceiling with a look of panic. The dog hurried over to lick Omie's face and she let out a gasp, holding a hand to her chest.

"Mamma, what's wrong? Is it your heart?"

Omie got her breath and cried, "I couldn't move! Ada, I was wide awake but couldn't move!" She looked at the dog. "Until he licked me. Good boy."

The dog snuggled close.

"Good, good boy."

Grace was lying quietly by Omie's side, looking at them.

When Omie had calmed down, she said, "Best the baby sleeps by you or Mamma for a while, Ada. Your daddy is up and gone to work so early. What would I do if she needed me and I couldn't move?"

Kate hurried into the room. "What is it, darlin'?"

Omie described for her mamma what had happened. "Have you ever heard of such a thing?"

Shaking her head, Kate said she'd not known a body could be paralyzed until someone touched them. "Could be from the lightnin'. I just don't know, hon. Best see what our Dr. Decker has to say about this."

"Let's wait and see if it happens again." Omie sighed. "Lord knows, Caleb has had his hands full with this family already."

There were no more such episodes for a couple of weeks. Omie began to think this was an isolated incident, but kept her bedroom door open when she laid to rest. Old Joe had taken to curling up at the foot of her bed.

During a mid-day nap, the dog sensed her distress. He whined and licked her feet until Omie sat up, trembling. She wept from the fear, the total helplessness she'd just felt. Old Joe moved up the bed to lick her face and she clung to him for a few moments.

"Ada!" she called.

Ada Kate came in from the kitchen. She knew instantly that the paralysis had happened again.

"I'm going to send someone for the doctor!" the girl declared. "Grandmamma, come quick!"

"No." Omie took her daughter's hand. "Emmie and Caleb will be here tomorrow. Let's wait, he'll likely know what this is."

Emmie could see the concern on her niece's face as soon as she got out of the car.

"What's happened?" she asked, looking from Ada to Omie.

"Come inside," Omie said. "Let's get settled at the table and I'll tell you then."

Caleb listened attentively to Omie's description of the incidents.

"I woke up and just couldn't move, Caleb! Not until Old Joe licked me. I don't know what to make of it, but it's terrifying!"

"I imagine it is," he gently replied. "I've heard of temporary paralysis but none that responded to touch. Or to licking." He smiled at the dog lying beside her. "This may come from damage caused by the lightning. I can't imagine there not being some sort of repercussions. Are you still having any other effects?"

"Only that I need to rest more. Also, that spot on the top of my head always burns. I have to put cold water on it several times a day."

"Well, keep your protector close by." Caleb scratched the dog behind his floppy ears. "I'll look into this problem when we return to Savannah. Dr. Campbell may have a theory to share with us."

Emmie was bouncing Grace on her knees and said, "Well, never a dull moment here!"

"No indeed," Caleb agreed. "I think I've learned as much from your unusual ailments as I did in medical school. Or since!"

"Glad to help with your education, Dr. Decker," Omie replied, with a wry smile for her brother-in-law.

After Emmie and Caleb had taken their leave, Ada Kate and Omie went into the herb room to tie up bundles of comfrey while Kate made crusts for pie. They heard the front screen door slam as Ezra entered the kitchen, letting fly a string of curses the likes of which no one had heard from him before.

Hurrying inside, Omie exclaimed, "Ezra Silar! What has gotten into you?"

"What's done got me, more like it."

He showed them his red and swollen hand.

"Damn ground bees. I was turning the tobacco field and they came swarmin' out. Didn't think it was warm enough yet for those little bast. . . bugs. Glad I had long sleeves on."

Kate motioned him toward the table and sat, then gently put her hand on his. "Ada, get my deer stone off that shelf yonder. Son, you were probably too young to remember when I used this on Polly after the rattlesnake bit her."

"I remember," Ezra said through gritted teeth as he took a seat.

Omie held Grace while Ada found the smooth, oblong stone and brought it to her grandmamma.

Kate nodded and said, "Now, wet it with milk and we'll put it on these stings to draw out the poison. Looks like two of them got you."

Ada took one of the pie pans and set it in the sink. She opened the ice box, took out the morning's milk, and filled the pan halfway. Turning the stone several time to be sure it was well coated she carried the pan to her grandmamma.

"Thank you, Ada. Now place it on his welts, just like that."

Ezra felt a slight suction on his skin. Shortly, the redness subsided and he was able to breathe normally.

"I never hurt so bad! Why are their stings more painful than others?"

"Probably because they have to live in the dirt and it makes them meaner!" Georgia Rose declared.

"Grandmamma," Ada asked, "why does this stone work? How can a rock draw out poison?"

Everyone turned to look at Kate.

"I guess I never asked you the why of it, Mamma," Omie said.

"All I can tell y'all is what my mamma said when she passed it down to me," she replied. "This is not a rock, Ada. It is a stone of sorts, found in the stomach of a deer. A white deer as I recall. My uncle shot it and brought this to Mamma."

"A white deer!" Ezra exclaimed.

"They're rare, but not unheard of in these parts. Anyway, a deer stone, or mad stone, as some folks call it, is made of minerals, hair and plants, things the creature eats but can't digest."

"Mad stone, Grandmamma?" Georgia Rose piped up.

"Folks say it can cure rabies and other sicknesses that drive you mad."

Ezra mused, "So, sometimes a collection of bad things turns into somethin' you can use for healing."

Omie had a sudden vision of Nate's face. *Lord, let me find some healing from our troubles.* She rose from the table and walked to the sink, but not before Kate saw the effect of Ezra's words in her daughter's tearful eyes.

Kate patted her grandson's shoulder. "You're a very wise fella, Ezra Silar."

He felt the stone release his skin and smiled.

"Thank you, Grandmamma."

She lifted it from his hand. "All right, Ada, I reckon the stone is done with him. Soak this in that milk for a spell to pull the poison out, so we can use it again. About an hour or so, then throw that milk down the outhouse."

Ada reverently put the deer stone back in the pan of milk, shaking her head at the wonder of the thing.

Soon, Ezra felt able to go back to work.

"I reckon I'll see y'all at supper time. Quicker if them bees are still swarmin' mad!"

Looking out the window, he saw Polly walking down the hill with a pile of books in her arms. "Reckon I'll go tell Miss Bookworm about my adventure, give them bees a chance to settle down."

He went out and met her by the back porch. "Carry those for ya?"

"I thought you were in the tobacco field. I was gonna sit under a tree and keep you company while I read."

He stuck out his hand, waiting for her to comment.

Polly squinted at it. "What?"

"Them stings! Ground bees got me."

She took his hand and rubbed the back gently. "Don't see nuthin. Where?"

He regarded his unblemished skin in wonder. And the hand that still held his.

"Grandmamma's deer stone. Sucked out all the poison."

Polly nodded. "She saved my life with that stone. Can't say I understand how, but that's the truth of it."

He reluctantly removed his hand from hers, noticing the color in her cheeks. "Anyways, watch out where you plop down." Taking in the amount of reading she had, Ezra asked, "Plannin' on sittin' out there 'til harvest?"

"No, silly. Sarah—Miss Gadsden—thinks I ought to consider becoming a teacher in a few years and gave me some books from her training to look through."

"That so? Well, you are awfully smart." He smirked. "For a girl, that is."

Polly went to swat him with one of the books, and he danced out of the way. They walked out to the tobacco field, where she settled herself beneath a nearby pine.

Ezra looked back over his shoulder as he walked to the plow. He hadn't considered the possibility Polly might have plans about her future that might not include him. They had gone through life together since they were babies.

*Will she have to go off to a teachin' school? Where would she teach after?*

With a furrowed brow, he hooked the mule back to the plow and gave the reins a shake. "Giddap!"


Later in the day, Ada Kate approached her mamma as Omie hung out the wash.

"Mamma, you look done in. Let me finish this for you."

"Well, you can help. Thanks, baby."

Ada picked up pins and placed them between her lips. When they had emptied the basket, she said, "Mamma, I should learn more about birthing babies so I can take some of the load off you. Since Grandmamma had to quit, you've been attending them all. Now that Aunt Julia has gotten too old to help, I want to take her place."

Omie searched her daughter's face. "I believe you can do the work, Ada, but sometimes tending these women and their babies is heartbreaking. Are you sure about this?"

"Yes, ma'am. I've seen my brothers and sisters come into the world. It was scary at times. But wonderful, too. I know there's still a lot for me to learn before I'm ready to deliver babies on my own. Let me go with you. Grandmamma is doing well now. I don't think she needs my help anymore."

Omie put her arms around her oldest daughter, resting a cheek against Ada Kate's sweet-smelling hair. "When did you get so grown-up?"

# 1939

## JUNE 20

Georgia Rose brought her easel up onto the porch and settled in a corner where the morning light was good. She had a mind to sketch each member of the family, then paint their portraits in her own time. *Not likely to see this bunch all together again soon.* Her mamma would love the paintings, and eventually they would become family history.

She'd managed to capture likenesses of her sisters and brothers, as well as nieces. All but Frank Thomas, who was deliberately on the move when he saw her. He never wanted to be photographed either. Why, she could not fathom. It wasn't as if his limp was visible when he stood still. Maybe if he and Ezra played music later, she could sketch him in secret.

Tess' younger brothers peeked over the edge of the porch railing. Cyrus piped up, "Whatcha drawin', Auntie G?"

"Monkeys. Would you two like to model for me?"

"Haw, you are not!"

"Well boys, I *would* like to draw each of you, but I don't think you can stay still long enough. Guess I'll just have to be satisfied with sketches of your sisters." Georgia Rose turned back to her easel.

The boys looked at each other, then back at her. Jacob asked, "You done drew them? When?"

"While y'all were off with your uncles."

"I reckon we got a little time now if you want to do us." Jacob tried not to look too interested.

Cyrus nodded nonchalantly but his eager eyes gave him away. "Me first!"

She had to sketch quickly, but managed to capture enough before they got too squirmy.

Lilly and Tess wandered over to see Georgia's progress.

"Not bad, Aunt Georgia," Lilly observed.

"You forgot their tails," Tess chimed in.

"We are not monkeys!" her brothers howled in unison.

Just then, Ezra and Frank Thomas wandered up the steps and headed for the kitchen.

Cyrus and Jacob ran to grab hold of them before they went inside. "Uncles, come play with us!"

"In a few minutes," Ezra said softly.

Frank Thomas put his hands over his ears. "Coffee."

The two men walked into the kitchen, looking sheepishly at their mamma.

"Mornin' boys." Omie reached for their hands.

"Mornin' Mamma." Ezra bent to kiss her.

Frank Thomas tried to do the same, but squinched his eyes in pain and stood back up. He patted her on the shoulder. "Mornin' Mamma."

"Need some herbs for that hangover?" Ada murmured as she filled his cup by the sideboard.

"I got some hair of the dog." He pulled a flask from his pocket and poured in a dollop, looking around to see if anyone was watching.

Omie looked out the window as if she hadn't noticed. "Give him some milk thistle, Ada. Ezra too. That dog must'a had some sharp teeth!"

Ada went out to the herb room and returned with a small bottle. "Speakin' of dogs Mamma, I was remembering earlier how Old Joe used to stay right by your side in case you had one of those fits. I wonder how he could tell one was comin' on?"

"I haven't had one since he passed. Oddest thing. I know he saved me more times than I can count."

Ezra grinned. "Old Joe. Best dog I ever knew. Smart as could be."

Ada grinned. "Remember when Georgia Rose won best picture at the county fair with her drawing of him? Came home with a blue ribbon and pinned it right to the dog's collar."

Everyone laughed.

"It was a big sacrifice for Willie to leave his dog with me when he left. He knew how much I needed him though."

"Dog never took to me," Frank Thomas muttered.

Ada squinted at him. "Wonder why."

Frank Thomas returned to his coffee.

# Chapter 14

## 1926

Georgia Rose dug her toes into the rich soil between the vegetable beds. A soft rain set free the scents of wet sandy clay, mixed with the remains of gardens long spent and turned back into the ground. Tiny earthworms, suddenly exposed, searched for a way back into their dark domain.

She sat beneath a canopy for string beans made of brushy sticks poked in the ground. On the back of a magnolia leaf, she began to draw the tiny world of bugs and worms before her.

"Georgia Rose!" Ada called. "We're goin' to the fields. Wanna' come?"

She hurried to catch up with her mamma and grandmamma. All spring, Georgia had been following the women as they searched for early plants to use as remedies. The little girl drew pictures of herbs on anything she found handy, the backs of thick magnolia leaves, tree bark, used scraps of paper that Sarah brought home from school.

Often, she would find the plants they were seeking before anyone else saw them.

Ada's curiosity finally made her ask, "Georgia Rose! How do you find them so easy?"

"I reckon 'cause they shine different. Um...like that patch of comfrey out there." She pointed to a place in the pasture a good twenty yards away.

"Shine?" Ada asked, as she walked toward the spot. Sure enough, the light green velvety leaves of comfrey came into view.

"Yarrow is brighter, and wintergreen don't shine so much. It's a darker color."

The little artist sat down and began to sketch a cluster of leaves. Ada shook her head in wonder, then went to tell her mamma of Georgia's explanation.

After an hour or so, Kate called, "Georgia Rose. We're done for the day."

On the way back to the house, Ada saw Sarah walking down with a package in her hand.

They greeted each other on the porch and walked into the kitchen together.

"Hi, ladies. More stationary here from my mother. I'll never be able to use it all, I still have some left from the last bunch she sent. May I give it to you?"

"Thank you! I'm overdue to write Emmie. She'll love this." Omie lifted the paper to her nose. "Scented with lavender too!"

Sarah smiled fondly. "That's my mother. By the way, I wanted to tell you how impressed I am with Georgia's drawings. She's actually quite talented, especially for an eight-year-old. Over time, I think our little Georgia Rose could become a true artist."

Omie thanked Sarah again as the young woman left, then sat at the table to begin a letter to her sister.

Georgia skipped into the house with a smudged face and a piece of an old envelope in her hand. "Whatcha doin', Mamma?"

"I'm writing to your Aunt Emmie. What do you have there?"

"Can I send Aunt Emmie my picture in your letter?"

"Sure, honey." Omie shook her head in wonder. "Oh my, look at those chickens! You got the feathers just right."

Georgia Rose smiled her pleasure, then skipped out the door again.

Emmie sent a package back to her niece containing a sketch book and pencils from Savannah. Inside was a letter for Georgia, praising her picture and saying, *Georgia Rose, did you know that your cousin Aaron likes to draw too? These are the same kind of supplies he uses.*

The girl was ecstatic.

Omie hugged her daughter and said, "Now, before you do anything else, I want you to write your aunt a thank you letter."

"I will Mamma, but let me go draw her something first." True to her word, she returned with a sketch of wildflowers and wrote a short note on it. After handing the letter to her mamma for an envelope and stamp, Georgia Rose took her new treasures and all but disappeared for a few days. Everything that caught her fancy was put to paper, and she began writing stories to go with them.

There was a likeness of Old Joe that Georgia Rose had hung on the wall of the kitchen, and when Sarah saw it, she encouraged the girl to enter it in the next county fair.

"Really?" Georgia asked. "You think it's good enough?"

"I think it's more than good enough!" Sarah assured her.

"Just don't forget that it's mine and Old Joe's!" Willie piped up.

On her aunt's next visit, Georgia Rose proudly showed what she'd drawn with her new supplies.

"Oh my!" Emmie exclaimed, with some surprise. "I do believe you have a gift, sweetheart."

Later, Omie saw them whispering at the table while she was preparing dinner and was not surprised when the girl piped up, "Mamma, can I go home with Aunt Emmie for a few days? She wants to take me to a mooseum. Aaron gets to go all the time. Please?"

Omie gave her sister a sideways look and said, "Honey it's a museum, not a mooseum. They don't keep cows there."

Georgia giggled.

"Now Emmie, don't go encouraging my daughter to hightail it to the city!"

"Oh, good grief, Omie. I just want her to see some real art, is all. It would do you good to have a little cultural exposure yourself. Come with us!"

Omie rolled her eyes but was secretly intrigued with the idea. Most of the planting had been done, so she could be spared for a few days. Nate would be too busy to miss her much.

*A trip away would be a welcome change.*

It was settled then.

Looking into Georgia Rose's hopeful eyes, she said, "Emmie, can you stay over tonight? I need a day to get ready. I need to go to Aunt Julia's today, too."

"I'll give Caleb a call from the store in town, I'm sure it won't be a problem."

Georgia danced around, then took Emmie's hand. "Come help me find some clothes to wear at the Mooseum."


Looking around her room to see if she had forgotten anything, Omie turned to Ada Kate with a worried expression. "Aunt Julia's granddaughter will take care of Grace while we're gone. She's nursing one of her own, so we'll take her there on our way. If any babies decide to be born, Aunt Julia can tell you what to do if you're willing, Ada. None are due, but as you know, they come when they're ready. That all right?"

Ada Kate seemed to stand a little taller. "Yes ma'am. We'll be fine. Y'all go have a good time."

Georgia Rose waved out the window until the auto had taken them beyond sight of the house. She settled between Emmie and Omie, commenting on everything she saw.

Caught up in the excitement of her freedom, Omie even gave in to a driving lesson.

Emmie looked at her sister with an encouraging smile. "Now, just watch what I do. I'll explain it all, I promise. Once you get going, it's really simple."

"Can I try next?" Georgia Rose piped up.

"Your legs have got to be long enough to reach the pedals, young lady. One day, I'll teach you too. All right, we're still running, so you don't need to learn about starting the auto yet. Let's get to the fun part."

Emmie pointed to the three pedals at her feet. "The one on the left is for going forward. This middle one is for going in reverse, and the right one is the brake."

"How will I remember which is which?" Omie asked, concern edging into her voice.

"You really only need to remember two for now—left for go, right for stop. The pointy one in the middle is reverse, no need for that yet."

First, Emmie moved a tall lever on the floor. "This is the hand brake. You release it forward." Smoothly, she pressed the left pedal to the floor while moving a smaller lever beside the steering wheel upward. "This little lever gives the engine fuel. It's called the throttle." They began to roll.

Gaining speed, she said, "To go faster now, we ease the throttle down a bit and let up on the left pedal. All the way. Now move the throttle up again. There. We're just driving. Easy. Right?"

"How do you stop?" Georgia Rose asked.

Emmie eased the throttle down and pressed the left pedal halfway with one foot and pressed the brake down with the other, then rolled to a stop. "The middle of the left pedal is neutral, use it along with the brake."

"Why is there a brake pedal and that other brake thing? The hand brake?"

"The hand brake is just for when you are parked to make sure the auto doesn't roll. Or to use if you get into trouble," she replied.

Omie put her head in her hands. "Trouble?"

"Don't worry, you won't need it. Now, come on sister."

Emmie pulled back on the hand brake. The two women got out of the vehicle and changed seats. Georgia Rose looked excitedly from one to the other.

Placing a hand on Omie's shoulder, Emmie said, "Hand brake forward. Good, now press the left pedal all the way down and move the throttle up. Perfect."

Omie's hands shook as she went through the motions and they began rolling along the road.

"Relax, or you're going to break the steering wheel in half!"

Taking a deep breath, Omie let her grip on the wheel ease. Slightly.

"Take your foot all the way off the pedal and we'll pick up a bit more speed." Emmie smiled. "See, I knew you could do it!"

Keeping up a light chatter, Emmie made slight corrections as Omie got used to steering. Omie tried to wave at other motorists as she'd seen them do. The best she could manage was to lift an index finger.

When they were a few miles out of Savannah, Emmie said, "I should take it from here. We'll be in the city soon." Pointing to the right, she instructed, "There's a good place to pull over."

"Oh," Omie replied, turning the wheel.

"Slow down first, hon."

"You didn't tell me how to slow down!"

Emmie reached over to decrease the throttle as Omie sped toward an oak tree on the right.

"Right pedal down and halfway down on the left."

Confusing the middle pedal with the right, Omie began to press.

"No, no, the right, not that one!"

"Mamma, stop!" Georgia cried.

As the tree loomed nearer, Omie grabbed the hand brake and pulled it back with all her might. Thankfully, Emmie had moved the throttle lever all the way down and their momentum slowed somewhat. The Ford jerked and spluttered to a stop, a couple of feet from the oak.

"Oh, My Lord!" Omie groaned, her head back against the seat.

Emmie looked down at her niece. "You ok?"

Georgia nodded. She patted her mamma's knee and consoled, "That's all right. You got the going fine. Just need a little work on the stopping."

"You'll get used to it," Emmie assured her.

"Yeah, Mamma!" Georgia Rose chimed in.

Opening the door, Omie got out on shaky legs. Emmie helped her to the passenger side, then slid back behind the wheel. "We'll try again on the way back."

Omie shook her head. "I am perfectly happy with my horse and buggy. Took long enough to find another good horse after the war. I reckon I'll stick with him until all he's good for is glue."

"Glue?" Georgia looked up at her mamma.

Omie replied, "That's just another way of saying 'going to heaven', honey."

"Will you and Aunt Emmie be glue one day too?"

The sisters looked at each other and Omie burst into hysterical laughter. By the time they got to Savannah, the others were giggling with her, tears running down their cheeks.

Both Omie and Georgia Rose took in the paintings at the Telfair Academy with wide eyes and open mouths. Caleb smiled at the two, enjoying their wonder. "Y'all are going to swallow flies," he whispered. "We come here so often I think the marvel of this place has worn off a bit for us. It's refreshing seeing it all through new eyes. What do you think, Georgia Rose?"

She looked up at her uncle. "I would never get tired of seeing these pictures."

Aaron acted as if this was all *old hat* to him. Bitsy wandered off to look at her favorite paintings. Danny sat on a bench, bored.

The visit to the museum was followed by a trip to the soda parlor. The adults sat at a table to talk while the children sat at the counter, spinning their stools and slurping egg custards.

"I think this is the bestest thing I ever tasted!" Georgia Rose exclaimed.

"It's the best, not bestest," Aaron remarked.

"Maybe yours is the best, but mine's the bestest."

At the table, everyone smiled at the grammatical banter between cousins.

Caleb swirled the malt in his drink and turned to Omie. "I think mine is the bestest."

When they returned to the Decker's home, Aaron showed Georgia Rose some of his drawings. She had her own sketch book, the one Emmie gave her, and the two were caught up in a world of their own. Aaron brought much of his art home from school. Georgia was astounded that students in Savannah got art classes, something Miss Sarah rarely did.

He showed her his color wheel, how some colors fit together better than others. "You're real good with colors already, cousin. You sure nobody taught you?"

Georgia Rose glowed under his praise. "Colors is—are—like people. Some of them like each other and some don't get along. Some of them make me want to stick my feet in the creek, some make me want to dig my toes in the dirt. I can't 'splain it, Aaron. They just do."

He stared at her, then shook his head. "I'll take your word for it. Guess I know which side of the family you take after."

Omie looked over their shoulders and listened to Georgia's excited chatter. Finally, she walked over, put a hand on the girl's shoulder and reluctantly reminded her. "Well, child. We best get home. Chores await us poor country folk."

"But Mamma, can't I stay? I could go to school with Aaron, we'd be in the same class. Please?"

Omie knelt down to look into Georgia's eyes. She knew, even without the *Sight,* that she would one day lose her daughter to this city. Little did she know she would lose two.

"I need you home for now, Georgia Rose. We all do. You can visit Aaron often, maybe show what he teaches you to the children at your own school! Wouldn't that be a help to Miss Sarah?"

The girl reluctantly picked up her tablet and hugged Aaron, then thanked her aunt and uncle for the trip to the museum.

"This was the best thing that's happened in my whole life!"

"I'll teach you everything I learn when you visit!" Aaron assured her. "Please feel free to return at any time." His formality had his siblings rolling their eyes, but Omie thought it charming.

Over the following months, the two children spent as much time together as they could manage. Bartie showed an interest in accompanying her little sister to Savannah, so Emmie came to get them both or sent Thomas in her stead.

Aaron preferred his house, saying he was not the barnyard type. On occasions when the boy did visit the farm, Frank Thomas and Ezra rolled their eyes, mimicking his declaration. Willy tagged along behind the two young artists, only agreeing to be their model if Old Joe was too.

# Chapter 15

Nate stared up at the sky as if he could will it to rain. Every afternoon, clouds would build up on the horizon and scud on by without releasing a drop. By mid-June, not even a cloud disturbed the blue haze above.

Ezra walked to his daddy's side. "What you reckon? Is it ever gonna rain again?"

"I'm thinkin' we best come up with a way to get water to the crops instead of waitin'. We got the river down there if we can figure how to get some of it up here."

Omie joined the men, concern etched on her face as well. "If we don't find a way to water the peanuts, we're going to lose them."

They stood side by side, pondering the predicament until Ezra spoke.

"I heard about a kind of pump fellas are using to fill tanks and haul water. It's called a ram pump. Works on pressure from fallin' water, no fuel or nothin'."

Omie turned to look at her son. "How do we get one of these things?"

"I'll ask around at the grange. We'd have to mill some cedar to build the tanks."

Nate looked relieved to have some plan of action.

"You go see what you can find out, son. I'll see to the wood. Find out how much the bands are gonna' cost us."

Ezra headed for the barn to saddle up.

"I do think we'll be fine with water for the house, Nate. That old well of Mama's hasn't gone down much. It never failed us during droughts when I was growing up."

"There must be a deep spring that feeds it," he replied.

"That or it's magic...it showed you to me." Omie kissed his cheek.

"Could be the devil's doin'." Nate kissed her back. "But you're stuck with me now."

In a few hours, Ezra returned with news from the grange. It seemed many folks had the same idea.

"If we join in with the rest of the fellas helpin' each other out, it shouldn't take too long to get ourselves set up. The mill is givin' everybody a break on sawin' the staves. There's a big order of steel comin' to the grange for bands."

"Couldn't hurt to dig a small pond for the cattle too, son. Keep 'em from goin' down to the river and messin' with things. Not so big we can't fill it easy."

"Could be there's a spring out there in the pasture. Wouldn't have to haul water for the cows."

"Worth a try I reckon."

The next day, Nate was in the pasture with a Y-shaped stick in his hands, walking back and forth. Georgia Rose came out to him with a mason jar full of lemonade.

"Whatcha doin' Daddy?"

"Why, I'm witchin' for water, darlin'. If there's a spring in the ground here somewheres, this stick will point straight down at it. If it's a good spring, the stick'll try to twist outta my hands!"

Georgia Rose was dumbfounded. "But, why does it do that?"

"I don't rightly know the why of it, but I been able to witch water my whole life. Used to do it for folks when I was a kid."

Suddenly, the stick swiveled downward, burning his callused palms.

"Damn! Run get Ezra, baby."

She ran as fast as her legs would carry her, shouting, "Ezra! Daddy found water."

Ezra put down his hoe and picked her up.

"What's this now?"

"Daddy's a witch! Did you know there were boy witches? He found water but I can't see it. The stick did though."

He let her jump onto his back and put her feet in his overall pockets.

"Hurry!" she shouted, and he galloped toward the pasture, her giggles trailing behind them.

"Hey Daddy. Looks like a good spot?"

"We might just get lucky, son. Tomorrow we'll start on the pond before it gets too hot."

Ezra figured the job of digging a pond would fall mostly to him, considering his brother's declaration to avoid their daddy and their daddy's tendency to disappear for days at a time. He was surprised, however, when Nate showed up every morning with a shovel and stayed until supper time.

All were surprised when they hit the spring early on. They had dug the perimeter of the pond but had to stop five feet down.

"Not as deep as I'd of liked," Nate said. "But if it keeps runnin' at this rate, we won't have to haul any water from the river for the cows. Sure would be a help. Waterin' the crops is goin' to take all our time as it is."

Omie came from the house to check their progress.

"See, you ain't the onliest witch around," he teased.

✦

# 1939

## JUNE 20

Finally, coffee and food subdued their hangovers, and the uncles seemed to be able to hold their heads up without wincing. Ada Kate's boys had done their best to be patient, but there was only so much bottling up of energy an eight and seven-year-old could manage.

"PLEEEEZE," Cyrus cried, "Let's go out to the pond and look for snappin' turtles!"

"I don't know." Frank Thomas winked at Ezra, "That's where I lost the toes of my foot."

The boys blinked in astonishment.

"Really? That's how come you got a limp?" Jacob asked.

"Sure is. Took 'em right off. Why, I can put my shoe on backwards if I want to."

"Come on, young'uns," Ezra spoke up. "Let's go before the s...tuff gets too deep in here."

Once they were all out the door, Bartie started laughing. The rest couldn't help but join in.

"I know it's not really funny," Ada Kate said, "but the image of Frank Thomas with a foot going one direction and the other another is hilarious!"

"That's kind of the way he was for a while," Bartie added.

When they'd all quieted down, Omie said, "Best the boys don't know the truth of it."

The women hadn't considered that the girls at the table didn't know the story either. Lilly looked at her mamma and Bartie sighed.

"I suppose we have to tell them, now. You girls are old enough to know about this, I suppose. But you are not to tell anyone. Promise?"

Tess and Lilly nodded.

Ada Kate began, "That was a hard time. Prohibition caused all kinds of problems. There was a terrible drought that went on for years. It just seemed like trouble had settled in to stay."

"And your uncle seemed bound and determined to send me to my grave!" Omie declared.

# Chapter 16

## 1926

Omie came out of the herb room and looked up the hill to see Willie going to Phoebee's barn. Figuring he was headed out for the morning milking, she grabbed a clean pail, hoping to fill it also. After old Dinah passed, Daisy became their new source for milk and settled into her mamma's stall. Phoebee took over the job of milking when she moved into Kate's old house. Willie was taught how to milk as soon as his hands were large enough.

Willie was sitting on a stool when Omie entered, his face against the animal's side. He looked up at hearing her footsteps and turned away quickly. She noticed the swelling above his right eye and his split lip.

"Willie, what in heavens name! Did she kick you?"

"No ma'am," he mumbled. "I just fell is all."

The boy waved away buzzing flies and kept filling the pail.

"I'll fill mine," Omie said, as he finished. "When you take that to Phoebee, ask her to come out here, would you?"

"Yes'm."

Watching him walk away, Omie noticed how tall Willie had gotten recently. Some of the playful child was gone from his demeanor, and she sensed this was due to more than turning ten. She saw Phoebee open the door and motion for him to take the milk inside, then look toward the barn as he relayed Omie's message.

After a bit Phoebee entered the barn with less than her customary cheeriness. "Hey there. Ever'thang all right?"

"Mostly." Omie moved her full pail out of the cow's way and turned to look at her friend.

"Phoebee, what is the story behind Willie's poor face? He didn't fall, did he?"

Phoebee looked out toward the house for a moment and turned back to Omie. "I been wantin' to talk to you 'bout this, but you've had so much on your mind. I didn't want to add to your worries." She settled herself on the ground and continued, "It's Frank Thomas. I don't know what's goin' on, but he's been pushin' Willie around of late. Willie finally got tired and pushed back. That's about all I can tell you."

Omie shook her head. "Why would he do that? I've never known Frank Thomas to be a bully!"

"I cain't get either one to talk to me about it. Maybe you can." Phoebee stood and put her small hand on Omie's shoulder. "I feel better that you know."

Walking back down the hill with the milk, Omie puzzled over the situation. Maybe Nate would have some idea of what was going on between the boys. Not that Frank Thomas spoke to his daddy.

She felt goosebumps on her arms that had nothing to do with the wind. An image of Nate's cruel daddy rose in her mind, though she'd never met the man. For months, his presence had been like a shimmer of dark smoke around the barn after Nate killed him.

*No! You don't get to claim my son, Old Man. I don't believe we pay for the sins of the fathers! Or the grandfathers. Every soul has its own purpose. I know that with every bit of my heart.*

Omie raised her chin and spoke to whatever angel hears a mother's prayers.

*My boy has something troubling him, is all. You know Frank Thomas has a good heart. Show me what I need to do.*

Near supper time, Omie watched out the window for the boys and their daddy. She soon saw them going toward the barn with the mules. Once the animals were unhitched and fed, Ezra and Frank Thomas headed for the back porch to wash up. She hurried out to catch her husband alone.

"Nate."

He turned to see her worried face. "Sumpthin' wrong?"

She told him about the situation between Frank Thomas and Willie.

"Any idea why he'd get up to such meaness, Omie? This doesn't sound like his kind of doin'. At least I don't think so. I hardly know the boy anymore."

"We have to take him to task and find out. After supper?"

"Yeah, I'll bring him out here."

Omie did her best not to show her anxiety during the meal. As she and the girls were clearing dishes from the table, she heard Nate ask Frank Thomas to help him finish chores in the barn.

"Why can't Ezra do it?"

"Because I didn't ask Ezra, son."

"I'll go." Ezra piped up.

"No, you will not."

Nate's look caused Ezra to sit back down.

Shortly after the two left, Omie took off her apron and told the girls to finish up. Ada Kate knew something serious was about to take place. Bartie raised her eyebrows at her sister, but Ada shook her head and turned back to the sink.

Voices coming from the barn grew louder as Omie made her way to the open doors. Frank Thomas stood just inside with clenched jaw, arms folded tightly across his chest. Nate stood facing the stalls, a half-head taller, hand gripping his son's shoulder. "Answer me!"

Omie shook her head. *My Lord, they look like boys about to go toe to toe in the schoolyard.*

Noticing her shadow move across the wall, Nate looked over his shoulder. Frank Thomas sullenly looked away.

"Let loose of him, please."

Nate took a step back and tried to calm his voice. "What do you have to say 'bout how you been treatin' Willie? We never known you to act like this, Frank Thomas."

The boy narrowed his eyes. "Might have known you'd take his side without askin' mine."

"He's still a boy and you're fifteen. Almost a man! What could he have done to you?"

Frank Thomas unfolded his arms and clenched his fists. "It ain't what he did. It's more what you did! Ever'body in town knows he's your bastard. You think I don't hear the talk? How do you think that makes Mamma look, or do you even care?"

There was a moment of stunned silence. Nate drew back to hit the boy.

Omie yelled, "Stop! Frank Thomas, Willie is *not* your daddy's."

"I know about that colored whore Minnie, Mamma. I remember about him layin' up with her. Him not comin' home for weeks. You tried to hide it from us, but we're not stupid."

Nate was breathing hard, glaring at his son.

Omie shook her head. "Never mind what you think or what people say, Frank Thomas. Willie's grandmamma is my dear friend. I know the truth of where that child came from. His mamma is buried in that cemetery right down the hill. Do you think I would have allowed her there if she was your daddy's whore!"

"One of his whores."

"Don't you disrespect your daddy that way!" Omie slapped her son hard across his face, which shocked them both. Frank Thomas put a hand to the red imprint she'd made, then abruptly turned and walked out into the night.

"Come back here!" Nate ordered, starting to go after Frank Thomas, but Omie stepped in front of him, pressing a hand to his chest. Nate panted with fury and his eyes kept looking from her to the darkening doorway. As his breathing slowed, all they heard were night noises of the woods and fields.

Omie covered her face with both hands and wept. She had never hit one of her children before. Now, she'd slapped this young man who had taken up for her ever since he was a child, who carried the weight of responsibilities when his daddy was off on a tear. She'd punished him for his words, though she could not say he was wrong about the other women.

Nate's voice was tired and gruff. "How long have you known Willie's not mine? That terrible thing I done with Minnie, I thought he could be. What did you mean about his mamma bein' in the cemetery?"

Omie stepped back and wiped her face with the hem of her apron. She looked him in the eyes and said, "I know who his daddy is. Sit down. I been needin' to tell you this."

She told him the story of what had happened between Aunt Julia's great-grandson Isaiah and the young white girl, Missy.

"You know how it is, what they would do to Isaiah for gettin' that girl with child. Wouldn't matter that they loved each other. So, his grandmamma begged me to help her make it look like the child belonged to Minnie and a white man who'd been with her. You."

"Why, Omie? Why didn't you just tell me, 'stead of lettin' the whole town believe I done this and then made you raise my bastard? I wouldn't a told nobody."

"Maybe partly because I don't know what you'll say when you're drinkin'. Maybe I wanted to punish you a little for Minnie. I don't know." She looked out at the night.

Nate stood, uncertain what to do. Then, he followed his son into the darkness.

There was no sign of Frank Thomas for a few days. Ezra always knew where his brother was, and Omie begged him to tell her.

"Listen, Mamma. He needs to lick his wounds awhile. It's been hard on him, all this talk. I don't believe none of it, but he does. He's got a gal in town, stays with her folks. He's all right."

"Please tell him I'm sorry for hitting him. Please."

"Yes'm."

Omie walked up to Willie in Phoebee's barn as he was pitching hay to the cow. "Can I talk to you?"

The boy tossed one last pile in the stall and put the hay fork down. "Yes ma'am."

"Listen, I am so sorry about Frank Thomas' behavior. Let me explain . . ."

"No need, Missus. Grandmamma talked to me about all this the first time me and Frank Thomas got into it. I understand why y'all took me in, tried to protect me. And I couldn't tell Frank Thomas it wadn't true. I been knowin' for some time."

Tears ran down Omie's cheeks. "We took you in for your grandmamma's sake Willie, but we've all come to care for you. I'm thankful that she would ask us, she's been such a good friend. Especially to my mamma."

Willie's own face was wet.

"I care 'bout y'all too, Miz Omie. And I thank you."

Omie pulled him close, felt the thinness of his shoulders. "We love you, Willie. It'll be all right. I promise."

They stood that way for a few moments while shafts of sunlight played through the loft window. When the boy stepped away from her embrace she saw a softer light around him, a release of the heavy burden secret sadness carries.

# Chapter 17

Emmie came to pick Georgia Rose up for a trip to Savannah. Aaron had new things to share with her from his art classes and begged for a visit. Bartie decided this was a good time to get away from the tension at home and joined them.

Along the way, Georgia Rose chattered on about school, about how she had helped Miss Sarah make time for art projects.

"Some of the other students draw really good too."

"Draw really well," Emmie corrected. "Don't forget about your grammar lessons too."

"When school starts back up, she's gonna put me in charge of art class! There's this one boy…"

Emmie and Bartie smiled at each other. The girl's excitement lifted their spirits like a tonic of joy.

Aaron was on the porch when they arrived, eager to sweep his cousin away from the adults. Georgia Rose wrapped him in a hug, then the two disappeared into the parlor to draw.

"Put your things in the guest room and let's have tea on the porch." Emmie suggested.

Once they were settled at the wicker table with refreshments, Bartie confided to her aunt about the tension at home.

"I can't hardly stand to be there anymore," Bartie muttered.

"Can hardly…," Emmie began to correct her, but Bartie spoke up.

"No, I can't! You don't know how bad it is. Daddy is on a tear. Mamma looks close to cryin' all the time, and Grandmamma is worried about her. Ada Kate is quiet as a mouse, takin' care of Gracie. Nobody is fun anymore, except Georgia Rose, but she's out drawing things all day."

"Well, why don't you and I go out for some shopping. That would be fun, yes? After all, you'll soon be seventeen. It's about time you had some dresses that suit a young woman instead of a girl."

Bartie's eyes got wide at the idea. "Truly, Aunt Emmie? Can we go now?" The girl got up and danced around the porch. "At least *you've* noticed I've grown up!"

Emmie imagined there were boys who had noticed the changes in her niece. She was sure this troubled Omie. Bartie had been finished with school for two years, and though she did her work on the farm, she had time on her hands. The girl was not one to be idle long, and had a mind for mischief.

"Let's go to the dress shop. Since it's Sunday, we'll have it all to ourselves. We can see if there's anything there that suits you, and if not, we'll come up with a design I can sew for you. Tomorrow, when the other businesses are open, we'll look for shoes and stockings."

Bartie glowed with pleasure.

Emmie gave her a fond smile. "I'll see if Maizie would mind watching our little artists. Bitsy will be at her piano lessons for a while longer and Danny won't be home for a few hours. I swear that boy loves baseball more than anything else in this world."

The two rose and entered the house. Sunlight lay across the parlor piano, and Bartie touched the honey-colored wood. "Bitsy must be pretty good now."

"She is," Emmie answered. "The girl practices all the time. Even when she should be attending to other things. Fourteen going on thirty, in her mind. She'll be the death of me yet."

As the Ford pulled up to the storefront, the first thing to catch Bartie's eye was a yellow silk sleeveless dress. It had the low waist and slim silhouette favored by young women known as *flappers.* Dozens of beads sewn onto the bodice and satin waistband shimmered in the sunlight. Folds of pale-yellow chiffon filled out the skirt. Bartie imagined how wonderful the material would feel, swishing around her legs as she danced.

She'd read in Emmie's fashion journals that jazz music and the *modern* woman had changed the modest styles of previous decades. Now, hemlines stopped just at the knee, revealing legs clad in silk stockings.

Inside the shop, Bartie immediately went to the window.

"Oh," Emmie laughed, "I should have known this dress would be to your liking!"

Bartie turned to her with a questioning look.

Emmie took her niece's hand and led her toward the dressing room. "I believe that one is a bit too mature for you, my dear. Step in here and I'll bring you a few things to try on that might be more appropriate."

Bartie expected the pleated skirts and long jumpers she'd seen on younger models in the journals. Or plain, shapeless shifts of durable materials. She sighed.

"Maybe not quite as stylish, but similar, I think." Emmie surprised Bartie with three of the same long-waisted types of dresses as the one in the window. They were like a bouquet in her aunt's arms. One was a color Emmie called *ashes of roses,* a pale mauve linen with a darker satin sash. Another was a layered, cream-colored chiffon, sprigged with tiny pink roses and a moss-green sash.

Bartie hung the first two dresses on hooks at the back of the dressing room so she could look closer at the third. It was the color of cornflowers, of clear spring skies. Like the others, it was sleeveless, but a tiny fringe of cobalt beads hung from each shoulder. The rippling skirt was decorated with rows of the same beaded fringe. Emmie helped her put it on.

"Oh my," were the only words to come out of Bartie's mouth.

"Don't think I've ever seen you speechless!" Emmie exclaimed. "I thought you'd like the blue best. It brings out the color of your eyes." She admired her niece's reflection in the mirror. "The dress fits you well." Emmie straightened the belt at Bartie's hips and stepped back. "You can take the others home, but this one will be for special occasions. I'll store it for you here until then. If you like it, that is."

"I have never seen anything so beautiful." Bartie turned to her aunt with shining eyes. "Could I really wear something like this? I'm just a girl from the country."

"Like I was?" Emmie replied.

Bartie stared at herself in the mirror, surprised to realize that her sophisticated, fashionable aunt had, indeed, been like her.

# Chapter 18

On the ride back to the farm, Bartie chattered about her new dresses and cloche hat, checking her image in the small, ornate mirror Emmie had bought for her as well. She wore the sprigged chiffon dress home, eager to show her mamma what a young lady she'd become.

"The hat does suit you well," Emmie commented, half listening.

"It would look much better if you'd let me bob my hair!"

"Bartie, you *know* I couldn't do that without your parent's permission."

"That's right!" Georgia Rose declared.

Bartie scowled at her little sister, then returned to admiring herself, a small pout on her lips.

Emmie was thinking about the state Omie was in. She'd heard most of the story about Frank Thomas from Bartie, and knew there would be a great deal more coming from her sister.

As soon as they arrived, Bartie was out of the Ford. She walked with sophisticated restraint until she was inside the house. Ada Kate turned from what she was doing and stared, open-mouthed.

"Who are you?" she exclaimed, and took Bartie's hand to spin her around.

Georgia Rose walked in, saying, "Ta-da!"

Omie came out of the bedroom, looking like she had just woken. Taking in the transformation of her girl, she cried, "Why, look at you!" Turning to Emmie, she said, "You shouldn't have. This dress must have cost you a month's wages."

"Sister, you forget. I am my own boss now since Elizabeth made me partner in the shop. Other than materials, all this cost was my time. And I need someone to model my new designs."

"What about me?" Ada Kate inquired with hands on her hips. "Next to her I look like somethin' Old Joe dragged in. Bein' the oldest, I should be the first to have a real, grown-up dress!"

Emmie walked over to her. "Just wait until you see what I have in mind for you, my girl. Can I tempt you into coming to visit?"

Ada Kate looked at her mamma.

"Go back with your aunt if you like, darlin'. Lord knows you deserve a break."

The two young sisters went off to their bedroom, giggling. Georgia Rose tagged along, telling Ada all about the trip.

Omie and Emmie sat down at the table. Emmie could see that Omie had lost weight again, and there were dark hollows under her eyes.

"What's troubling you? Bartie told me some of what happened between you all and Frank Thomas. I gather it's bad, looking at how tired you are."

"Oh Emmie, I hit him!" Omie buried her face in her sister's shoulder and sobbed.

Emmie quietly rubbed Omie's back and looked out the window. She saw Nate standing beside the porch, uncertain whether to come in or not. Finally, he turned toward the barn.

As Omie's crying subsided, she told Emmie the whole story.

"He hasn't come home in weeks. Ezra tells me his brother is all right, but I need to see him. To tell him I'm sorry. I know this situation with his daddy has got him drinking."

Emmie started to protest, but Omie raised a hand to stop her.

"I know it in my bones, sister. I worry about what'll happen to him if he doesn't stop. He sees what Nate struggles with. Why would he even start?"

A few moments passed in silence as Emmie thought what to say. "The boy just doesn't understand what Nate has to contend with."

Omie lifted her head. "Do you think Frank Thomas will turn out like his daddy?"

Emmie hugged her sister close. "He doesn't have the same demons to deal with as his father. Perhaps that will be his saving grace. You could not have shown him more love than you have, sweetie. He'll come home. You wait and see."

When it was time to return to Savannah, Ada Kate had her valise packed and was ready to be gone. She hugged her mamma and sister, then went out to the vehicle. As Emmie slid behind the wheel, Ada said, "I've hardly ever been in an automobile, Aunt Emmie."

"What? Surely, you've ridden with us…"

"It's always somebody else going. Always me staying behind to look after the others."

Emmie turned to face her niece. "Ada Kate, I am so sorry. Sometimes the oldest child gets the short end of the stick. I know. You are so strong, no one thinks to ask what you need or want."

Ada looked down at her lap. "Not that strong."

"Well, it's time for a change, then. Before we go to Savannah though, there is one thing I would like to do. Do you know where Frank Thomas is?"

The few streets of town made it easy to find the house Ezra had told them about. A small, pretty cottage overhung by live oaks came into view. On the porch swing sat Frank Thomas and a young woman. When he saw who was parking in the yard, the swing stopped and he half-stood. The young woman held him back.

Emmie and Ada Kate got out. Emmie called, "Frank Thomas."

"Aunt Emmie, Ada Kate."

In the awkward silence, the girl spoke up. "I'm Ellie. Won't you please join us? I'll go in and get us some tea."

As they climbed the steps, Emmie could see an older version of Ellie through the screen door, listening to her daughter. She nodded, and they went into the kitchen together.

Taking seats in the rockers, Ada Kate and Emmie faced Frank Thomas, who would not look them in the eyes.

"Are you tryin' to kill Mamma?" Ada Kate asked angrily. Her brother looked shocked for a moment.

"What do you mean?"

"Since you ran off, she can't eat. She doesn't want to talk. She sleeps half the day. I don't know what you did or said to her, but you need to come home and apologize."

"Me?" he exclaimed. "I didn't do nothin'. She slapped me across my face! *They* run me off, dammit!"

Emmie sighed. "No, son. Your mamma has cried her heart out over what she did. The mark on your face has faded, but she'll never stop hurting until you forgive her."

"Daddy," he began, but Emmie cut him off.

"I'm not talking about your daddy. What is between the two of you is yours to deal with, but your mamma needs you. Nothing else she's been through has been as hard on her as this guilt. Not the lightning strike, not any of your daddy's monkey business. Please, Frank Thomas. Go home."

While they were talking, Ellie paused at the door but pushed through when they were done. She set a tray on the small table between chairs.

"Please, have some tea. My mamma sliced us some pound cake as well."

The girl sat beside Frank Thomas again and took his hand, looking up at him with concern. He looked down at her and kissed her forehead. "You've heard me say plenty about my daddy. Let's talk about sumpthin' else."

Emmie asked how Frank Thomas and Ellie had met. Ellie grinned.

"He followed me home from Mrs. O'Dell's, like a lost puppy."

"I *walked* you home, you mean!" He laughed, and Ada Kate thought how good it was to hear that laugh again.

"Anyhow, he kept hangin' around 'til my mamma invited him for dinner."

He groaned with pleasure over the cake. "Her mamma is the best cook." Ada Kate gave him a look. "Well, the best cook in town."

"I figured he wasn't goin' away, so I might as well let him court me."

Frank Thomas rolled his eyes.

Ellie ignored him. "I hope to meet the rest of y'all soon. Everybody sounds so nice." At his scowl, she amended, "Mostly."

Emmie and Ada soon took their leave, calling thanks to Ellie's mamma and telling Ellie to please come to the farm soon. Frank Thomas was civil but distant. As the auto pulled away, he gave a short wave of good-bye. Seeing the conflicting emotions on his face, Ellie put a hand on his shoulder.

"Everything will be all right, Frank Thomas. Every family has its falling outs. If you didn't love them so much, it wouldn't matter. Time will find a way to heal things between you and your mamma."

"How'd you get so smart?" he asked.

Ellie kissed his cheek and led him inside the house.

# Chapter 19

Omie sat in the herb room, gazing out the window as she braided stems of onions to hang and dry. A whisper of air lifted a spider web tucked in the corner. Hanging from a branch outside, a leaf spun, suspended on a silkworm thread.

She felt suspended herself, outside of time. Ada Kate was in Savannah. Mamma was making dinner for the children. Bartie was at her friend Jewel's house, in town. Yet even in the silent peace of the herb room, Omie still felt the recoil of her words and the fire in her palm where she'd slapped Frank Thomas.

She sighed and shook her head to free herself from the thoughts that kept circling in her mind.

Kate opened the door with a plate of food in her hands. "You need to eat."

"Not now, Mamma. Soon as I finish this last basket of onions, I'll come in."

Kate nodded and returned to the kitchen.

Omie leaned over to gather another bunch and took a deep breath. The bulbs had a comforting earthy smell. One of the few things that never changed. When finished, she walked into the kitchen and washed up, then found a cloth to dry the dishes as her mamma laid them on the drainboard. A jar slipped from Omie's hands into the enamel sink, shattering, sending slivers into the wash pan.

"Oh! Mamma, I'm so sorry. Let me get you fresh water and clean this up."

Kate turned to her daughter. "No, I'll take care of this. I'm afraid you'll cut yourself, the state you been in."

Omie started to cry softly. Kate held her close a moment, and said, "Go on outside and find some peaceful place to sit in the sun. Just empty your mind and listen. Sometimes that's when you'll hear His voice tellin' you what to do." She slipped a biscuit into Omie's apron pocket. "You have got to eat, Omie. And here." Kate reached above the sink for her deer stone. "Hold this close to your heart."

Offering a small smile of thanks, Omie took the stone. Trusting her feet to find the right path, she walked. Things seemed blurry lately, everything had a haze about it. She found herself at the well beside her mamma's old house. Omie settled on the bench Nate had built beside it. This had been her favorite place to rest in the months following the lightning strike.

She breathed deeply, trying to clear her mind. It did no good. Standing, Omie turned and slid back the well's cover, resting it on the bench. Coolness bathed her face, and the smell of damp moss brought up memories of the years this was their only source of water. She'd been a young girl then, unaware of the troubles ahead, the heartbreaks love brought with it.

In the still surface, she saw only reflections. Trees. Clouds framing her face with its sorrowful expression. *Why can't you show me something to ease my soul?*

The deer stone felt warm in her hand in contrast to the coolness rising from the well. She closed her eyes and tried to imagine its comfort flowing into her aching heart.

A twig snapped behind her. "Mamma."

She turned, and fell into Frank Thomas' arms, saying his name, over and over.

"Mamma, stop." He held her up by the arms and looked in her eyes. "I am so sorry."

Tears ran down both their faces. Tears for the hurt and time lost between them. Tears of forgiveness, of relief.

"It's me needs to say I'm sorry, son."

"Can we just put this behind us, Mamma? I don't really want to talk about it right now. I'll apologize to Willie too. Though I don't expect he'll forgive me."

Omie gently touched his face where she had left a mark. The imprint of her hand was long gone, but would always remain on her heart.

"Willie is a good soul, Frank Thomas. He understands more than you know, for his age. I imagine he's forgiven you already. Go find him, then come to the house."

As Frank Thomas rounded a corner of Phoebee's house, Old Joe saw him first and raised his hackles. Willie turned to see what the dog's warning was about. The boy rose to go inside, but Frank Thomas called softly, "Willie, please. I just want to talk."

Willie sat back down on the porch steps with Old Joe at his side.

Frank Thomas looked at the ground and cleared his throat. His eyes were still damp and his voice hoarse, but he continued. "I been punishing you for sumpthin' that ain't true. And even if it was, none of it is your fault. I don't know how I'll make it up to you, but I will. If you'll let me."

Willie sat a few minutes without speaking, then stood up and nodded his head, briefly meeting the other boy's eyes. He turned and walked into the house with his dog.

Frank Thomas stood there a moment more, then walked away.

Phoebee watched the scene unfold from the barnyard. She breathed a sigh of relief, and went back to feeding the chickens.

In the field, Ezra stopped working and looked at the house. Polly was seated near him under a pine, and followed his gaze.  A wisp of sweetness lifted into the air along with smoke from the cookstove pipe.

Bartie and Georgia Rose rounded the barn and looked at each other. "Bartie, I smell Mamma's lemon pound cake!"

"Frank Thomas is home!" They began to run.

# Chapter 20

Ada Kate woke up drenched in sunlight. She couldn't recall ever having slept this late before. Stretching slowly, she felt like a pampered cat and decided she rather liked the feeling. Sounds of morning commerce drifted through the window, the clopping of horses' hooves on the cobblestones of River Street, delivery men calling to shopkeepers, and all manner of footsteps hurrying here and there on the sidewalks below.

A scent of cinnamon wafted up the stairs, enticing her to rise and put on the soft morning gown left for her at the foot of the bed. She made her way down to the kitchen.

"Good morning, sleepyhead!" Bitsy called to her cousin.

Emmie rose and planted a kiss on Ada's cheek. "I'm so glad you were able to rest until you felt ready to rise, sweet girl. I don't imagine that's a luxury you get to experience often."

"Uhm." Ada Kate put a finger to her lips as if trying to remember when she'd last slept in. "Never?"

They all laughed. Maizie set a cup of coffee on the table and said, "Welcome, Miss Ada! I made you some of my special morning buns. The Campbells are up to Charleston, so I'm going to stay with the boys while you all have an adventure."

Her warm brown eyes shone with happiness for Ada Kate, who blushed at all the attention.

Emmie took a sip of coffee and sat back with a sigh.

"The Campbells are thinking of traveling to Europe this summer, and I'm hoping we can convince Maizie to come work for us while they're gone. I'm enjoying being spoiled by her."

"My pleasure." Maizie grinned. "Just try gettin' rid of me!"

"Having you here certainly makes it easier for me to get caught up at the shop with Elizabeth gone. I have a feeling she's going to talk Dr. Campbell into retiring."

After breakfast, Emmie drove them to the dress shop, where she and Bitsy got to work on Ada Kate's new look. Her niece was a lovely young woman, Emmie thought, with a figure too full to suit the boyish styles in vogue at the moment. Emmie sensed those would not be Ada Kate's preference anyway.

Bitsy sat outside the dressing room, waiting for her cousin to model the dresses they'd chosen for her. "Ada, are you gonna come out of there?"

Ada Kate shyly parted the curtains and stepped out. Emmie stood behind her, beaming.

For this niece, Emmie picked lovely print dresses made of rayon, a much more practical material than silk. The bodices were loose enough to allow for Ada's full breasts, the side seams tucked to fit the young woman's curves.

"Look at yourself in the mirror!" Bitsy exclaimed. "Who knew you were so beautiful!"

Ada Kate was, indeed, surprised by what she saw. Shapeless house dresses were what she'd mostly worn, embarrassed as her bosom showed signs of being like her Grandmamma Kate's. Now, though, she thought perhaps they might be an asset.

Emmie looked over both girls' shoulders. "You are very womanly, my dear. Never hide the loveliness of what God has given you. To be honest, I don't really understand the attraction of these fashions made for a boyish body."

Bitsy rolled her eyes at her mother, but could not deny how lovely Ada Kate looked.

Holding up a green and gold print, Emmie said, "This one will bring out the special beauty of your eyes."

Where Bartie had the strawberry blonde hair and blue-eyed look of her father, Ada Kate had inherited her mamma's green and gold-flecked eyes and Grandmamma's dark, thick waves of hair. The combination was stunning.

Ada Kate went back into the dressing room to try on this latest frock. When she stepped out, her aunt and cousin both nodded their approval.

"So, is there a boy you want to impress with this dress?" Emmie asked through a mouthful of pins, as she made a few alterations.

A small smile lifted the corners of Ada's mouth.

Emmie nodded. "Mhm." *That young man won't stand a chance now.*

"You also need something for everyday wear. Sturdy cotton. Still, you don't have to look like an old washerwoman to do farm work."

When Ada's wardrobe was complete, Emmie suggested, "Let's try some new hairstyles on you."

"Can I unbraid your hair and brush it?" Bitsy asked.

The rest of that day was spent experimenting with Ada's hair. It was a delicious feeling, being fussed over. One Ada Kate had never experienced. Her mamma always had a tug-of-war getting tangles out of the thick locks and insisted her daughter wear braids. This was sheer bliss in comparison.

Emmie and Bitsy could not resist the temptation to show off their gorgeous ingenue.

"Let's go to lunch!" Emmie exclaimed. They took Ada Kate to the Marshall House, which she had not visited since Emmie's wedding.

"I remember everything being so much bigger!" Ada exclaimed. "It still feels like I've stepped into another world. So beautiful." She was too nervous to eat much. It was an effort not to keep looking around in astonishment.

*Don't be the country cousin come to the city!*

If anyone noticed her discomfort, they certainly didn't show it. Many heads turned as they walked by the table. Emmie smiled as she greeted customers and acquaintances, knowing there would be much gossip and speculation as to who this lovely young woman might be. Ada was pleased and embarrassed at the attention.

Caleb came in from work that evening and stopped to hang up his coat. As he turned to greet them, he was met by the vision of a beautiful young woman sitting at the dinner table. Emmie walked over to take his coat before it dropped to the floor.

"Hi, Uncle Caleb," Ada Kate said, blushing.

He looked at Emmie in astonishment, and Bitsy laughed. "Yes, Daddy, it's Ada. Close your mouth or say hello."

Danny and Aaron giggled.

"Hello Ada." He walked over and kissed her cheek. "You look lovely."

Ada Kate blushed at the unaccustomed attention, but was obviously pleased.

"I say let's show her off to Savannah, Daddy!" Bitsy declared.

"Splendid idea," he agreed.

During the next week, Caleb took the family to vaudeville performances and movies at the Lucas Theatre. A new phenomenon called air conditioning had recently been installed. The lovely coolness inside was a welcome retreat from humid walks in Savannah's verdant parks.

When it was time to return to the farm, Ada's head was swirling with all she'd seen and experienced in the city. As she was packing to go, Bitsy sat on her bed.

"Think you might want to move to Savannah? You could share my room with me."

Ada sat beside her and considered the offer.

"I've had the most wonderful time. You all have shown me a world I never knew before." Ada patted the girl's hand. "But I'm a country girl, Bitsy. I love my life there. Not very romantic or interesting to you, I'm sure. Following in Mamma and Grandmamma's footsteps, learning to be a healer like them, feels like my calling. Do you understand?"

Bitsy leaned against Ada's shoulder and sighed. "I guess so. Only, please say you'll come back to visit us sometimes? I'll design clothes just for you!"

"Well, how can I say no to that! Now, I better get packed." She hugged her cousin and said, "Thank you, Bitsy. Thank you for everything."

On the ride back to the farm, Ada Kate was washed in a mixture of emotions. Familiar landmarks looked different, somehow. She felt as if a girl had left home and a woman was returning in her place.

# Chapter 21

## 1927

"Daddy, can I ride to New Abercorn with you? Mamma needs me to run some errands."

Nate looked down from the wagon at Ada Kate. "Why shur, I could use the company."

He watched as his oldest walked back toward the house to get her things.

She returned and climbed up on the buckboard. Ada Kate had not seen much of her daddy through the winter. He tended to have more episodes of drinking, being gone for days at a time. Sometimes more. Her mamma seemed to understand that the dark days brought out more of a darkness in him as well.

They headed toward town, reveling in the warmth of the sun on their backs. The silence between them was comfortable, broken only by the rejoicing of birds. He kept giving her sideways glances, and finally she turned to him.

"What is it?"

"You and Bartie. Y'all just surprise me, is all. Turned into women when I wasn't lookin'."

Ada blushed. "Don't be silly, Daddy."

"No, I mean it. You've acted growed most of your life, been a big help to your mamma and all. But you always been my little Ada. I reckon I'll be losin' you to some fella soon."

It was so uncharacteristic of her daddy to speak this openly about his feelings, Ada wasn't sure what to say.

"Every boy in this county is scared of you, Daddy. I'll probably end up an old maid!"

This made him grin. "A'right with me!"

Ada Kate *was* sweet on someone. But she had questions about love, ones her mamma wouldn't be able to answer. How could you know if a man was steady and would be there for his family? Grandmamma told her it was part common sense, part the Lord's will, that made you choose a husband. This did not inspire Ada's confidence in the whole business.

Near town, they met up with other farmers on their way to buy seed and such. Wives and children came along as well, drawn out by the spring sunshine. For most, other than school, this was the first trip off the farm since winter had finally shaken loose. The atmosphere was merry.

"You can let me off here, Daddy, no need to go out of your way. I'll be at the dry goods store when you're done at the grange."

"Stay out of trouble," he jested, and she rolled her eyes.

Ada Kate wore one of the new dresses Emmie had gifted her and felt lovely as the day. She didn't have Bartie's confidence or brashness. Bartie didn't care what she said in front of any boy and was still capable of landing a good punch if one sassed her. But the way boys had looked at Ada other times she'd come to town assured her that she would *not* be a spinster.

As she walked between the dry goods store and the new post office, James Dillon sidled up beside her.

"Hey, Ada Kate. Where you headed?"

"Well, I reckon I have about three choices, James. There, there or there!"

They both laughed.

"Can I walk you to whichever it is?"

She nodded and asked, "How's your mamma an' them?"

"Fine, fine. She appreciates the potions your mamma brung her. Swears your mamma is better than any doctor."

"Don't tell Doc Pritchard so, though I think he knows it too."

"Say, you wouldn't be of a mind to go to the dance at the grange with me Saturday, would you?"

Ada Kate looked at him sideways as if she was sizing him up.

"I s'pose I'm free. You might want to ask my daddy first."

James paled slightly at the thought.

"He's at the grange now. He'll be picking me up directly."

"I'll go find him. How 'bout I come to get you at six?"

"If Daddy says yes, that will be fine."

She smiled to herself. Any boy willing to face her daddy and ask permission to court her had some backbone.

James paused a moment before going. "Ada, I don't know if I should be the one to tell you this, but I saw your brother Frank Thomas hangin' out by the river with some rough lookin' boys. They was all drunk."

She stopped and turned toward him.

"Frank Thomas? Really?"

"I'm 'fraid so. I won't tell no one else, but I thought you ought to know."

Returning home later in the day, Ada Kate saw Frank Thomas, Ezra and Polly on Phoebee's porch. She walked up to them and stared sternly at her brother. "Frank Thomas, could I speak to you a moment?"

He looked at the others, then said, "Sure."

When he didn't rise to come with her, Ada Kate said in a slightly firmer voice, "Walk with me, please."

As soon as they were out of hearing, she hissed, "What are you doin' drinking? You were seen by the river with some ruffians, drunk as Cooter Brown! Haven't you learned a thing from Daddy?"

"Oh Ada, it was just a little fun. I won't never be like Daddy, trust me. I know when to quit."

"Sounds like you been at this for a while!"

"You are not my mamma, Ada. I'm old enough to know what I'm doin'."

She moved closer.

"I may not be your mamma, but if you don't stop, I'll *tell* Mamma."

For a moment, his bravado faltered, then he shrugged and said, "You do what you want."

As he walked away, Ada's heart sank.

She sought Ezra out when he came down the hill alone. Her youngest brother had trouble meeting her eyes, so it was evident he knew about the drinking.

"Ezra, are you part of this too?"

"No, sister! I have more sense than to follow in Daddy's footsteps. I've knowed about Frank Thomas' drinking, though. Didn't tell nobody 'cause I'm hoping he'll listen to reason. Mamma and Daddy fussing at him will just make things worse."

Putting his hand on her shoulder, he looked in her eyes. "Let it be, Ada. I know where he hides his 'shine. I been waterin' it down. He ain't got money to buy more right now."

She hugged her little brother. "I know how close you two are, Ezra. And I trust your judgement. Please promise me though, if things get out of hand, you'll tell me?"

"I will, sis. I promise."


Ezra was not the one to discover Frank Thomas drunk, however. Nate was coming home in the wagon along the river road, having a few pulls on a jug himself. He heard the laughter of boys coming from over the bank and recognized the slurred voice of his son.

"Gimme that, Buddy!"

"Not 'til you swing off the rope too, chicken. Cluck, cluck, cluck."

Nate heard a splash and Frank Thomas called out, "Ah might be a chicken, but you look like a duck!"

Nate pulled the wagon over and climbed down. Quietly, he approached the bank in time to see Frank Thomas drain the jar and throw it in the water. The boy in the river saw Nate first.

"Uh oh." He half-walked, half-swam toward the shore.

Frank Thomas turned and squinted his eyes. "Hey Daddy. I'd offer you a drink, but I finished the last of it." He began to laugh. The other two glanced at each other, uncertain whether to run or join in with Frank Thomas. The look in Nate's eyes decided them, and they grabbed their things, then ran to the trail they'd come down.

"Where y'all goin'?" Frank Thomas stared in the direction they'd gone.

"Don't matter where they're goin', son. You're comin' home with me."

Frank Thomas sat down hard on the dirt. "Am not."

"The hell you say!" Nate jumped down and grabbed him by the arm.

"Let me go, you son-of-a-bitch! You got no call to preach to me about drinkin'." Frank Thomas stood and took a swing at his daddy. He missed, ending up in the river.

"Maybe that'll cool you off!" Nate waded out and grabbed the drunken boy before the current took him.

Sputtering and coughing, Frank Thomas struggled to get out of his daddy's grip. Nate lost patience and lashed out with a fist, knocking his son out cold. He loaded the unconscious boy into the back of the wagon and headed for home.

Omie saw Nate arrive at the barn, taking little notice until she spied Frank Thomas sitting in the back with his head in his hands. She ran out to them, crying, "Nate, what's happened? Are you hurt, son?"

"He cold-cocked me is what happened, Mamma!"

She turned to glare at Nate.

"I found him down by the river. Drunk. Tried to get him to come home with me but he wouldn't."

"Couldn't you have handled this without hurting him?" Omie helped Frank Thomas out of the wagon, cursing under her breath.

"Lord a'Mighty, you don't have the damn sense God gave a billy goat. What in tarnation were you thinkin'? Not thinkin', by the looks of it. Can't I have one single day of not worryin' what you'll be up to next? I swanny, I don't know what I ever did…"

Neither father or son knew who she was giving a tongue lashing to. They figured it was probably aimed at them both.

Later that spring Frank Thomas nearly died from bad moonshine, despite his promise that he was done with drinking. With prohibition causing folks to drink corn liquor instead of whiskey, men saw an opportunity for quick money and turned their hands to brewing. Some knew too little, or cared less, about the right way to distill spirits. The result was an epidemic of blindness and death the likes of which no one had seen before.

Frank Thomas and his friends had been steadily getting cheap moonshine from men who had a still back in the marshes. An older brother taught one of the boys a secret whistle which would allow them to approach the still without being shot. These men cared not a whit about the ages of their customers, only the color of their money. Within weeks, all three of the boys had succumbed to the effects of poisonous alcohol.

One morning, Ezra found his brother beside the barn, trying to drag himself to the house.

"Mamma! Come quick!"

Omie looked around to see where Ezra was calling from and dropped her hoe. She ran to Frank Thomas' crumpled form and knelt beside him, calling his name.

The boy looked up helplessly, unable to speak.

"Do you know what's happened, Ezra?"

"No, Mamma. He was near the feedlot. I thought he was a critter out to get the chickens. Then I saw it was Frank Thomas. Why cain't he walk?"

"Let's get him inside, then you go fetch your daddy."

Each managed to get one of his arms over a shoulder and hoisted the limp body up, dragging him toward the house. A flurry of women ran from the fields to help, and Ezra took off to find Nate. He found him pitching hay from the wagon into Phoebee's loft.

"Daddy, we need you! It's Frank Thomas," Ezra gasped.

Nate jumped down from the wagon and ran toward home, not waiting for an explanation.

Inside, his son lay pale and unmoving on the bed, eyes closed.

"Is he dead?" Nate cried.

"No." Omie's voice shook. "I don't know what this is, Nate. I don't know what to do!"

Nate bent close to Frank Thomas and sniffed.

"Likker. Omie, I think he's got hisself poisoned."

"Likker? But he promised..."

Ezra spoke up. "I thought he'd quit. I woulda' told y'all if I knew he kept drinkin'."

Nate's voice was tight. "Do you know where he got it, son?"

Ada Kate spoke up then. "James told me awhile back that he saw Frank Thomas with some other boys by the river, drinking."

"The same ones I caught him with, I reckon. And neither of you thought to tell me?"

Omie turned to him. "Nate, to be fair, you're out drinking half the time. Do you expect the children to come to you with this? Go get Doc Pritchard!"

Nate took a moment to calm himself. "Let's get the boy to town. It's quicker. Ada, you come with us and talk to James. See if he knows the others."

Omie and Kate padded the back of the wagon with as many quilts as they could put their hands on. Ezra and Nate lifted Frank Thomas into it, then Omie and Ezra climbed in beside him. Ada sat on the seat beside her daddy.

Kate stood on the porch holding Grace and praying. Phoebee hurried up to the wagon and asked what she could do.

"Just let the girls and Willie know what's happened when they get back. I'm not sure where Sarah took them to pick berries. Thank you, Phoebee. And see to Mamma. We'll get word to you soon as we can."

By the time they got to the doctor, there was no need to ask James about Frank Thomas' companions. The two other boys were on beds in Doc Pritchard's clinic.

"This has got to be stopped, Mr. Silar." The older man took off his glasses and rubbed his eyes. "I'm seeing cases every week. One of these boys may not make it. The other is likely blind and that's his brother sittin' in the house with my wife. He's the one told these young fellas where to get the stuff. I don't know why he ain't sick too."

Nate went into the Pritchard's parlor and grabbed the young man by his collar. "You're gonna' take me to that still, and I mean now!"

Doc Pritchard came in, saying, "Whoa, Mr. Silar. The sheriff is on his way to do just that."

Nate ignored the warning. "Ada, call Emmie and tell Caleb he needs to come. I'll be back directly. Doc, will you give them whatever they need? I'll pay you as soon as I can."

He marched the brother out the front door, where they ran into Sheriff Turner. The two men looked at each other a long moment.

"Put him in the back of my wagon, Mr. Silar. Let's go."

For once, they were of a common purpose.


Caleb arrived at the clinic as Omie was administering everything she could think of to dilute the poison in Frank Thomas' body. The boy was more aware of his surroundings but still could not stand. As her brother-in-law walked in, Omie threw her arms around him, sobbing.

"Caleb!"

He rubbed her back for a moment, then leaned away to look in her eyes. "Tell me."

Between what he learned from Doc Pritchard and what he observed in his nephew, Caleb knew this would not be an easy recovery. Possibly, permanent damage had been done.

"Omie, there've been many cases of tainted alcohol paralyzing and killing people since this damned prohibition." Doc Pritchard nodded in agreement. "Whiskey that is supposed to be reputable has been tampered with too. A number of people in Savannah are crippled with what they call 'Jake Leg', due to the stuff. I thought folks were at less risk drinking moonshine."

She gasped and put a hand over her mouth. "You don't think Frank Thomas will be crippled for life?"

"Trust to time and your good healing work, Omie. That's all I can say."

Omie closed her eyes. She was revisited by a vision from years before, the day of Nate's return from the war. Dark portents, a gathering of crows, followed her to the field below the house. She was sure Nate was dead. When he walked up from the river road and found her, she clung to him, filled with joy and relief. The children ran to greet him too, and as the family walked home, Omie stopped suddenly, *Seeing* a different scene. Dead corn. Circling crows.

Omie stayed with Frank Thomas a few days until Doc Pritchard deemed the boy able to go home.

"There really isn't anything more I can do for him, Mrs. Silar. I much imagine he'd rather be in his own bed."

Nate brought the wagon to fetch them, figuring it would be easier than trying to get his son into the buggy or a car. Once he was settled in his room, either Omie or Kate stayed by his side. Ada left the room only to make potions and teas for him. The women took turns laying hands on his body, moving slowly from place to place, lingering on his legs. A gentle light emanated from them, seeming to seep into Frank Thomas as he slept.

Bartie helped Ada cook and care for the rest of the family until at last, Frank Thomas was able to stand, then take small steps. Eventually, he got about on his own with a cane.

History would reveal that during prohibition, the government had a hand in the deaths of over ten thousand of its citizens. Officials endorsed poisoning industrial alcohol. The belief was that this measure would discourage bootleggers from distributing illegal whiskey. What the regulators had not figured on, was the power of money over men with little conscience.

It pained Ezra sorely that he could not reach his brother. Frank Thomas had pulled so deeply into himself that the light had left his eyes.

Polly tried to be of comfort, keeping Ezra company when she wasn't studying the teacher-training books. Often, they sat quietly together at the old well, gazing out toward the fields and woods. Ezra softened his focus to see different 'lights' around the trees and plants, the animals that ranged into view. He tried explaining this to Polly when they were children, but after squinting her eyes for long moments at a time, she gave up trying to see them too.

Occasionally the vague forms of spirits who had passed would find their way to him, emerging from the tree shadows. Some were very old, barely there. Indians, he imagined. Perhaps revenants of something earlier.

On a Sunday afternoon, the two of them were sitting by the well talking, when Ezra suddenly sat up straight and turned to Polly.

"Buddy's spirit wants to tell Frank Thomas something."

Polly raised an eyebrow. "Buddy?"

"Frank Thomas' friend who passed."

"Do you know what he wants to say?"

"Not yet. I expect he wants to wait until we're with Frank Thomas." Ezra sighed. "Guess I'll go find him."

Polly started to rise, but he placed a hand on her shoulder.

"I best do this alone, Pollywog." He only resorted to her childhood name when he was troubled.

"You come here after, all right? I'll be waiting."

When he looked back, she had her nose buried in a book again.

Ezra found him inside the barn, looking for butts to smoke from their daddy's cigarettes.

"Hey, Frank Thomas."

His brother turned, but said nothing. Just behind Frank Thomas, a quivering shadow hovered. As Ezra's eyes adjusted to the dim light, he felt more than saw Frank Thomas' friend, Buddy, who had died from alcohol poisoning.

"What're you starin' at?"

Ezra just pointed.

Frank Thomas looked over his shoulder. He'd never before seen any of the ghosts that seemed to visit Ezra often. "Buddy? Wha...what's he want? Why is he here?"

A few moments of silence passed before Ezra replied, "He wants you to know he's all right. He's going away to a better place, he's seen it. But he needed to tell you sumthin' first. Says not to blame yourself. Get on with your life."

Frank Thomas limped to a hay bale and put his head in his hands. Ezra stood a moment, watching as his brother's body began to shake. Unintelligible words poured from Frank Thomas between deep, rasping sobs. Whether they were prayers or curses, was not clear. Ezra left him to his grief.

Late afternoon light filtering through the hay loft above settled easy on the boy's honey gold hair and bathed his heaving back. There was a gentle pressure on his shoulder for a few moments. Then, it was gone.

"Bye, Buddy," he sobbed.


Nate walked to the barn to feed the mules and horses, when he heard crying inside. Peering into the gloom, he saw a huddled figure on one of the bales against the feed room wall.

"Frank Thomas?"

The boy grabbed his cane, stood up unsteadily and snarled, "What do you want?"

"Easy son, I just wanted to see if you were all right."

"No, I'm not all right! My friend is dead. One is blind. I cain't walk worth a damn! Likker has ruint everything. Look at you!" He flung the words in his daddy's face.

Nate clenched his fists. For a moment, the heavy silence was broken only by Frank Thomas' ragged breathing and the uneasy stamping of the horse.

Nate lowered his head. "Might be you're right. But *you* don't have to be ruint. At least now you'll leave it alone, son."

With those words he walked over to the mule's stall and grabbed a bridle. He slipped it over her head as Frank Thomas watched, a slurry of emotions crossing his face. Part of him wanted to lift his cane and strike the man until he begged forgiveness. Another part wanted to throw himself into his daddy's arms and beg forgiveness. Before either one could win out, Nate led the mule outside and jumped on its back, riding toward the river.

Bartie walked into the barn. "Where's Daddy goin'? I heard shoutin'."

"None of your business, daddy's girl."

"Why are you so hateful, Frank Thomas? Nobody got you in this mess but yourself! You're always bitin' my head off if I even say hello, and I'm tired of it."

He turned away from her without a word.

Years later, the cane would no longer be needed, but Frank Thomas would always have a limp, marking this terrible misadventure in his youth.

# 1939

## JUNE 20

That afternoon, Omie and Bartie went to Phoebee's to help shell peas. Lilly had tagged along, hoping to catch more stories, but soon tired of sitting. She went back down the hill in search of her cousins. Ada Kate was at the old stove, greasing cake pans.

"Aunt Ada, where's Tess?"

"Oh, she'll be back soon. I sent her to collect eggs for a cake I'm making. What do you two have planned?"

Lilly shrugged, then cleared her throat. "Since it's just us, I wonder if I could ask you about somethin'. Mamma won't talk to me about Grandpa, about what happened between him and her. What did he do that was so awful?"

Ada folded her dish towel slowly, then looked at her niece.

"Sweetie, I don't know if I should be the one. . ."

"That's what Grandmamma says too. I don't think anybody is gonna tell me! This would be a good time while they're all up at Aunt Phoebee's."

"Ok, calm down. Let's go sit on the porch and watch for Tess. Can you keep what I tell you to yourself?"

"Yes'm, I swear."

The two sat side by side on the steps. Ada began, "I blame myself for what happened. I should have been watching out for Bartie more. Your mamma was willful and a bit wild at seventeen." She took Lilly's hand.

"That was the summer James and I were courting.We were at a square dance and suddenly Bartie disappeared. I didn't think much of it at the time, just figured she got bored and was off with her friends. By the time I learned what she was up to, it was too late."

Ada Kate paused.

"And?" Lilly asked.

"Honey, I'm just going to tell you the short version of it. Now that your mamma is here, maybe she'll find some healing from all that. We shouldn't stir up the past or she might just turn her back on it again."

Lilly took her aunt's words in, then nodded.

"Daddy had told her not to go somewhere. It was very important to him that she mind him about this. He'd never refused Bartie anything before, they were that close. Well, she went anyway."

Closing her eyes, Ada continued, "Daddy was drinking a lot those days, not being his best self, I guess you could say. He caught her. And he was in such a rage that he struck her."

Lilly asked, "Was it that bad?"

"It was bad. She went to Savannah and refused to come home again."

"Did Grandaddy get punished?"

"He did, Lilly. But I think he punished himself most of all. For the rest of his life."

Lilly sat quietly for a few moments after hearing the story. She chewed on her thumbnail and gazed out at the fields, lost in thought. Finally, she asked, "Is that the last time Mamma ever saw him? Didn't she come to your wedding?"

"She came once more, but not for my wedding. Daddy didn't come either. I was upset with her at the time, but she was so young, you know? Young and hurt and afraid of facing him. I understand that now." Ada Kate squeezed Lilly's hand. "I've missed my sister. The few times we saw you all in Savannah was just not enough. I hope you'll come often after the summer is over. It's not so far."

# Chapter 22

## 1927

"Daddy. I need to ask you something." Bartie had found him in the barn where she figured he'd be this early in the day. Chores limited Nate's intake of alcohol to a splash in his coffee until evening came around. He was more apt to listen and agree with her before his nightly stupor.

"What's on your mind, baby girl?"

"Well, I wanted to ask you first, because Mamma will tell me to anyway. There's a dance next weekend in Savannah. I could stay with Aunt Emmie and Uncle Caleb. A real nice boy asked me. In fact, he's Uncle Caleb's cousin, Jackson Decker. He moved to Savannah to work at the newspaper. They introduced us the last time I went to visit them. You'd like him. Please say it's all right with you and you'll talk to Mamma about it!"

Bartie had been so busy reciting the words she'd rehearsed for days that she didn't notice the thundercloud her daddy's face had become.

"No daughter, I cain't let you do that."

"But Daddy, why not? I'm seventeen, goin' on eighteen, and Jackson is real responsible. Uncle Caleb would skin him alive if he didn't get me home on time!"

Nate turned away, removed his hat and raked his fingers through his hair. After a moment, he seemed to come to a decision and motioned her to sit on a hay bale. He replaced his hat and sat down beside her.

"I don't know nothin' about these city dances except what I hear from folks in town. They say that music is of the devil, makes young people want to drink and carry on the way they oughtn't. Girls wear their dresses so short you can see half their legs and they put rouge on their knees for who knows what reason. Cain't be good. Jumpin' around like monkeys. That ain't dancin' anyhow."

"Oh Daddy, it's not that bad. Jackson wouldn't take me any place where there might be trouble, he's a good Christian boy and I really like him."

"It ain't just the dance, Bartie. I don't want you gettin' mixed up with a Decker boy. Just mind what I say. That's the end of it." He got up to resume his work, dismissing Bartie, who felt confused at his stubborn stance on the matter. Truth was, she knew she was closest to him of all her brothers and sisters and had never been refused anything by him before.

"Daddy, what have you got against Uncle Caleb and his brother? I never have understood why you act like you do to them. I'm not back-talking, I would just like to know."

Nate looked out into the feedlot, quiet so long that Bartie wondered if he'd heard her.

"I'm goin' to tell you somethin', daughter, that I never wanted you young'uns to know. I ain't proud of this, and it is not to be told to anyone outside this family. Reckon your sisters need to know it too."

He returned to sit beside her and she looked up into his face. Not wanting to meet her eyes, Nate looked down at the ground, rubbing his chin like he was figuring out how to start.

"That Decker boy is kin to you. And not by marriage. He's a cousin or some such."

Bartie shook her head as if to deny this could be true, but her daddy said, "Just listen to me until I'm done. I ain't never lied to you, have I?"

She reckoned this was true.

Nate told her the whole story of his birth and upbringing, how he ended up here at her mamma's farm. And later, the shock of finding Emmie engaged to his half-brother.

When he was finished, he turned to look at Bartie, expecting to see disgust at finding out she was the daughter of a penniless bastard. What he found instead was her tearful face gazing at him with such sorrow and love that he could hardly bear it.

"Oh Daddy!" Bartie threw her arms around his neck. "I am so, so, sorry. It was not your fault. You deserved better than that!"

Nate gently pulled her arms away and said gruffly, "Well, now you know. We'll not speak of this again."

He walked out of the barn.

Omie was walking to Phoebee's when she saw Bartie heading toward the house with a stricken look on her face.

"Bartie, what is it?"

They returned to the kitchen. Omie made her a cup of chamomile tea as Bartie repeated the story.

"Why did no one tell us this, Mamma?"

"Well, why would they, child? This's a painful thing for your daddy to admit. No one would fault him for it, but he doesn't see it that way. He's ashamed. Please be mindful of who you confide this to. I understand you'll want to tell your sisters but you know how it is with your brothers and their daddy. Don't give them more reason to think badly of him."

Nate did not come back for a couple of days. Needing, Omie supposed, to numb the emotions his confession to Bartie had stirred up. The girl had been pulled in two directions ever since. She still wanted desperately to go to the dance, but did not want to upset her daddy again.

"Mamma, what if I tell him I'll just go with Jackson as a friend? What can he find wrong with that? It would be like having a brother escort me and no one would be the wiser."

"I don't believe that will set any better with him, honey. Best just leave it alone."

Bartie couldn't though. She'd met Jackson when visiting her aunt and uncle. They went walking along the riverfront and stopped to hear the jazz music at a speakeasy he knew of. She watched couples dancing with wild abandon. It was intoxicating. She knew this was where she had to be.

"Hey, Daddy." Bartie set a cup of coffee on the lid of the corncrib near him along with a couple of hot buttered biscuits from breakfast. She'd put a dob of sorghum syrup on them, just as he liked.

"Hey, Snake."

He doctored his coffee from the flask in his overalls bibb and settled down to eat. They talked about the day's work ahead and the possibility of fitting a little fishing in there somewhere.

"We still got to catch 'Big Jack'."

She laughed. "More like, 'Big Whopper' is what I think of that story!" As she collected his cup and napkin to take back to the house, she made her case for going to Savannah the following Saturday.

"Bartie Silar, I said no and I don't want to hear no more about it! Trouble is all that will come from it. I'll not have you gettin' a reputation as one of those floozies."

She stomped toward the house with tears of frustration in her eyes.

By the next day, she had come up with a strategy that was only a partial lie.

"Mamma, I'd like to go spend the weekend with Mrs. O'Dell's granddaughter Jewel if you don't mind. She and some friends are going to a square dance at the grange tomorrow night."

Omie looked at the resigned face of her daughter and said, "Let me talk to your daddy, but I'm sure it will be fine. Ada and James will be there. At least you'll get to dance, hon."

When Omie approached Nate about it, he nodded in agreement. Some of the guilt he'd felt since denying his girl what she wanted, lessened.


Bartie found her sister sitting in front of their mirror on Saturday, already dressed for the night.

"Ada Kate, want me to fix your hair?"

"Why sure. That's mighty sweet of you to offer. What's up?"

"Nuthin' really, I just wanted to know if I could ride with you and James to the dance tonight. I can find my own way home if you want him all to yourself after."

She wiggled her eyebrows, and Ada Kate shot her a warning look in the mirror.

"Now don't you go saying things like that in front of James. He's a nice boy."

"It ain't James I'm worried about."

Ada tried to reach back and swat her sister, but Bartie backed away giggling, still holding the dark tresses in her hands.


James picked them up in his folks' buggy. Ada Kate introduced him to the family, and he promised to bring the girls home as soon as the dance was over.

Her younger sister fidgeted the entire ride to town, causing Ada Kate to glare at her.

"What bee has got in your bonnet?" Ada asked, but Bartie just smiled and wiggled her eyebrows again, causing Ada to look straight ahead and ignore her.

Bartie had heard from Jewel about some other young folks who intended to go dance to a jazz band in Savannah. They couldn't stay long if they were to get back to the grange by midnight when the square dance was over, but one of the older kids had a car, so it was doable.

The girls had put petticoats and long skirts on over the short dresses they intended to wear in the city. On her previous visit to Emmie's, Bartie had hidden the blue beaded dress and brought it home for this occasion. They would slip the square dance clothes off and store them in the boot of the car before leaving. Jewel had taken a pot of rouge from her grandma's store to paint each other's knees.

Soon after Bartie found Jewel at the dance, they waited outside, breathless with excitement when their ride pulled up. Bartie opted to sit up front with the driver and his girl, while Jewel snuggled with a boy in the back. A bottle went round, and for the first time in her life, Bartie knew the taste of whiskey and freedom.

She'd managed to put a letter in the mail to Jackson the week before, explaining that she would be arriving with friends and would meet him there. The dance was to be held in one of the old warehouses along the river front.

By the time they got out of the vehicle at River Street, the merrymakers were all a bit unsteady walking the cobblestones leading to the dance. Bartie giggled as she partially fell into the arms of Jackson, waiting outside the dance hall.

"Are you drunk?" he asked, unsure if he should be concerned or laugh it off.

"Not yet!" she replied, grabbing his hand and following the others inside.

The night passed by in a flurry of sound and color. Bartie had never danced or laughed so much. By the time they were ready to leave, she was not drunk on whiskey anymore, but on sheer joy. Taking Jackson's arm as he led her toward the cars, she tripped over the trolley tracks and he caught her.

"Let me drive you home," he whispered, holding her close.

Bartie felt the mood of the evening slipping away as she realized it was time to tell him the awful truth that lay between them.

"All right, but Jackson, there's something I need to tell you on the way."

"What could be so bad?" he asked with a grin, then saw how serious she'd become.

"I'll tell the others to go on," Bartie said, turning her face away.

It was hard to read Jackson's expression in the dark vehicle as the story poured out. Bartie waited for him to say something, to tell her he wanted no more to do with her disreputable family. She held her breath waiting for the worst when Jackson reached over and took her hand.

"I'm so sorry, Bartie. This certainly is not how I wanted things to go. It's a pity what your father has gone through. S'pose we have to be satisfied with being good friends. I do care a great deal about you."

Jackson pressed her hand to his lips and turned to give her a reassuring smile.

Nate sat in the shadow of the grange, brooding and drinking from a mason jar.

*How in hell could she do this? My own daughter I've loved and trusted. Never has disobeyed me before.*

He took another long swig. He'd thought to come by the dance to see her, maybe even join in, to make up for not allowing her to go to Savannah.

Ada Kate had told him, "She was here earlier, Daddy. She's probably just outside with her friends."

Nate went back out to sit in the wagon beside the building and pulled a jar from under the seat. He watched as two automobiles pulled up. Bartie got out of one with a strange boy, and walked over to the other girls. They were retrieving their skirts and petticoats from the boot when Bartie's daddy approached.

"Just what the hell have you been up to?" Nate asked in a seething voice. Bartie spun around, face drained of color. She looked up at his glaring countenance.

"Daddy, wait, I . . ."

Nate saw her rouged knees and backhanded her to the ground.

"You crawl on them knees until ever' bit of that stuff is off 'em, you hear? Crawl, I said!"

Bartie tried to crawl away on hands and knees but he jerked her up by the arm.

"No ma'am! Like this!"

He half dragged her on her knees until they got close to the wagon. Tiny cobalt beads lay in the road, mixed with blood-smeared dirt.

"Stop!" Jewel screamed, but he paid her no mind.

When he dropped her arm, the young men tried to get between Bartie and her daddy. Nate grabbed his whip and struck them, then turned back to his daughter.

"Don't you tell me what to do! I'll teach you to disobey me!" He struck her across the shoulders and back, beating her harder as she tried to get away. Bartie grabbed the horse trough and pulled herself up but her daddy was in a red rage and knocked her back down with his fist. She hit the corner of the trough with a loud crack and fell, holding her arm to her side. She watched blearily as more beads fell into the water.

Nate stood over her, ready to swing again, when he saw his reflection in the trough. He stopped, momentarily frozen and confused. In the lantern light, his face and raised fist had become those of his stepfather's.

Ada Kate heard the commotion and ran down the steps to Bartie. James and the other boys grabbed Nate, pulling him away from his sobbing daughters. He flung them off and stumbled to his wagon, climbing aboard and whipping the frightened mule into a gallop.

Ada Kate, Jewel and Jackson knelt beside Bartie's shivering form as James ran to get Doc Pritchard. They returned with a stretcher and laid the girl on it gently, then carried her to the clinic.

The doctor attended to her broken arm and assessed that there were no obvious internal damages. He let his wife begin cleaning the girl's wounds and turned to James.

"Y'all need to go get her mamma."

"I'll drive you there," Jackson offered.

Ada cried, "I want to stay with her. Please hurry."

Jewel put her arms around Ada and sobbed.

When Jackson and James left, the other two boys went to fetch Sheriff Turner.

The sheriff looked up as they entered the jail. The boys tumbled over each other's words trying to tell him what had happened.

He held up a hand. "One at a time. You—Ted Johnson, is it? Tell it to me slow."

"But he's gettin' away, Sheriff!" the other boy cried.

When Sheriff Turner had gotten the full story from the boys, he sat a moment thinking over his course of action.

"This is a terrible thing. Do you know how the Silar girl is doing?"

"Not yet sir, we came straight here after we took her to Doc Pritchard's."

"Now you boys listen. You're not gonna like what I have to say. I can find Nate Silar and throw him in jail for a few days, maybe a few weeks if the judge allows. But unfortunately, unless he's killed her, the law won't allow me to do much to a man for the way he disciplines his family."

The sheriff looked hard into the Thompson boy's eyes.

"There's nothin' *legal* to be done, you get my meaning?"

The boys looked at each other for a moment and nodded, then went back out into the night.


Omie woke in a sweat with her stomach clinched tight. She scanned through all the images of those she loved and knew immediately that Bartie was in trouble. Throwing off the covers, she dressed and went to wake her mamma.

"I can't *See* what, but I know something has happened to Bartie, Mamma."

Kate rose and lit the lantern, ready to do what needed to be done. Just then they heard an automobile pull up outside. Jackson jumped out, hurrying to the door.

"Ma'am, please come with us quick. Bartie needs you."

"Is she hurt, son?" Kate asked.

"Doc says she'll be all right, but her daddy whipped her pretty bad."

Omie grabbed the medicine bag and kissed her mamma on the cheek, then ran out the door. "I'll let you know something soon as I can."

James stood holding the front passenger door open for her. "Mrs. Silar, I'm so sorry."

She nodded wordlessly and put her bag on the seat, then climbed in beside it. James closed her door and got in the back.

On the ride to town, James introduced Jackson and between them, they recounted what had happened, telling her that Bartie was now resting in the clinic at the front of the doctor's house.

James concluded, "Ada Kate and Jewel are with her now."

Jackson looked over at Omie. "I didn't know she wasn't allowed to come to the dance in Savannah. I swear it, Mrs. Silar."

"I believe you, son. Bartie has a mind of her own. Let's just get her situated and we can talk more later. Thank you both for coming to get me."

"Of course," James said, fighting back tears. "I'll get Ada home."

"No, I need to stay!"

Omie looked up at her daughter. "Please, Ada. I need you to go tell everyone what's happened."

"But Mamma, I can help."

"And you will, daughter. But right now all she's going to do is sleep and you're needed at home."

Jewel said, "I'll be here, Ada. If anything changes, I'll make sure someone comes and gets you."

Ada reluctantly kissed her sister's forehead, hugged her mamma and went with James.

Omie sat up all night, stroking Bartie's hair and sponging her cuts and bruises with a tea of boiled herbs. Salves had been applied to the worst cuts on her knees, a few of which needed stitches. The doctor had set the broken arm and given the girl a goodly dose of laudanum. Mrs. Pritchard brought cups of tea to Omie and made Jackson a pallet on the rug beside the fireplace so he could spell Omie when needed. Doc Pritchard was still a bit concerned about the broken ribs he'd found and wanted to be sure there was no problem with Bartie's breathing in the night.

"If you hear any rattling at all, call me. We'll leave the door into the house open and I'll hear you."

"Thank you so much, Doctor," Omie replied. He laid a hand on her shoulder and bid them goodnight.

The following morning, Omie asked Jackson if he would go to Savannah and get Caleb to see what should be done. There was a large nasty bruise on Bartie's hip that concerned the doctor as well.

"You want to watch that," Doc Pritchard said. "If the swelling doesn't go down soon, we may have a broken hip to deal with."

As the dose of laudanum wore off a bit, Bartie was able to speak of what happened. At least, what she remembered. Jackson had given Omie the whole story but Bartie needed to unburden herself, so her mamma listened. The color was fading from Bartie's face, both due to her broken ribs and, Omie imagined, a broken heart. She stroked the girl's hair until her sobs became short, soft breaths.

By day's end, Caleb arrived along with Emmie. He decided that Bartie should go to Savannah for assessment and treatment. There, an x-ray machine was available.

After determining it was safe to move his niece, Caleb and Doc Pritchard carefully laid her in the back seat of his motorcar. Even with a dose of laudanum heavy enough to render Bartie unconscious, an occasional bump in the road brought moans from her. Omie reached back and stroked the girl's forehead the entire ride, barely able to hold back cries of sympathy.

Emmie put a hand on her sister's shoulder. "Omie, I swear to you Caleb and I had no knowledge of Jackson and Bartie's plans."

Caleb said in a tight voice, "He'll answer for this, believe me. My cousin may be young, but he should have known better than to introduce her to what goes on down at River Street."

"It's not the boy's fault." Omie turned to face her brother-in-law and sister. "He told me he didn't know she was there without permission. She and her friends cooked this up and Jackson was just trying to watch out for her."

They were silent for the rest of the trip, each lost in thought about events of the past evening. Familiar landscape passed by, farms and small towns edging toward the city. Little had changed, but Omie felt as if nothing would ever be the same.

Fortunately, no breaks or fractures were seen in x-rays of Bartie's hip. A cast enclosed her arm and the broken ribs were snugly bandaged. Caleb was certain everything would heal in time.

The bruising and swelling were soon reduced by Omie's comfrey poultices. She gave Bartie a tea of nettles and yarrow for the bruises also. Mixed in were St. John's wort and lavender for the bruises on her heart.

Omie knew when the days of deep sleeping were done, there would be much tending of Bartie's spirit. Jackson came every day before and after work, endearing himself to Omie and Emmie. The women gave the two young people some time alone to talk. Bartie seemed soothed by his presence. There was even an occasional laugh coming from the room, followed by a groan of pain. It was a welcome sound, nonetheless.

Emmie walked over to Bartie's bed where Omie was watching the girl sleep. She sat behind her sister and began unbraiding her hair. "Omie, let me drive you to the farm to get a few of yours and Bartie's things. I know everyone there is anxious to hear news and the children are missing you. What do you think?"

"I suppose that would be a good thing." Omie sighed. "Maybe I'll stay there a few days. I want Mamma to come back with you, though. To tend Bartie while I'm gone. Caleb is a fine doctor and all, but what comes through Mamma's hands is a healing greater than his or mine."

"That's true." Emmie brushed out her sister's hair and re-braided it. "I'll tell Caleb we'll be going shortly."

The ride to the farm was mostly a silent one, though Omie did tease Emmie about her driving.

Emmie remarked, "I'm better than you!"

Omie attempted a wan smile and turned her head to look out the window.


Ada Kate wrapped her mamma in a fierce hug as she walked into the house. She was frantic with worry and wanted to know every detail of Bartie's condition. The rest of the children listened with solemn faces except for Frank Thomas.

"I been tryin' to find him. I'll kill his sorry tail if I do, Mamma. Ada hid the shotgun, but there's other ways."

"No, Frank Thomas. If you do, you'll go to jail, and I need you too much for that to happen."

He struggled to speak, nodded, then got up and went out the door.

She looked at the others and said, "Ada Kate, why don't you go back to Savannah with Mamma and Emmie? I know your sister will be glad of your company. I'll talk to Phoebee and Sarah, set things in order here so I can return to Emmie's later."

Georgia Rose' face looked stricken at the thought of her mamma leaving again.

She put an arm around the child's thin shoulders. "Just until we know Bartie is able to come home, sweetie. Emmie, would you come get me in a few days?"

"Of course, I will."

Georgia Rose stayed close to her mamma, never letting Omie out of sight.

"Don't you worry, darlin' girl of mine. When I go again, I'll need you to take care of your baby sister, all right? Let me show you how to do some of my chores so you can be a big help to your brothers too."

Georgia seemed to like the idea of being in charge of the house and bossing her big brothers around for a change. She nodded with a serious expression, lifting her chin in importance.

# Chapter 23

Nate had lost all sense of time since the nightmare of his actions. By day he lay in back of the wagon sleeping off the night before. He'd been drinking himself senseless to rid his mind of images of Bartie's crumpled body. Jars of moonshine meant to be sold were quickly disappearing into his gut.

But the liquor was losing its power, and moon-cast shadows had begun crowding around the wagon, taunting him. Finally, he gave up trying to find peace.

He was stumbling along one evening, letting the road take him where it would. Sometimes, a fish could be heard splashing in the river. As the moon shone between a gap in the trees on its banks, Nate stopped.

*I should jest throw myself in, be done with it.*

He lurched in the direction of the water but stopped when he heard the sound of horses on the road. He searched for somewhere to hide, but was too late. A group of men carrying torches, dressed in sheets and hoods, surrounded him as he squinted up at them.

"Well, there he is," one of them said. "We been lookin' for you. Been hidin' out like the sorry dog you are, ain't ya?"

"What you want with me?" Nate growled. "I got no business with you."

"Oh, but *we* got business with *you*," a younger voice answered. "Any man does what you did to his own flesh and blood needs punished. You deserve a dose of what you give your poor daughter."

The men jumped down from their horses and began raining punches and kicks across Nate's body. He was too drunk to fight them off and too ashamed of himself to try. One of the men, the younger voice he'd heard, picked up pebbles from the road and began to stuff them in Nate's ears, then his mouth and nose, so that he could hardly breathe.

"That's enough, son. We want to teach him a lesson, not kill him."

"Be better for everybody if we did," the boy replied.

The men hoisted Nate's unconscious body across the back of one of the horses. They didn't have far to take him, as he had almost made it home.

"Omie! Omie, wake up and put some water on to boil. They've near 'bout kilt my son!"

Omie sat straight up in bed at the sound of a woman's voice calling her. She lit the lantern and looked around, but no one was there. Still, she knew she'd heard it loud and clear. Had to be Nate's mamma, who else? Her scalp tingled and darkness blotted out the lantern light.

*Can't breathe!* She closed her eyes again and tried to feel for the bedclothes, but felt only sand and clay beneath her fingers.

A hand shook her. Omie gasped and opened her eyes, still seeing no one. She dressed and carried the lantern to the kitchen. As she poured water from a bucket into a large pot, there came the sound of a horse's hooves and a loud thud as something heavy hit the ground.

"Nate!" Omie flung open the door and hurried out when she saw the barely recognizable face of her husband.

Frank Thomas and Ezra woke when they heard their mamma's cries and ran to her side.

"Get Phoebee and Sarah, hurry!"

Frank Thomas just stood looking down at his bleeding father with disgust until Omie yelled. "GO!"

The women came down the hill in night gowns and shawls. Willie followed with a fireplace poker in hand, ready to fight whatever this was.

Phoebee covered her mouth when she saw the condition Nate was in. Omie checked to see if he had a pulse and hurriedly began removing the rocks from his nose and mouth.

"Do y'all think we can get him in the house?" she cried.

"Of course," Sarah replied, taking charge. "Phoebee, you and Polly lay out some blankets on the floor. Willie, take his other arm. Frank Thomas, Ezra, grab his legs."

They each grabbed a limb and managed to half-carry, half-drag Nate's body inside. Frank Thomas dropped his hold and went out the back door.

Omie said, "Let him go. Willie, would you and Georgia please take Grace to your house?"

They took Grace's hands and walked the sleepy girl up the hill.

The women cleaned Nate's wounds and wrapped his ribs tightly. He appeared to have a number of broken ones. It remained to be seen what other damage had been done. There were bruises in his kidney area the shape of boot heels.

When Omie had managed to get some laudanum down his throat and Nate was taking regular raspy breaths, she sat in a chair and put her head in her hands. "It's too much. It's just too much."

Shock or something deeper had enveloped Omie once her tending to Nate was done. Sarah reached for Omie's slumped form and pulled her up.

"We'll take care of him, Omie. You need to be there for your daughter."

Omie raised her head, looking gratefully into Sarah's eyes. What frightened Phoebee was the dry stoniness of her friend's face. Omie's eyes grew hard as she fought for control of her voice.

"Not in this house, though. I want him in the barn where he belongs. With the other animals. Have a pallet made for him there, the kids can take food and water to him. Anything else, I'll leave that up to you to decide if he's worth it."

As Omie moved to go to bed, she turned with a defeated sigh. "I'm sorry, Sarah. I didn't mean to be so gruff with you and Phoebee. I appreciate your help, I really do."

Phoebee and Sarah wrapped their arms around Omie, their kindness unlocking the tears that had been dammed up. Omie laid in her bed weeping through the night.

The sun was high when Omie rose the next morning, and there was no sign of Nate or anyone in the front room. Coffee had been made and a slice of honey cake sat on the table waiting for her. She'd slept through it all. Weariness knotted her muscles so that she could barely carry her cup to the table. Outside, she saw Sarah directing Phoebee and the children as they carried things into the barn and forked dirty hay into the feedlot.

Frank Thomas was not among them.

# Chapter 24

On the ride to Savannah, Emmie filled Kate and Ada in on Bartie's state. She was still pretty bruised and broken, she told them, but what concerned her most was Bartie's lack of tears.

"Her anger is like a fever that's burning in her heart. I don't know what to do. Honestly, Mamma. I'm hoping your hands can reach that place inside her we can't. It doesn't seem healthy to keep such emotions locked up."

Sitting between them, Ada was quiet. It took a moment for Kate to realize tears were running down the girl's cheeks.

"Honey, whatever is wrong?"

"It's all my fault, Grandmamma."

Emmie looked over. "How is this your fault, sweet girl?"

"If I'd paid more attention, I would have known she was up to something. All I thought about was dancing with James. I didn't even miss her until the dance was nearly over and Daddy came in."

Ada began to sob.

Kate reached over and took her granddaughter's hand. "Listen to me. You and your sister are different people. She's almost as old as you are, old enough to know better."

"But..."

"Think about the roses in my garden. Theres my Mr. Lincolns and my Seven Sisters. They're both roses, but not nearly alike. And each rose is different from the other in some way. The same is true with you and Bartie."

Emmie added, "You were not born to be your sisters' and brothers' keeper, Ada, though you've done just that all your life."

"But why did this happen y'all? Why did it have to be so awful?"

Kate was a quiet a moment, then replied, "The Lord gives us hard lessons sometimes, but that doesn't mean He doesn't love us. When I prune my roses, I don't do it to hurt them. I do it so they'll grow and bloom better. Maybe that's not a good comparison, but you get my meaning?"

Ada nodded and rested her head on her grandmamma's shoulder.

For the rest of the trip, Kate and Emmie tried to keep the conversation light between them.

"How've you been holding up with Elizabeth and Daniel gone? This trouble with Bartie must be a lot on top of running the dress shop by yourself."

Emmie shrugged. "Having Maizie with us full time now has made life much easier. I can spend more time taking care of mine and Elizabeth's customers. Bitsy is becoming a big help too."

"Think she'll join you at the shop when she's done with school?"

"Who can tell with that girl! I know she likes being there right now. If not Bitsy, maybe I'll find some country bumpkin like I was to train."

"You were never a country bumpkin! Caleb must be working longer hours since Dr. Campbell retired."

"He is. But it seems our Danny is going to follow in his father's footsteps. He spends quite a lot of time at the hospital after school doing what tasks he can."

Kate put a hand on Ada's. "They're all growing up, aren't they?"

Emmie gave her a sad smile. "They certainly are, Mamma."

The three of them arrived at the Decker's home just before supper time. Emmie pulled up in front.

"Y'all go get settled and I'll park the car."

Ada gathered their bags from the back seat and helped Kate up the porch steps. Maizie opened the door, gave each a hug and told them how happy she was to see them. Her eyes said more, but they figured she didn't want Bartie to overhear.

"I know y'all are tired. When you're ready, come on in the kitchen and let me show you what I've got cookin'!"

Then she nodded toward Bartie's room, and Kate smiled gratefully.

It took Bartie a few moments to realize they were in the room. From deep inside her dreams, she felt her grandmamma's hands on her, warm and soft. She would love to have stayed in that comforting, safe place, but Ada's sobs drew her up to the surface. Bartie opened her eyes.

Ada Kate wrapped her sister's hand in hers and cried, "I'm so sorry, honey."

Bartie turned her head toward Ada and asked, "What do you have to be sorry for, Ada Kate?"

"I should have done something to stop him, I should have..."

Bartie looked sharply at her. "No, this is all on him. I didn't deserve to be beat like a damn mule—sorry Grandmamma. He might 'a killed me if it weren't for James and Jackson!"

She winced and took a moment to slow her breathing.

"I don't want to talk about it, or hear his name."

Bartie took her hand back and slipped it under the covers. She turned her back to Ada and closed her eyes again.

Kate's eyes pleaded for Ada to be patient. The girl stood and walked out, shaking. She went to the kitchen looking for Emmie and found Maizie stirring a pot of something that smelled delicious.

"Come sit," Maizie said softly. Her dark eyes were troubled, and Ada figured she had heard Bartie's declaration.

Wiping her eyes, Ada sighed. "What can I do for her, Maizie? She doesn't want to talk about what happened."

"Just be there, hon. Time is the Lord's great healer. How is your mamma doing?"

"Oh, she's a mess. Everybody is. I have no idea what's happened to my daddy either. Likker is pure evil, isn't it? I can't believe he would do such a thing if he wasn't under its spell."

"The devil loves whiskey, that's for sure. Makes it easy to find those weak parts of a person and poke 'em, so a body cain't stand it. 'Stead of turnin' to the Lord, some folks just find it easier to tell their troubles to that bottle."

Emmie came into the kitchen and sat beside her niece.

"So, how did it go?"

"She turned her back on me. Didn't want to talk or listen."

"That's the way it's been, Ada. I guess she just needs more time." Emmie paused a moment and then said, "Why don't you read to her? That might be soothing. Jewel came to visit a few days ago and brought some magazines."

Ada Kate nodded. "After supper, I'll see if she'll let me read to her."

In the hallway, they saw Kate come out from Bartie's room. She closed the door quietly.

"Hey, Mamma." Emmie kissed her. "You have any luck with our wild child?"

"Oh," Kate replied, "she's sleeping again. I think something shifted inside her. Body or spirit, though, I'm not certain."

"Well, let's see what a feast Maizie has made us. Everyone's home but Caleb, and he called to say he'd be late. We're to start without him."

Bitsy, Danny and Aaron were already seated at the dining room table. They got up to hug their grandmother and cousin, then Danny said, "Y'all come sit. I'm starving!"

Emmie removed his ball cap and tousled his hair. "Starving. You have not gone hungry a day in your life, young man."

"Playing ball is hard work, Mamma!"

Maizie came through the kitchen door with a large bowl of chicken and dumplings. The smell was intoxicating. She set it down and went to fetch another large bowl of steaming collards with bits of ham floating in them.

"May I have some pepper sauce, please?"

Kate smiled at Aaron's proper manners.

"You sure can, I'll bring a bottle with the okra."

Maizie's okra was, to Emmie, the best in town. She dropped chopped okra into hot bacon grease and dusted it with salt, pepper, cornmeal and flour.

"Oh, my!" Kate groaned when she ate a forkful. "Maizie, you are a wonder in the kitchen!"

"Thank you, ma'am."

"It's all Elizabeth and I can do to keep someone from stealing her out from under us!"

"Never happen," Maizie declared. "Y'all are family. No amount of money can buy that."

Slices of pecan pie threatened to fill their bellies to bursting. The adults settled back with a second cup of coffee while the children went outside.

Kate declared, "I'm going to have to put myself to bed after that meal. It's been a day."

"That it has," Emmie agreed. "Ada Kate?"

"I think I'll go read to Bartie if she'll let me. Can I help clean up here?"

"Don't worry about it, go see your sister."

Ada gently knocked, and Bartie said, "Come in."

Maizie came in behind her to retrieve Bartie's tray.

"That was so good. Thank you, Maizie."

"Of course." She winked at Ada on her way out.

"Hey. I thought I might read to you some if you don't mind."

Bartie rolled her eyes. "You're not going to read the bible to me, are you? I am not in the mood to be saved."

"No. Aunt Emmie said Jewel brought you some things."

Under a stack of Vogue magazines, Ada found a book with a scowling couple on the cover.

"What's this? F. Scott Fitzgerald. *The Beautiful and the Damned.* They don't look very happy. What's this about?"

"Oh, just something Jewel thought I'd like. It's too heavy for me to hold with one hand and read, though."

The truth was, Jewel had managed to have the book sent to her grandmamma's store and retrieved it before Mrs. O'Dell checked the post. She and Bartie had spent many hours already devouring its descriptions of the care-free flapper lifestyle.

Bartie sighed. "All right, read if you want. It'll put me to sleep, I imagine."

Ada Kate settled into a chair as her sister closed her eyes.

Ada began reading but as soon as Bartie seemed to be asleep, she got bored and muttered, "Sounds like a spoiled, rich brat to me. Does he get any better?"

Flipping through the pages, Ada gasped. "Oh, my word. I can't read this!"

Bartie knew without seeing that Ada's face was red as a beet. When she heard the door close, a big grin spread across her face.

The next morning, Kate returned to Bartie's room. Through the open door, Emmie and Ada watched as Kate's hands moved gently from the broken arm to Bartie's ribs and her hip. She settled at the girl's feet and began humming a soft song. They closed the door and left them in peace.

When Kate was done, she rose to leave and heard Bartie quietly call her back.

"Grandmamma," she said, taking Kate's hand. "I'm not asking this to be mean, but could you convince Mamma not to come back for a while? I feel like I need some time alone to work this through without her fussing over me. Can you understand?"

Kate patted her hand. "I do, honey. Some things medicine don't fix."

"You've helped more than you know, though. I really appreciate you and Ada coming. I don't want you to think I'm ungrateful."

"It's fine, baby. You rest."

Kate found her daughter and granddaughter sitting on the porch.

"Come join us, Mamma." Emmie patted the arm of the chair next to her. "How's our girl?"

"She's better." Kate sighed. "I believe she needs to deal with things in her own way, though. No doubt this'll change her. I see it already. She'll still be our Bartie, but ...different."

The others rocked quietly.

"Ada, honey, maybe we should go home tomorrow. I need to talk to your mamma."

The Decker household woke to thunder rattling the window panes. Lightning cracked the sky above the old live oak trees as their heavy boughs swung in the wind. Aaron had climbed into Kate's bed, 'just to make sure she wasn't scared'.

"Just the devil draggin' his old bones across the sky. It'll be done soon," she assured him.

In the early hours before dawn, Ada came and sat on the bed next to them, listening as Kate told stories her daddy had made up for her when it was dark and stormy out. Before long, the sun chased the dark-bellied clouds westward. Glistening drops of water clung to the Spanish moss like glass beads.

"I smell pancakes!" Aaron cried, and jumped off the bed. He turned to look back. "C'mon y'all!"

Danny and Bitsy were in the kitchen, stuffing their mouths with plump, golden pancakes full of pecans and topped with generous dobs of butter. There was a puddle of syrup on Danny's plate nearly flowing over the sides.

"Good morning," Emmie greeted them. "Have a seat, I have more ready."

"Well, look at you cooking, daughter. I can't believe Maizie lets you near the stove."

"The Campbells get back this morning, or she wouldn't! She'll be over to say goodbye."

"Where's Uncle Caleb?" Ada asked.

"An early surgery, I'm afraid. He said to give you his love."

The whole of earth seemed washed from the storm. Small branches lay here and there on the road as the women drove out of the city.

"Mother nature doing her cleaning," Kate said.

As they emerged into the countryside, there was a sense of hope in the lilt of light dancing over fields of corn, beans and the rusty red heads of sorghum.

Kate asked, "Can I count on y'all to help me talk Omie out of going back to Savannah for a little while? She's not going to want to hear that."

"Yes ma'am," they answered.

# Chapter 25

Emmie's boys didn't quite know what to make of this new version of their cousin Bartie. They were used to the crackle of mischief that accompanied her through the door whenever she visited. She made time for them and laughed at their jokes, whether they were funny or not.

This Bartie stayed tucked beneath the covers in the same room their aunt had occupied after the lightning strike. This Bartie slept most of the time, groaning in her sleep as her broken body went about mending.

They had heard whispered conversations among the adults and murmured voices coming from behind the door when their father checked on the girl. The boys knew something awful had happened, involving their Uncle Nate drinking and beating Bartie. The why of it was lost on them. And no one would explain.

Bitsy was old enough to gather the information she'd heard into a passable truth. Bartie had misbehaved by coming to Savannah without permission, but that was no reason for her to earn such a beating. Bitsy knew her uncle had a drinking problem. Alcohol was not something often indulged in at her home, other than wine at dinner occasionally. Bitsy decided that 'spirits' must contain 'evil spirits' as the minister said, and she vowed never to come under their spell.

Each day, the girl would go into Bartie's room, bringing dolls she was sewing outfits for. The cousins seemed content in companionable silence. Sometimes Bitsy would offer news of the world outside. She also liked to describe what she would fashion next for the fine china dolls Emmie brought her from France.

Mostly, Bartie stared out the window with a faraway gaze, showing little interest. Bitsy did occasionally catch the ghost of a smile turning up the corners of her cousin's mouth.

"Today Mamma gave me some leftover satin and lace from a bridal gown she's making!" Bitsy excitedly held the finery in front of Bartie's face. When there was no response, she continued, "I'm going to make a dress for Amelia and marry her to the nutcracker on the mantle. He's a fine-looking soldier, don't you think?"

She continued, "But then, she might become an old maid like Miss Haversham in Great Expectations. Nothing to eat or drink but cobwebby cake and moldy wine." She gave Bartie a sideways glance, then in a doll's voice, said, "Might I interest you in some rotten refreshments, my dear?"

A small sound came from Bartie, the suggestion of a giggle.

"Truly, my dear, it is a most gruesome vintage."

Bartie turned to look at her cousin then and gave a wincing chuckle.

"Stop," Bartie rasped, "it hurts to laugh."

"Well," Bitsy replied in an affronted doll's voice, "I suppose that's a no."

Afterwards, there were days when Bartie was more engaged, listening, if not commenting. This was fine with Bitsy, who loved an audience.

Danny and Aaron began making an appearance daily, though they weren't sure what to say. They brought her flowers, plucked from neighbors' gardens, she imagined, and showed her their favorite rock collections. Soon, Bartie's voice grew stronger. Her spirits seemed to lift as well, and the cousin they knew began to re-emerge.

Omie had agreed to giving Bartie a couple of weeks by herself. After that, she insisted on returning regularly with a fresh batch of herbs and poultices. When the children asked how their sister was doing, Omie told them, "I don't know as she'll ever be the sassy-fras she was, but there's vinegar in her yet."

After convincing her mamma she needed more time under Caleb's care, Bartie stayed in Savannah until the end of summer. Omie returned when the day came for the cast to be removed.

"I am so glad to get that itchy thing off!" Bartie exclaimed, scratching furiously.

Omie scolded, "Stop. Now stop! You'll scratch it raw and get an infection!"

Caleb nodded. "Then I'll just have to cut the arm off." He winked at his niece. "This is going to be a bit uncomfortable, Bartie. Your arm has been in that sling for a long while. Just breathe deeply and we'll go slow."

Bartie winced as Caleb straightened her arm.

"Look how puny it is, Mamma!"

"That's to be expected, hon. We'll work on it and get you up to snuff in no time."

After returning to the Deckers' home, Omie massaged a salve made with comfrey and boneset into the muscles and joints of Bartie's arm. Immediately, relief spread through the tissues, whether from the herbs or her mamma's touch, Bartie did not care. She was sick of being an invalid. Her ribs and hip still pained her some when walking, but having the use of this arm again cheered her immensely.

"Mamma, there's no need of you staying. I know you're needed at home. I'm all right with Aunt Emmie and Uncle Caleb. Isn't that right Aunt Emmie?"

Emmie had just come into the room and sat on the bed.

Omie brushed the hair back from her daughter's face. "Well, I was thinking you could come back home with me in a day or two. You don't need to do anything that will tax you."

"Mamma." Bartie looked up, eyes shining. "I'm not coming home. I can't be around . . . him. Not ever again."

Tears of grief coursed down the girl's cheeks, but her voice stayed firm.

"I want to stay here and go to secretarial school. There's really no reason for me not to. Aunt Emmie already said it would be all right if I stay with them meantime."

Bartie looked to her aunt for confirmation.

Omie looked at Emmie too, and said in a tight voice, "So, y'all have decided this without talking to me first."

Emmie pleaded, "Please don't be angry, sister! Caleb and I told her we would support her decision, but only with your blessing."

Omie stood up. "Let me think on it some. I'll be back in a week with my answer." She walked toward the door. "I'm going to ask Thomas to drive me home now."

"Mamma!" Bartie called.

They heard the front door slam and Omie was gone.

Kate walked in from the herb room and found Omie sitting at the kitchen table, still wearing her shawl and hat.

"My baby girl wants to leave us, Mamma. You have a potion to fix *that*?"

"Tell me," Kate said.

When Omie had finished relaying Bartie's decision to leave home forever, Kate took her hand.

"First of all, daughter, the hurt is still fresh, physically, and emotionally. It's too soon to know if she'll change her mind, but she needs to heal from this on her own terms. It's not about you, it's about her daddy."

Kate tilted Omie's face to look in her eyes.

"She's in good hands. We will all miss her, sweetie, but Savannah's not so far. We'll visit often." Kate groaned as she stood. "You may have to use a block and tackle to get me up in the buggy though."

# 1939

## JUNE 20

Tess walked up to the porch carrying a basket of eggs.

"Hey Lilly, Mamma. What are y'all doin' out here?"

Ada Kate fanned herself with the dish towel. "It's hot in that kitchen. We're just gettin' some fresh air." She took the eggs from her daughter, planted a kiss on the girl's cheek, and returned to her baking.

"Wanna go to my house?" Tess asked. "At least there's some big fans on the porch."

The girls wandered toward the river and out into the field where James and Ada Kate had built their home.

Lilly stood on the porch taking in the serene landscape of grasses and wildflowers leading to the wood's edge. The yard was bordered by azaleas and forsythia bushes. A neat array of washtubs was planted with zinnia's—Grandmamma Kate's favorite flower, Tess told her—along with medicinal herbs. Ada Kate's vegetable garden held as many flowers as vegetables.

"This is wonderful!" Lilly exclaimed.

Tess looked around. "It is if you don't have to weed and water it. Come on in, let's get some lemonade."

As her cousin went into the kitchen, Lilly wandered around looking at photographs on the walls and on top of the piano. She picked up a portrait taken of her Uncle James and Aunt Ada Kate on their wedding day.

When Tess joined her, Lilly exclaimed, "Your mamma is the most beautiful bride I ever saw!"

Tess smiled. "Wish I took after her."

Lilly regarded her cousin a moment. "You do, Tess. Least I think you will more as you get older."

This seemed to please the girl greatly. She handed Lilly her drink, then they went out to sit in the porch swing.

"When we go back to Grandmamma's, do you think we could get your mamma to tell us about her wedding?"

Tess responded, "Prolly so." Lulled by the gliding of the swing and sound of the fans overhead, she turned sleepily to Lilly and said, "Wonder what the poor folks are doin' now."

Soon, the smell of sugar, cinnamon, and vanilla roused the girls. They strolled back toward their grandmamma's house, picking up pecans along the way.

Tess remarked, "You know we're gonna' be the ones to shell these, right? My brothers are lazy as pigs."

"Well, they won't get any pralines, then." Lilly grinned. "It's the one thing I'm better than Mamma at making."

Before the girls got to the porch, Cyrus and Jacob ran past them, yelling, "We get to lick the bowl."

"Speaking of the little devils," Tess said.

After the boys licked both the batter bowls clean, they were out the door again.

"Whoa!" Lilly yelled as she was nearly knocked down.

"There go my two little tornados." Ada laughed. "What have you girls been up to?"

"Oh, we were just sittin' on our porch swing,"

"I got to see the picture of you at your wedding, Aunt Ada. You were beautiful! Still are."

Ada turned to smile at her niece. "All right, you must want something."

"No, truly," Lilly replied. "I wanna hear all the details about your wedding. Was it just perfectly romantic? I bet James was the handsomest man there."

"Yes, ma'am. He sure was a sight up there, waitin' for me beside your Uncle Ezra."

"How about the uncles, were they handsome too?"

"They cleaned up pretty well." Ada laughed. "It's a rare thing to see the men in this family in other than overalls."

"How about Grandaddy?" Lilly asked.

Ada turned back toward the stove. "I better take these out before they burn!"

Tess looked at her cousin and shook her head slightly.

Lilly mouthed back, "Oh."

Ada Kate turned back to Tess and Lilly.

"It's all right, girls. No, my daddy did not attend my wedding. Nor did your mamma, Lilly. I admit, it took me years to find it in my heart to forgive them. But the happiness James and I found filled much of the emptiness those two left, and when this one came along," she kissed Tess' cheek, "there was no room for anything but joy."

Tess blushed with pleasure. Lilly could see how close her aunt and cousin were. A small bubble of sadness rose in her chest, and she wondered what had shaped this distance between herself and her mamma. Maybe, being an only child, something had been missing. Something she didn't even realize she needed.

"I don't know why we moved all the way to Atlanta," Lilly said. "I could've had a bunch more time with y'all if Mamma had stayed in Savannah."

"But then, she might not have met your daddy," Tess replied.

"Well, yeah. He is pretty great."

"We all liked him from the start." Ada smiled. "Even Mamma, really. She just wasn't ready for what was to come. I think she scared him a bit!"

# Chapter 26

## 1927

Once Nate had recovered enough to fend for himself, he disappeared. There was no sign of him throughout the last days of summer. Ezra, as always, was the one who kept track of his daddy's whereabouts and reported to Phoebee that Nate had moved into the red shack near the grange. He was doing odd jobs for anyone who would hire him.

Frank Thomas, Ezra and Ada Kate took over the chores that had been their daddy's so that Phoebee and Omie could focus on the peanut crop. Ada's beau, James Dillon, became a fixture around the farm, lending a hand whenever needed.

Omie approved of the boy. She knew his family, often ministered treatments to his mamma for arthritis. The Dillons were good folks. His father and brothers worked for the railroad and were often away.  Mrs. Dillon helped care for her grandchildren in spite of the pain in her swollen joints.

Young James seemed to have more of an affinity for working the land than being a railroad man. He and Ezra had become good friends and she was glad for her son to have the company. It had become apparent to Omie that Frank Thomas would find a different path than farming.

It was not a surprise, then, when James came to her to ask for Ada Kate's hand.

"I will be good to her as anyone ever could be, Mrs. Silar. My family already love Ada like she's one of us. I know she's a big help to you here with . . . with her daddy gone, but we'll be close by. We'll both come help every day."

Omie took his hand in hers and sat quietly for a few moments. He felt a warmth along his spine, then she smiled at him.

"Welcome to our family, son."

James whistled as he walked back to the barn where, Omie knew, Ada Kate waited for his news.

She felt a flutter in her stomach and wondered if this was the *Sight* coming to warn her of something about this young man that she had not sensed. Maybe it was just the oncoming loss of her girl about to become a woman.

*Where would they live? Would Ada leave her, like Bartie?*

Omie stood up and walked to the porch rail, looking out towards the river. Beams of sunlight broke through afternoon clouds and fanned across the hay field, turning the ripening seed heads gold. A wavering image came to her. A house, bathed in sunlight. A home, filled with love. Land was what she would give the couple as a wedding gift.

Omie made no attempt to contact Nate about the wedding. He'd heard the news from Ezra though, and stood beneath trees at the edge of the churchyard, still as a shadow. Through blurry eyes he watched as the church filled with family and the couple's young friends.

*I'm not welcome at my own daughter's weddin'.* He passed a shaking hand across his face. *But I done this. I wish't I could take it all back. The drinkin'. What I done to Bartie.*

Emmie and Caleb arrived with their children and the Campbells. Nate noticed Bartie was not with them.

Bartie had sent Ada a long letter when she heard news of the wedding, begging her to understand that it was too soon to travel. The jarring of the car on rough roads would be very painful. It was all she could manage to go to school at this time. Ada tried to understand, but was hurt all the same. She had always thought her sister would be her bridesmaid. Polly took Bartie's place.

The ceremony was simple, the small church only big enough to hold immediate family and closest friends. The smell of herbs and wildflowers, set in vases along the alter, filled the room.

Ezra and Polly entered first as best man and maid of honor. Polly left behind her studious expression and shone with happiness for her friends. Ezra had not been able to speak when he offered his arm to escort her down the aisle. In place of his best friend was a young woman in a blue satin dress that showed her petite curves and brought out the color of her eyes.

They took their places and turned to face the back of the church. James entered and came to stand beside Ezra. As the preacher's wife played the first notes of the wedding march, everyone stood.

Frank Thomas walked in with his sister on his arm, his cane in the other hand. Ada Kate carried a bouquet of the Mister Lincoln roses her grandmamma loved so much. She smiled as she passed the pews, but her eyes were only on James.

She wore the ivory gown her mamma and grandmamma had been married in. Emmie managed to cover areas where the satin had yellowed with white lace and tiny pearls.

Kate's heart swelled to see her namesake in the same dress she had worn at the altar beside her own husband.

*Look at our first grandchild, Frank. She's grown into a beautiful young woman, inside and out.*

She heard his voice as if he were in the pew beside her.

*Spittin' image of you, Katie.*

Tears coursed down her cheeks and Kate put a hand to her heart.

"You all right, Mamma?"

"I'm fine, Omie, just fine."

Omie's face was wet with tears of her own. They clasped hands and watched as Ada Kate married the boy she loved.

James was handsome in his daddy's suit. He looked like he was afraid he'd wake up any moment and find that this ravishing creature smiling at him was only a dream. The best dream he'd ever had. Finally, after they'd kissed as man and wife, he managed to relax and enjoy his wedding.

Outside, the churchyard was filled with many of Kate's, Omie's, and Ada Kate's customers who'd come to express their appreciation. Folks had brought a bounty of food to celebrate Ada Kate's wedding, grateful for this fourth-generation healer who would continue caring for them in years to come.

Frank Thomas and Ezra were smiling like polecats. Everyone knew the brothers had spent the greater part of the morning in the barn where James' buggy was parked. The groom hoped that whatever mischief they'd been up to would not do permanent damage to his parent's property.

Ezra saw his daddy standing under the trees and made brief eye contact. He could feel the man's misery, sense the weight on his shoulders.

Nate stayed until his daughter and new husband emerged from the church, happy and smiling. He didn't want Ada to know he was there, didn't want to see either pity or scorn in her eyes.

Omie saw him, though. The lengthening shadows seemed to reach for Nate as he turned and walked slowly into the woods.

*I can't believe we're not sharing our first daughter's wedding.*

She swallowed her tears, refusing to allow anything to dampen the joy of this day.

# Chapter 27

## 1928

Omie had offered the newlyweds twenty acres near the river to build their house on. James' family paid to have the house built as their gift to the couple. Work began early that spring, and by summer, Ada and her young husband moved into their home. James worked the farm alongside the family, learning much from Ada's younger brother. Ezra had taken on more responsibilities while Frank Thomas learned to accommodate the weakness of his leg, and was glad of the help. A bond grew between James and his brother-in-law that made them feel like true brothers. This did not escape Frank Thomas' attention. He grew distant, sometimes surly towards them. Ezra was at a loss to figure out what to do about the situation.

Concern over his brother's state, and doubts about how the farm was faring, worried Ezra, deepening the crease of his brow. What weighed on his heart most, though, was what might become of Polly if she became a school teacher. Where would she teach? Would she move from the farm and leave him? They had been together since birth. Ezra hardly knew who he was without Polly beside him.

He often sat on a rise overlooking the river where gravestones of Mr. and Mrs. Rhymes  stood. The old man had gifted his farm to Omie and Nate when they were first married. He'd joined his wife on this hill shortly thereafter. It was a place where Ezra could escape with his worries at the end of a day. He did not see their ghosts there, but felt a peaceful presence that soothed him.

One quiet afternoon, his gaze took in the sparkle of light on the river as he sat with his thoughts. Tall cypresses lifted their heads above the oaks and willows along its banks. In his younger days, Ezra took his troubles to the river. He'd had more time to slip away then.

A memory came to him of a fishing trip he had taken by himself, years ago.

He'd packed a frying pan along with some cornmeal and lard to fry up his catch on the bank. The river was low then from a late summer drought and he knew the chances of anything biting were slim. Still, he looked forward to some solitude.

Walking along that day, Ezra had seen something pale low in the far bank. He laid down his pole and gear, then lowered himself to the water, holding on to branches and scrub. Wading across the muddy river bottom, he stooped to see what had caught his eye. Bones. They were old and yellowed, but still distinct. Part of a skull with vacant eyes stared timelessly out at the world. How many centuries had they seen go by?

Ezra knew there had been encampments of Indians in these parts for as far back as anyone could remember. He had turned many arrowheads up as he plowed the fields in spring, rains having brought them closer to the surface. Contemplating the people who had lived on this land long before his kind claimed it, Ezra left the old bones to rest where they were. He waded back to the other side and, finding a deep pool near the bank where water eddied in lazy swirls around cypress knees, he dropped in his line.

# 1939

## JUNE 20

Tess asked why Lilly's daddy had not come to the funeral.

"He had to take care of the club. Uncle Frank Thomas and Aunt Jewel help out when they're not traveling, but both of 'em wanted to be here for Grandaddy's funeral."

Ada Kate imagined Bartie wanted to face her past alone, as much as anything. Lilly was not going to be left behind, however.

"Shad has never been here," Ada said. "I hope that will change now, though."

"Why didn't he come for Great-Grandmamma Kate's funeral?" Tess asked.

"Bartie had not met him yet. She was still living in Savannah, but Mamma made her come home for that. She left as soon as the service was over though. Snuck away before anybody knew she was gone."

"That was the last time she came home?" Tess asked.

"Yep," Ada Kate replied. "Then she moved to Atlanta, married Shad. You came along." She kissed Tess' cheek.

"And you came along." She leaned over and kissed Lilly's cheek as well.

"Life just got busy. We did meet in Savannah when we could, though, so you two would at least know each other. Cousins are important."

"Like you and Aunt Bitsy," Tess remarked.

"Your Aunt Bitsy got busy too, helping her mamma in the dress shop. When her brothers were old enough, they found their own lives. Suddenly, we were all grown up."

The girls sat with chins in hand, taking all this information in.

"All right, I have work to do, you two. Go find someone else to tell you stories."

"But Mamma."

"Shoo!"

"Whatcha want to do?" Tess asked.

The girls were walking toward the river, watching the afternoon sun slip between the trees below. As they neared the old cemetery, they saw Grace sitting on one of the old headstones. She seemed to be deep in conversation with someone.

"Hey," Lilly called.

Grace looked at them and smiled, motioning them over. The marker she sat on was nameless. Whether the rains of time or lichen had worn it away, was hard to tell. The odd, bubbling artesian spring scented the air with sulphur, and Lilly scrunched up her nose.

"Phew!"

Tess laughed. "Who are you talking to, Grace?"

"Aunt Grace," Lilly corrected.

Tess rolled her eyes. "Hard to call her aunt when I been wearin' her hand-me-downs all my life. There's just a few years between us."

Lilly raised her eyebrows. "So, I don't need to call you aunt either?"

"Nope," Grace answered. "Like Daddy used to say, I don't care what you call me, long as you call me to dinner!"

"Grace talks to the dead," Tess offered.

"Mostly, they talk to me."

"Guess I shouldn't be surprised," Lilly said. "This family is full of unusual talents."

"This is where Leila Rahn was buried," Grace told them. "Course, she's not there now, just a bunch of bones. She's been tellin' me about this place from a long time ago. There were Indians living down by the river then, just aways up towards town. She says they taught her about plants and such, how to make baskets, where to find quail eggs."

"Indians?" Lilly shuddered.

"They were just people tryin' to live their lives, like we are. Most were willin' to share what they knew too, until white people drove them out. We're the ones to be feared of, Lilly."

"Does your Grandma Kate talk to you too? And your Grandpa Frank? Where are their graves?"

Grace walked them over to a sunnier part of the cemetery, where marble headstones gleamed.

"I was little when Grandma Kate passed. Grandpa Frank had been gone for years before that. They haven't spoke to me. I feel her close though, especially around Tess."

Tess' eyes widened. "Really? Why me?"

"Dunno," Grace replied. "Maybe she's your guardian angel."

"We have guardian angels?" Lilly asked.

"Of course." Grace chuckled then. "Whoever yours is says they should get paid overtime."

Lilly and Tess had a skipping contest on the way back to the house. They were sweaty and hot, thinking of taking a dip in the river. They slipped through the screen door and plopped onto chairs.

Ada passed a frosting bowl to the girls. "Saved you some. Hurry and lick it before the boys figure out I did. They'll be sniffin' around like coon dogs."

"I bet Grandmamma was not happy to find out about me," Lilly said.

"Oh, hon," Ada Kate replied, "she was upset at first, just because Bartie was so young, and we missed out on having a wedding. Mammas live for that, you know."

She gave Tess a stern look, but smiled.

"Once your grandmamma got used to the idea, though, she was over the moon. It was hard for her with Bartie in Atlanta. She didn't get to experience you becoming part of the family until she delivered you."

Ada ran her hand over Tess' hair.

"This one just slid out into the world without a worry, but Bartie had a bit of trouble. It was a good thing Aunt Emmie came to get Mamma when she did."

Lilly looked up questioningly.

"It was all fine, though. Two grandchildren, eight months apart! Mamma had lost Grandmamma Kate before Tess was born, and Aunt Julia just before you were born. New life makes losing loved ones more bearable."

Ada bent down to kiss each girl on the head.

"Never doubt that you both were a blessing."

"Were?" the girls said simultaneously.

"Are!" Ada laughed. "Now, go see what your brothers are up to."

"Can we go swimming at the river, Mamma?"

"I need you to look after your sisters right now, Tess. But when I'm done, you can go."

Lilly and Tess heard screeching as they rounded the corner of the house. Jacob had managed to tie his little sisters' braids together and was leading them around the yard.

Cyrus followed his brother laughing. "Giddyup! Make 'em gee and haw, Jacob."

Tess grabbed Jacob's arms and yelled, "Let go!"

"Ow, yer hurtin' me!"

"I said, *let go!*"

Jacob dropped Olivia's and Naomi's hair. "We was just havin' fun. No need to get so all-fired hateful."

Tess held onto one of Jacob's arms. "Was this fun for you, girls?"

Olivia sniffled and answered, "NO! I hate you, Jacob Nathaniel."

Little Naomi took her big sister's hand and said, "Cyrus was mean too. He started it."

When Tess turned to look for him, he was down the road, running toward Sarah's and Phoebee's place. Jacob managed to wrench out of her grasp while she was turned away and followed behind.

Lilly took Olivia's hand and said, "Why don't we go down to the river and see if we can catch some crawdads. Tess said they're the best eatin' around."

"They are!" Naomi looked up with her big blue eyes.

Tess smiled at her sisters. "Maybe we'll take you swimmin' later, too."

Lilly shuddered. "What about those crawdads, won't they pinch your toes?"

"Just don't touch bottom!" Olivia said.

Lilly looked at Tess for confirmation.

"Or wear your shoes," she offered. "Don't hurt as much."


Bartie was walking down from Phoebee's and had stopped behind the old oak. She watched the children's scene unfold and considered intervening, but was reminded by Tess of how Ada Kate would always manage to take a troublesome situation in hand.

*Looks like the acorn didn't fall far from the tree. Those boys are tough nuts to crack.*

Frank Thomas and Ezra had been angels in comparison.

She slipped into the house and saw Ada Kate watching out the window.

"I don't know what I'd do without Tess, Bartie. I spoil the boys. I know that. It's just..."

"You came so close to losing them both, honey. I understand."

Ada turned and embraced her sister. "Won't you stay a couple more days? Please say you will. I miss you, sis. And we still have so much catching up to do without all the others around."

Bartie was seized by memories of the two of them when they were girls. She suddenly wanted to go back in time and feel that closeness again.

"All right," she whispered into Ada's ear. "All right."

# Chapter 28

## 1928

"I'm sorry sister, but Bartie's determined to move to Atlanta. She's done with secretarial school and will soon be nineteen. What can anyone do?"

Omie sat at Emmie's table looking down at her folded hands.

"Didn't she know I would be here today, Emmie?"

"Oh, she knew all right. She figured I would break the news to you before she came home if she was late. As far as I know, she's out walking with Jackson and her friends from school."

"How is Jackson?"

"He's fine. He tries to keep an eye on her without seeming like a chaperone. Caleb hears from him occasionally, just to let us know she's all right. I don't imagine he's tried to dissuade her from going to Atlanta, though. You know how she is, that would make her more determined than ever."

"Well, I am her mamma. We'll see about this."

Bartie came in the door soon after. She hung up her coat and called brightly, "Mamma, you're already here!"

Omie gathered her emotions close and said, "Come give me a hug, honey."

Bartie glanced at her aunt, surprised not to be in trouble, but Emmie's face gave nothing away.

After an afternoon of pleasantries and catching up, Bartie had relaxed her guard. Then Omie said, "Sounds like you have some things to tell me, daughter."

Flustered, the girl stammered out her plans.

Omie said, "What made you think I would agree to let you move so far from home, Bartie? You're a young girl who's hardly been anywhere. You don't know what life is like in a city as big as Atlanta. It's a dangerous place for an unchaperoned young woman."

"How would you know. Mamma? You've never been there!"

Bartie took a deep breath.

"Sorry Mamma, I don't mean to disrespect you. I just need more than Savannah has to offer. I'll always wonder what else there is if I don't go see."

Bartie looked at both her mamma and aunt with pleading eyes.

She continued, "My friend Jewel is moving there and staying with her aunt and uncle. They've agreed to me coming, as well. Jewel says there's lots of work opportunities for us. I can always come back here if things don't work out. Can't I, Aunt Emmie?"

There was no doubt she would not return to the farm and her daddy.

"I'll think about this," Omie said wearily. "Now tell me news of Jackson."

Emmie agreed to go with Bartie to meet Jewel's aunt and uncle in Atlanta, and determine if the circumstances would be suitable for her niece.

"This does not mean your mamma is agreeing to let you go. Be patient, young lady, you don't know how much you're asking of her." Emmie smiled at the girl on the seat beside her.

"Might not be a bad thing for you to learn how to drive if we're going to be traveling back and forth, seeing as how you'll be visiting us often." She gave Bartie a meaningful look.

"Really? You'll teach me to drive your car?"

"Let's see how this meeting goes first."

Bartie rolled her eyes, then grinned.

Jewel's relatives proved to be kind, reassuring people. They were of modest means, but had a lovely little home in Virginia Highlands, with an extra room for the girls.

"We are truly excited to have them both," Mrs. Harper assured Emmie. "We weren't fortunate enough to have children of our own, so Jewel is just that to us. A jewel."

"My niece and I can't thank you both enough for your generosity," Emmie replied. "I'll talk with Bartie's parents and let you know of their decision as soon as I can."

Back on the road, Bartie held her tongue as long as she could, noting Emmie's blank expression. "Please, please tell me you liked them! Say Mamma will let me come!"

Emmie pulled over and turned to face her niece.

"Get out."

"What? What did I say?"

She handed the girl her keys and flashed a big smile.

When Emmie visited Omie a few days later with a good report, her sister seemed to wilt a bit, giving in to the inevitable.

"She'd go anyway, whether I agree or not. At least this way, we'll know where she is and can keep in touch. I wish the *Sight* would set my mind at ease, Emmie."

The sisters embraced and Omie let her tears flow. When she felt cried out, Omie sat back and wiped her face.

Emmie squeezed Omie's hand. "I can't imagine what I'd do if Bitsy wanted to leave us, hon. It worries me a good bit. Right now, she's with me in the shop every day after school. The girl has gone from sewing doll clothes to designing and making a few of her own dresses. With small adjustments from me, of course." Omie could see the pride in Emmie's eyes. "I'm trying not to pressure her to become a seamstress if it's not what she wants to do, but she's good, and I could use her at the shop, now that I've bought the shop from Elizabeth. Besides, it gives us something we can do together without me getting my head bit off! Why do girls go through this awful stage?"

Omie offered a sad smile. "I reckon it's so we can let them go, Emmie. Maybe you should call her Bit-Me."

# Chapter 29

Life found a steady rhythm at the farm and Omie took comfort in it. Over the past months, she had come to accept Bartie's absence, though she felt like part of her heart was missing.

All seemed as well as she could hope without Nate's presence. On a fine April morning while Omie was turning over the garden, Ada Kate came running out from the house with Grace on her hip, calling, "Mamma, Mamma, it's Grandmamma!"

Throwing her hoe to the ground, she ran behind Ada, bursting through the doorway to find Kate sprawled on the floor.

"She just moaned and fell!" Ada Kate put a hand over her face and whispered, "She was gone so fast."

Omie sank to the floor sobbing.

"Mamma! Oh no! Mamma."

The rest of the family soon entered the house. Phoebee ran in and dropped down beside Omie's heaving body. The children knelt next to their grandmamma and cried.

Willie buried his face in Old Joe's neck and sobbed.

James stood in the doorway, giving the family space for their grieving. He rode to town to send a telegram to Emmie and Caleb, tears tracking his dusty face. On the road he met Aunt Julia and her granddaughter Alberta riding toward the farm. The old woman looked as if she was barely holding on to life herself, too weary to look up at him.

James nodded to Alberta and went on, not knowing what to say.

Omie ran to Alberta's wagon as soon as she saw it pull into the yard. Frank Thomas helped Aunt Julia down from her seat, and Omie wrapped the frail body in her arms. There were no words for the sorrow flowing between them. Alberta helped her grandmamma to the house, offering a quiet nod to Omie.

Kate's body lay on her bed. Aunt Julia gently curled up next to her old friend and wept. Omie sat beside her, stroking the old woman's shaking shoulders while Alberta stood among the young ones, with her arm around Willie's shoulders, crying quietly.

Omie looked at Ada Kate. "Children, would you give Aunt Julia and Miss Alberta a little time alone with your grandmamma?"

Ada Kate herded her little sisters into the kitchen. The boys quietly followed.

After many long moments, steeped in sorrow, Aunt Julia raised herself from the bed and said in her husky voice, "Alberta, you best go home and tell the people."

"All right." Alberta placed a kiss on her grandmamma's head. "Y'all bring her home?" Omie nodded and their eyes held for a moment. "Mizz Kate was shore a good woman. We all be sorry for her passin'. Anything I can do, you hear?"

Omie thanked her, then turned to Aunt Julia. They held hands and gazed at Kate's still body. Pale light came through the window. Shadows of blooms from the dogwood tree danced lightly across Kate's body, caressing her face.

"Mamma loved that tree. She told me the legend of the blossoms, how each petal bears blood from where Jesus was nailed to the cross, the crown of thorns in the center."

"Your mamma was a good Christian woman, best I ever knew. Best friend I ever had, too." Aunt Julia blew her nose and turned to Omie. "You and me will lay her out. Tomorrow, folks will be coming by to pay their respects and this is the only time we'll have her to ourselves again."

"What do you want to put in the water for washing? I'll get Ada warming a big pot full. I have some dried lavender."

"Yes, lavender would be fine." Aunt Julia thought a moment. "Get the girls to fetch some dried petals from Kate's Mr. Lincoln roses. She dearly loves them. There's usually some hanging in the herb room, yes?"

Omie nodded.

Ada opened the door a crack and peeked in the room. "Mamma, can we come back in now?"

"Course, honey."

Ada sat little Grace on the bed next to Kate, and Georgia Rose climbed up beside her. Polly and Phoebee came into the bedroom, standing on either side of Ada Kate. Polly's eyes were red and swollen behind her glasses. "She was the only grandma I ever had."

Phoebee gasped, then covered her mouth and began to cry. She looked like a child, leaning against Ada's shoulder. Willie walked over and took her hand.

Ada Kate spoke quietly, "Frank Thomas and Ezra are in the barn working on a casket, Mamma."

Omie covered her face, realizing her sweet mamma would soon rest beneath the earth. This time, Aunt Julia caressed the young woman's back, softly humming a song of solace passed down through generations of her people.

As supper time approached, Ada Kate took the girls back into the kitchen. "Georgia, would you gather some of the dried roses hanging in the herb room?" She handed her a basket. "Fill this full."

Polly and Phoebee offered to take Grace with them to feed the chickens and milk the cow. Ada gave them a grateful nod. Phoebee put a hand on Ada's back. "Sarah should be gettin' in soon and I'll come back to help you."

Ada Kate turned suddenly and wrapped her arms around Phoebee. "Thank you so much," she sobbed.


Aunt Julia and Omie heard the family leave for Phoebee's after supper. The two women worked in silence, both lost in memories. When finished, they pulled a scented sheet over Kate and went into the kitchen. Aunt Julia sat down at the table and Omie collapsed to the floor beside her. She laid her head in the old woman's small lap, hiding her face in the soft folds of the well-worn skirt. Gentle hands stroked Omie's hair until her sobs subsided.

Aunt Julia spoke into the stillness. "Listen to me now. You got to take all this hurt, all the sorrows stored up in you and find a place to put them. A woman's heart holds not only her own, but the pain of every woman in the family who came before her. This is where the *Knowin'* comes from. We are guided by those on the other side."

Omie lifted her face. "But how, Aunt Julia? I feel like I can't breathe, like my heart is going to break right through my chest."

"You go sit out on the porch. Set that pain in the chair beside you. Listen to what it has to say. Then leave it there. Go out to talk with it when you have a need, but do not let it follow you around all the day. You have a life to tend to. Folks who need you." Old Joe began to lick Omie's face. Aunt Julia reached down to rest her hand on his warm head. "There you go. Animals are here to help take away our pain. They know how to bury it like a bone."

Outside, the birds had ceased singing. Crows flew in on silent wings to hold vigil, filling the pines trees. Only the sound of sawing and hammering echoed in the air as Frank Thomas and Ezra worked on Kate's coffin.

Frank Thomas held his sorrow behind a clinched jaw, focusing on the task at hand. Ezra wiped his eyes constantly, trying to see what was before him.

"Just go on inside if you need to, Ezra. I can finish this."

"No, brother. I'll get myself pulled together. I just can't imagine Grandmamma in this box."

Frank Thomas replied, "You of all people should know she's not going to be in this box. Only her bones, and one day, not even them." He put down the saw and took a deep breath, then stared out the barn door. "What do your ghosts say, Ezra? Can they see her? Can you?"

Ezra took a moment before answering. "Nothin'. I ain't sure if I'll see her. I really don't know how death works. Why I see some people and not others. Ghosts don't answer my questions, Frank Thomas. I wish they would."

The boys returned to their work, each caught up in their own thoughts.

Phoebee heard the murmur of their voices as she walked toward Omie's house. She saw her friend sitting in one of the rocking chairs, talking to herself. As Phoebee began to climb into the closest chair, Omie said, "Not there. Sit in this one."

Phoebee went to the other rocker, casting a worried look at Omie.

"My troubles are sittin' here." Omie pointed her thumb at the chair and told Phoebee about Aunt Julia's advice.

Phoebee nodded and took the other rocker. "That sounds wise." She hooked her little feet under the rungs and began to rock. "Dang, I shur hope my troubles have longer legs than me, else I'll have to get Ezra to build me another short chair."

Omie gave her friend a small smile. "He and Frank Thomas are in the barn now, building Mamma's casket."

"God bless 'em. I don't know how they can stand to." Phoebee said.

"Men need somethin' to do when they're hurting, I suppose."

"Y'all eat sumpthin'?"

"No, I'm not hungry." Omie sighed. "Aunt Julia took some tea, but that's all she was up for. She's resting just now. I'll get us both a plate directly. Ada left some food in the warming ovens."

Phoebee reached out and took Omie's hand. They rocked in easy rhythm with each other, staring out at the trees full of crows until it grew too dark to see the still, black shapes.

Aunt Julia expressed a wish to sit at Kate's side through the night. Omie found her dozing in the chair and tucked a quilt around the small woman. When the grieving children had gone to bed, Omie went once again to the porch. A light flickered beside the barn. She put on her shawl, knowing who this would likely be.

It was Nate. He stood with a lantern in his hand, wick turned down low.

"Omie," he said in a choked voice.

She came to him and they stood in a long embrace. No words were spoken. They let their tears fall for Kate, for themselves, for all the things gone unsaid.

At last, he pulled back and held her arms.

"I just heard. I am so, so sorry about your mamma. In spite of all I did, she was good to me. Better than I deserved."

Omie looked up at him. Grief had deepened every line of her face and cast shadows beneath her eyes.

"Omie, I been sober for most of a year now. I know that don't count for much, but I am tryin' my best to stay this way. Not so's you'll take me back,

I don't imagine you ever could after . . . after what I did to our daughter. I just want to be a better man. If not for you, I prolly would have died before I was old enough to shave. I want you to know that's the truth of it."

She looked away a moment. "Thank you for that, Nate. What you did to Bartie was about the hardest thing I have ever had to find my way through. But losing Mamma is like losing my heart. She was my strength, I always knew she'd be there when I couldn't find my way in this world. Now, I just feel lost."

"If there's anything I can do..." He screwed up his courage to ask, "May I come to the funeral?"

Omie struggled with her thoughts. Her sorrow and need for comfort won out in the end, and she nodded. He held her hand while they sat on a hay bale side by side, looking out into the night until the stars began to fade.

The small church could not hold the mass of people who came to pay their respects to Kate Lee. She had been at the births of many and delivered their children as well. The ill, the dying, anyone who needed comfort knew they could count on this wise and gifted woman. Some might have entertained thoughts that she was a 'witch' with her gift of the *Sight,* but they could not deny she used it for God's work.

Just as Omie arrived, an automobile pulled up in the churchyard, carrying her uncle Asa and cousin Ralph. She was shocked at the changes in them both. Asa could barely get out of the car, even with his son's help, and Ralph himself looked none too steady. Omie remembered her Aunt Wilda's letter after the war, speaking of the injuries that sent her son home.

Omie walked toward them and reached out her hands.

"Uncle Asa. Ralph. I can't believe you came all the way from Tennessee. It's been so long!"

Each pulled her into a gentle embrace.

"Kate was the last of my kin. I never should have stayed away so long," the old man said.

"It's my fault, not yours," Ralph assured his father. "If I'd of bought that car sooner, I coulda brought you here while she was livin'."

Omie put a hand on each of their arms. "Well, you're here now and I appreciate it."

Omie could only sob in the face of her mamma's death. She did not try to be strong, but buried her face in Nate's shoulder.

*I can't bear it! Mamma!*

She heard the condolences friends and neighbors expressed, managing to give a small nod in return. Emmie stood at her side, barely able to do much more. Caleb and all the children were gathered beside them. The Campbells, Maizie and Thomas, and Marion had come from Savannah, all deeply saddened by the loss of this dear woman Emmie brought into their lives.

Omie had insisted that Bartie come home for her grandmamma's funeral. The girl hung back from the others, leaning on a cane. She would not meet her daddy's eyes, and he did not try to approach her. His shame was palpable, but Bartie had no forgiveness in her.

As soon as the service was over, Jackson offered her a ride back to Savannah. She took it, knowing her absence would not be noticed for some time.

"Thank you, Jackson. I want to get gone before Mamma tries to guilt me into staying. Jewel and I are moving to Atlanta next week and I want to put this place behind me as fast as I can."

Nate watched his daughter ride away, a mixture of emotions playing across his face. He knew deep down that this was likely the last he would see of her.

"She's took him back!" Frank Thomas shouted at Ezra as they stood behind the church. He lit another cigarette off the last one. The funeral procession had begun moving toward the cemetery and Nate was one of the pall bearers.

"Easy, brother. This is a hard day for Mamma. For all of us. You don't know that she forgave him, so don't make trouble for her now."

"Oh, I won't. Believe me. But if he's around after this, you won't see much of my hide."

Frank Thomas threw down the cigarette and crushed it angrily.

Ezra followed him to the gravesite, shaking his head.

Back at the house, tables were laden with food from friends and neighbors offering condolences. Omie held a plate on her lap but could not seem to get a bite past the lump in her throat. Emmie sat beside her with a full plate as well. The sisters nodded their heads and thanked those who came to offer a few words of comfort. Neither remembered much of this at the end of the day.

When Omie rose before dawn the following morning, Ezra sat at the table with his face in his hands.

"Hey, son." Omie kissed the top of his head. "Did you sleep?"

"No ma'am. I just cain't get it in my head that Grandmamma's gone. I keep trying to see her, but I cain't." He began to weep.

She sat and pulled his head to her heart, stroking the dark hair that was so much like her daddy's. "It's hard to know what happens when those we love pass over. I imagine they want to comfort us, but maybe it's easier to feel their spirits than to see them. I still feel her close. Do you?"

Ezra looked up. "Yes, Mamma, I do. I know she's here. But I miss her sweet hands on mine." He sniffed. "She could make everything better with a touch. And the way she would look at me when I talked to her. Like I really didn't need to say a word. She already knew what was in my heart."

"Well, darlin'. She still knows. Don't stop going to her with your troubles."

Omie rose to put on the coffee, but turned back to him. "Ezra, you know you can talk to me too. About anything."

He wiped his face with a sleeve. "I do know, Mamma. It's just that you got so much on you with Daddy and everything. I don't want to burden you."

She walked back to the table and took his chin in her hand. "Baby, a mamma's shoulders are wide. I'll set down any cares I have about your daddy to make room for yours. Never forget that."

After the coffee was perking, Omie walked into her mamma's room and came out with an old fiddle case.

"Uncle Asa wanted you to have this, son. I reckon Mamma wrote him about you and Frank Thomas making music."

Ezra opened the case and pulled out a fiddle the color of dark honey.

"That was their daddy's, my grandpap's. I was only about ten when he passed, but I remember how much we all loved it when he came to visit. Half the county would show up to hear him play, and we'd dance in the barn until the sun came up."

"I cain't believe this! I been wanting one. It's tuned the same as Frank Thomas' mandolin. He's been givin' me lessons now and then. I just gotta figure out this thing." He waved the bow around.

The fiddle looked natural in Ezra's hands, as if it had always been there. Omie saw a light dancing around the bow and had a sense of the old man guiding it across the strings.

# Chapter 30

Omie listened to the faint notes of Ada Kate playing Sarah's piano as the wind carried them down the hill. Something soft and sweet in the tune spoke to Ada's mood.

*I expect my girl might be in a family way. Music flowed out of me like a stream of clear water every time I had a baby comin'. Reckon that told me even before I counted the days since my menses.*

Ada Kate's small rounded belly became more apparent as the warm days peeled winter clothes away. She wanted to wait until her third month to announce their news to the family. Knowing the story of her mamma's miscarriage with her first baby, Ada wanted to spare them grief if something went wrong.

As everyone sat on the porch shelling the first peas and enjoying the evening air, James blurted out, "Guess what y'all. We're gonna' have a baby!"

Ada slapped his knee playfully and cried, "We were going to tell them together!"

"Congratulations!" rang out and hugs were given all around.

Omie just rocked and shelled peas, a quiet smile on her face. "I thought you were going to keep it a secret until the little one told us herself."

"You knew already?" Ada asked in surprise.

Her mamma stopped rocking and looked at Ada.

"Of course you did," Ada laughed.

"Herself?" James asked.

"Prepare to be hen-pecked," Ezra announced. A chorus of clucks rang out from the porch, causing the hens in their pen to look up in confusion.

"When will the baby come?" asked Georgia Rose.

"October," said Ada and Omie in unison.

"We'll go find her in the pumpkin patch!" Ezra hugged his little sister.

"Ezra," Georgia Rose replied, "do I need to tell you where babies really come from?"

# Chapter 31

Since moving to Atlanta with Jewel, Bartie had sent several letters begging Omie to come see her. Partly from guilt at leaving her grandmamma's funeral so quickly, but she also wanted her aunt and mamma to see that she was doing well.

Finally, Emmie convinced Omie to go. "The trip would be good for both of us, sister. I miss Mamma so much. Maybe a change of scene would help loosen this stone in my heart."

They packed for the trip and Omie's excitement at seeing Bartie was apparent, though she tried to hide it.

Grant Park still hosted a pastel maze of azaleas, bordered by peonies and iris.

"I never thought to see so many flowers in my life!" Omie declared.

"See Mamma." Bartie linked arms with her mamma and aunt as they strolled along the path. "Savannah is no match for this city. Everything is bigger and better."

Omie looked and replied, "I don't know about better, but it certainly is bigger."

"Look, there's the Cyclorama!"

A large stone building stood on a hill, commanding the attention of all passers-by.

"Let's go in, you'll never see anything like it outside of Atlanta!" Bartie led them through the door where they were greeted by a man in confederate uniform.

"Hello, ladies!" His smile was hidden behind a large salt and pepper mustache.

"Mamma, Aunt Emmie, this is my friend, Shadrach Cain. He's a host for the museum."

"Shad, please." He kissed their hands in turn, like the gentlemanly officer he portrayed. "I'm delighted to give you your first tour of our beloved Cyclorama."

*How does he know this is our first tour? It certainly doesn't seem to be my daughter's.*

They were led up a flight of stairs to an entrance through the floor. Suddenly, the women were enveloped in The Battle of Atlanta.

"The largest oil painting in the world. Forty-nine feet high, three hundred and fifty-eight feet long. It's quite impressive, don't you think?"

Emmie and Omie were speechless. The brutal reality of the battle was all around them. Faces of the soldiers from each side were a study in misery, pain and fierceness. Emmie felt tears welling in her eyes.

*All these loved ones, gone. Boys, mostly. No woman from either side would willingly consent to sending their men off to die without completely exhausting any other means of resolving our differences.*

She prayed that no one she loved would ever come to this again.

After Shad's narration of events leading up to and during the battle—biased a bit toward the south, Omie imagined—the three women went in search of lunch.

"Appears to me you know this 'Captain Shad' pretty well," Emmie ventured.

Bartie blushed but quickly recovered as she casually looked at the menu.

"We've met before."

Omie tilted her head. "You spend much time at the museum, daughter?"

Bartie put down the menu and said, "All right, I wasn't going to tell you about him yet. Shad plays the piano and sings at a jazz club in the evenings. We actually met in Savannah when he was playing for dances there. I did *not* decide to move here for him though." She gave them a defiant look. "The Cyclorama is a volunteer position he holds during the day. He has a passion for history."

Omie said sternly, "I thought you were chaperoned by Jewel's aunt and uncle. What are you doing in speakeasies at your age?"

"Her relatives take us, Mamma. They know we love to dance and would rather go with us than worry about us going alone."

"Which you would," Emmie retorted.

After ordering lunch, Bartie continued, "He's a nice man, y'all. The Harpers like him. Shad studied classical piano in school, he's not just a bar musician. I like him too, but don't know that we'll be much more than friends."

"Well, he is a bit old for you, don't you think?" Emmie gave Omie a concerned look.

"Just ten years older." Bartie raised her chin. "He says I'm very mature for my age, and I tend to agree."

They left it at that, as lunch was served, and talked of Ada Kate's good news.

# Chapter 32

Ada's bump continued to grow through the hot summer months, leaving her tired by mid-day and looking to escape her mamma's kitchen as soon as dinner was done. Once the men went back to the fields, Omie would tell her to go rest a few minutes. The afternoon sun gave way to shade on the back porch, sometimes trailing the blessed whisper of a breeze in its wake. Ada enjoyed this slight reprieve whenever she could.

Georgia Rose noticed this pattern in her sister's behavior and decided to take advantage of it. She'd been cooling her feet in the pond Nate and Ezra had dug, watching turkey vultures circling above, when the idea came to her.

*I could sneak around the corner of the house and hide behind that forsythia bush next to the porch.*

She gathered her drawing supplies, slipped around the corner of the house and under the arching cover of leafy branches.

Ada Kate came out of the screen door and lowered herself onto the back steps. She closed her eyes, tilting her face toward the sky. A faded light was bathing Ada's belly as she dug tired feet into the dirt, looking for coolness in the clay.

Georgia stared, transfixed. *My sister is downright beautiful.* She drew her sketchbook and pens from the big apron pocket Emmie had sewn onto it.

Quietly, so as not to disturb her subject, the young artist captured as much as she could of Ada Kate in this moment. The chance might not come again. Ada had shooed off any mention of being sketched before. Soon, the baby would come and there would be few moments of relaxation for the new mamma.

Omie watched her girl through the window over the sink, remembering how many times she had sat on those same steps when pregnant. She knew how important these stolen moments of rest were.

"Hey sweetie, you doing all right?"

Georgia Rose slipped away unnoticed.

"It's SO hot, Mamma."

Sitting on the step below, Omie took Ada's swollen feet in her lap and pulled out the jar of liniment she carried in her apron pocket. "This is what Mamma used on my feet when I was carrying. She came up with the recipe herself. 'Course, her hands were the best at pulling out the soreness anyway."

Ada Kate groaned with pleasure and swore she would be useless for the rest of the day.

"You go rest, I'll clean up here. Your job now is to grow that grandchild for me."

"When you put it that way..." Ada smiled and stood up, then slipped on her shoes and headed for home.

Georgia Rose kept her sketch tucked away. From time to time, she found a hidden place to sit and fill in the rough edges with the soft features of her sister. What she wanted to capture, she wasn't quite sure. More than just a good likeness, something of the change pregnancy was working on Ada Kate. She'd gone from girl to grown woman, seemingly overnight.

Omie came upon her young artist beside the well one afternoon, deep into her drawing. Georgia Rose had not heard her mamma approach in time to hide the picture. Omie took in a quick breath and covered her mouth. She sat down on the bench, staring as tears coursed down her cheeks.

"Mamma, are you all right?" Georgia looked up at Omie with concern. She started to put down her sketch pad, but Omie reached out a hand to stop her.

"Baby, this is beautiful! Oh, my. You caught her so well. That color all around her, she really glows like that, doesn't she?"

Georgia Rose grinned. "Yes, ma'am. She does. Like the light I see around plants."

"Are you going to give this to her?"

"I was thinkin' I'd give it to her for Christmas. I need a frame for it, though."

Omie hugged her daughter's slight shoulders. "Maybe we'll have to make a trip to Savannah and ask Emmie to help us find just the right one!"

Ada Kate snuggled deeper into the covers as James rose to light a fire in the stove. She found it harder and harder to rise early on these late fall mornings when the sun had not yet slipped through their bedroom window.

She woke again to the smell of coffee being waved beneath her nose.

"Mmph," she moaned.

"Come on, my sleepy girl. Let me set this down and I'll help you sit up."

Ada smiled as James slipped his hands beneath her arms and pulled. He tucked both pillows behind Ada's back, positioning them until she was comfortable. Her eyes reluctantly opened and she reached for the cup.

"Can I stay here until the baby comes? I'm so cozy."

He sat on the bed and lifted a strand of hair away from her face.

"I swear you get purtier ever' day."

"I get bigger, that's for sure. Pretty soon you can just roll me around like a barrel."

"How you feelin' this mornin'? You were makin' noises in your sleep. I don't know if you were cussin' me or singin' to the baby."

"Believe me, you'd know the difference." She laughed and handed him the cup so she could shift weight. "James, I think she's coming today."

His eyes danced as he cried out, "Really? You think so or you know so?"

"Well, if you're referring to the *Sight*, you know I don't have it, but these pains I'm starting to feel are a good sign she's ready. Maybe you should tell Mamma ...?"

He was headed out the door before she had time to say, "Not right now!"


Leaves from the sycamore tree danced around Omie as she headed down to Ada's house with her birthing bag. She felt light as a leaf herself.

*A new baby in the family! Oh Mamma, I wish you were here.*

Warmth spread around her body, and she knew it was from more than the weak October sun.

"Hey, sweetie!" she called, entering the bedroom.

James had Ada Kate's feet in his lap, rubbing in the liniment Omie had given him.

"This is for more than just swollen feet," she'd told him. "It will help Ada relax for what's to come."

James was more relaxed also, having something to do. A circle of light embraced the young parents, and Omie imagined the baby must feel it too.

"How close are the pains now?"

Ada Kate looked apologetically at her mamma. "Still a good bit apart. I tried to tell James to wait until my water broke to come get you!"

"Oh, I don't want to miss any of the fun," Omie reassured her. "I'll make some more coffee and bake a pan of biscuits to hold us awhile."

James grinned. "Mamma Silar, I do love your biscuits!" He looked up quickly at Ada. "Almost good as yours, hon."

"You don't have to lie to me, James. I know...ugh!" Ada panted. "That was a doozy. James, help me walk a bit."

He supported her so she could swing her legs over the side of the bed.

"One, two, three!"

Ada Kate stood unsteadily. James hugged her to him and they began to walk around the small kitchen. Omie smiled to herself, pleased with the devotion her son-in-law showed for this precious girl. Ada Kate asked for little in life, but deserved so much.

"Take me outside, please." Ada was panting again. "It's too close in here, I need some air."

Omie slid the biscuits into the oven and began brewing a pot of coffee.

"Oh Gosh! My water!"

Omie hurried to the front door to see James holding Ada up as she stood spraddle-legged, her water gushing so hard she looked like a cow peeing on a flat rock. The two of them began to laugh and Omie joined in.

Knowing what to do, Ada Kate was able to instruct James as to what would be needed when the baby came. He brought her back inside and set her in a chair, then spread extra blankets and sheets on the mattress before helping her back onto the bed.

Omie was free to finish making breakfast and fill a couple of pots with water to put on the stove. All that was left was for the little one to make her entrance into the world.

The pains were coming more regularly now, but there was still some time to go yet. Knowing how much his wife loved music, James began to sing to her. Omie joined in, and the two went through a half-dozen songs before Ada arched her back and yelled,

"Would y'all please sing in the same key! Owwwww."

Omie fished around in her bag. "Easy, honey. Here's a piece of wood to bite on. You know how to do this, just breathe like you taught every mamma you've helped birth a child."

James mopped his wife's forehead with a cool cloth. "I'd like to stay and help if that's all right with you, Mamma Silar. I'm not squeamish, can't be worse than watching a cow give birth!"

"Did you just call me a cow?" Ada tried to grin around the stick, but it turned into a grimace as a fierce contraction hit.

Fortune smiled on the young couple, and before long, Omie put James into position to catch the baby.

"There she is! Ada, there's our little girl!"

A red-faced bundle slipped into his waiting hands.

"Oh my God, she's beautiful!" he cried.

Omie saw the face of her mamma reflected in the child's features and was lost in the wonder of it for a moment.

The tiny eyes seemed to search their faces, as if asking what was next.

"Why isn't she crying, Mamma?" Ada looked down at James with a worried expression.

Omie took the baby and turned her over, rubbing her back with a warm cloth. She was rewarded with a small mewl, whether of pleasure or indignation, it was hard to tell.

"She's just bein' polite, I reckon," James said.

When the baby was cleaned and swaddled, Omie put her against Ada's breast. The two women shared a long look that Omie would remember as long as she lived. *Some feelings are just too big to be bound in words.*

"We want to name her Teressa Kathrine, Mamma. For both our grandmammas. Tess for short."

James came to sit on the bed beside his girls, and Omie went into the kitchen so they could bask in their joy privately. She looked out the window over the sink to see her sons standing together by the barn, staring down at James and Ada's house. She could tell they were in earnest conversation, but could not guess what it was about. There had been a space between her boys she'd never felt before.

*Hope they figure things out themselves before I have to have a 'come to Jesus' talk with them.*

Ezra found busy-work to keep him close to the barn as sounds of his sister's moans carried up the hill. So much went through his mind. Memories of Ada Kate, the big sister, always near at hand to care for her sisters and brothers. Even as a young girl. There were times, he knew, when she was the only balm soothing them when Mamma and Daddy were at odds.

*She's been our 'little mamma' her whole life. Wonder why we never thought about what she might need.*

Caught up in his musings, Ezra didn't hear Frank Thomas approach.

"If Ada doesn't live through having this baby, I'll kill him!"

Ezra turned quickly, flashing an angry look at his brother that Frank Thomas had never seen before.

"Would you please shut up!" Ezra hissed. "You ain't gonna' kill nobody. What the hell is wrong with you?"

Frank Thomas looked taken aback. "I'm just worried, is all."

"That's not your problem and you know it! You been a horse's ass to James ever since he come here. He's been nothin' but help to us. And good to Ada too."

"He sure has made hisself at home. I reckon the farm belongs to you and him now, don't it?"

Ezra looked at his brother a long moment. He closed his eyes and took in a deep breath.

"You and me both know your heart's not in farmin'. I've always knowed that."

Frank Thomas began to protest.

"No, brother, let me finish. You love makin' music, it's what you're meant for. I cain't run this place by myself, Frank Thomas. You should be thankin' James for givin' you a chance to go do what you really want to do."

From down the way they heard their mamma call, "You have a niece!"

The two turned to wave at her. They were silent as this news sank in.

Frank Thomas looked sheepishly at his brother and said, "Uncle Ezra."

Ezra began again in a softer tone.

"You are the onliest brother I will ever have. You know me, Frank Thomas. Ever'thing about me. James is a friend, but he ain't you."

"I'm sorry, Ezra. This has been tearin' me apart and I shoulda' talked to you instead of actin'...like a baby." Frank Thomas looked toward Ada and James' house again. "We're all family, and that's what matters most. Let's go welcome the newest member."

"A'right, Uncle Frank Thomas. That's a lot for a young'un to say, wonder what she'll shorten it to."

"Well, don't you go given' her any ideas."

# Chapter 33

Omie wrote to Bartie often. Emmie had called her niece with news of the baby, but it gave Omie pleasure to describe the birth in detail. Pressing the girl to return home would not work, she knew, and would drive a wedge between them. Guilt was a useless weapon, one Omie never wanted to wield. Bartie was good about writing back though, her letters pouring over with the excitement of city life, so she was never far from Omie's thoughts.

Just before Thanksgiving, Emmie drove up in the yard. The look on her sister's face assured Omie this was not a visit for pleasure.

After greeting Phoebee and making a fuss over Georgia Rose and Willie, Emmie took her sister aside.

"I need you to go back to Savannah with me. There's no emergency, hon, but Bartie is there and wants to see you."

"Well, I just got a letter from her two weeks ago. What could be the matter?"

"She's brought Shad with her. They're married."

Omie sat in a rocker and took a deep breath.

"And, she's pregnant."

"Oh, my Lord!" Omie rocked angrily. "Knew this would happen. Knew it, knew it, knew it. That girl!"

Emmie sat beside her.

"It's not as bad as all that. They both seem happy and very excited about the baby."

Omie closed her eyes for a few moments, then said, "Let me pack some things."

While she waited, Emmie filled Phoebee in on the news, asking her to let Ada Kate and the others know.

Bag in hand, Omie returned, saying, "I want to get going before any of them come ask why. Georgia will be home from school soon, please let her know everything is all right."

"I will," Phoebee assured her. "You just go see your girl. They's worse things could happen, Omie. Remember that before you tar and feather her."

As the car pulled into the carriage house behind Emmie's home, Omie was of two minds about the situation. She wanted to be happy for her daughter. She was hurt and angry though. All of the family would be hurt not to have been part of the wedding. They would have accepted the fact of her pregnancy, except for Nate, of course, but he would not have been invited anyway.

Taking a deep breath, she wiped her eyes and opened the car door.

"Mamma!" Bartie threw her arms around her, sobbing and laughing at the same time.

Omie could feel the slight swell of her daughter's belly and gave in to the embrace. Then she held her at arm's length, taking in the changes.

Bartie took Omie's hand. "Come say hello to Shad."

When Omie walked inside, Shad made as if to embrace her. He felt a chill that had nothing to do with the cold air that clung to her coat.

She glared at her new son-in-law. "I don't know if I want to strangle you or congratulate you."

"I think I'll give you some time to decide, ma'am." He nodded at her, gave Bartie a wink, then walked out the door, wrapping a scarf around his neck.

*I'll find the measure of him later.*

Emmie passed Shad on the porch and gave him an encouraging smile before she walked into the house. She quietly closed the door and watched the situation unfold between her sister and niece.

Omie took a deep breath and turned to her daughter. "I called you from here a month ago. You knew then?"

"I had no idea, Mamma. You know how irregular my monthlies are."

"You obviously knew how to get this way though."

Bartie looked down.

"Couldn't wait until you were married?"

Bartie raised her chin, temper flaring. "I thought you of all people would understand about that, Mamma."

"What are you talking about?" Omie turned to glare at her sister.

"I've never said a word!" Emmie declared.

"I saw in the family bible that you lost a baby before Ada. Not too long after you got married." Bartie lowered her head and took her mamma's hand. "I'm sorry. I don't mean to be hurtful. Forgive me?"

Emmie said, "Why don't we all have a seat. I'll make coffee."

Bartie and Omie sat across the table from each other. Omie would not look at her daughter.

"Mamma, I was a mess when I met Shad. I didn't want to worry you with it, but Daddy did more than break my body! He broke my heart so bad, I never thought it could hold love again. I pretended to be all right but I wasn't. Shad's kindness and his goodness found a way to put the pieces back together. And this baby is our blessing. I hope you can come to see it that way too."

Omie deflated suddenly, and her eyes filled with tears. She lifted her daughter's chin. "I love you, honey. I just wanted you to have more freedom before you settle down to have a family."

"I know, Mamma. We're happy though. I can't wait to hold this little one in my arms, dance with her and Shad. I feel certain we're having a girl. Can you *see . . .*"

"No, I cannot. But I like the idea of a girl for you. Have you picked out a name?"

"I thought I would let Shad name him if it's a boy, but if it's a girl I want to name her Lilly."

Omie did her best to be civil to her son-in-law over the next two days. His warm humor and obvious love for her daughter won her over by the time she left for home. He declared his intent to make Bartie and the baby the most important parts of his life. Recently, a music school had offered him a full-time teaching position and he would no longer be frequenting the speakeasy bars for work.

Emmie was happy to see a smile return to her sister's face on the ride home. They let the windows down and breathed in the sweet cool air. Omie stuck her hand out and let it weave along with the wind. Emmie did the same and before long they were laughing, talking about everything and nothing. Omie's heart swelled at the thought of another grandchild. She began singing songs from childhood and Emmie joined in, their voices trailing like bright ribbons behind them.

*Oh, I went down south for to see my Sal*
*Singin' Polly Wolly Doodle all the day*
*My Sal she is a spunky gal*
*Singin' Polly Wolly Doodle all the day*

*Fare thee well, fare thee well,*
*Fare thee well, my fairy fay*
*For I'm goin' to Lousiana*
*For to see my Susianna*
*Singin' Polly Wolly Doodle all the day*


When Emmie pulled the car up to the house, they saw Nate leading Georgia Rose and Grace around on the back of a mule. Omie could tell by the scowl on his face he had heard the news.

*At least he's not run off and dove into a whiskey barrel.*

He helped the little girls down and they ran to Emmie's window.

"Aunt Emmie, come see the new goats!"

"I need to get back, my little puddle ducks, but I'll return soon. Give me a kiss."

Ada Kate came out and shared a look with her mamma, then took the girls inside.

Omie turned to her sister. "Thank you. For everything. I'd lose my mind if I didn't have you."

Emmie kissed Omie's cheek. "Try not to worry, sister. I'll see you at Thanksgiving."

Nate opened the car door for Omie.

"Emmie." He nodded a greeting.

When the automobile was out of sight, the couple stood, taking a breath and measuring their words.

Nate growled, "Who is he? I'll kill him."

Omie slapped him hard, surprising them both. "No, you will not! You nearly killed our daughter, so don't act all high and mighty." She took a shaky breath. "Bartie is pregnant and they're married. This can't be undone."

Nate put his hand to his face and started walking away, but Omie called in a tired voice, "Don't go."

He stopped, considered a moment, and returned, taking her in his arms as she sobbed against his chest.

The months that followed were an agony for Omie. Her second-born was soon to be a mother and, by all rights, Omie should be there to deliver her grandchild. Emmie and Bartie spoke regularly, both having the luxury of a telephone now. News was reported back to the farm in letters penned by Bartie once a week. Occasionally, Emmie would surprise Omie with a visit and the sisters would talk for hours. These times made the pain of separation more bearable for them both.

# Chapter 34

## 1929

Planting a new batch of peas in the garden, Omie was enjoying the feel of the sun on her back. Not hot enough yet to burnish her forearms where the sleeves were rolled up, but soothing. She'd felt a chill all morning and was glad for the warmth.

*Might be coming down with something. Hope not, I got no time for sickness.*

Willie was working at the other end of the rows and they both looked up when they heard a horse's hooves clopping up the road in their direction. The familiar face of Alberta's husband, Rufus, came into view. Omie wondered what would send him this way on a Friday. He usually came to take Willie to Thistle Town on Sundays.

A certainty came to her then. The chill she'd had was not from illness.

"Oh no," she said.

"What is it Miz Omie?" Willie looked over the fence as Rufus approached. Then he dropped his bag of seeds.

"It's Granma, in't it?"

"Yes, son. She passed in the night. Peaceful like. Alberta went down to take her somethin' and found her still curled up in bed."

"Oh, Willie," Omie cried and pulled the boy close.

The rest of the world fell away, the garden, the wagon, the gathering crows. The sun felt cold and lifeless on her back now as she wrapped her arms around the sobbing boy who had lost so much already. Omie knew she must try to contain her own grief until Willie's could be eased. She feared what would come when she came face to face with the loss of Aunt Julia in her life.

Rufus cleared his throat. "Ah'm on my way to send a telegram to your daddy, Willie. He'll want to come for the services." Tears rolled down the man's broad face. "Wanted to let you know first. You can go wid me or I can come back for you."

He looked at Omie, "If'n you want to help Alberta lay Miz Julia out, she says that would be fine. She's a proud woman, that one is, but I think she could use your help, Miz Omie. I never seen her grievin' so hard."

Omie wiped her face on her apron.

"Of course I'll come. And I'll bring Willie with me. Please tell Alberta we'll be there as soon as I let my family know and gather up some things."

Willie went out the garden gate to the wagon, and Rufus got down to embrace him. Then the boy ran to find his dog.

Omie left him to the solace of his old friend while she went into the herb room to gather what was needed for washing Aunt Julia's body. Her sobs escaped like hiccups as she tried to do what needed doing.

Phoebee heard Willie crying and found him in the barn with his face buried in Old Joe's ruff. She put a hand on his heaving back. "Granma" was all he could manage to say. Hearing a wagon pass by, she looked out to see Alberta's husband going down the road.

*Aunt Julia!*

She found Omie sitting on the back steps with a basket of plants on her lap and her head in her hands. Phoebee sat close beside her friend, putting an arm around her shoulders.

"She's gone, ain't she?"

All Omie could do for a moment was nod. Then she lifted her face.

"You got to help me with this, Phoebee. I've got to be strong for Willie and I don't...know...how."

"Not just yet, you don't," Phoebee said softly. "Get shed of all you can. He's up there talkin' to his dog, and that's where he'll want to be for a while."

The two wept together for the woman who had given so much to them and everyone she knew. Her old, worn hands were the first to touch many a child in this county. She had fought death's grip on the least and the largest of folks, and none of her like would be seen again.

Slowly, Phoebee pulled away as Omie's sobs subsided. "I'm gonna check on Willie and then we'll come down to do whatever you need. Take as long as you want, darlin'. A'right?"

Phoebee got up, dipped her apron in some cold water from the well to wash her face, and headed toward the milk barn.

Omie breathed deeply, stood and washed her face also.

*Help me Mamma. I need you now.*

A deep warmth gathered around her. She felt a soothing hand on her heart.

*Thank you.*

Omie went down to Ada Kate and James' house to give them the news. James and Ezra were just coming in from the fields for dinner as she joined them on the road.

Ezra looked at her red eyes and stricken face.

"Mamma! What's wrong?"

"Aunt Julia," she managed to say, and Ezra wrapped his arms around her.

James put a hand on her shoulder, saying, "I'm so sorry, Mrs. Silar."

She heaved a great sigh and drew back, looking hopelessly into Ezra's eyes.

"C'mon Mamma, let's go tell Ada. Then I'll go find Frank Thomas, I believe he's at Jewel's house. Should I go to the school and let Sarah and Georgia Rose know?"

"Yes, thank you, son."

Ada had the baby on her hip while she stood at the stove making dinner. Grace was sitting on a kitchen chair with her feet dangling down, making dolls out of twigs and moss.

"Look!" she cried, when they entered. "Look what I made."

"Ada." James said quietly. He went over and took Tess into his arms. She looked at him questioningly, then saw her mamma in the doorway.

"What is it?" She ran to the door and led Omie to a chair.

"It's Aunt Julia, sis."

Ada looked up at Ezra, then back at her mamma. "When?"

"In her sleep. Alberta found her this morning," Omie replied. "I've got to take Willie there and help Alberta wash...the body for laying out."

Omie covered her mouth, trying to keep the river of tears from flowing again, then asked, "Would you see after everybody until I can send word of the funeral?"

"Of course."

Grace got down and climbed in her mamma's lap. "Don't cry," she said, patting Omie's arm.

Omie turned to James. "Would you go tell Nate? He's down at the river working on the pump. And tell him Ada has dinner ready."

"Yes'm."

Ezra turned to go back out the door. "I'll head for town, then."

Ada said, "Eat something before you go, brother. Sit." She took little Tess back and James headed down to find Nate.

"Mamma?" Ada asked.

"No, hon, not for me. I can't swallow a bite."

Shortly, they all walked up to Omie's house. Ezra went to ready the horse and buggy for his mamma.

He hitched the mule to the wagon. "Be back soon as I can," he told them.

Phoebee and Willie walked in. Ada hugged him close and said, "I'm so sorry Willie."

Grace hugged him too, then hugged Old Joe.

"You want me to drive you there, Mrs. Silar?" James asked.

"No, we'll be all right. Won't we Willie?"

The boy nodded his head without looking up.

"You want to help Old Joe into the back seat?" Omie asked.

"Yes ma'am," Willie replied gratefully.

The dog rode with his head on Willie's shoulder, licking his boy's face from time to time.

"You reckon my daddy will come, Miz Omie?"

She looked over at the hope in his reddened eyes.

"Why, yes, I'm sure of it."

"Think maybe he'll take me back with him?"

"I would not be at all surprised if he does."

She patted his shoulder and they rode on in silence.

*I suppose I should have expected this to happen soon. Surely Isaiah is ready by now.*

She looked again at the young man beside her, for he had grown into a young man in the eight years he'd lived with them. Omie knew he got letters regularly from his daddy, but they went to Aunt Julia's house, so she did not know what had passed between them.

The lane in front of Aunt Julia's house was crowded with wagons and people. Omie pulled the buggy around back where she and Willie could enter unnoticed.

He put a hand on the dog's head and said, "Stay here, buddy."

The small house was so full, it was standing room only. Most of the folks in Thistle Town were family in one way or another, and those who were not milled around in the yard between the picket fence and flower beds.

Rufus spotted them and led the way back to the bedroom where Alberta stood with some of her sisters around Aunt Julia's body. Willie ran to the bed and buried his head against the old woman's neck.

Alberta put a hand on his back and said in a soft voice, "She went real peaceful. The Lord took her in her sleep. She's with the angels now."

Omie looked at the small figure wrapped in quilts on the bed.

*Such a tiny body for such a strong soul.*

Turning to the women around her, Alberta said in a voice choked with sorrow that nonetheless brooked no argument.

"Me and Miz Omie will wash and lay her out. Y'all go help with the folks comin' by. Tell 'em we'll have her ready for the visitin' tomorrow afternoon, give time for folks travelin' to get here."

Each stepped up to kiss their grandmamma on the forehead before walking out of the bedroom. One of the sisters took Willie by the hand and led him out as well.

When the room was cleared, Omie shut the door. Alberta began to tremble.

"Thank you for comin' Miz Omie, I..."

Omie went around the bed and drew Alberta into a chair.

"You don't have to be strong around me, Alberta. I know you are, but you need to grieve too."

Her broad shoulders shook like a child's as the woman dropped her head to the bed. She bunched up a handful of quilts and held it to her mouth, trying to silence the wails that could be held back no longer.

Omie sat quietly, being present for Alberta. It was all she could do.

When Alberta's raspy breathing slowed and she raised her head, Omie told her, "I'll see to getting some water warming. What do you want in it? I brought some of Mamma's lilacs. Did Aunt Julia like those?"

"Yes, she did." Alberta sniffed and scrubbed the tears from her face with the heels of her hands. "There's still some jars of dried herbs and things in the pie safe. You'll know what's best."

Omie went out into the kitchen to ask for help in heating water and to give Alberta time to collect herself. Looking out the window, she saw Willie sitting with Old Joe on the porch steps, an uncle on either side.

*He needs the comfort of men in his life. I'm afraid we haven't given him much of that.*

When the water was heated, she found a couple of pans to pour it into and searched the pie safe for scents she thought Aunt Julia would like. Something calming for Alberta and herself as well. She found dried lavender, lemon balm and mint, and sprinkled them over the pans, then added lilac flowers.

They worked in silence, washing Aunt Julia tenderly. Words just seemed to float weightless as dry leaves on the surface of their grief. When the body was clean and dressed in a favorite dress, Omie put an arm around Alberta's shoulders, gave her a gentle hug and left the room.

She told Willie if he wanted to stay, she would bring him clothes for the visitation tomorrow and the funeral Sunday.

Rufus said, "I reckon we can find something for him Miz Omie, don't worry none. He's a strappin' young man now, 'bout the size of his cousin, Clem."

Willie stood and walked her back to the buggy. He struggled for words and Omie took his chin in her hand, looking into his eyes.

"I know. It's hard to believe this now, but in time you'll be able to think about your grandma without being sad. Try to think of all the good times you had with her. Know too that she is guiding you from the other side, hon. You'll hear her as surely as I hear my mamma sometimes."

"You think so?"

"I know so." She bent to hug the dog and then climbed up on the buggy. "Bye Old Joe. See you both Sunday."

Omie turned for a moment to watch the boy step back into the arms of his people.


Sunday morning, Phoebee, Sarah and Polly rode with Omie and Nate, while the rest of the family joined James and Ada in their wagon. As they approached the lane to Thistle Town, carriages, wagons and buggies stretched as far as they could see. White families had pulled over to the side so that friends and family of Aunt Julia's could get by.

Omie got down and said, "Let me see what the situation is before we go on."

All along the way she was hailed by folks she and her mamma had treated or birthed children for. Aunt Julia had ministered to all of them.

A stream of people waited to pass through the door and pay their respects. Omie walked around to the back door, quietly waiting for a chance to catch Alberta's eye. Willie stood in line with family, thanking the folks for coming, receiving condolences. He looked so grown up in his cousin's clothes that it brought tears to Omie's eyes.

Aunt Julia's body was laid out on the trestle table with a fine ivory cloth beneath her. So many flowers filled the room, the air was heavy with their perfume.

Alberta saw Omie waiting and excused herself for a moment to speak.

"Hey Miz Omie."

"Hey Alberta. How you holding up?"

"I'm still standin'. 'Bout all I can say."

"I think everyone in the county is here. Maybe it would be best if some of us went on to the cemetery instead of trying to come in."

They both knew that by 'some of us', Omie meant the whites that had come to see Aunt Julia off to her reward.

"That might be best," Alberta agreed. "Soon's the Homegoing service is done, we be there."

Omie smiled and nodded, then held up a hand to say hello to Willie. He saw her and waved, then turned back to greet people.

As Omie walked back toward her family, she suggested to folks waiting that they might want to head on down to the small churchyard at the end of the lane.

Nate gave her a hand up and they followed the others to the small whitewashed church. Amongst the headstones, neighbors, both farmers and townsfolk, milled around talking with each other. Nate joined a group of men he knew from the grange while Georgia took Grace by the hand and went in search of schoolmates. Ezra followed Frank Thomas in the opposite direction from what their daddy had taken, with James at his side.

Sarah walked among the stones, reading those that were still legible. Ada stood beside Omie, holding the baby with one hand and taking her mamma's hand in the other.

"Can I hold that young'un?" Phoebee asked.

There was an easy silence among them as they waited for the minister and Aunt Julia's family to arrive.

The sun had begun a slant toward afternoon when they heard the singing. A swell of voices came up the road. Soon, four men, including

Willie, were seen carrying a small casket draped in magnolia leaves and flowers of every color. Alberta and her sisters followed close behind with a seemingly endless stream of folks trailing them.

"Ada, would you find all our bunch and bring them back here?"

"Yes, Mamma," she said, and moved toward the group of white folks at the cemetery's edge.

After the mourners had passed, Omie and the family drew as close as they could to hear the minister speak. Omie imagined most of the things people had to say about this woman they held so dear had been said at the Homegoing. She wanted a moment to share what Aunt Julia meant to her also, and hoped the family wouldn't mind.

Easing her way through, she caught Alberta's eye. The woman nodded and motioned for folks to step aside and make room. Ada Kate and Phoebee came to stand beside her.

"I've known Aunt Julia all my life," she said. "She was my mamma's closest friend. Everything I learned about healing came from those two women, several of my children were brought into the world with Aunt Julia's help. I owe her more than I can say."

She began to cry and covered her mouth. In the silence that followed, Ada Kate lifted up her sweet clear voice and began to sing.

*I am a poor wayfaring stranger*
*Traveling through this world below*
*There is no sickness toil nor danger*
*In that bright world to which I go*

Frank Thomas and Ezra joined them in harmony. Soon, voices all throughout the gathering rose.

*I'm going there to meet my father*

*I'm going there no more to roam*

*I'm only going over Jordan*

*I'm only going over home*

*I know dark clouds will gather o'er me*

*I know my way is rough and steep*

*But beauteous fields lie out before me*

*Where God's redeemed his vigils keep*

*I'm going there to meet my mother*

*She said she'd meet me when I come*

*I'm only going over Jordan*

*I'm only going over home*

The sound carried through the towering live oaks draped in moss, down the bank to the Savannah River, across marshes where all the birds stilled to listen. It wove through the cypress trees and along the muddy water, past herons that ceased their hunting for frogs, that had gone silent as well, past the still forms of gators sunning on the bank, until the last note traveled on toward the sea.

# Chapter 35

Willie sat on the porch with his head in his hands. Omie and Ada Kate looked at him helplessly, wishing there was something they could say or do to ease his pain.

Isaiah had not come.

Alberta received a telegram from him saying he would be there as soon as he could, but it had been two days since the funeral and Willie was inconsolable. The chuffing of an automobile came up the road, but the boy was so deep in his misery, he didn't hear it until the engine stopped nearly in front of him.

"Willie?"

A tall, well-dressed man stepped out of the car, his black face shining with sweat and a huge smile on his face.

"Daddy?" Willie jumped up and hurried over, wanting to throw himself into his daddy's arms, but stopped himself and offered a hand instead.

Isaiah shook it, then wrapped the boy in a tight embrace.

"I'm sorry it took me so long to get here. It was a six-day drive from Philadelphia in my old jalopy. Let me look at you!"

He held his son at arm's length.

Willie was grinning from ear to ear.

"I left a baby here and came to find a man in his place. How did that happen?"

Old Joe ambled over to sniff at the stranger's shoes.

"This is my dog, Daddy. His name's Old Joe."

Isaiah squatted down and rubbed the dog's head. "Why, hello there, Old Joe!" This earned him a face washing.

"Guess he thinks you're all right," Willie said.

Isaiah looked up at the house and waved a hand. Omie and Ada Kate stepped out and greeted him.

"Goodness, Isaiah, I wouldn't recognize you!"

"It has been a while, Mrs. Silar. And this is?"

"I'm Ada Kate. Pleased to meet you. This is Tess."

The baby stared at him with calm eyes, then looked down at Old Joe with a smile.

"You have a grandbaby then, Mrs. Silar. Wonderful."

"Please, come have a seat."

Isaiah put his hands on Willie's shoulders. "If you don't mind ma'am, I'm in a bit of a hurry to get to Alberta's and see the family. I haven't been there yet. I wanted to see my boy first."

Willie turned and looked up at him with pleasure.

"Let me get some things and I'll go too," the boy said. He ran in the house before anyone could say a word.

"I want to take him back with me, Mrs. Silar. I cannot tell you how grateful I am for all you've done for Willie. I'm just sorry it took me so long to get him."

"You've been doing what you needed to do to make a good life for the both of you, Isaiah, we know that. It's been nothing but a joy to have Willie here these years. We will miss him sorely."

Isaiah looked at Old Joe. "I live in the city, Mrs. Silar. I don't think it's the place for a big dog who's used to the freedom he's had. He does look like he's getting pretty old."

The dog looked up at Omie as if he knew they were talking about him. She thought about this for a moment. It would break Willie's heart to leave him, but what Isaiah said was true. The face that was once yellow had become white, and Old Joe's hips had begun to give him trouble.

"Let me talk to Willie when you bring him back. He doesn't need to worry over it now, just let him be happy in your company while you're here. How long are you staying?"

"I need to get head back in a couple of days. I'll bring him for the rest of his things on Sunday if that's all right with you."

"I'll have them ready."

"Thank you, ma'am."

Willie came dashing out of the house with a sack of clothes.

"Can Old Joe go to Alberta's with us Daddy?"

"Sure. He can ride on the seat between us."

Willie looked happier than they had ever seen him as he waved out the window.

Ada Kate sighed and said, "I'm happy for him. Sure will miss him, though. Maybe we can have a little going away party for him Sunday. I'll talk to everybody about it."

She briefly put a hand on her mamma's arm, then left to give Omie some time to take in this new loss.

By noon on Sunday, there were plank tables in the yard covered with all Willie's favorite foods. Omie had gotten word to Alberta of her plans and hoped they were acceptable to Isaiah.

By one o'clock the auto pulled up the road and everyone on the farm was there to greet Willie. He got out laughing and helped his dog down from the seat. Georgia Rose tied a festive bandana around Old Joe's neck and Grace stuck flowers in it. Her little hands had liberated many of the blooms from their stalks, but the effect was jolly nonetheless.

"Hey, y'all! This is my daddy, Isaiah."

"Willie has told me so much about you all, I feel as if I know you already." He gave Frank Thomas a look that made the young man turn his head away.

Omie noticed and said, "Y'all get some food and let's sit on the porch. I want to hear all about your life in Philadelphia, Isaiah. Everything!"

The hours passed quickly, with stories going back and forth about big city life and the farm. Before they knew it, the time had come for father and son to get on the road, hoping to put some miles behind them before nightfall.

Willie's face became serious. He took a deep breath and turned to Omie.

"Miz Silar. I don't think the city is a good place for Old Joe. The trip would be hard on him too."

He held the dog's grizzled muzzle between his hands as he spoke.

"I know he's a help to you too when you have those spells."

The boy could say no more as tears welled up in his eyes. Omie wondered how many times he'd practiced this speech in his head, trying to prepare himself for parting with his old friend. She was grateful he'd come to this decision on his own.

She put a hand on Willie's shoulder. "We would be honored to take care of him for you, son. I think you're being very wise."

Georgia Rose spoke up, "I'll draw pictures of him and send them to you, Willie. Once a week."

She held out the one she'd drawn of Old Joe that won first place at the county fair.

He looked at her in appreciation.

"It was always yours," she said, and gave him a hug.

Each one had a gift for Willie, just like his family in Thistle Town had so long ago. Ada Kate gave him a soft linen shirt she'd sewn, the first new piece of clothing he'd ever owned.

"You gotta look like a city boy now!"

Little Grace handed him a turtle shell she'd found.

Polly put a copy of Moby Dick in his hands, knowing it had been his favorite.

Phoebee handed him a parcel wrapped in paper. "There's a jar of honey and some cake for your trip." She hugged him tightly and whispered, "We love you."

Sarah gave him a fine blank journal to write of his travels and new life.

Nate had whittled a ball inside a cage from a single piece of wood.

"Thank you, Mr. Nate!"

Isaiah said, "That's a fine piece of work there, sir."

Nate thanked the man and shook Willie's hand. "You be good for your daddy, hear?"

Willie looked up at his father, then smiled at Nate. "Yes sir."

Frank Thomas had hung back while the others said their goodbyes. He stepped up to Willie and extended his hand. In it was a fine Old Hickory pocket knife.

"But that's yours," Willie said, surprised.

"Well, now it's yours." Frank Thomas put it in the boy's shirt pocket and held out a hand. They shook without a word.

Omie spoke up, "Better give him a penny, Willie. Else a knife will cut your friendship."

Isaiah reached into his pocket and handed the boy a coin, who gave it to Frank Thomas with a grin.

Ezra said, "Here. A good knife needs a good sharpenin' stone. I ordered it from Arkansas."

Omie waited until all the rest had given Willie their tokens of goodwill. Then she handed him the quilts women in Thistle Town made for him to bring to the Silar's farm when he was a small boy.

"I mended them for you, hon. You and that dog gave 'em a rough time, but there's a lot of love in every stitch. I thought you might need something to keep you warm up north."

Willie was overcome with emotion, and Isaiah put an arm around him.

"Guess we best go, son."

Hanging out the window and waving as they left, Willie's face was bright with tears and with joy.

Georgia Rose and Grace called to Old Joe and he ambled toward the house with them.


As the months went by, Georgia kept her word and sent Willie sketch after sketch of his dog; Old Joe letting Grace lay on him, being followed by a band of ducklings, standing beneath the oak tree staring up at a cheeky squirrel.

Her final sketch was of Old Joe curled up under the dogwood tree, nose tucked under his tail with a pair of angel wings on his back.

# Chapter 36

In the early hours, Omie woke with her heart beating rapidly. She heard a car coming down the drive, and she knew Bartie must be in labor. She dressed and was on the porch with her birthing bag before Emmie had time to get out.

"Don't bother, I'm ready."

A plan had been made already for Phoebee and Nate to watch over the children when this day came.

"What have you heard?" Omie asked.

"It's too soon to know much. She began last night. I just pray the baby isn't born before we get there. I came as quickly as I could. The roads are a bit slippery."

"I know you did, hon."

They said little while the sky lightened and a rosy glow captured the horizon.

"She'll be fine, Omie. They both will."

Omie responded, "I'd give anything if the *Sight* would show me that's true, Em.

A nagging sense of unease was pooling at the bottom of Omie's stomach.

Emmie navigated the streets of Atlanta carefully. They soon pulled up beside the small bungalow in Virginia Highlands Shad had bought for his new family.

*She's been here before. Without me.*

Before Omie could give this realization much thought, Shad came out to welcome them. The stress around his eyes revealed more than words would have.

"Her doctor has been with us all night, Mrs. Silar. I told him about you and he was pleased to have a midwife coming."

When she entered the bedroom, Omie saw a man sitting at Bartie's feet with his head under the sheet. Omie went to her daughter's side, laying a hand on the girl's sweaty, tired face.

The doctor sat back and looked up at Omie.

"This is Doctor Meyer Epstein." Shad offered. "Plays clarinet in our band. He's taken care of Bartie throughout the pregnancy. Meyer, this is Omie Silar, Bartie's mamma, of course. And her aunt, Emmie Decker."

The doctor nodded to Emmie and to Omie. He said, "Hello, ma'am. Your daughter told me you would come. She's had a long night of it. I've encouraged her to rest before pushing again. I'm glad you're here."

"I appreciate you, sir." Omie said, and turned back to her daughter. "Baby, how're you doing?"

"Mamma, is it supposed to take this long? It hurts so bad!"

"I know darlin', but you're a brave girl. You've seen many a birth and you know that this will all be behind you soon. Once that sweet baby is in your arms, you'll forget the pain. For now, I need to check how far along you are, all right?"

This seemed to fortify Bartie, and she nodded.

Doctor Epstein stood and excused himself for a moment, relinquishing his seat to Omie. She looked beneath the sheet and felt for the baby's head. The child was stuck in an awkward position.

Omie looked at Bartie. "I need to turn this little one to get the shoulder free. That should make things go easier, hon."

The doctor returned and watched as she pushed on Bartie's belly, manipulating the tiny body beneath her hands like Aunt Julia taught her, then reached inside to ease the baby's shoulder into position.

"There now. Take a few deep breaths and let's get this baby into the world!"

Omie stood, motioning for Doctor Epstein to sit. She worked in tandem with Bartie's breathing, pushing from above as the doctor sat ready to catch the child. Soon they were rewarded with a high-pitched squall. He held a red-faced, squirming baby girl while Omie cut and bound the cord.

"I must say, Mrs. Silar, that was most impressive. I've never seen that maneuver done for turning an infant. I hope I can replicate it, should the need arise."

Omie gently handed her granddaughter to Bartie.

"Here is your darling Lilly."

The two of them smiled at each other with tears streaming down their faces, speechless with love for the tiny miracle before them.

Doctor Epstein waited for the afterbirth to come. After thirty minutes, he looked at Omie with some concern. She came to his side and said, "Let me see what I can feel."

He watched as she reached inside while pulling gently on the umbilical cord. After a moment, the afterbirth came sliding out and they studied it. "It's not whole, is it?" he asked.

"No, sir. I've never seen only part of it come out. Wonder why?"

"Sometimes, if there is scarring in the uterus, the placenta may stick to it. We've got to remove it or infection and fever can set in fast. There is the danger of hemorrhaging when we scrape the wall of the uterus, though. Often can't be stopped."

Omie considered the situation for a moment and said, "I have a tincture I keep in my bag that may help her push more of the tissue out. And yarrow to help stop the bleeding. Maybe we should try that first."

"Very well, Mrs. Silar. But we shouldn't wait too long to act if this doesn't work."

Reaching in her bag, she pulled out two dark brown bottles.

"Emmie, give her two tablespoons of this one." Omie handed her the first bottle. "Follow that with a goodly swallow of the other if she starts bleeding. I'll let you know."

"Mamma, is everything all right?"

"Yes, Bartie. We're just making sure everything is out, don't you worry."

She shot the doctor a hopeful look and turned her attention to kneading Bartie's abdomen.

"What is in that tincture, ma'am, if I may ask?"

"Red raspberry leaf, blue cohosh, and shepherd's purse," Omie responded. "They help move the afterbirth along. The other bottle is yarrow, to stop the bleeding if we should need it."

The doctor nodded and bent to see if there was any sign of discharge.

After a few moments, Omie said quietly, "Give a little push now, sweetie. Easy does it."

A small bit of bloody tissue emerged. All seemed well until a trickle of bright red blood began to seep onto the sheets. It grew.

The doctor looked up and engaged Omie's eyes.

Not wanting to worry Bartie, Omie asked, "Perhaps a dose of yarrow, doctor?"

"I believe so, Mrs. Silar."

Bartie's face was growing pale. Her eyes fluttered and closed.

"Mamma?"

"Emmie, go ahead and give her some. Hand me that boiled cloth, please. I'll pour a bit of yarrow on it too."

Omie came around to join the doctor once again. She saw the spreading stain and quickly slid the cloth in as far as she could reach. She pressed it against the slippery wall, trusting her instincts to direct her fingers where they needed to be.

Minutes went by, seeming like hours. At last, he looked at her and nodded.

"The bleeding has stopped."

Omie realized she had barely breathed while she waited to see what her daughter's fate would be. Removing the cloth gently, she dropped it in a pan, then rose and kissed Bartie's cheek before going to wash.

The sisters kept vigil together, wiping Bartie's face as the baby fed. Emmie picked Lilly up after she had nursed so that Omie could get some broth into her exhausted daughter.

Once the doctor was satisfied all would be well, Shad walked him to the door.

"I can't thank you enough, Meyer. I'll pay you as soon as. . .."

"You play at my son's Bar Mitzvah and we'll call it even." The doctor clapped his friend on the shoulder, then stepped out into the sunshine.

Emmie called Caleb to let him know all was well.

"You have a great-niece! Her name is Lilly."

"Lilly. I'm sure she's just as beautiful as her namesake. You tell her I can't wait to meet her, and give Bartie my love. All went well, then?"

Emmie explained about the afterbirth and bleeding, with assurance that Omie had things under control. He promised to go inform the family.

Caleb drove to the farm as soon as he could get away from the clinic. Sarah, Phoebee and Ada Kate gathered around him as he stepped out of the automobile. Comforting them all first that mother and baby were well, he told the women of Bartie's complications. Nate hung back listening, then walked toward the barn as Caleb drove away. His thoughts were troubled and he could not seem to concentrate on any chores for distraction.

When Phoebee came out to let Nate know supper was ready, she found him sitting on a hay bale, elbows on his knees with his face pressed into a damp handkerchief.

"Nate, you all right?" Phoebee gently laid a hand on his arm.

His stricken face looked wordless and worried.

"She'll be fine. You heard Caleb. Your girl's in her mamma's hands, the best ever there was, you know that. Come in and get some food, you'll feel better for it."

"Thanks Phoebee, but I think I'll just stay here awhile."

She sat beside him. "What's troublin' you?"

"What if what I done to her...what if that's why she had trouble with the birth?"

"Women have trouble all the time, Nate. Remember how it was for me? Try to stop worryin' and study on being a grandaddy! Imagine that!"

"I'll never get to see that baby. Bartie won't come anywheres near me anymore."

"You wait and see. Babies can heal old wounds." She patted his shoulder. "I'll save you a plate."

Georgia Rose and Grace walked the dirt road to the mailbox every day, hoping for a letter from their mamma. Their bare feet made little puffs in the soft sand.

Omie wrote often, sending news of Bartie's recovery and stories about Lilly. Her latest letter ended with,

*I will be home soon, children. Take care of each other until I return. I look forward to your letters. Gracie, you're learning to write your name so well!*

*Love to all, Mamma*

Nate wondered if he was part of the 'all'. He hoped so, anyway.

Each of the children wrote a line or two to their mamma on stationary Sarah supplied. Georgia Rose drew pictures of them doing various tasks. Once a week, Nate took them all to town in the wagon so they could post their letters as he bought supplies.

The day came when Emmie's car pulled into the yard with Omie in the passenger seat. Georgia jumped on the running board for the last few feet of the drive. As Omie stepped out of the car, Frank Thomas picked her up and swung her around. Then Ezra took a turn.

"Let me down!" Omie shouted, laughing at their antics.

Grace held her arms toward Omie, wanting to be picked up. "Did you miss me the most, Mamma?"

"I missed every one of you the most!" Omie replied.

Grace pondered the unfairness of the answer as Frank Thomas carried his mamma's bag into the house. Everyone gathered around the kitchen table while she answered questions about their new niece.

"Her name is Lilly," Omie began.

"Walk with me, Nate." After supper, Omie followed him out the door into the gathering darkness. She took his arm and steered them toward the river, listening as a woodcock peented and whistled in the field.

"What's on your mind, Omie? Should I be worried?"

"No, I just wanted to think out loud. Tell you what's been runnin' through my mind."

She was silent a few moments, then said, "All the hardships we've been through, with you and me. The children. Mamma and Aunt Julia. It's come to me that I have a choice whether to let them harden my heart like Mamma's deer stone or teach me to be a better person. Take some grains of wisdom from those troubles to heal the ones around me. Does that make sense?"

He blew out a breath and answered, "You make it sound so easy. To choose. I don't know as I can bend that much. I'm like an old pine knot."

She stopped and turned toward him. "Maybe we shave just a little off at a time."

He wrapped her in his arms, saying, "I'll try."

# Chapter 37

Caleb came through the door at the end of the day with newspaper in hand, calling Emmie's name. He found her in the kitchen, standing over a simmering pot of soup. Steam fogged the windows, blotting out the gray autumn sky.

She turned to look at him, her face flushed from the heat and loose strands of hair curling against her cheeks.

"Caleb, what in the world?"

"There's been terrible news, Emmie."

She sat down and watched him pace the kitchen as he spoke.

"Wall Street has crashed. There's chaos in New York…"

"Well, we've heard the news reports of trouble in the stock market, but…"

"No, darling. This is a disaster like no one has seen before."

He laid the newspaper on the table in front of her. "Many people have lost everything. Banks are closing. The outlook is very bad for the country."

Emmie read the reports, trying to take in what they were telling her.

"How awful." She looked up at him. "What does this mean for us, Caleb? We don't have investments to lose, do we? We've not discussed this."

"No, no, sweetheart. Perhaps we're fortunate not to have the kind of money these people had to risk. I fear what this will mean for the country's future, though."

"Daniel and Elizabeth?

"Daniel invested everything he could in the new hospital. I believe they will be all right."

The following weeks and months revealed a chain of devastation that spread throughout the country. Omie heard the news from Mrs. O'Dell. Many local farmers were losing their homes as loans were being called in from banks everywhere in the state.

The shopkeeper shook her head in frustration. "How in the world can folks be expected to come up with that kind of money?  They had to borrow it in the first place just to get seed in the ground."

"I know," Omie agreed. "We all thought this was a problem for cities in the north, not poor farmers."

Mrs. O'Dell nodded. "I believe we're blessed to be a farm community, though. My customers don't need for much but what they cain't grow. We're just goin' to have to take care of each other best we can. If I have to do trade for 'taters and corn, so be it."

She turned a concerned face to Omie. "You all goin' to be ok?"

"I believe so. We don't owe the bank anything. The peanuts did real well this year. Enough so we don't have to buy any to plant. Ezra and James have had good luck with the sorghum and corn too. If nothing else, we'll be able to feed ourselves and the livestock."

Omie paid for her purchases and left the store. Her mind was troubled at the thought of so much uncertainty. She'd heard about many banks closing and farmers in the mid-west going bankrupt despite having the best wheat harvests in years. It was difficult to understand the effects of finance and commerce when her community seemed so far removed from it all.

When Omie arrived back at the farm, she asked the girls to put away the groceries while she went in search of Ezra and James. Omie could see Nate plowing under the cornstalks out in one of the fields as she approached the boys at the smokehouse, hanging hogs they'd butchered that morning.

"Hey, Mamma." Ezra kissed her cheek as he held his bloody hands away. "Don't get too close. We'll clean up here in a minute."

James nodded in her direction. "Ever'thing all right Mamma Silar?"

"I suppose so, though the rest of the world seems to be falling apart."

"Bad news in town?"

"A lot of banks in trouble, James. A lot of farmers too. I'm so proud of you boys for keepin' us clear of debt."

"Daddy did too," Ezra reminded her.

"Yes, your daddy too."

It was sometimes hard for her to forget the position he'd put them in once, over-extending credit with the bank before the war. Hard to forget too, the way the banker had treated her and her mamma, as if they had no right to know their own financial situation.

"The only ones holding on are the few that didn't have to borrow against their land."

Ezra finished scrubbing his hands and arms in the leftover water they'd used to scald the pigs.

"Startin' to get chilly out here. Freeze tonight accordin' to the almanac. How about the women y'all help with their peanut crops, Mamma. Have you heard anything from them?"

"Mostly through Mrs. O'Dell. A good many of the ones whose men died in the war have managed to hold on to their places by themselves. I guess there's something to be said for being a woman, since the banks don't think we have enough sense to give us loans. Who's smarter now!"

# 1939

## June 21

The following morning, Omie rose early to have a few quiet moments to herself. The day brought with it a sense of peace, of life finding its way back toward the familiar. She sat at the kitchen table looking out the window.

*Mamma used to say, loss only seems to slow time for a precious few breaths, then settles into the heart as a companion to the life remaining.*

Soon, Bartie and Lilly joined her. After making pancakes for them, Bartie suggested a walk to the mailbox.

"Not me," Lilly declared. "It's too early."

"Well, sleepy head, I'll go without you!"

"I better get to those tonics I've been putting off," Omie replied. "I still have folks in need of help."


After breakfast, Tess went to find Lilly. Her cousin was finishing off some biscuits and honey, washed down with a cup of milky coffee.

"Hey there," Tess called.

"Hey yourself!" Lilly grinned and offered to fix Tess a cup of coffee.

"Yuck! No thank you. Where is everybody?"

"Don't know, I think Grandmamma is outside.

Lilly gulped down her coffee and popped the last crusty bit of biscuit in her mouth.  The girls walked out the back door. There was a strange scent coming from the herb room on the porch. Something pungent and medicinal, but not unpleasant. Through the door they could see their grandmamma sitting at the old plank table crushing leaves in a bowl.

"Can we come in?" Lilly asked.

"Of course, girls. You can even help me."

She stood and reached for another bowl and pestle. "Here ya go."

Lilly turned the carved piece of wood around in her hands. "What's this for?"

"That is called a pestle. It's for breaking up leaves and seeds. The bowl there is called a mortar."

Omie took a bundle of leaves and laid them on the table.

"Follow what I do. You got to free the oils from the leaves to make a tincture out of them."

"But what *is* this?" Lilly took a deep breath. "And what is it for?"

"Mugwort," her grandmamma replied. "Your Aunt Grace is troubled by menstrual pains. You'll want to learn how to make some for yourself, when your time comes."

"I don't never want mine to come!" Tess declared.

"You do if you ever want to have babies. Isn't that right Grandmamma?"

"Yes, Lilly. It's all part of becoming a woman. Which is not so bad when you know what to do, Tess."

"Hmph," was her reply.

On the end of the table was something covered in old oilcloth. Tess recognized it as the book her mamma studied sometimes, taking great care when she unwrapped it.

Tess pointed. "Is that where you learned to make tinctures?"

Lilly looked up. "What is that, Grandmamma?"

"That, my darlin' is somethin' more precious than gold. My great-grandmamma's healin' book. A journal, I reckon you could call it.

She brought it from Austria with her and it made its way down to me. To your mamma really, Tess. She uses it the most now."

"Will it be Tess' one day?"

Tess screwed up her face. "No, thank you. I don't want to take care of sick people and deliver babies."

"I suppose that leaves you, Lilly."

"Can I look at it?"

"Be very, very, careful. The pages are faded and crumbling in the beginning. They are also in German, so you won't understand them, but you can read my grandmamma's and my mamma's writings. Mine too. I suspect Ada has also started some pages of her own."

Reverently, Lilly rose and touched the oilcloth cover. She gingerly removed it. Careful to avoid the oldest pages, she turned to the middle of the book. Drawings and pressed leaves were surrounded by notes in a careful script. Her great-grandma Kate's.

"To answer your question, Tess, I did learn to make this tincture there. Mugwort grew in Austria too, apparently."

Lilly was quiet for a bit, her eyes glued to the pages.

"I almost feel like I know her," she whispered.

"You remind me of my mamma sometimes. The way you laugh. How you look when you're studying on something. Like now."

"But I never knew her."

Omie smiled and went back to her work.

"Anybody home?" Phoebee came up the back steps and peered in the door.

"I got a letter from Sarah today. She says Emmie got hold of her. Told her about Nate. She's terrible sorry she couldn't be here."

Omie raised an eyebrow at her friend.

"Terribly sorry. Excuse me." Phoebee waved a hand. "Anyway, she's still takin' pictures way over in Africa. I reckon Rusty got a job reporting on sumpthin' there."

"I bet they've seen elephants and rhinoceros and monkeys!" Tess exclaimed. "Maybe she'll send us pictures of them."

"What if one of them rinotsseresses eat her!" Phoebee cried. "I wish't she'd come home."

"Who's Rusty?" Lilly asked.

Phoebee rolled her eyes.

"Rusty is not going to let anything happen to her, Phoebee."

"Well, what's he gonna do, Omie? Scare 'em off with his banjo? Now that I think on it, he prob'ly could."

# Chapter 38
## 1930

*Down in some lone valley*
*In a lonesome place*
*Where the wild birds all whistle*
*And their notes do increase*
*Farewell Pretty Saro*
*I bid you adieu*
*And I'll dream of Pretty Saro*
*Where 'ere I go*

Sarah and Polly were sitting at their kitchen table discussing one of Sarah's texts from teaching school when they heard singing outside the window. Phoebee was at the kitchen sink and turned to look at them.

*My love, she won't have me*
*So I understand*
*She wants a free-holder*
*And I have no land*
*I cannot maintain her*
*On silver and gold*
*And all of the fine things*
*That a big house can hold*

"Rusty!" Sarah cried, hurrying out the door,

Phoebee and Polly were close behind her. They leaned out from the porch railing to stare up the road. A young man walked towards them with a rucksack slung across his back, strumming a banjo. He stopped at the bottom of the porch steps, smiled at Sarah and took up his song again.

*If I were a merchant*
*And could write a fine hand*
*I'd write my love a letter*
*So she'd understand*
*I'd write it by the river*
*Where the water o'erflows*
*And I'd dream of Pretty Saro*
*Where'er I go*

"Rusty Crutcher! As I live and breathe. What in the world brings you here?"

The handsome fellow removed his hat, freeing up a mop of thick blonde hair, and bowed to the ladies. When he looked up, Phoebee noticed one of his eyes was green, and the other blue.

"Why, I've been searching the world over for my old true love, that's all!"

"Oh, Lord," Sarah replied, blushing despite her feigned indifference. "*Old*? You have a 'true love' in every county south of the Mason-Dixon line."

Sarah turned to the women and made introductions.

"This is my *old* friend and neighbor Rusty, from Virginia. This is Phoebee and her daughter Polly."

"Best come in," Phoebee said, "I reckon you'll need feedin' after your long journey."

She turned and gave Sarah a quick wink before stepping inside. Polly giggled and followed her mamma.

Rusty grinned, motioning for Sarah to enter first. Already Sarah was angry with him and didn't know why.

Phoebee fired up the woodstove, then mixed batter for cornbread. Once she'd set the heavy skillet in the oven, she began to fire questions at the young man, hardly waiting for an answer in between.

"How long you known Sarah? Wuz y'all sweethearts? Did she break your heart and you come to take her back with you? You cain't you know, she's our teacher here at the school and we need her."

Throwing back his head to laugh, Rusty put both hands in the air as if to ward off a blow.

"Hold on Miss Phoebee—or is it Mrs? I ain't here to cause anybody trouble! The short answer is, I've know'd Sarah since we was tadpoles. I tried my best to court her, but she wouldn't have it."

Polly looked at her teacher with a raised eyebrow.

"Now, stop. We were only ever friends. Besides, I wanted my independence. And so did you." She pointed a finger at him. "You'll never set down roots anywhere, I know you."

He sighed. "It's true, I do love to roam. Don't want to get too mossy. Me and this banjo have seen some things, I'll tell ya."

After the hot cornbread was set on the table, Phoebee brought out a jar of her best sourwood honey.

"I robbed this from the bees just last week."

Rusty looked like he would faint from delight. "Miz Phoebee, you are surely a wonder."

She smiled from ear to ear and cut him a generous slice of cornbread, slathering it with butter.

After an hour or so of small talk, Sarah said, "Walk with me Rusty. I'll show you what I'm working on."

"All right." He stood and bowed. "That was some of the best vittles I've had since leavin' Virginia. Thank you kindly, Miz Phoebee."

He picked up his hat and turned to follow Sarah, giving Polly a quick wink. As soon as the two were down the porch steps and out of hearing, Polly and her mamma hurried to the window.

"He is so handsome!" Polly exclaimed. "How did she ever turn him down?"

Phoebee's brow furrowed. "A purty man is just a pain in the backside. Don't let 'em fool ya. I hope she has sense enough to turn him away now. Else I'll have to shove him head first down the outhouse hole."

"Oh Mamma, you don't mean it!"

Phoebee turned from the window with a secret smile on her face.


Sarah told Rusty about the work she was doing with cataloguing plants and their uses. As they walked, the air was filled with a bouquet of scents from their footsteps.

"I've learned so much about the medicinal value of these plants from Omie, the owner of this farm, and her mother Kate. Sadly, Kate died a couple of years ago."

"It's not Phoebee's place?"

"No, she rents Kate's old house and I rent a room from her. It's quite a nice arrangement. Now, tell me why you're really here, and don't try to use that hillbilly charm on me."

"You always did hate me talkin' this way."

Sarah glowered at him. "I became a teacher to help lift the next generation toward a more literate life. It doesn't help when someone as educated as you are chooses to sound like a backwoods banjo player."

"Well, nobody takes an eloquent banjo player seriously."

She had to laugh at that.

"Truly though, Sarah, I like my life. For now. I wasn't lying when I said me and this banjo...this banjo and I...have seen things you wouldn't believe."

He plucked a dry stem of grass and chewed in thoughtful silence.

"Might be I'll travel to Europe and other countries. I've been thinking of becoming a journalist, find a paper that will hire me if I can. The world is getting smaller, and I want to be a part of what comes next."

Sarah stopped walking and turned to look at her friend.

"Is this why you came to see me, to tell me you're running off to the ends of the earth and I may never see you again?"

"No, Sarah. I came because your mother asked me to."

He took her hands.

"Your father is not well. He doesn't want to tell you so, and your mother knew if she wrote to you, he'd be suspicious. It seems to be his heart."

She put a hand over her mouth, then asked, "Has he seen a doctor? Pappa's so stubborn when it comes to admitting any weakness."

"He's getting the best care possible, but the doctors think he may have some kind of inherited problem. There's no way to know how much time he has, but she wanted you to come home for a while in case things get worse fast."

They resumed walking in silence as Sarah ingested this news.

"I'll need a little time to get my teaching replacement ready and collect my wages to pay for the train fare."

Rusty knew the best course of action for Sarah was to busy herself with details. She hid her emotions beneath tasks at hand. Such as leaving Virginia, and him, years ago.

"Don't worry about the train fare, your mother sent that with me. I'll wait until you're ready and go back with you."

Sarah flung her arms around his neck and sobbed, "Thank you."

"But Miss Sarah, I'm not ready! I don't have a teaching certificate!"

Polly wrung her hands and paced.

"Yes, you are. I've talked with the county school supervisor. You do not have to have a certification if you can pass a simple exam, which I know you can. I've given you a high recommendation also, which counts for much with the board."

Polly stopped walking.

"A test?"

"Yes, Pollywog, one you will breeze through, believe me. I've seen it. And I'll be there to help. This is only temporary until I know how things are with my father. It will give you a chance to get your feet wet until your own teaching post comes available."

The girl took a deep breath, then stood straighter.

"What do I need to study?"

Ezra wasn't sure how to react to Polly's news. He wanted to share her excitement, but he feared what this would mean in the future. Would she leave her home, him, all she'd ever known, to go teach somewhere far away?

"So, who is this Rusty fella anyway?"

"He's Sarah's friend from back home. More like a suitor I think, at least from his side of things. Sarah doesn't seem much inclined to take him seriously. A wandering banjo player? Not her cup of tea, I'm sure."

Polly went on to describe Sarah's friend, saying he had a fine voice too, and maybe Ezra and Frank Thomas would like to make some music with him while he was there.

Ezra didn't much like the tone of voice Polly used while describing the man. He went to find Frank Thomas and tell him about the visitor.

"I thought I heard banjo music comin' from Phoebee's barn!"

"Reckon that's where he's sleepin'."

"Well, let's go investigate this fella. Grab your fiddle."

Frank Thomas went to get his guitar and the brothers trudged up the hill. Hearing strains of *Ebenezer*, Frank Thomas stuck his head in the barn and called, "Howdy."

Rusty stopped playing and looked up. When he saw instruments in the men's hands, his face split into a wide grin.

"Welcome! I didn't expect to find more musicians here." He stood and offered his hand. "I'm Sarah's friend from Virginia. Rusty Crutcher. Glad to make yer acquaintance."

"We heard." Ezra grudgingly shook hands.

"I'm Frank Thomas Silar and this is my brother Ezra, Phoebee's neighbors." Frank Thomas set down his guitar and opened the case. "I believe we know that tune. Right?"

Ezra set his fiddle case on a hay bale and took the instrument out. He silently rosined up his bow while the other two made small talk. When he was done, Ezra stuck the instrument under his chin and began a romping version of the song.

Frank Thomas picked up the rhythm and base line, then Rusty joined in.

Several tunes later, Frank Thomas said, "I been asked if Ezra and me would play at Red's Barn this Saturday night. What do y'all think, me and you and Rusty here, make a little pocket money?"

Ezra scowled at his brother.

"You know they sneak likker in there! We'd get thrown in jail if revenuers come pokin' around."

"Likker, you say?" Rusty waggled his blonde eyebrows.

An automobile drove up in the yard. The car had been a gift from Jewel's grandparents for her seventeenth birthday, but Frank Thomas was usually at the wheel.

Ezra and Rusty appeared with their instruments.

"All righty, fellas. Put your instruments in the trunk and let's GO!"

"I can't believe I let you talk me into this," Ezra muttered as he looked out the window.

"C'mon now brother, where's the harm?"

Frank Thomas snugged Jewel a little closer to him and she kissed his cheek.

"Red's Barn!" Frank Thomas crowed. "It's the best money in the county for playin' music. We may as well get paid for doin' what we love to do anyhow."

"Polly will skin me if she finds out I been there."

"Oh sugar," Jewel said, "she won't give a hoot where the money comes from when she sees that engagement ring you got in mind."

"I don't know. I haven't asked her yet."

Frank Thomas looked at him incredulously. "You two haven't been apart since the day she was born. Who else is she gonna marry?"

A little smile played across Ezra's lips, and Jewel winked up at him.

Rusty figured this was a good time to keep his mouth shut.

                    

Inside, the barn smelled of tobacco from years ago, before "Red" figured he could make more money using the place for dances, along with likker and gambling in a back stall.

Jewel went to find them a table as the boys carried their instruments to a make-shift stage in the corner.

Frank Thomas clapped his brother on the shoulder. "Now, just let me do the talkin'. All you fellas got to do is play that fiddle and banjo like I know you know how. We'll be fillin' our pockets with cash dollars!"

He went to find Jewel, and Ezra looked cautiously around.

*This place looks like trouble. I don't know why he has to go lookin' for it, trouble seems to find him just fine at home.*

Ezra often grumbled about his brother's antics to Polly, but he was there whenever Frank Thomas asked him to be. Usually, it was the four of them together, riding the backroads in Jewel's car. Polly had begun to beg off as alcohol became more involved in their outings. She might as well have gone, since her evening was spent worrying about what they were up to.

Frank Thomas returned with a couple of mugs of homemade beer. "It's only beer, Ezra. Just to whet our whistle. I'm done with anything stronger, you know that."

He took his guitar out of the case and Ezra pulled out his fiddle. They tuned to each other, and waited for Rusty.

"I'm as tuned as I'm gonna' get fellers. You know what they say, a banjo player spends half his time tunin' and the other half playin' outta tune."

The trio stepped up onto the platform. A single microphone on a stand left them just enough room to lean into it as they broke into a rousing rendition of 'Cotton-eyed Joe.'

*Where did ya come from*
*Where did ya go*

*Where did ya come from*
*Cotton-eyed Joe*


Next, they slid into 'The Girl I Left Behind Me'.

Some old-timers who'd served in the Confederacy put hands over their hearts. After a few more fiddle tunes, Frank Thomas was ready to move on to what he loved best.

"Howdy folks, we're the Silar Brothers from over in Chatham County and this here's Rusty from out Virginia way."

He leaned over to Rusty and asked, "You play swing tunes?"

"I know Sweet Georgia Brown. But I can follow most anything you throw at me, brother."

"A'right now folks. We got a big treat for ya. Get ready for the latest and greatest swing music to cross the Georgia line! A one, a two…"


*No gal made has got a shade on sweet Georgia Brown*
*Two left feet, but oh so neat has sweet Georgia Brown*
The crowd went wild.


Then, they were off on a version of "Yessir, She's My Baby." Frank Thomas' strong, whiskey-smooth voice carried across the dancers as Rusty's syncopated rhythms drove them on. When Ezra took his fiddle breaks, the yells and whistles of the crowd nearly drowned him out.

Jewel joined Frank Thomas singing 'Goodnight Irene' to close out the evening.


*Irene goodnight*
*Irene goodnight*
*Goodnight Irene*

*Goodnight Irene*
*I'll see you in my dreams*


Sweaty and grinning, Frank Thomas received back slaps and compliments as Red counted out the band's earnings into the young man's hand.

"I've not seen my brother this happy in many a year," Ezra said, as he and Jewel watched from the stage.

"He needs this, Ezra. Your daddy makes him feel so low and worthless."

"Why does he let Daddy get to him like that? He should know better."

"Still, Frank Thomas has got to have something to make him feel better about himself with his limp an' all."

Throwing an arm across both men's shoulders, Frank Thomas guided them toward the car. He set down his case and threw his hat up into the air.

Rusty danced a jig while Frank Thomas did a stilted waltz with Jewel around the parking lot. Then he danced with Ezra, who fell down laughing.

"Oh Lord, I'm gonna' be in a world of hurt tomorrow!" Ezra exclaimed.

Frank Thomas held a hand out to help his brother up and replied, "You just show them greenbacks to Polly and she'll fix what ails you!"


Polly was at the kitchen sink when Ezra stepped up onto her porch. She heard Jewel's car drive away and dashed out the door to see if everything was all right.

"Hey, Polly."

She could smell the beer on him from ten feet away.

"Ezra?" It was not like him to over-indulge. In fact, he rarely drank at all.

"Look!" He tossed his earnings into the air and Polly caught him as he started to fall.

"What is all this?" she exclaimed.

"This," he replied, "is what I'm gonna' buy you a ring with!"

She helped him inside to the sofa and found him a pillow and quilt, figuring he'd wake up every soul at his house. As Polly went to bed, she worried about how to break the news to him.


"What do you mean, you cain't marry me?" Ezra exclaimed the next morning, then put his aching head in his hands.

"Drink your coffee and hush, it's too early to wake Mamma and Sarah.

She lowered her voice. "Now Ezra. We've never talked about this. You never told me you felt like that about me!"

"Well, Pollywog, I just thought you knew. Don't you love me too? Is there somebody else?"

Polly sat beside him and put a hand on his shoulder. "I do love you, Ezra Silar. Always have. But you know I'm not allowed to teach if I'm married."

Ezra looked up. "Why?" he yelled, then moaned, lowering his head back into his hands.

"It's always been that way. I thought everybody knew."

# Chapter 39

"Ezra." Rusty walked out to where the young man was hacking at weeds between the corn rows. "I reckon them weeds must'a done somethin' unpardonable, my friend. You all right?"

The hacking continued as Ezra sputtered, "No, I am not all right, thank you very much. If it wadn't for your girlfriend, Polly wouldn't want to be a teacher. Now she cain't marry me."

He turned to Rusty and threw down the hoe. "Why'd you have to come here, anyway?"

Rusty said in a low voice, "You know why, Ezra. Her daddy's ill."

"Couldn't she find somebody else to take her place? Why Polly?"

"I think this is what Polly chose."

Ezra picked up the hoe and continued chopping at weeds. Rusty imagined some of them resembled his face.

"If you try to stop her, Polly won't marry you, anyway. Sarah will be back, I'm sure. Give the girl a chance to see if teachin' is really what she wants."

He put a hand on Ezra's shoulder. "You'll work it out. I seen the two of you together. She loves you, Ezra. Likely she'll want children of her own to teach one day."

"You think so?"

"Of course she will. Now rest a minute. I got somethin'—someone I want to talk to you about. I met him just before I came here."

Below the train trestle near New Abercorn, three men huddled around an iron pot of stew. It was hot out, too hot for a fire, but everyone was tired of tinned beans, and Isa had managed to snare a rabbit. Into the pot went ramps, poke salad, cattail roots and a bit of salt he had stashed inside his bundle. Peppergrass gave it a spicy smell and just a touch of river silt reddened the gravy.

"Where'd you learn how to cook all that stuff?" An old man asked, inhaling the fragrant steam.

"Oh, my granny, I suppose," Isa replied. "Wasn't much else to put on the table where I come from."

Rusty came upon the men on his way to the Silar place and took off his hat before sitting down.

"I don't suppose you could spare a cup of that?"

"The Lord always provides enough, stranger. Welcome. I'm Isa Sparrow. This here's Talbot and his brother Hank."

"Pleased ta meet ya. Rusty Crutcher is my name." He slung off his banjo and pack, then rooted around for his tin cup.

Isa's eyes lit up. "Whoa now, a travelin' minstrel! Reckon you could play us a tune while this rabbit finishes cookin'?"

"Sure thing."

Rusty strummed the strings, tuned a couple, and broke into a jig. The other men smiled at each other. After a few more, Isa asked, "Know any hymns on that thing? Somethin' to bless this food with?"

"You a preacher?" Rusty asked.

"Some might say so." Isa smiled. "You know 'Bringing in the Sheaves, son?"

"I surely do."

*Bringing in the sheaves*
*Bringing in the Sheaves*
*We shall come rejoicing*
*Bringing in the sheaves*

Surprising harmonies mingled in the air from the gruff-looking trio sitting around the fire, and Rusty reckoned this was not the first time they'd sung together. With so many men traveling the rails in these desperate times, songs passed from hobo camp to hobo camp with a few embellishments along the way. Excepting hymns. There seemed to be no lack of memory as to their lyrics.

Isa dipped a wooden spoon into the pot. "I reckon she's done, boys. Come and get it."

As they ate, the men talked of the places and families they'd left, looking for work. Rusty had availed himself of the trains from time to time, collecting stories to weave into songs. Most were similar, but this preacher's story seemed to carry a bit more mystery. Not that he was very forthcoming, but Rusty sensed something all the same.

"Where you headed on this fine day?" Isa asked.

"I'm headed for a farm where a friend is staying. The Silar place, do you know it?"

None did, but one of the men offered, "The grange is right near. Might be they can tell you where to find it."

Isa added, "When you do find it, ask if they need a hand there. We're all good workers—and godly men. Any kind of work would be a blessing. We're not lookin' for handouts."

Rusty said he would, and rose to gather his things.

"Walk with me Preacher?"

"Why, sure. I was goin' to the grange today anyhow."

One of the others spoke up, "We'll clean up here, Preacher, and be there directly."

The two walked companionably for a while and Rusty asked, "Pardon me Isa, but you don't strike me as a farmer. You're an educated man, am I right?"

Isa gave him a small smile and replied, "I'm not sure I'd characterize myself as educated, but I've studied more than the Good Book in my time. You don't miss much, do you?"

"S'pose that's what storytellers do, pay attention to folks. And music is mostly tales of triumphs and troubles."

"I'm so used to folks telling me their troubles, I don't think much about my own. It's the paradox of preaching."

Rusty laughed. "Paradox. Now there's a two-dollar word! I'll raise you a dollar if you're not too parsimonious, Parson."

"Whoo hoo! Now, let me see...I am categorically not, sir. I don't have much of value in this world, so I might as well draw from my stores of locution. And, I appreciate your camaraderie."

They laughed for a moment, then Isa continued, "My father wanted a very different life for me. Wanted me to become a banker, sit behind a desk and get rich. I'm afraid I've failed him as well."

Rusty gave him an inquisitive look.

Isa paused a moment. "I take you to be a trustworthy sort, Rusty Crutcher. Am I wrong?"

He looked deeply into Rusty's eyes.

"You can trust me, Mr. Sparrow. I got no cause to betray you."

"Been preachin' the Lord's word since I was a boy. Seems I been tasked with His work from the beginnin'. I just...know things, Rusty. See things before they happen sometimes. I know what plants are healin', how to use 'em. My granny taught me a bunch, but some of it I taught her. Don't know the why of it."

They walked on in silence a moment.

"Somehow though, I couldn't *See* what was comin' for my wife, Nessa. She was too sensitive for this world, I reckon. We lost a baby, then two. Seems like all the life went out of her then, no matter what I tried to do."

He passed a hand across his face and sighed. "One day I come home from a revival to find she'd drunk a bunch of laudanum the doctor had given her for melancholy. I should have known she needed more watchin', Rusty. After that, I just didn't have the heart to minister to the townsfolk anymore. The way they looked at me. I do what I can for these men, but it will never make up for what I didn't do for Nessa."

Rusty was silent for a moment, then stopped walking and put a hand on Isa's shoulder.

"I'm sorry for your loss and your burden. This story goes no further. Believe me, there's no judgement here."

"I thank you, sir. Sharin' makes the load lighter, it surely does."

They continued to follow the path and soon came to the grange. Isa reached out a hand to Rusty. He shook it and the two parted ways.

When Rusty finished telling Ezra his tale, he continued, "I heard from Sarah you see ghosts, Ezra. I'm wondering, if I bring this preacher here, would you just tell him if his wife is at rest? It would bring the man such comfort."

Ezra thought a moment and said, "I can't guarantee anything. He's welcome to come though. Sounds like a good man. I'll speak to the family about finding him some work."

Rusty replied, "Thank you."

Hoping to find Isa and his companions still there, Rusty walked along the river toward the trestle. He heard soft whistling coming from the bank and stopped to listen. The tune floated on the air like a sweet summer breeze. It was a gospel song his mother loved to hum, 'The Old Rugged Cross.'

Rusty began to sing along.


*On a hill far away stood an old rugged cross*

*The emblem of suff'ring and shame*

*And I love that old Cross where the dearest and best*

*For a world of lost sinners was slain*

*So I'll cherish the old rugged Cross*

*Till my trophies at last I lay down*

*I will cling to the old rugged Cross*

*And exchange it some day for a crown*


"Rusty!" Isa called out. "How are you, my friend?"

"Right as rain. Where are Talbot and Hank?"

"There was some work to be had loadin' grain and I left it to them. They need the money more than me, I reckon. I got no one to send it home to."

After pleasantries were passed, Rusty brought up the subject of the Silar family. He told the preacher of their unusual 'gifts'.

"Ezra Silar talks to ghosts, Isa. I don't know that he could talk to your Nessa, but maybe there'd be some comfort in tryin'. I confess, I did mention your situation, but didn't say who you were."

Isa hung his head and thought for a bit. When he looked at Rusty, there were tears traveling down his cheeks.

He took a deep breath. "All right. When might we go?"

"No time like the present. I made sure Ezra would be around today."

The two men kept to the shade of trees lining the river bank until the road up to the Silar's farm appeared. Rusty could see Ezra in one of the upper fields and pointed him out to Isa.

The preacher stopped to take in the farm. "Looks like a right nice place."

"It is. Nice folks too, you'll like them."

As they drew closer, Rusty called out, "Ezra. Got someone I'd like you to meet."

Isa held out a hand to the young man before him. "Isa Sparrow, pleased to meet you."

Looking around with admiration, the man remarked, "Looks like y'all are doin' all right despite this drought."

"Yessir, we're lucky to be so close to the river. Me and Daddy dug that pond over there for the cattle in twenty-six when things got so dry. Found a good spring there."

The men fanned themselves with their hats and Ezra said, "Y'all come on to the porch. We'll get a drink of cold water. Mamma might even have some lemonade."

Omie saw the three men walking toward the house. A searing sadness filled her heart, and she took a deep breath, then slowly let it out.

*There's a troubled soul if ever I knew one.*

Yet, she also saw a gentle light surrounding him, extending to the others.

*They look mighty thirsty. I'll chip some ice and bring out a pitcher of lemonade.*

She added lemon balm to it for comfort, like her mamma taught her.

As the men drew near, Omie waved them inside. "Y'all come sit in the kitchen. It's a bit cooler."

Rusty cleaned off his boots before stepping through the door. He removed his hat and smiled. "Hello, Mrs. Silar. This is my new friend, Preacher Isa Sparrow."

Isa nodded to Omie as he came in. "Pleased to meet you ma'am. Don't know as I claim to be a bona fide preacher anymore."

"Well, you're welcome here, bona fide or not!" she exclaimed.

The men took seats at the kitchen table and she filled their glasses.

When they'd drunk deeply, Isa said, "This lemonade is truly nectar for a thirsty body, Mrs. Silar. Something else in it as well, for the spirit. Balm of Gilead?"

She shook her head. "Just lemon balm, Mr. Sparrow. As close as Mamma could get."

Omie looked into his eyes and saw recognition there. This man had gifts of his own. Kate would have known what they were without a word spoken.

Rusty explained how he and Isa met when he was looking for the Silar farm.

"Sounds like you have some interesting stories to tell, Mr. Sparrow. No family back home?" Omie asked gently.

He turned to look at Rusty, then Ezra, seeing only kindness in their eyes.

Isa spoke of his wife. Of the sorrow that had led him to take to the roads and rails across the country, spreading gospel to weary souls he met along the way.

"Rusty here told me about Ezra, said he might be able to contact Nessa." Turning to face Ezra, he continued, "I don't want to put you on the spot. I just thought..."

"I wish it was that easy." Ezra looked down at the table, then back at Isa. "They find me, seems like, not the other way."

The preacher nodded. "Well, if she does find you son, please tell her I'm sorry I failed her."

The screen door slammed after Grace as she ran in. She asked, "Can I have some lemonade too, Mamma?"

"Course you can, honey. This is my youngest daughter, Grace, Mister Sparrow."

"Mister Bird!" Grace went to the man and looked up at him.

Isa's face had gone pale.

"The lady wants me to tell you. She's up in heaven. Don't worry. She can help you better now."

Omie stood looking at the girl, stunned.

Grace skipped over to her mamma, took the cup from Omie's hand, and was out the back door before anyone could speak.

Finally, Isa sobbed, "Mr. Bird. That's what Nessa called me."


When the men left, Omie went out to find Grace. Like as not, she was probably playing with the young goats or feeding the older ones greens from the garden. Sure enough, the girl sat in the pen with a black spotted kid on her lap. Its mamma was chewing on a handful of collards.

"Honey, don't be feeding those goats our good greens! Or they'll get your share, do you want that?"

"I don't care, Mamma. Look how they chew sideways." Grace mimicked the goats, grinding her little teeth together.

Omie picked the child up and swung her around, pretending to nibble at her belly.

"Maybe I'll just gobble you up!"

Grace squealed with delight. When her mamma set her down, she couldn't walk straight and plopped to the ground. Another of the baby goats climbed into her lap.

*Lord, she's just like me at that age.*

"Gracie, I wanted to ask you something. How did you know those things you said to Mr. Sparrow?"

"I told y'all, the lady asked me to tell Mr. Bird she was fine. I reckoned he was the one, since a sparrow is a bird. Right?"

"But who is the lady? Is she someone you met somewhere? At church maybe?"

"No, Mamma. She just whispered in my head. I never saw her."

"Do other people whisper in your head?"

Grace scratched the furry little face in front of her while she tried to recall.

"Once when I went to town with Ada Kate, a boy's voice said he wanted me to tell his mamma he was in heaven, but when I told her she acted like she was mad at me. I don't know why."

Omie considered what trouble this kind of *gift* could bring with it, especially in one so young who could not anticipate the outcome.

"I tell you what, baby. If somebody you can't see whispers to you again, come tell me, and I'll make sure the message gets delivered. That sound good to you?"

"Yes ma'am."

The baby goat looked at Grace with adoring eyes.

"BAA."

"I guess he says yes too, Mamma."

# Chapter 40

Rusty had agreed to accompany Sarah home on the train to Virginia. They took their leave after many goodbyes and promises to write. Polly was visibly nervous about the responsibilities being placed on her small shoulders, but Sarah hugged her and assured the girl that all would be well.

"You have another month before school starts to ready yourself, Polly. You're ready now! The school board has agreed to let you teach in my place until you take the test, then you'll be a certified teacher."

Phoebee wrapped her arms around her friend. "Please let us know 'bout your daddy soon as you can, hear?"

"Of course I will! Don't worry. I'll be back as soon as I'm able."

Frank Thomas and Jewel drove them to the train station in Savannah.

"You take care of her, now." Frank Thomas put out a hand to Rusty, who shook it heartily and gave the younger man a clap on the shoulder.

"Save up some tunes to teach me. You just never know when I might be back around."

"Hope so," Frank Thomas replied.

He and Jewel stood watching the train until it was gone from sight.

"Think you might want to take a ride to Atlanta, honey babe?"

"My gramma will shoot me if I'm gone too long!"

"We'll call her from Bartie and Shad's. It'll be all right. Especially if we tell her we're gonna' elope."

Jewel looked up at him. "You mean it? Really?"

Frank Thomas pulled a box from his pocket and placed it in her hand.

"I would drop to my knee if this old leg would let me, darlin'."

She opened the case to find a slender gold band inset with a small, sparkling diamond.

"Yes! Yes, yes, yes!"

In the car, Jewel kept turning the ring around on her finger as if it might disappear, should she take her eyes off it. Frank Thomas put an arm over her shoulders and pulled her close.

"You know what a no-good rascal you're marryin', don't you?"

He was only half-jesting, Jewel knew. His self-worth was always in question, as his frequent jabs at himself showed.

"I wish you'd stop that," she admonished.

"What?"

"Frank Thomas, you got to let go of the past, else it will own all your tomorrows. Mine too. Do you think so little of me that I'd agree to marry someone 'no good'?"

He drew his arm back. "I didn't mean, I wasn't....," he stammered.

She turned toward him and put a hand on his.

"There's no sin in what you love. Me, music, the world beyond where we grew up. A bunch of what happened when you were growin' up was your daddy's fault. Mrs. Silar would say the same."

Frank Thomas was quiet for a while, taking this in.

He put an arm back around her and smiled his appreciation.

"She'll soon be Mamma Silar to you."

When they pulled up in front of Shad and Bartie's bungalow, Jewel was out of the automobile as soon as it stopped. Bartie stood on the porch, surprised to see her best friend and brother coming up the walk.

Jewel held her hand out for Bartie to see the ring, and they hugged each other, jumping around in a circle like the school girls they used to be.

"I'm gonna be your sister for real!" Jewel squealed.

Shad joined them with the baby in his arms and a big grin on his face.

"Congratulations, brother."

Frank Thomas looked at him questioningly.

"I could hear those two from the back of the house. Lilly did too."

Her little eyes stared up at them as if wanting to know what all the fuss was about. Jewel came over and touched the baby's soft cheek.

"Hey little one. I'm gonna be your Aunty Jewel."

"When do these nuptials take place?" Shad inquired.

"As soon as we can go to the courthouse!" Frank Thomas replied.

Shad and Bartie looked at each other.

"It's not quite that easy," Shad said. "You two have to go apply for a marriage license and wait at least five days. There's paperwork to be done first."

Barite spoke up. "You don't get to just jump the broom, brother!"

"Five days, huh?" Frank Thomas turned to Jewel. "Guess we better go to the courthouse and head back home. I don't want your granny comin' after me with a shotgun."

"I 'spect Mrs. O'Dell would, too!" Bartie laughed.

Jewel took Bartie's hand. "When we come back, would y'all stand with us at the courthouse? We don't need a church wedding, though Granny is going to pitch a hissy fit. She'll get over it though."

"You gonna tell Mamma?" Bartie asked her brother.

"I imagine she'll know before we even get home."

Once back in the auto, Frank Thomas turned to Jewel. "There's another place I need to stop by first. I think I know what will soften Mamma up."

# 1939

## JUNE 21

The afternoon offered a chance for a lazy doze, and Lilly curled up on the sofa next to Omie. Soon, they woke to sounds of fiddle, banjo and guitar at Phoebee's house through the open window. Ada opened the back door and looked up the hill. Frank Thomas and Ezra had brought their instruments to the porch and a group had gathered around them. Jewel was sitting next to Frank Thomas with her banjo on her knee. Lilly darted out the door to join in the merriment.

Tess called, "Come dance with us Lilly!"

Polly was clogging, as was Tess, while they swung each other around. Lilly stood by with unaccustomed shyness, trying to figure out the steps. Tess came up to her, and said, "It's like this." She did a little shuffle in place she called 'the Tennessee walking step' and before long, Lilly was keeping up.

"Once you know that one, you can do all kinds of stuff!"

Tess and Polly tried to outdo one another, showing off their skills, until both were completely out of breath.

"Uncle Ezra made me this here dancin' board." Tess dragged over a three-foot by three- foot platform with holes drilled in the sides. "You sprinkle some cornmeal on it like this." Lilly's cousin scattered a liberal amount on top. Then she stepped up onto the platform and the rhythmic sound of her feet came to life. Ezra stood close and Tess kept time as he played 'Turkey in the Straw', then 'Arkansas Traveler'.

Omie had risen from her nap and joined Ada Kate on the back porch. They watched the goings on for a few minutes, smiling.

Ada nodded toward Phoebee's porch. "Ezra and Polly are like a tale from a storybook," she remarked.

Omie agreed. "They are, aren't they? Born so close together, and tight as twins their whole life. Almost like they're one spirit in two bodies. I'm glad they had a proper wedding. I could have skinned Frank Thomas for wanting to run off to Atlanta and elope."

"Well, Mamma, you made him listen. He and Jewel had a nice little ceremony. And, we sure threw a fine hoop-dee-doo for Polly and Ezra!" Ada replied.

The women made their way up the hill to the others.

"Hey y'all," Jewel called. She put down her banjo and stood to embrace Omie, then Ada.

"So sorry I couldn't be here for the funeral, Mamma Silar. I hurried back as soon as I could."

"Well, your grandmamma needed you, sugar. How's she doin' up there in Kentucky with her sister?"

"She's as well as could be expected. They take care of each other and seem to be getting along."

"Grandmamma, give us a little jig!" Tess begged.

"Go on," Ada Kate encouraged.

Ezra did a 'one potato, two potato' introduction, then broke into his mamma's favorite tune, 'The Red- Haired Boy'.

Omie hiked up her skirts to dance and gave them a show until she ran out of breath as well.

By supper time they were all happy, tired, and hungry. The smell of chicken and dumplings had been floating out of Phoebee's kitchen door all the while. When the scent of hot cornbread mingled in as well, the music-makers put away their instruments and hurried inside. Everyone filled plates, then settled on the porch to eat. Phoebee came out with her own plate and sat next to Omie.

As night closed in and the fireflies rose over the fields, Omie leaned her head on Phoebee's small shoulder. "I love you, ya know."

Phoebee kissed the top of her friend's head and whispered, "I love you too."

# Chapter 41

## 1930

Frank Thomas and Jewel pulled up in front of the house. They looked at each other, took a deep breath and got out of the auto.

"Hey Mamma," he called, and stepped up onto the porch.

"Hey, Mrs. Silar," Jewel greeted Omie with a kiss on the cheek.

"Come sit a spell. Where are y'all off to, son?"

"We just came by to see you and talk to Ezra. Is he home?"

"I am," came the reply from behind the screen door.

"Come look at this guitar I picked up for myself! I been learnin' some new licks from them boys down at the mill. They get together for a pickin' every Tuesday after work."

Frank Thomas brought the guitar over to show his mamma. Before long, she got her harmonica and was playing as Jewel sang 'Red River Valley'.

Ezra brought his fiddle and joined in.

When the rollicking tune was done, Jewel walked to her car and came back holding two banjos.

"What in the world! You gonna' play them at the same time?" Omie asked.

Jewel crouched down beside her. "No, Mrs. Silar. One of these is for you."

Omie looked at Frank Thomas, then back at Jewel, as a banjo with lovely mother-of-pearl inlay was set in her lap.

"I remember you said you used to play one at church when you were a girl. Thought you might like to give it a try again," Frank Thomas said softly.

Omie smiled as she ran her fingers along the intricate blossoms inlaid on the neck. Before long, she was frailing a simple tune she remembered her grandaddy playing on the fiddle when she was small.

*Waterbound I can't get home*
*Waterbound I can't get home*
*Waterbound I can't get home*
*Down in North Carolina*

Jewel joined in on her instrument and sang along.

Omie laughed with pleasure as the song came to an end.

"Well, you sure 'nuff made your old mamma happy, son. Looks like you have some good news to tell me, too."

Frank Thomas looked at Jewel.

"You said she'd know." Jewel held out her ring for Omie's inspection.

"Well, I'll be," was all Ezra could manage.

"It's beautiful, honey. I'm happy for you both. Now when's the wedding?"

"Uh, about that, Mamma. Me and Jewel don't really want a big wedding. We'd be happy just going to the courthouse to get married." He turned to Jewel. "Ain't that right?"

Jewel smiled back at Frank Thomas, but Omie saw the conflicting waves of light around the young woman.

"Son. You know that would break her grandmamma's heart."

He started to say something, but Omie cut him off.

"It's your decision, I know, but hear me out first. Mrs. O'Dell lost her daughter and son-in-law when Jewel was just a baby. Her only child, and Jewel is her only grandchild. She would want to see you wed. Would you rob her of that too?"

The porch was silent for a time. Frank Thomas held Jewel's hand and gazed at the floor while he took this in. Looking up at Jewel's troubled face, he resigned himself to the truth of it. There would be a wedding.

"Do you think we could at least keep it small, Mrs. Silar?" Jewel asked. "Grandmamma knows everybody in three counties! If she invites them all it will be huge."

"I'll talk to her, hon. Reckon you might as well start calling me Mamma Silar."

With that, she stood and embraced them both. "Y'all go tell Ada and James. I'll cook us up something special for supper."

James saw the two of them walking up the path. "Here comes trouble," he joked.

Before they were through the door, Jewel shouted, "Guess who's gettin' married!"

Ada Kate clapped her hands and threw her arms around Jewel. "You gonna make an honest man out of my brother?"

"Wait a minute," Frank Thomas said, "Isn't that supposed to go the other way 'round?"

"Not with you, baby brother. Not with you."

James laughed and shook both their hands. "I'm truly happy for y'all."

Jewel pulled away from Ada with a knowing look in her eyes. "How far along are you?" she whispered.

"Just about three months. Shhh!"

Before beginning supper, Omie went to find Nate in the field. He leaned back on the traces as she told him about their son's engagement to Jewel. He nodded and thought a moment before giving her a sad smile.

"I'm happy for them, Omie. I am. I don't reckon he'll want me at the weddin', but tell him I wish them the best."

He clucked at the mule to begin again, but Omie put a hand on his arm to stop him.

"I'm going to have a talk with Frank Thomas. I want you there beside me, Nate. We didn't get to share Ada's wedding or Bartie's. Can we not miss this one together, too?"

"Up to him. Love you." He leaned over and kissed her, then picked up the reins again.


After supper, the family gathered on Omie's porch to make some music. Laughter rang out as the children chased each other in the yard. Phoebee joined the crowd, sitting on the steps so she could tap her toes.

Nate sat in the shadows at the back of the barn, smoking. He thought about the tension between himself and his oldest son. None of his attempts at reconciliation seemed to bear fruit, so they settled for a sullen tolerance of each other. Tonight was Frank Thomas' time to celebrate though, so he'd made himself scarce.

Settling back in the hay with his arms behind his head, Nate felt something of himself knit back together. His feet began to tap against each other as he listened to a lively rendition of 'Has Anybody Seen My Gal'.

# Chapter 42

Frank Thomas and Jewel decided on a September wedding, when most of the harvest was in.

Mrs. O'Dell agreed to settle for a small wedding as long as she could have a big celebration at the store beforehand. She closed shop and had tables set all along the walkways for food folks brought. There was plenty of cider and lemonade, which some of the men took out back and doctored with a dollop of whiskey.

Frank Thomas and Ezra played music on the porch, joined by Jewel whenever she could break away from well-wishers. James had taken up playing a washtub base at Ada Kate's insistence that he learn an instrument. She wasn't sure the tub, fitted with a broom handle and string, constituted an instrument.

"Well darlin', it's real useful. We can use it around the farm when I'm not playin' it!" James declared.

"Doubtful, once you put a hole in the bottom for that string!"

Still, Ada was pleased to see him on the porch of the store, having a good time with her brothers.

Omie linked her arm through the shopkeeper's and said, "Walk a bit with me."

The women wound through the crowd, nodding and accepting congratulations, until they were far enough down the road for a little privacy.

"Omie," the older woman said, "I'm so proud our families are going to be joined together. I just wish your mamma and daddy were alive to see it, I surely do."

"Me too, Mrs. O'Dell. I never thought to see Frank Thomas marry at all. Jewel is like a sister to Bartie, what could be better?"

"You think those two will give us any grandchildren?"

Omie shook her head. "You know I can't *See* the future for my family. I do believe they'll be happy together though."

Mrs. O'Dell sighed. "Well, that's what matters most, I guess. I sure would like to hold another little one before my time is over."

"Let's go find Ada Kate and steal that baby from her for a while!"

"Jewel, I can't."

"Bartie, your daddy most likely won't even be there!"

"I'm sorry, I just can't take that chance."

"Not even for me? Not even for your brother? I want you to be my maid of honor!"

"Let me think about it, ok? It's only August. I'll let you know before September."

When she got off the line, Bartie went over to Shad and sat on his lap.

"Jewel is so angry with me. She just doesn't understand!"

She got up, walked over to the bed, and took the baby in her arms.

"I might have an idea," Shad assured her. "Maybe we could get them to come here as previously planned and marry at the courthouse without telling anybody. Later, they could have the wedding in New Abercorn. That way, you'd still be her maid of honor. What do you think?"

She sat in his lap again, hugging him with her free arm.

"What a wonderful, sneaky idea, Mr. Cain."

Shad tickled Lilly's chin and was rewarded with a smile.

"Just like to see my girls happy, ma'am!"

"Hold Lilly, I'm going to call her back."


Frank Thomas and Jewel showed up the following day, papers in hand.

Shad sat at the kitchen table with Lilly on his knee. He waved Frank Thomas over. "Join me, brother. They've got girl talk to do."

Bartie grabbed her best friend's hand. "Come with me."

They took a seat on the bed and Bartie asked, "What are you going to wear?"

"Oh, gosh. I hadn't thought about it! We just jumped in the car and came soon as we could. I told Grandmamma I wanted to look at china and silver with you here in Atlanta."

Ruffling her hands through the closet, Bartie pulled out the two dresses Emmie had given her.

"I think either of these would suit you. The cream chiffon would show off your beautiful skin. The mauve is maybe a bit more sophisticated. Whichever one you don't choose could be your going-away dress after the church wedding."

"Oh, Bartie, I can't! Emmie meant those for you!"

Bartie looked down at her belly. "Jewel, I'll never fit into these dresses again. I'd rather you have them than give them away."

Jewel only hesitated for a slight second, then took the chiffon in her hands.

"These tiny roses are so lovely! I'll wear this one today."

She held Bartie close and cried softly, whispering, "Thank you so much. You're the closest to a sister I'll ever have."

"Always will be. Couldn't get rid of me if you tried!" Bartie replied with a catch in her voice. She stepped back and said, "Now let's get you married."

In the courthouse, Bartie bounced Lilly in her arms to quiet her fussing as she watched her brother and best friend tie the knot. Lilly did not like the new lace bonnet tied under her chin and couldn't figure out how to pull it off.

The judge pronounced Frank Thomas and Jewel man and wife. Then he walked over to Bartie, lifted Lilly's chin and cooed at her. The baby reached up and grabbed his beard.

"She likes you!" Shad remarked.

"Got three grandchildren at home to spoil. Best part of my day."

# Chapter 43

Just after their engagement was announced, Frank Thomas had convinced Ezra to play music every chance they had to make a little money. He wanted to take Jewel to Nashville for their honeymoon and didn't want Mrs. O'Dell to pay for it. There were plenty of opportunities in the secret road houses throughout neighboring counties, though Ezra resisted.

"You keep my share of the money for your weddin' too, brother. The sooner we can stop this foolishness, the better. I cain't afford to get arrested, and neither can you."

The Silar boys' reputation as musicians earned them a measure of admiration in the community. Not only for their toe-tapping dance tunes, but for their sweet hymns as well. They were much in demand for church socials, weddings and funerals. No money was accepted at the small churches or gravesite services where the dead were laid to rest.

Omie asked them to play for a particularly somber funeral. A woman and her daughter had perished when a chimney fire sent sparks to their old shake roof and set the house aflame. The women managed to crawl to the porch, but between the smoke inhaled and severe burns, they were beyond saving. Mr. Kendrick and his sons ran in from the fields when they saw smoke and pulled the women clear, but their old heart-pine house was too far gone.

Doc Pritchard was summoned, but to no avail. The old physician would take nothing for his time, as the husband's mistrust of banks insured that every dollar, stuffed inside the mattress ticking, perished also. A neighbor came to tell Omie of the tragedy and asked if she would be willing to prepare the dead for burial. After agreeing to the task, Omie enlisted Nate's help.

The bodies of the Kendrick women lay in the woodshed, wrapped in sheets donated by nearby families. Omie had Nate set up sawhorses and boards to lay them on. She hoped the two of them could manage the job of lifting the corpses, so as to spare the family more horror and heartbreak.

"My God. Omie, I cain't do this!" Nate gagged, nearly fainting.

Omie coughed as well, but sputtered, "Not so different from the smell of the smokehouse. Try to think of that."

He set his end of the bundle down.

"No, Omie. I smelt more burnt bodies in France than I care to remember. Not all of them dead, neither." Closing his eyes for a moment, he fought back the memories and the nausea. "All right, let's get this over with."

When the women were lifted onto tables, Omie sent Nate for buckets of water, then told him to wait outside for her. She cleaned and dressed them as best she could, to be placed in their simple coffins. Closing the door behind her, she joined Nate on the wagon seat, where he sat with his head in his hands.

Laying a hand on his shoulder, she spoke softly, "I tried to wash the smell off darlin'. There's naught to do about these clothes, though."

"Let's just get home." Nate could not face her, shame welling up such that he nearly choked on it.

"Nate, I didn't know . . .."

He patted her knee and signaled the horse to go.

As more requests came from poorer neighbors in need of help burying loved ones, Omie found herself away from home more often. Disease and the natural passing of the aged did not affect her as strongly as deaths in childbirth.

*So many women lose their lives trying to care for their families and bring new lives into this world. Most sorrowful when both mother and child perish. Lord, please. Give me strength to do what must be done and to give comfort where I can.*

Nate occasionally went with her when there was a male member of the family that needed preparing. It seemed to Omie that he was trying to pay penance for something. She could see the emotions writhing around him, leaving a gray cast to his being. Like different shades of leftover paint mixed together for the porch floor.

A few days after the women's funeral, Frank Thomas asked Omie, "What's ailin' Daddy?"

She was surprised by his use of the word 'Daddy', it had been so long since he'd said anything about him. Nate's state was apparent in the gauntness of his face and the silence that followed him like a shadow.

Omie told her son what had happened that day they laid the woman and her daughter out.

"Oh my God," Frank Thomas said. "That must have been terrible."

"He hasn't had the dreams as much as he used to, but I think this stirred up memories he can't shake."

She turned to Frank Thomas. "I need you to do something for me. I want you to ask your daddy to the wedding. He needs something to pull him back to the present, something to look forward to. I don't know how much forgiveness you can find in yourself for him, but please, son. He's like a ghost these days."

They stood looking out at the field where Nate was harvesting corn, wrapped in quiet solitude.

"All right, Mamma."

Frank Thomas picked a day when Ezra and James were off to the grange and his daddy was sitting alone, having a smoke.

"Got another one of those?"

Nate looked up in surprise. "I can roll you one quick."

They were silent for the minute it took to put the tobacco in a paper and twist it up.

"You're fast," Frank Thomas remarked.

"Lots 'a practice," Nate replied.

"I guess you heard me and Jewel are gettin' hitched?"

"I did. Glad to hear it, son." Nate waited to see if his use of the word 'son' would make Frank Thomas angry.

All he said was, "We're hopin' you'll be there."

"Wouldn't miss it."

Frank Thomas stood up, nodded, and walked away before his daddy could see the emotions on his face. Or before he might see his daddy's. It was the best he could do.

# Chapter 44

"Do not mess up Jewel's car! I'm warnin' you two."

Ezra winked at James. "Now, Frank Thomas, what makes you think we'd do such a thing?"

"Yeah, especially since y'all were so considerate about my folks' buggy when Ada and I got married." James winked back.

"Oh, Lord," Frank Thomas moaned as he walked toward the church.

"What goes around, comes around!" they called to him.

Nate snuck around the corner of the barn when the coast was clear and handed Ezra some strings of cans he'd tied together. He'd filled them with enough rocks to create a racket and wired the lids shut.

"That's good, Daddy! Let's tie 'em on with so many knots he'll never get shed of 'em!"

Georgia Rose took a bar of soap and drew caricatures of the couple on the doors of Jewel's car. Then she'd written *Just Hitched* everywhere else. After surveying her work, she ran inside the church and sat innocently in the pew beside her Savannah cousins.

Though the bride had managed to limit the number of people her grandmamma could invite to the wedding, a crowd milled around outside. They patted Nate and Ezra on the back as they entered the church along with James, promising to keep their handiwork on the automobile a secret.

Ada Kate and Omie were with Mrs. O'Dell in the small room at the back of the church, making a fuss over Jewel.

"My weddin' dress fell apart years ago," Mrs. O'Dell told them. "It had been my mamma's, so you can imagine how fragile it was. So, we ordered this one from the Sears and Roebuck catalogue."

"I don't want to look like I'm from another century anyway, Grand-mamma. Don't feel bad about it."

Omie sighed. "It's a beautiful dress, Jewel."

*I'm sure her grandmamma's gown would not have shown off her figure as well, either!*

Ada Kate said, "Jewel, I'm so sorry Bartie isn't here to stand with you," She looked down at her rounded stomach. "I know you'd rather have her than a big-bellied bridesmaid like me!"

"Not true, Ada. I knew Bartie wouldn't come. She's hard-headed, but she's my best friend, and I have to forgive her. Besides, you're even more beautiful when you're pregnant!"

Omie could see that her daughter was secretly pleased to be in her brother's wedding. She was, truly, beautiful.

Ada Kate caught her mamma's eye and pulled something from behind her back. "Jewel, we hope you like what we've made for you. It's nothing fancy..." She placed a lace cap in which fresh flowers had been woven on Jewel's shiny, bobbed hair. From the cap, a long veil trailed.

"It's perfect!" Jewel cried.

Mrs. O'Dell held out a string of delicate pearls with a ruby pendant in the center.

"This was my mamma's," the old woman said softly.

Jewel looked at the necklace with shining eyes.

"It's the most beautiful thing I've ever seen! Grandmamma, why have you never shown me this?"

"I was savin' it for your special day. Now turn around and let me fasten it on you."

Ada and her mamma slipped out quietly to give the other women a few moments of privacy before Jewel walked down the aisle. Omie took her seat between Nate and Emmie as Ada Kate went to stand beside the altar. Ezra stood on the other side, looking hot and uncomfortable in the suit he had borrowed from James. He kept fidgeting with the collar.

Frank Thomas smirked as he came to stand beside his brother.

Ezra muttered, "Once again, you talked me into somethin' I do not want to do. Feel like I'm stuffed into a turtle shell."

"Oh hush. It don't hurt you to get out of them overalls once in a while. Maybe even wash 'em. Bet Polly would like that."

Frank Thomas was dressed in a handsome suit Emmie had made for the occasion. She'd tailored it to fit him perfectly.

"Doesn't your son look dashing on his wedding day!" she commented to Omie.

"Good job of hiding his pointy tail," Omie murmured.

Caleb chuckled.

Mrs. O'Dell was escorted to her seat, as she wiped her tear-filled eyes on a lace hanky.

Grace turned around on the pew to look at the church entry. "Look!"

They all stood as the wedding march was played.

Emmie sighed. "Well Omie, he may be a devil, but look at the angel he's marrying!"

Jewel glided through the door on the arm of her uncle. She was indeed beautiful. Omie's heart swelled to see the happiness on her son's face as he watched his bride walk toward him. Knowing that he would have someone to spend his life with, someone to love him deeply, was such a blessing.

Nate took her hand and squeezed it tenderly. He was obviously fighting back tears, and she remembered how he'd cried openly at their own wedding.

When the newlyweds hurried out the door to cheers and a shower of good wishes, Jewel's Ford was in front waiting for them. Grace giggled and danced around it, pointing out her sister's artwork.

Frank Thomas picked his little sister up and gave her a big kiss. "You get her back for us, hear?"

He opened the door for his bride and then got in on the driver's side.

"Just wait," Ezra said to Polly. The crowd waved goodbye and the automobile took off with a terrible clatter. The men slapped their knees and congratulated each other on their fine work.

"They'll be heard all the way to Atlanta!" Nate guffawed.

Frank Thomas calmly pulled over, took out his pocketknife and cut the cans free. Then he saluted them and drove off.

"He skunked us," Nate admitted. "He surely did."

# Chapter 45

Ada smiled to herself as she rode toward the Ellis farm. Mrs. Ellis was carrying a new life inside her as well. There was an instant connection between pregnant women that crossed all borders of race and station in life, she thought.

Resting one hand on her belly while holding the reins in the other, she felt the baby's round bottom nestle against her palm. The first frost had turned roadsides into a pageant of yellows, peaches and reds. The autumn sun felt good on her aching back.

*Just a few more months, little one, and you'll see this big, beautiful world for yourself.*

Up ahead she saw the little Ellis girls, Mable and Ruthie, waiting for her by the mailbox.

"Hey, Miss Ada!" they called, reaching up to rub the horse's long neck.

She got down from the buggy and tied the reins to the porch post. Reaching in her bag, Ada brought out two apples.

"Here, you can give these to Horace if you want to. But put them flat on your palm, like this."

She placed a small apple on the oldest girl's hand and watched as Horace gently took it with his lips. The child giggled.

"Me! Now me!" cried Ruthie. After offering Horace the treat, she snatched her hand back and wiped it on her dress. "He slobbers a lot!" she declared, and the girls ran into the house laughing.

Ada Kate put her hands on the small of her back, stretched, then reached for her medical bag before entering the house.

Mrs. Ellis was at the cookstove making coffee and greeted the young woman with a hug.

"Would you like a cup? I got some persimmon cake too."

"We picked the 'simmons ourselfs!" Mable declared.

"Yes, you did, my good girls. Now, give Miss Ada room to sit."

A steaming cup of coffee and a slice of cake were put in front of her. Ada noticed the woman's bump had not increased much in the month since she'd seen her last.

"How have you been feeling, Helen?"

She watched as the girls were given slices of cake also before their mamma sat down. There was so much tenderness on Helen's face as she bent and kissed the tops of the girl's heads. There was also an audible wince when she stood back up.

"Everything all right?" Ada tried to keep the concern out of her voice so as not to worry the children.

Helen gave Ada a cautionary look and said, "Oh, I'm just fine. A little gas, probably. You know how it is when these babies push on your belly."

When the cake was eaten, the girls went back out to see the horse, and Ada asked, "How are you, really?"

"I don't rightly know," she answered. "I've not felt any movement. Seems like I ought to by now, don't you think?"

"It's been what, six months since your menses stopped?" Ada asked.

"Bout that."

"Let's put you on the bed and let me see what I feel." Dread reached deep into Ada's own belly, but she tried not to let it show on her face. Pressing gently on the firm mound of belly, she did not quite know what to think.

There was no definition of the child's head or body. Something should have been discernible, even if the child was dead.

"Maybe this one is just a late bloomer, you might not be as far along as you think. Let's give it a few more weeks and see if things change."

She helped Mrs. Ellis up to a seated position and began talking about things that might be soothing to them both.

"You know, Mamma was just sayin' how she'd like to see your girls before they get too much bigger. I'm so fortunate that she watches my little one while I do my rounds, but I know Mamma misses the company of her friends. Maybe we could visit tomorrow? Would that be all right?"

"Me and the girls would love that. Raymond too." As Helen stood, she winced again. "Like I said, I'm sure it's nuthin' but gas. No more beans for me!"

Ada Kate handed her a gentle tea for settling the stomach and promised to visit the next afternoon.

When rounds were finished, Ada made her weary way home and stopped at her mamma's house to get Tess. Omie met her at the door and saw the fatigue in the diminished light around her girl. More than physical, she thought. There's trouble there too.

"Hey darlin'. Come sit for a minute and let me rub those feet."

"I won't say no to that," Ada replied. "It's been a day." She sat and took Tess into her lap. "Hey, baby girl."

Omie got Kate's special salve out of the cupboard, remembering all the times her mamma had done this same thing for her. The scents of mint, meadowsweet, witch hazel and beeswax mingled together, taking her back to her own pregnancies.

"Oh, that is pure heaven," Ada crooned, as Omie rubbed the healing herbs deep into the tired feet and calves resting on her lap. Tess fell asleep listening to the sounds of her mamma's moans of pleasure. Ada nearly dropped off herself.

Omie asked softly, "Anything troubling you today?"

"You remember Helen Ellis, Mamma?"

"Sure do. Those little girls were the last births I attended. She pregnant again?"

"It seems so, but something isn't right. She should be bigger. The baby should be moving at least a little. I didn't feel anything. Truth is, I didn't feel a baby at all."

"Don't say. Hm. Want me to take a look at her?"

"That would be wonderful, Mamma. I've not encountered anything like this before. I told her we might visit them tomorrow."

Omie nodded. "I'll pack a lunch to take with us and bring my birthing bag. About one o'clock good for you?"

"Yes ma'am."

Ada Kate headed home as soon as her foot rub was done, eager to see James. Remaining at the table, Omie thought a while of the situations she'd seen that might give her a clue as to what could be Mrs. Ellis' problem.

*I'm gonna need your guidance, Mamma. You and Aunt Julia. Help me understand what my hands are feeling.*

The warmth around her let her know she'd been heard.

After supper, Omie went in search of Phoebee and saw a light in the honey room off the porch. Bees surrounded the doorway and windows, drawn to the scent of their pilfered bounty. Omie waved at the window and Phoebee came out, quickly closing the door.

"Hey! Go on in and I'll clean up so we can visit. Be just a minute."

Omie marveled at the way the little insects landed on Phoebee's head and bare arms without stinging or causing her to flinch. Omie went into the house and took a seat at the table. Memories of her daddy in the very same chair filled her heart with a longing she'd not had in years.

*I miss you, Daddy. I know Mamma's with you now, and that's a comfort. I reckon a body never stops feeling like an orphan though, no matter what age.*

Phoebee came through the door with a fresh jar of honey and put it in Omie's hands. "You look like you could use some sweetnin' up. Ever'thing all right?"

"Oh, fine, fine. Just thinking about growing up in this old house. Memories tucked in every corner."

"Well, you weren't much bigger than a peanut when you got married. Must feel like a long time ago."

Omie sighed. "It does. Listen, I didn't mean to interrupt your work, I just wanted to know if you could watch Tess tomorrow. I'm going with Ada Kate to see one of her customers. There might be a problem with the pregnancy, she's not sure."

"Poor woman. I hate to think of anybody going through somethin' like I did when I had Polly."

"You and Polly made it, though. I expect this will turn out fine too, Ada just hasn't run into many difficult births yet."

Phoebee got up and retrieved another jar of honey.

"Of course I'll watch Tess. Take a jar of honey for that family, too."

The women talked further, of this and that, over cups of tea, then Phoebee said, "I best be getting' back to it. The sooner I drain them combs, the sooner I can take 'em back to the tree. Them bees'll have all the honey off 'em lickety-split."

Ada Kate came to the door the next afternoon, pale but steady.

Omie kissed her cheek. "Sick again? Did you eat anything this morning?"

"Can't yet, Mamma. I'll have a biscuit later. I'm fine."

"All right then, sweet girl. Let's take this little one up to Phoebee's and we'll go to the Ellis'."

They each took one of Tess' hands and helped her walk up the hill. As soon as she saw Phoebee, she started calling, "Beebee! Beebee!"

Phoebee scooped her up and tickled her under the chin. "We're gonna' have us a good time, ain't we sweet pea?"

"Don't spoil her too much," Ada joked.

"Just never you mind. Me and this one have bid'ness!"

The little girl waved goodbye and toddled inside the house.

Once again, the Ellis girls were waiting at the mailbox. They ran alongside as Ada pulled up to the porch.

"Miz Omie!"

She got down and hugged each of the girls, declaring, "You've gotten so big! I bet you're a lot of help to your mamma."

"Yes'm," Ruthie replied.

"We're gonna' have a baby!" Mable cried.

"I know! Now, let's go see about that baby."

At the stove, Mrs. Ellis was taking bread out of the warming ovens.

"Why, hello Omie, Ada Kate. Just let me slide this in to bake and I'll pour us some coffee."

"None for me," Ada said. "Just some hot water if you please. I have some tea with me to calm my nausea."

"She's been sicker with this baby," Omie explained.

"Same tea as you gave me yesterday?" Helen asked.

Ada nodded.

"So, tell me about how you're feeling, Helen. Ada Kate says you've been having a little pain when you bend and straighten up. Did the tea help?"

Helen sat next to Omie. "You girls go see if you can find any more pecans in the orchard. I'd like to send these ladies home with a sack full."

"Yes, Mamma."

Once the children were out of hearing, Helen confided, "I think it's worse today. I nearly couldn't stand up when I got out of bed this mornin'."

"Why don't I have a look before we have our coffee, hon? Let's get you to the bed."

Helen took off her apron and shoes. Ada Kate helped remove her heavy skirts, then Mrs. Ellis settled onto the bed, with some discomfort. Omie could see that the mound of belly was offside and small for six months. She said a quick prayer as she warmed her hands.

"All right, let's see what we have here." Omie placed her hands on either side of Helen's stomach, gently feeling for any part of the baby's body. When she pressed below the navel, Helen winced sharply.

"Is this where you usually feel the pain?"

Helen took a deep breath and nodded.

Closing her eyes, Omie tried to *See* what was beneath her hands. No movement occurred, she felt no warmth or sense of spirit at all. A gentle voice in her head said, *There's no soul here. Never was.*

After a moment, she heard Helen's worried voice. "Is something wrong? Is the baby dead?"

Omie opened her eyes, looked at Ada, then at Helen.

"You're not pregnant. This is likely a cyst. It happens sometimes, hard to tell the difference until you're on along like this."

Helen asked softly, "I'm not having a baby?"

"No, but if this is just a cyst, we might be able to shrink it with some herbs. Let's get you started on a tincture, three times a day for a week. If your stomach gets smaller, then we're on the right path. That sound good?"

She could see a mix of emotions cross the woman's face. Disbelief. Fear. Possibly relief. Four boys and two girls was a good-sized family. Might be enough for Mrs. Ellis, though she would probably not say so to her husband.

*Or say no*, Omie imagined.

"We'll need to go home and make the tincture. One of us will bring it around tomorrow if that's all right with you."

"And we'll bring Tess to visit, too." Ada smiled.

"The girls will surely love that. I thank you both for your trouble. Don't know what I'd do without you."

"No trouble at all, Mrs. Ellis." Ada turned toward the kitchen. "I'll go check the bread while you get dressed."

The women had thick slices of warm bread slathered with butter and Phoebee's honey along with their coffee. Ada's appetite seemed to return and she ate three pieces. The door opened and Mable entered with Ruthie behind her, dragging a burlap bag.

"My goodness!" Omie winked at Ada. "Did you bring us the whole crop? You've been working hard."

"Near 'bouts," Ruthie answered. Both girls beamed with pleasure at the praise.

"I better feed these workers," Helen declared. "Bread and butter, girls?"

"Honey too, please." Mable replied.

On the way home, Omie talked with Ada about what to use for the situation. "You know that low growing plant in the garden with the little white flowers? That's chamomile. My grandmamma Ida Ruth brought it with her when she and your great-grandaddy came here. Cared for the little pot of herbs all the way from Austria. Chamomile tea is good for nausea, and I'm sure many people had sea sickness on the boat coming over. She wrote in the book that it was good for women's troubles, like cysts too. Something about the flowers shrinks them and helps get menses flowing again."

"Certainly worth a try," Ada said.

"I've been steeping some in alcohol for a few weeks. Stole several jugs of your daddy's corn likker way back for us to use."

Ada Kate laughed. "What'll we use when those run out?"

"He may be back on the wagon right now daughter, but I expect he'll take a tumble eventually."

The following day, Ada stayed home to rest, and Omie took Tess along with her to deliver the tincture. She let the toddler help hold the reins and call, "Giddap" to get Horace moving. The warmth of the little body on her lap and the warm sun on her back were a balm to Omie's soul. Along with the scents of crushed leaves and woodsmoke, the sweet baby smell of Tess brought memories to Omie's mind of earlier years passing, of other children.

The Ellis girls danced around as Omie pulled up to the house.

"Tess! Tess!"

"Can we walk her into the house, Mrs. Silar?" Mable asked.

"Of course."

Each girl took one of Tess' small hands and guided her up the steps to the porch.

"Why, hello there, little one," Helen called.

"Mornin'," Omie returned the greeting. "Here's your medicine."

Helen took the little brown bottle and uncorked it. The fumes made her cough and her eyes water.

"We never took to the drink, Omie. What will this do to me? And what will Raymond do when he smells it on my breath?"

"It's only a few drops in water or coffee, hon. Not enough to matter. Take it three times a day, and we'll see how you are in a couple of weeks. Should help with the pain, too. I'll talk to Raymond, don't worry. You just get better."

They sat down at the table and Omie made sure the woman measured out her first dose correctly. Helen made a face at the taste but drank her coffee and promised to repeat the dose that evening.

After a bit, Omie said she needed to get Tess back home, and said her goodbyes. Mable and Ruthie said goodbye to Horace, then ran to the rope swing out back. Their bright laughter reminded Omie of when Ada Kate and Bartie were so small.

Her heart was both filled with tenderness for those days and saddened by time's inevitable claim on the past.

*Autumn reminds us to cherish the moment, for everything passes in its season.*

Raymond and the oldest of the Ellis boys were in the field, chopping corn stalks into fodder for the cows. Their movements were nearly synchronized, father and son so familiar with the task that they conversed in a rhythmic cadence.

Raymond straightened when he saw her and both turned to wave.

"Howdy Miz Omie. How you doin' today?" He wiggled his eyebrows at Tess.

"Right as rain, Raymond. Hello, Paul."

"Sure do thank you for takin' care of my wife. We never would have know'd such a thing could happen. Women's a mystery, they surely are."

"I hope the medicine I brought will take care of things. I wanted to let you know there's a bit of alcohol in it to draw out the oils in the herbs. Not enough to notice, I promise. Helen's worried you'll be upset about it."

"If that's what's needed Miz Omie, I trust you know best."

Paul grinned. "I think I got a stomach ache too, ma'am. Can I have some?"

Raymond laughed, and the men got back to work.


As autumn folded into winter, Mrs. Ellis' cyst had all but disappeared, and she seemed to be in good health. Omie knew that often the reasons for a false pregnancy were not as easily treated. She felt grateful for all the knowledge passed down from generations of women before her. Grateful too, for the gifts she'd been given, her sense of purpose in the world.

# Chapter 46

Omie did not know how they got along before the telephone was installed. She'd been excited and uncertain about it as the men put up the lines and poles. Something about these physical changes to their farm gave her a sense of unease she couldn't explain. Soon, however, the novelty of it all faded into familiarity. Emmie called often, though long-distance cost her a pretty penny. Calling Bartie was something Omie was only able to do occasionally, but she felt much better for it.

Some of her clients had telephones now, which made it so much easier to check on them without having to ride from farm to farm. She had taken on more of the visits to clients who did not, letting Ada stay home and rest. This pregnancy was more fatiguing for her than with Tess. Most likely because the nausea persisted longer, as happened sometimes. Omie wasn't worried, but decided to check her out just the same.

On the walk down to Ada and James, Omie took in the brilliant beauty of sunlight dancing on frosted leaves. She felt the delicate crunch of grasses beneath her feet. The air carried a sense of melancholy as the year neared its close, but also, a brisk promise of rest and renewal.

"Hey, Mamma." Ada Kate was washing up the breakfast dishes when Omie rapped on her door.

"Good morning, sweet girl. Can I have a cup of that hot coffee?"

"Yes ma'am, you can. Have a seat." She set a cup on the table and sat as well. "What's up?"

"I was thinking we should give you a quick look-over, see how things are coming. How do you feel?"

Ada blew out a breath. "Tired. It's not even ten o'clock and I'm ready to go back to bed."

"Well, why don't you lie down on your bed for me."

In the bedroom, Ada removed her shoes and settled back with a sigh of relief. Omie sat Tess on the bed beside her and took a moment to warm her hands. She placed them on Ada's belly, softly pressing, feeling for the baby's head. She paused.

"What, Mamma? I felt movement this morning. Or rather, my bladder felt it."

Omie sent a message to Kate. *Is this what I think, Mamma?*

She felt, rather than heard, a confirmation and opened her eyes.

"I believe you have a matched pair, daughter."

Ada's eyes grew large. "Twins? We don't have a history of twins in the family, do we?"

"Not as I know of," Omie replied. "Let's see if we can get Caleb to listen for two heartbeats, but I'm pretty certain you're in for double trouble. Especially if they're boys!"

"Will you call him for me?"

"Of course. Why don't I take Tess with me, give you time to rest."

"Thank you so much, Mamma."

Ada's eyes closed and she was asleep before Omie and Tess were out the front door.

Caleb and Emmie arrived the following Saturday in a new car.

"Whoo-hoo," Omie cried, admiring the deep blue roadster.

Emmie got out and wrapped an arm around her sister's waist. "Isn't she pretty?"

Caleb stood beside them with a grin on his face. "And why, may I ask, is it a she?"

"Anything that gorgeous has to be a she," Emmie responded. "I wanted a yellow one, but Dr. Decker here decided that was a bit flashy for his profession. Hop in, we'll ride down to Ada's."

"Let me tell Georgia to watch Grace. I'll be right back."

James came out onto the porch with Tess wrapped in a warm shawl. Ada Kate followed close behind, hands supporting her belly.

"I want a ride when it's warm enough to put the top down and I don't have a blimp for a belly!" Ada declared.

"As you wish, Madame." Caleb kissed Ada's cheek and shook James' hand.

"Come on in," she said.

After catching up on recent news, Ada looked at Caleb.

"Can you listen now? We can't wait to know."

"Certainly. Let's go to your room."

Everyone crowded around the bed as Caleb put on his stethoscope and held it to Ada's stomach. He moved it around, listening intently, then removed it from his ears.

"Two heartbeats, no doubt about it."

Everyone laughed, but Omie noticed the concern on his face.

"What is it, Caleb?"

Suddenly, the room grew quiet.

"Because you are so knowledgeable Ada, I want to be up front with you. One of the heartbeats is much weaker than the other."

She looked at him questioningly. "What does it mean?"

He sighed. "Since there's no history of twins in your family, I suspect these are identical twins. That means a single egg split in two. Sometimes there isn't enough blood flow for both of them."

"Will one die?" she cried.

Caleb took his niece's hand. "Not always. I would be prepared for that possibility, however. I'm sorry to worry you dear, but it's best to know."

Emmie and Caleb soon took their leave, promising to return in two weeks for Thanksgiving. Before getting in the car, Emmie took Omie's hands.

"Try not to worry?"

"Fat chance, hon. But I'll try."


Little had changed by Thanksgiving. Ada Kate continued to gain weight, as she was ravenous all the time. Her energy was consistently low though, which concerned Caleb. By her seventh month, she began to feel a bit better and hope rose in her heart.

James came in the house from feeding the animals one evening to find Ada at the stove making supper with a smile on her face. Tess was sitting on the floor playing with her rag doll.

"I'm so glad you're feelin' better, darlin." He hugged her from behind, resting his hands on her belly.

"I am, James. Truly. I thought I'd never get out of that bed again! But here I am."

She turned to kiss him and bumped him backwards with her belly, sending Tess into a fit of giggles.

# Chapter 47

Omie figured she was due for a visit to Savannah soon, before Ada's baby came. Georgia Rose was also anxious to see her cousin Aaron before Christmas. She had not shared the contents of her letters to and from Aaron of late, and Omie suspected there was something afoot.

One morning while in town, on impulse, Omie stopped at Mrs. O'Dell's to call Emmie. She could hear the older woman talking in the back room where the new switchboard had been installed.

*I bet she spends half her time talking and half of it listening in on other folks' conversations.* Omie had to smile. *This was the perfect job for a lonely old woman...Bless her heart.*

A young man stood behind the counter. He nodded at Omie and introduced himself as Mrs. O'Dell's nephew, Micah.

"Mr. O'Dell was my grandaddy's brother. Aunt Biddy's my great-aunt or something like that. I've just called her Aunt Biddy all my life. Can I help you Mrs.?"

"Silar. Omie Silar."

"Pleased to meetcha. Can I help you with something?"

"Oh, I'm hoping to place a call to my sister in Savannah. Could you let Mrs. O'Dell know I'm here?"

The young man seemed a bit crestfallen at not making a sale. He turned to go to the back and Omie called after, "I do need a thing or two now that I think about it, Micah."

His face lit up and he replied, "Yes'm, I'll be right with you."

Mrs. O'Dell instructed Omie on how to use the telephone, as if she'd forgotten the Silars had one of their own. It gave the old woman pleasure though, so Omie let her go on. After a brief chat with Emmie, probably to be relayed down the gossip chain by Mrs. O'Dell, the visit was planned for the following Saturday.

*Maybe Emmie and I can figure out a way to make our calls more interesting and mysterious for the ladies' entertainment.*

Emmie had offered to come get Omie, and she agreed. Chilly winds had driven most creatures into their dens and nests to curl up, noses tucked under tails. This was not buggy weather.

Saturday promised more of the same, but the Ford held wool lap blankets for a cozy ride.

"Hello, Georgia Rose!" Emmie gave her niece a hug and tucked a blanket around her.

"Hello." There was an unmistakable gleam in the girl's eyes as she asked, "Did you get your Christmas tree decorated yet?"

"Yes...but Aaron has asked for one of his own. Would you know anything about that?"

Georgia clamped her lips together and would not speak another word. Omie smiled at Emmie over her daughter's head.

Bare fields passed by, the skies a mercurial gray suggesting rain, as the sisters caught up on recent events. They were startled by the form of a swift red fox crossing the road with a rabbit in its mouth.

Georgia Rose twisted around to watch as it ran into the woods. "Oh, I wish I could paint her."

"Perhaps on our way back we could bring our new camera." Emmie replied. "You never know, we might see her again."

"You have a camera?" Georgia exclaimed.

"It was our family Christmas gift. We decided to open it early so we could take photographs during the holidays."

Georgia Rose squinted her eyes. "Aaron didn't tell me that."

"Seems like you two have a few secrets."

Georgia grinned, then clamped her mouth shut again.


The Decker home was a picture postcard of holiday cheer. One tree stood in the parlor window, another in the dining room.

Emmie hung their coats in the hall and said, "Aaron declared his brother's and sister's decorations to be boring and without any style. He wanted a tree of his own, but he wanted to wait for Georgia Rose to help him decorate it."

The tree in the parlor was festooned with strings of popcorn and cranberries, an array of ornaments Omie remembered seeing grow over the years, and the newest addition, electric lights.

Emmie turned them on, and Omie was astounded at the sight.

"I can't take my eyes off those lights, Emmie. What a wonder!"

"Lovely, aren't they?" Emmie put an arm around Omie's waist, and the sisters stood gazing at the tree for a moment.

Aaron emerged from his bedroom to greet them. "It's ok, but just you wait!"

He took Georgia's hand and led her to the dining room where a tall spruce nearly touched the ceiling. His cousin's mouth dropped open.

"This one is ours?"

"Yep. Come to my room, I'll show you what we're doing. Mom, no fair peeking until we're done. You too, Aunt Omie."

He shut the double doors leading into the dining room and drew the lace curtains across them.

"Well, sister, I guess we've been dismissed!" Emmie laughed. "Come along, let's go to the kitchen and see what Maizie left us. She wants to see you while you're here, when you have time."

"I haven't seen Maizie since Aunt Julia's funeral," Omie said.

"Her grief seems to be easing some. Maizie was so close to her aunt. But let's talk about Ada Kate. How is she?"

"Better, I believe. Her strength has returned and the nausea's eased up. She feels encouraged about the weaker twin's chances. I just wish I could sense more about the situation. It's vexing to me not to be able to give her more than just hope."

Emmie hugged her.

"What else can we offer, really, but hope."

They walked into the kitchen and were greeted by the delicious aroma of Maizie's Brunswick Stew simmering on the stove.

"Sit, I'll make us a cup of hot cider. How is Polly faring as a new teacher?"

"She's doing well. Phoebee's so proud of her. We all are. Even Ezra, though he's miserable knowing they can't marry as long as she's teaching."

"And your brood?" Omie asked.

Emmie told her of Danny's increased interest in going to the clinic with his father after school. "We're trying not to get our hopes up too soon, but it seems that Danny has decided to follow in Caleb's footsteps when he finishes high school."

"Where would he have to go to study medicine, Emmie?"

"I believe that would be in Augusta. Not terribly far, but still..."

"Well, you have a year or so to get used to the idea. At least Bitsy and Aaron will still be at home. Right?"

Emmie smiled fondly. "It's been a joy to work with Bitsy, now that her rebellious years have settled. Somewhat. She's a talented seamstress and designer. Quick to assert her own sense of what's in style. I'm afraid she's made me out to be an old matron when it comes to fashion."

Omie rolled her eyes. "I honestly don't know which is harder to raise, boys or girls. I have two hellions, Bartie *and* Frank Thomas."

"Well," Emmie replied, "it remains to be seen what direction our Aaron goes in. He's a sensitive boy, as befits an artist, but there is a bit of devilment behind those blue eyes."

"Speaking of, should we check on our young artists?"

Trying to walk softly, they approached the dining room doors.

"Go away!" Georgia Rose called. "We can hear you."

Caleb and Danny came home just before supper and were duly informed of their banishment from the dining area.

"Well, where are we supposed to eat?" Danny asked, in earshot of the closed doors.

"Just a few more minutes," came Aaron's reply.

Over coffee in the kitchen, Caleb described his day. "Mostly the usual maladies for the season; coughs, fevers, an occasional mishap on the ice."

Danny excitedly told them how he'd been allowed to watch his father sew up a nasty cut on a patient's leg.

"The man slipped and fell on the edge of his shovel, trying to scrape the sidewalk clean. There was so much blood! Dad asked the man if I could watch him sew the leg up, and he said yes. Did you know there are lots of different kinds of stitches?"

"Yes," Emmie said with a smile. "He learned most of them from my sewing."

They heard Bitsy come through the door, and Emmie rose to guide her toward the kitchen.

"What's going on in there?" Bitsy pointed at the closed doors.

"Aaron and Georgia Rose have been decorating their tree all day. They've promised to unveil it soon. Come on in to kitchen. Oh, do I hear music?"

Grinning like Cheshire cats, the two artists entered the kitchen, singing carols. They gestured for the family to follow them and stood back as everyone stopped to stare at their work.

The tall spruce was crowned by a porcelain and satin angel. Yards of wide, silver satin ribbon wound around and around the tree in a perfectly spaced spiral. Red velvet bows were tied to branches and among these, hand-painted, wooden ornaments hung. Candles in silver holders were placed carefully, shining with a soft light.

There was a collective sigh, and Emmie put an arm around them both. "It's perfect!"

# Chapter 48

Phoebee and Polly walked to the mailbox in falling snow so light, it was nearly mist. The tiny scalloped flakes melted quickly as they landed on fences, tree limbs and their upturned faces.

"I wonder if it's snowing in Savannah," Polly mused. "I hope they get a real snow, one that will stick."

"Long as it don't freeze and Omie cain't get home."

"Can't Mamma. Not *cain't*."

Phoebee shrugged.

"You can act like you don't care, but wait until Sarah gets back and hears you."

Phoebee scowled. "Seems like she's been gone a coon's age."

The mailbox was dusted with a fine powder of snow. Polly opened the hinged door and reached inside. There was a letter in a silky blue envelope.

"Sarah!" she cried. "Here Mamma, it's addressed to you!"

"That means it's addressed to us. You read it, I'm too scared of what she might say. I miss her like the dickens and if she says she's stayin' there, I'm gonna pitch a fit. Don't tell me if it's bad news."

"Well, it's some bad news and some good news. Her pappa has died. One week ago, she says."

"Oh," Phoebee said, wrinkling her brow. "That is bad news."

"He died in his sleep, though. It was a peaceful passing."

"Well, that's good news."

"She needs to help her mamma get settled in with her brother and his wife, so she'll be there a few more weeks."

Phoebee sighed. "More bad news."

"But she'll be back as soon as she can."

"That's good news! I guess. Is she gonna stay?"

"They need to sell her folks' house, and Sarah will have to go back for that."

"Shoot. More bad news."

"Mamma!" Polly put her hands on her hips. "Would you stop! Bad new, good news, bad news, good news. You sound like an old hen cluckin' around the coop!"

"I am *not* old!"

Polly burst into tears and Phoebee looked at her in alarm.

"I'm sorry I upset you, honey. Here." She wrapped Polly in her arms and patted the girl's back. "I'm a pill, I know. I just want Sarah back, is all."

"Oh, it's not you, Mamma. Though you are a pill sometimes! I don't know what to do. Ezra wants to get married, so part of me wants Sarah to come home and take over the school again. The other part of me wants to keep teaching, and when she's back, I'll have to choose between Ezra and leaving here to find another position."

Phoebee pondered this dilemma for a moment. "Y'all will figure things out."

Polly pulled away and wiped her eyes.

"Let me finish reading." She broke into a smile. "Sarah will be driving herself from Virginia in her daddy's automobile. Says her mamma doesn't drive and her brother has one, so this will be hers. Maybe she'll teach me to drive!"

Phoebee laughed. "Better get a sack full of them Sears and Roebuck catalogues to sit on first!"

# Chapter 49

Georgia Rose wanted to replicate the Christmas tree she and Aaron had created in Savannah. Instead of a tall, proud spruce, however, she had to make do with the usual tree they'd always had. A cedar, as full as could be found, but only about six feet tall.

"Think about it this way," Omie said. "You can reach the top just by standing on a chair. Here, I'll hand you your angel."

"It's just not the same!" Georgia wailed.

Omie picked the girl up and sat her on the chair.

"Now, listen. What you and Aaron did was beautiful. But Christmas is not just about you. This is the family tree. All the ornaments you and your brothers and sisters have made through the years are going on it. Do you understand?"

Georgia ducked her head and replied, "Yes ma'am."

"Now, let's get the ribbon and bows your Aunt Emmie gave us and use those. Ok?"

The girl brightened up and stood on the chair again.

Omie put her arms around Georgia's slim shoulders.

"I'm so proud of you, darlin'."

"Thank you, Mamma. Just. Do we have to put that squirrel tail Ezra tied with a ribbon on the tree? It's old and ratty."

Laughing, Omie relented. "I agree. Old Joe had his way with that one. Maybe we should send it to Willie!"

Ada Kate called 'hello' as she walked in with Tess. Georgia Rose hopped off the chair and declared the tree was ready for the ornaments. Omie had pulled out the Christmas basket she stored in the cupboard from year to year. Reckoning it would be difficult to get the whole family together at once to decorate, she left it up to each person to come hang their own when they could.

"Oh, my Lord," Ada exclaimed as she sorted through the basket. "We thought our creations were so pretty. How did you keep from laughing, Mamma?"

"Now, they are all beautiful to me. I wouldn't trade a single one for all the fancy trimmings in Savannah."

Georgia Rose rolled her eyes.

Tess held a corn husk doll in her small hands "Pretty!" she declared.

Omie lifted her up so she could place the doll among the branches, and they all clapped.

Ezra stuck his head in the door. "No need to clap for me, but thank y'all anyway." He winked at Georgia Rose.

"We are clapping for your brilliant niece, not you!" Ada retorted. "She hung the first ornament on the tree."

"Well, I'm gonna hang the next one," he said, looking through the basket. "Hey, where's my squirrel tail?"

"We sent it to Willie for his new dog," Georgia told him. *We're gonna. It's not really a fib!*

Omie knew this Christmas would not be the same. Their lives had all become bigger in some ways. Smaller in others. The world was claiming her children and there was nothing she could do about it. Frank Thomas had come to her a few days ago, asking to be excused from the family doings Christmas morning.

"Mamma." He took her hand in his. "I know how much Christmas means to you. I need to ask if you would mind for Jewel and me to be with her grandmamma to open gifts in the morning. Jewel is really the only family Mrs. O'Dell has here. We don't want her to be alone."

Omie gazed into his eyes. "I understand, son. Won't you bring her here for dinner? The more the merrier. We're all family now."

Frank Thomas sighed with relief, obviously having dreaded this ask.

"That'd be great, Mamma."

"We'll likely eat about two o'clock, but come anytime."

"Thank you." He kissed her cheek, then went to tell Jewel.

Bartie's absence was a given, but it still left a hollow place in Omie's heart. She imagined the three of them, Shad, Bartie and Lilly, sitting beside their own small tree in Atlanta. Omie allowed herself a few bittersweet tears, then pulled herself up.

*What will be will be.*

The Decker family joined them late in the morning of Christmas Eve, as Caleb was to be on call at the clinic Christmas Day. Aaron was gracious in his praise of Georgia Rose's tree, though she knew theirs in Savannah was much more impressive.

Caleb and Emmie gifted both the Silar house and the Dillon house with a beautiful mantle clock.

"You have to wind them with a key," Danny instructed. "Like this."

Omie could not get over how tall the boy had become. As tall as his father. At sixteen, he'd become a quiet, serious young man.

*Suited to the study of medicine.*

She saw the pride shining from Caleb's eyes as he watched his son.

Bitsy laughed with her cousins, teasing the little ones and engaging Georgia Rose in conversation. She had Emmie's sweet nature and natural ease with people, making her an asset to their shop in Savannah.

There was a reserved manner to Aaron that Omie wondered at. He seemed fully himself with Georgia Rose, but did not speak unless spoken to with the others.

Omie felt a prickling on the back of her neck. It did not last long, but when Aaron met her eyes, he looked quickly away.

After all the gifts were exchanged, they enjoyed slices of Phoebee's honey cakes. She and Polly had made two; one traditional, one soaked in brandy for the adults.

"Wherever did you get the brandy?" Emmie asked.

"Santa," Phoebee replied, wiggling her eyebrows.

A light snow began to fall, gracing the boughs of the trees. It lent a quiet sweetness to the day. Omie lit candles, and the table glowed with warm light.

Ada Kate sat on the parlor sofa, absently running her hand over the swell of her belly. She leaned against James' shoulder as they watched Tess and Grace play together.

"That's a mighty purty picture," Nate said nodding in their direction.

The others at the table agreed, smiling over cups of coffee and slices of cake. Ada looked up to see them all staring at her and called, "What?"

"We're just takin' bets on when you're gonna pop them young'uns out!" Ezra called back.

James pretended to pull a wallet out of his pocket. "Count me in! I'm hopin' for sooner rather than later. She can't even put her shoes on now! The things I have to do for this woman."

Ada reached over and gave him a playful swat. The love between the two of them was so apparent, Omie thought her heart would burst. She knew they were concerned about the twins, but tried not to let on.

*I pray their children are all born into such love.*

Caleb wanted to get back to Savannah before the roads became icy, so the Deckers declined an invitation to an early supper.

"I'm still full of cake!" Danny exclaimed. "Thank you, Aunt Phoebee."

Phoebee's face shown with pleasure at hearing herself referred to as 'Aunt Phoebee' by Emmie's boy.


Christmas morning found Georgia Rose and Grace up before everyone else, seated beneath the tree.

"What are you stinkers up to?" Omie asked, rubbing her eyes.

Georgia Rose gave her mamma a stern look, and said, "Well, someone had to make sure Santa ate his cookies. Seems like everybody had too much of Aunt Phoebee's cake, so I got up early to check."

Omie mouthed, "Thank you," and went to the stove to make coffee.

Soon, Nate and Ezra joined them. Polly and Phoebee came down the hill singing, with baskets of gifts and goodies on their arms. As the family sat at the table for coffee and biscuits, James came in the door carrying Tess. Ada Kate followed them, yawning loudly.

Omie wrapped her arms around Ada, saying, "Poor darlin'."

"And I didn't even have any brandy cake!" she complained.

Everyone had agreed that gifts to each other were to be hand-made. Santa delivered presents for Tess and Grace, however.

Ada had embraced knitting during her spells of fatigue and nausea, when she could do little else. As a result, each of them received a new pair of socks. Georgia Rose contributed by creating natural dyes for the yarn, so that each pair was different.

Ezra declared, "I am not wearing pink socks, sister."

"They were meant to be red! Just faded some is all."

He offered to trade for Nate's blue ones, but was adamantly turned down.

Nate, Ezra and Frank Thomas had all worked secretly in the barn to craft a dollhouse for Tess and Grace. Omie sewed curtains for it. Polly had made miniature books to line the shelves Georgia crafted, and Phoebee braided tiny rugs for the floors.

The girls had gifts for the adults, as well. Georgia Rose had taken the two young ones on foraging trips, collecting rocks, feathers, and any items deemed treasures.

Grace came over and sat on her daddy's lap. "Did you like your present from me most?" she asked.

"Why, a'course, Grace Bug. Nobody ever thought to give me a turtle shell before. It's just right to carry worms in for fishin'. Soon's the weather gits warm, we'll go dig us some!"

Omie thought about how often he and Bartie used to fish together. She pictured the two of them back then, and tried not to go beyond gratitude into grief. There were so many good memories to choose from instead.

Near noon, Frank Thomas and Jewel arrived along with Mrs. O'Dell. They all carried packages in their arms.

"Welcome, welcome," Omie called as she met them at the door. "So good to see you," she said, kissing the older woman on her cheek.

"Mighty glad to be here!" the shopkeeper declared.

"Looks like you brought the whole store with you," Ada Kate said. "I thought we weren't buying gifts this year, y'all."

"Actually," Jewel replied, "these are for Tess and Grace. And for you." She smiled at Georgia Rose.

After all were seated, Tess and Grace opened the gifts, with a little help from their Aunt Jewel. Inside each box were exquisite pieces of furniture for the doll house. Carved and tufted, there were divans, tables and chairs for the living and dining rooms.

The little girls' eyes grew large with wonder.

"Look!" Grace squealed. In one box were beds with pillows and quilts.

Ada Kate looked at Mrs. O'Dell. "Oh, this is too much!"

"Nonsense," she said. "I only ever had Jewel to spoil once Mr. O'Dell and I had the store and the means. You know, I lost Jewel's mamma a long time ago."

"Yes, I know." Ada touched Jewel's arm and smiled. "From what I hear, you spoiled this one pretty good."

"I miss havin' a young girl about. Reckon I enjoy a doll house full of pretty things as much as they do. Never had one myself, growin' up."

Grace took Tess' hand and they walked over to Mrs. O'Dell.

"Thank you."

"T'ank you."

They each gave her a kiss and went to place the furniture carefully in their doll house.

"And now for you, Georgia." Frank Thomas had snuck out to the auto and come back in with a tall easel, graced with a red ribbon.

Georgia gasped. "Really?"

"Really." Her big brother smiled fondly. "Just remember us when you're rich and famous."

She jumped up to hug him, then Jewel and Mrs. O'Dell.

"It's nicer than Aaron's!"

# Chapter 50

## 1931

New Year's Day arrived shining and mild.

Omie stood on the porch, breathing in the fresh air.

*A promising sign for the days to come.*

Everyone gathered at Ada and James' house for dinner.

Phoebee was feeling melancholy after the excitement of Christmas was over and begged off. She claimed to be coming down with a cold, though she didn't feel sick. Just out of sorts.

This was not a typical state for Phoebee to be in, and she didn't like it one bit. Every task she considered doing made her tired before she began. Grabbing her coat, she headed for the woods, knowing there was no honey to be found, but wanting comfort from the trees anyway. The scents of dry pine needles and oak leaves mingled with wintergreen berries crushed beneath her feet. Despite the chill, she walked barefoot to feel a connection with the land.

Head down, deep in thought, she nearly bumped into the dark form of a black bear pawing at a rotten log for grubs. It was hard to tell who was more surprised. She began to back away slowly. The bear stood up and Phoebee sunk to the ground, pretending to be dead.

*Lord, Lord!*

Ambling over, the creature's cold nose began to sniff around Phoebee's back and head.

*I ain't but stringy muscles and bones, bear. Not worth your time.*

Finally, it dropped down beside her.

*What in tarnation am I supposed to do now!*

The bear rubbed up against her as if she was a small stump. She tentatively reached her hand out and touched the bristly fur. The bear responded by pushing back against her pressure. Phoebee gave it a small scratch. The bear pushed back even more. She scratched harder.

A muffled groan came from its snout as its red tongue slipped out. Phoebee began to explore the wide back, pulling out twigs as she rubbed. Finally, it heaved itself up, shook, and waddled into the trees, looking back once as if to thank her.

Phoebee sat still for a few minutes and then lay back on the ground, laughing until tears ran down her cheeks.

*Bears n' bees!*

She thought she might keep this adventure all to herself.

Phoebee walked out of the woods and into the field, still chuckling. Close to home, she saw a handsome blue automobile parked beside the house.

*Sarah! Gotta be!*

She ran to the porch. Sarah came out and swept Phoebee up in fierce hug.

"I've missed you so much! I didn't know what to think when you weren't home, Phoebee."

"Maybe I'll tell you what I been doin' later, but I want to hear everything you been up to first. I ain't gonna let you go off so long ever again!"

Sarah stepped back and looked deeply into her friend's eyes.

"You're part of the reason I've been gone so long. Come in, I have something to show you."

She took Phoebee's hand and pulled her through the door. Phoebee stopped and gasped. It took her a moment to find her voice. "Mamma! Granny!"

The women rose from the table and circled her in their arms. All they could do was sob for a while. Twenty years of tears and sorrow melted into a joy so large, there were no words to embrace it.

"How? Where?" Phoebee turned to stare at Sarah, whose own face was wet with tears.

Her mamma answered. "She found us, honey. I don't know how. Miss Sarah come drivin' up to the house in that fancy automobile and I thought she was a revenuer. Or somebody comin' to give us bad news."

Granny chimed in, "When she got out, I had yer daddy's old shotgun pointed at her. Like ta' scared her somethin' silly!"

Phoebee felt like the world was spinning around. She sat at the table with her hand over her mouth, crying silently. Her mamma came and put a hand on the slight shoulder.

"When you run off with that Ephram, the law come lookin' for y'all. After so much time went by, we took you for dead. Why didn't you get word to us you were here after he died, baby?"

Phoebee cut her eyes over at Sarah, then looked up. "I was ashamed, Mamma. Granny. I didn't think y'all would ever want to see me again. 'Specially after we cost you your wagon and horse."

"Good Lord, child! You think a damn horse and wagon mean more to us than you?" Granny looked for a place to spit her snuff. Sarah found an empty can and handed it to her.

"Sides, the sheriff couldn't keep 'em. No likker in the wagon. Nuthin' and nobody to charge for a crime."

Sarah said quietly, "After my father died, all I could think about was how much family matters. I'd taken it for granted mine would always be there for me. But I wasn't there for them." She reached for Phoebee's hand. "I went to Stone Mountain to find your people. I didn't know your maiden name was Winder, but I figured someone would remember a bee charmer named Phoebee. Folks at the general store did, and told me where to find your family."

"I don't know how to thank you, Sarah." Phoebee stood and looked up at her friend. They smiled at each other for a long moment. "This is the best gift ever."

"You don't need to thank me. You're my sister and I love you. Now, I'm going to let you all catch up, and I'll go say hello to Omie and her bunch."

"They're at Ada and James house. Would you send Polly home to meet her family?"

"Of course." Sarah waved to the women and walked out to her auto.

At the Dillon house, everyone heard the vehicle drive up and swarmed out the door like a hive of bees.

"Sarah!" Polly cried.

Nate let out a long, low whistle as he rubbed a fender on the Pierce Arrow. Ezra, James and Frank Thomas nodded in agreement.

Sarah rolled down the window and Jewel leaned in. "Are you some famous movie star in her fancy car, Miss?"

Watching the rest of them make a fuss over the auto, Sarah laughed and replied, "I don't think I'm the star of this show! Hop in."

She leaned out the window and called, "Who wants a ride?"

Omie picked up Tess, then she, Polly and the other little girls hurried into the back seat. Jewel and Ada Kate sat up front.

"Sorry, boys! No more room." Sarah revved the motor and took off toward the river road, laughing at the sight of the bewildered men standing in the yard.

Georgia Rose let out a *"Whoopie!"*

"Your daddy sure had good taste," Jewel exclaimed. "Two-tone blue on the outside, blue leather upholstery on the inside. You sure you're not from famous people?"

"It's only money," Sarah replied.

Omie laughed, "Said like somebody who's got some!" She put a hand on Sarah's shoulder. "I can't think of anybody that deserves it more."

About ten minutes later, Ada said, "I hate to break up the party, but I have to pee. Again!"

"All right, little mamma. We'll head back." Sarah turned the car around. The men scattered as she zipped up into the yard. "Pregnant woman. Got to pee!"

She got out and told Frank Thomas to get behind the wheel. "You all go for a ride. We have women talk to do."

"Gladly!" he replied.

The girls reluctantly got out.

"I call front seat!" James pulled open the passenger door. Nate and Ezra climbed in the back.

"Teach us how to drive, brother," Ezra said. "We been talkin' about getting' a truck for the farm."

And so, he did.

"First, I have some important news for you all," Sarah said.

Polly sighed, "You're going to marry Rusty and move back to Virginia."

Sarah squinted at the girl. "Marry Rusty? Heavens, no."

Just then, Ada walked in the door. "You're going to marry Rusty?"

"No! I am not! Now listen."

She told them about her search to find Phoebee's family, including how Granny had pointed a gun at her as she got out of the car.

"I thought she was going to shoot first and ask questions later."

Polly was listening intently. "I have family there still?"

Reaching out for the girl's hand, Sarah said, "Honey. You have family here, now. I brought your grandmother and great-grandmother back with me."

Polly jumped up and was out the door before anyone else could digest this news.

Omie put her arms around Sarah and the others joined her. Even Ada managed to get an arm around Sarah's shoulder, despite her belly getting in the way.

Grace asked, "Why is everybody crying?"

Georgia Rose took her little sister's hands and danced her around. "They're happy tears, Gracie."


Sarah gave up her room for Phoebee's mother and grandmother to stay in, figuring they would want to be together as much as possible. Omie invited her to stay in Ada's and Bartie's old room at her house. She looked forward to having some private time to hear more about this feat Sarah had pulled off.

After Georgia Rose and Grace had gone to bed, Sarah and Omie sat at the table with cups of chamomile tea.

"This is just what I need," Sarah sighed. "I'm exhausted but too keyed up to sleep!"

"How in the world did you do this, hon? I really am impressed at all you went through to find Phoebee's family and bring them here."

"Honestly, Omie, it was as if I was guided to them. And what characters! That acorn didn't fall far from the tree, no matter how far she rolled. Sometimes I had to ask them to hush so I could drive without wetting myself. Especially Granny. We stopped to stay at a hotel on the way here, and let me tell you, the owners will never forget them."

"I imagine so." Omie smiled. "I'm looking forward to spending time with them, hearing some stories about Phoebee as a child. So much time wasted, Sarah. It breaks my heart."

Sarah looked down at the table. A sadness enveloped her like a pale light.

"We all waste valuable time when it comes to the ones we love, I suppose. I should have made more time for my father. Now he's gone, and taken the things I wanted to learn from him, with him. Such an intelligent man. I got my love of nature from Father."

Omie put her hand on Sarah's. "How is your mamma holding up?"

"Oh, Mamma is fine. Grieving, no doubt, but she's tough under all that city refinement. She'll be busy with my brother's children, once they've moved her in with them. Her garden club and charities give her a full social life."

"Why haven't they ever visited you here?"

"Daddy and my brother Michael were so busy with their business. To be honest, Mamma did not want me to take this teaching job. I think she felt visiting me would give the impression of approval, or at least acceptance that I am not returning to Virginia."

In the days that followed, Phoebee's family and the Silar family came to know each other. It was easy to be with the Winder women. They were funny, friendly and so grateful that Phoebee had been taken in and cared for. Polly was like a happy child, not opening a single book in their presence. Omie wondered if both Polly and Phoebee had experienced a sense of something missing from their lives, despite being part of the Silar family for so long.

As everyone sat in Omie's kitchen one morning after breakfast, the Winder women announced they wanted to make a meal for their hosts.

"We ain't used to bein' waited on. Don't feel right." Granny spit snuff into a tin can and looked at Welda. "Reckon we could cook up a possum if we could borrow a gun ta git one."

Welda nodded. "You are the best shot on Stone Mountain. If'n anybody could nail one, you could."

Ada looked at Phoebee, who stared down at the table and sipped her coffee.

"Maybe shoot two," Welda said. "There's a passel of folks to feed."

"Y'all got some onions put up? Sweet taters? Ain't nuthin good as a big ole greasy possum cooked with taters and onions." Granny spit again.

Phoebee glanced at the queasy expressions on the faces around her and began to giggle. Welda and Granny grinned at each other, then guffawed.

"Jest look at y'all!" Granny slapped her thigh.

Welda wiped her eyes and said, "Maybe we best stick to fried chicken, Mamma."

Omie grinned back. "Well, those we've got. I'll have the boys kill a couple."

She looked at Nate.

"Best take Grace to town or she'll pitch a fit. She loves those birds. It's a struggle every time we have chicken for dinner."

"We can fix sumpthin' else," Welda offered.

"Naw," Nate replied. "I'll catch her a fish. It's what we always do."

"Sometimes we eat gator!" Ezra told them.

Welda looked shocked. "A alligator?"

Phoebee nodded. "Tastes like chicken."

"Well, I never!"

Granny looked at Nate. "Can I shoot one?"

"I'll see if I can stir one up, ma'am."

"Hot damn!" she shouted, then looked around her apologetically.

"That's pretty much how it feels," Nate said.

One evening, Omie got up for a glass of water and found Phoebee sitting with Sarah at the kitchen table after everyone else had gone to bed.

"Can't sleep?" she asked Phoebee.

"Too excited. I'm wound up like a racoon with a burr on its butt."

Omie sat. "I haven't had chance to talk to you since your mamma and grandmamma came. What of the rest of your family?"

"Mamma told me my daddy passed a couple years after I left. Feels like I just lost him. Reckon me and Sarah have that in common." Phoebee looked at her friend and took a deep breath. "But my three brothers are still on the farm. Two of 'em married with young'uns. Hard to imagine; they was just boys when I took off with Ephram."

Sarah put a hand on Phoebee's. "I was thinking that I'd take you and Polly back with me when I take your folks home in a couple of days. I can leave you two there, and then head on to Virginia to take care of mamma's house. I'll pick you up on the way back. How does that sound?"

"What about the school?" Phoebee asked. "It starts back up soon."

"I think if I tell the school board that I want to return to teaching but need to finish family business first, they'll agree to put it off for a couple more weeks."

Tears welled up in Phoebee's eyes. "Thank you, Sarah. Lord, I thought I was cried out!" She wiped her cheeks and smiled.

"Omie, there's something else I'd like to talk to you about. It seems my brother has already found a family who wishes to buy the house. I would like to take some of my share of the money and build a house for Phoebee and me. Ezra and Polly ought to have your family home. What do you say?"

Phoebee's eyes grew so wide, Omie had to laugh.

"Of course! I'll talk with Nate right away and we'll figure out a good spot."

"Well, knock me down with a horse feather!" Phoebee exclaimed.

Sarah made plans to leave in two days' time. She went to New Abercorn to send a telegram to her brother, giving her permission to sell the house, taking Polly with her. It was obvious the girl was struggling with emotions. The discovery of her relatives and the relinquishing of the teaching position were pulling her in different directions.

They made small talk as the fields and farms slid by, then Sarah brought up the reason for inviting Polly along.

"I have a proposition for you, honey."

Polly turned to look at her mentor. "For me?"

"There is funding available to establish libraries in rural towns now. I think you would make a wonderful librarian, Polly. You're intelligent, well-read, and you'd have the freedom to choose what books to introduce to the community. There are a lot of older people here who don't know how to read. You could have a special class for adults, so you'd still be teaching."

Polly thought about this for a few moments. "But, what would I have to do to become a librarian?"

"The Savannah library has an apprenticeship program. It would only be a few weeks in the summer. What do you think?"

"Can a librarian be married?"

"Yes, my dear. They can."

Sarah could see Polly warming to the idea. By the time they were driving home, she was talking about ideas and books to include in the library. Sarah felt a maternal warmth toward Polly. She'd been present for most of the girl's life. To be able to help her felt like a gift Sarah was receiving, as much as giving.

When they pulled up to their house, Polly got out and turned to go down the hill.

"I need to find Ezra."

"Of course, sweetie. Go give him the good news."

Polly found him in the barn tossing hay to the horse and mules.

"Hey," she called.

He nodded at the pitchfork and grinned. "Hay."

She took Ezra's hand and led him out toward the cattle pond. The sky was a mid-winter blue, reflected in the water, etched here and there with wispy clouds. They stopped to watch a small green heron fishing at the edges, spearing minnows.

"Well, there goes my bait," Ezra said half-heartedly.

Turning to face him, Polly said, "Ezra, you've been so patient and understanding about my wanting to teach. I appreciate it more than I can say."

He steeled himself for the news that she would be leaving to teach elsewhere. Maybe in Stone Mountain, now that she'd found her family there.

She gazed into his eyes. "But that's done now. Sarah wants to bring a library to New Abercorn. And she wants me to be the librarian."

"What? That's great! At least I think it is. Can a librarian be married?"

"Yes, Ezra."

He took her up in an embrace so tight she could barely breathe. They stood that way for a long time, outlined against the coming dusk.

Omie was seated at the table, looking out the window. Her heart clenched tightly with concern for these two young people she loved so much.

*Is this good news, or goodbye?*

She smelled the soft scent of roses and felt her mamma's warm hand on her back.

*I believe there's another wedding comin', daughter.*

Ezra took Polly's hand and dropped to one knee. "Now, Polly Miller, will you be my wife?"

She pretended to think about it for a moment, and then laughed. "Of course, silly! How could I not."

They walked toward her house hand-in-hand.

Phoebee opened the door and said, "Y'all are grinnin' like mules eatin' briars! Mamma, Granny, looks like our girl is gettin' hitched!"

The three women wrapped their arms around Polly and she felt as if she'd never known so much love. Ezra was pulled into their circle too, towering above their heads.

The following day, Omie insisted on riding to town to buy supplies for a celebration dinner.

Nate looked up at the clouds rolling across the sky. " Colder than a well-digger's a...hind end today. Cain't this wait 'til it warms up?"

"No, husband, it can't."

Once they were on their way with quilts across their laps, Omie smiled. "Isn't it something, Nate? Ezra and Polly getting married."

"Sure is. Seems like they was both babies not so long ago. Shame Ephram wasn't a better daddy, he's missin' out."

"He wasn't any kind of daddy. Polly's better off not knowing that scoundrel."

"What did Phoebee say happened to him?"

Omie told him about the story Phoebee gave Sarah when they first met.

"She said he died in the tornado, head first in the outhouse hole?" Nate had a good long laugh at that. "Sounds like Phoebee. She didn't tell that to Polly, did she?"

"I've never asked her. I expect she claimed he's dead, though. I never heard Polly ask any questions."

Nate laughed again and Omie joined him.

# Chapter 51

The gleaming bald dome of Stone Mountain was visible from miles away. Phoebee's breath caught. She never thought to see the big granite rock again. Her last view had been the day Ephram took her away from home, and the memory of their leaving sat heavy on her heart.

*Lord knows, he was all I could think about at the time, but it didn't take long for that shine to wear off.*

"You OK?" Polly put an arm across her mamma's shoulders.

Phoebee nodded, wordless for the moment.

"That's our big 'ol rock!" Granny said. "Your family goes back a long time here, Miss Polly. My grandaddy and his grandaddy was here before settlers come and laid claim to most of the land."

Welda nodded. "Daddy was half Cherokee and Granny here is mostly Muscogee. What white folks called Creeks. Stories say our people traded the mountain for a horse or some such silliness, but we know it was really took."

"You know that sayin', 'Good Lord willin' and the Creek don't rise'? Weren't about no water," Granny cackled.

"We got some English blood too, some Irish and Scottish." Welda turned to look back at Polly. "You look a good bit like Daddy's Irish side of the family, don't she Mamma?"

Polly looked at her braid of reddish-brown hair and said, "I wish my hair was like Mamma's."

Phoebee looked surprised. "Really?"

"Didn't my daddy ever tell you how pretty it is?" Polly asked.

Phoebee shook her head. "He was more the type to say it looked like 'kind' hair. The kind you'd find on a mule's rear end. Thought he was real funny, that one."

"Well then, I'm glad he died in the outhouse!"

Welda turned back to face forward and grinned.


The road to Phoebee's old home wound around the base of the mountain and up a hollow. Despite the cold, she opened her window, drawing in a deep breath of mountain air.

As they turned up the drive, Polly shouted, "Mamma, look!"

The yard was full of wagons, a couple of automobiles, and a passel of people gathered around them. As Sarah's car drew near, a large cheer came from the waiting crowd. Phoebee covered her mouth, laughing and sobbing at the same time.

Phoebee's brother Kurt opened the car door, reached in to help Polly out, then swept his niece off the ground in a bear hug. "You gotta be Pollywog!" he shouted.

Phoebee had never heard Polly laugh with such joy before.

Jamie opened his sister's door and did the same.

"Put me down, ya big galoot!" Phoebee cried.

"Not til I'm done squeezin' the stuffin' outa you!" he replied.

Finley took her from Jamie's arms and swung Phoebee around until she yelled, "I mean it! Y'all are gonna' make me lose my breakfast!"

Finley had been a young boy when she'd disappeared from their lives. She was surprised that he remembered her.

"Oh, Lord, Finley!" Phoebee opened her arms for a hug. "You're so growed up now."

Sarah felt her heart swell, watching the scene.

*If you're there, God. Thank you. Thank you for this.*

Sarah had called with word of their arrival to the general store. The owner promised to get a message up the mountain right away. Word spread quickly to family and friends so that before long, folks began to arrive at the Winder farm. Tables were set up for food by the men, and benches placed near a big fire built to keep the chill off.

Phoebee sat to catch her breath. She motioned for Polly to join her. "These great big fools claim to be my brothers, Kurt and Jamie. But the brothers I left was just a little taller than me, 'cept for Finley."

"We was born taller than you, Phoebee."

Folks came up in polite groups of two and three to introduce themselves and welcome Polly into the family. Phoebee stood to hug their necks, marveling at the changes twenty years had made.

Welda brought over her grandchildren to meet them, Kurt's boys and daughters and Jamie's sons. "This here's your Aunt Phoebee and your cousin Polly."

The children ranged from eight to eighteen. The boys were shy in the face of this newcomer, but the girls surrounded Polly on the steps, questions ready.

"How far a piece did you come, cousin? Did you get to see Atlanta?"

Finally, Phoebee walked away from the gaggle of girls and went to fix herself a plate of food. At the table, her sisters-in-law introduced themselves, taking Phoebee under their wings and telling her who was who in the crowd.

Kurt's wife Julie was eager to fill her in on family gossip. "That redhead over there? That's cousin Rhonda. Married a car salesman from Marietta. Thinks she's somethin' special now 'cause she drives her own automobile and moved uptown. She'll be the first one to load her plate up with chicken feet though, you watch. Cain't get them in the city."

Next, she turned toward the preacher and his wife. "Just 'cause he carries that bible in his hand don't mean you can trust Preacher. He's got a eye for the ladies, likes to get a little feely when he hugs you. She pretends she don't see, but she does."

Jamie's wife Linda snorted. "His breath could melt paint off a barn. Speakin' of barns, that big 'ol girl there is Widder Sacket. She sells Avon. Wears enough of her own product, she probably has to scape it off with a straight razor at night."

"Who's that?" Phoebee pointed to a leathery-skinned old woman who had been staring the whole time, but made no move to greet her.

Julie glanced over to where Phoebee pointed. "That's Granny Jones, from your daddy's side. Nobody knows how old the woman is. Full blood Muscogee, still knows the language. She walked over here from up on the mountain. Some kind of witch, folks say. I don't know. Keeps to herself mostly."

Linda said, "Looks like she's here to meet you, though."

Phoebee felt a pull toward the crone. A warmth spread through her chest and belly as they locked eyes.

"I'll see y'all later. Thanks for the food."

She carried her plate over and sat on the bench beside Granny Jones. The woman's dark eyes shone with interest, taking in more, Phoebee could tell, than just her appearance.

"So, you're the bee charmer, eh?"

The toothless grin aimed her way set Phoebee at ease, and she replied, "That's what they say. Don't understand it exactly."

"They's much we aren't meant to understand. Don't really matter."

Granny Jones' voice was surprisingly deep, accented with the cadence of her native language. "I reckon you been seeing a lot of unusual things where you been, eh?"

With a forkful of food half-way to her mouth, Phoebee paused and raised her eyebrows.

"Shinin' all around you." A look of concern came into the old woman's eyes "You been troubled by ghosts?"

"No ma'am, not troubled. My future son-in-law does see them though. Helps them move on from this world. His mamma is my best friend, Omie. Has the *Sight*. She's a real good woman, a healer like her mamma was."

"Yes, I *See* that."

They sat in comfortable silence as Phoebee ate and Granny Jones smoked her pipe. The tobacco had a sweet, woodsy scent, and Phoebee asked what was in it.

"Kinnikinnick."

"Kinn? What? It sure smells good."

"Made from bark and plants, such as that. This recipe was handed down through the women in my tribe. Come see me before you leave. I'll give you some."

With that, the old woman rose and grasped her carved hickory staff. She gave Phoebee one more deep look, then turned and disappeared into the trees.

After a couple of hours enjoying the food and listening to Phoebee's relatives talk, Sarah decided it was time to leave. She rose, stretched, then went to stand behind Polly and Phoebee.

"I better shove off, got miles to go before I stop for the night. I've really loved being a part of this reunion, Phoebee."

The women stood and each took one of Sarah's hands.

"This is a blessing you brought to us, Aunt Sarah," Polly replied. "We can never thank you enough."

Phoebee reached up and put a hand to her friend's cheek. "You always been family to me and Polly. Now, you got family here for life." She laughed. "Whether you want 'em or not!"

Sarah made the rounds, saying her goodbyes, then climbed into the Pierce Arrow and drove off.

Finley came to stand beside his big sister. "She married? Or got a boyfriend you could run off fer me?"

"She's too old and too smart to be courted by a rascal like you. Forget about it!" Phoebee stuck her tongue out at him.

"Yep, that's the Phoebee I remember."

This earned him a swat. They went to sit beside the fire and its warmth seemed to draw out memories for them both.

"I worried a bunch about you when you left. Didn't know where you was, or if that no good Ephram hurt you. We was all sad, Phoebee. I'm not tryin' to make you feel bad. Well, maybe a little. I just want you to know we never forgot you."

Phoebee gave her little brother a peck on the cheek.

"I never stopped thinkin' about you all, Finley. I hope I can make it up to you somehow, leavin' like that without a word. I was ashamed, is all."

He blushed a little at the intimate turn the conversation was taking.

"It's all right, sister. I got my own room when you left."

She swatted him again. "Well, it's my room again while I'm here. You can sleep in the barn."

Phoebee went to fetch Polly so they could say goodbye to kinfolk who were packing up. There were many invitations to come visit before they left.

"Y'all don't be strangers now, hear?"

Phoebee knew if she was to see any of her people again, it would be here. Doubtful many of them left the mountain, certainly not to travel as far as New Abercorn.

She stepped in front of Polly as the preacher and his wife came to say their farewells. Phoebee immediately reached out to shake their hands, not giving him the chance to get too near. Linda and Julie grinned at her from the porch.

"This was your old room, Mamma?" Polly sat on the bed beside Phoebee.

"Yes, darlin'. I expect Findley was made to get his stuff out so Mamma could make it as near to mine again as she could."

She brushed her fingers over the bright quilt on the bed. "Mamma and Granny sewed this for me when I was just a little 'un. All the ladies near 'bouts came to quilt it for me. They set the frame on chairs and I sat underneath while they worked." She sighed. "Pollywog, don't do nuthin' you'll regret, like I did. Stayin' away so long was the worst of it. No matter what you do, you never have to doubt that I love you."

Polly wrapped her arms around her mamma and held on tight.

Kurt, Jamie, and their families spent as much time with Phoebee and Polly as possible. The boys took turns chopping firewood for Welda and Granny and mucking out the barn while they were there.

At the table one night, talk turned to what prohibition had done, how revenue from moonshining increased.

Granny said, "It ain't like anybody here was buyin' fancy likker anyhow, but folks come from Atlanta lookin' fer shine."

Jamie looked down at the table. "We heard Ephram come back around a few years ago, sister. Lookin' to get in on the shine business here I reckon.

Me and Kurt looked for him, tryin' to find out what happened to you, but he disappeared again pretty quick."

"Didn't find much welcome on the mountain, I don't imagine." Welda looked at Granny. "Prolly knew we'd a skint him alive if we could."

"I'd of skint him and made a rug out of his hide. Then I could beat it ever' chance I got," Granny agreed.

Phoebee fell into an old rhythm of waking before dawn, milking the goats and feeding the stock. She saved gathering eggs for Polly, knowing she would want to help. When chores were done, the two of them took long walks, as weather permitted. Phoebee took her to the creek where her mamma was so badly stung when she was pregnant.

"Course, the old log is long gone where them bees was livin."

They sat on the bank and turned their faces up to the pale sun.

"I don't like to think about what would have happened if Grandmamma hadn't made it back home before you started coming!" Polly was quiet for a few moments, then said, "I'm a little worried about having babies. You had so much trouble, and Grandmamma did too, with you. I know it was the bees and all, but still."

"Sweet Pea, set your mind to rest about that. I come so early, I think I hadn't grown enough." Phoebee shook her head. "I wadn't built for havin' babies 'cause of that. Makin' babies wasn't easy for me neither."

Polly teared up and said, "Did I cause you nothin' but pain, Mamma?"

Phoebee took her daughter's hands and looked straight into her eyes.

"Pollywog, I would go through every bit of it again just to have you. Put that thought out of your head right now!"

Polly wiped at her cheeks.

Phoebee assured her, "Look at them big boys my mamma spit out. She didn't have a bit of trouble with them. You'll be fine too."

Sarah sent word again that she would be back in two days to get them. Phoebee was considering how she might visit Granny Jones before then. Somehow, it seemed important to.

Over breakfast the next day, she asked, "Mamma, could I ride one of the mules up the mountain? I want to go see Granny Jones."

Welda looked surprised and glanced over at Granny.

"What fer, honey?"

"I don't know. She asked me to come. And somethin' tells me I should."

"Well, I reckon we could get a saddle on Amos, he's pretty good with bein' rid."

"I don't need a saddle, just a blanket and bridle's enough."

Phoebee turned to Polly. "Wanna come? I can show you more of the Rock too."

"Sure." Polly grinned. "When do you want to go?"

Welda said, "Best be soon if'n yer goin' today. It's a goodly piece to get there. Make sure you're headed home well before dark, though. There's painters up in them woods."

Polly looked at her mamma quizzically.

"Panthers," Phoebee said.

Once Amos had been fitted for travel, Phoebee brought him close to the porch so she and Polly could get up on his back. She could see Polly's hesitation, now that danger was part of the adventure.

"Don't you worry, honey. All my years roamin' this mountain I never come across a big cat. Amos here will protect us."

Welda laughed. "He'll be back to the barn lickety-split if he gets a whiff of a big cat!"

"Don't tell my brothers we went, Mamma. They'll likely come lookin' for us."

"We won't," Welda assured them. "Here's some vittles fer the ride."

Phoebee put the sack in front of her and turned to look at Polly.

"You ready?"

With a deep sigh, Polly replied, "Ready as I'll ever be!"

An old trail wound up the mountain through the trees, then along its bare flank. The day was warm and clear for January, with no breeze to chill them. High above, a hawk called out.

"How do you know where to find Granny Jones?" Polly asked.

"Mamma's been there a few times for ginseng. She told me landmarks to look for. I used to know ever' bit of this mountain. Cain't imagine it's changed too much."

Phoebee pointed out the places she spent time as a child, picking flowers and looking for turtle shells. She'd collected milk weed pods, and set them sailing down the creeks like boats.

"I lived in paradise and never knew it!" she declared.

On the backside of the mountain, they started to descend. Just after passing back through the tree line, Polly started noticing things hanging from trees. Clusters of small bones and feathers tied together. Twigs fashioned to look like people.

"Mamma, look!"

"We must be close. Them are to warn and protect against outsiders."

Soon, a path opened up beside an old oak, just wide enough for the mule and his riders.

In the middle of a small meadow, Granny Jones' cabin sat near a creek. The water glistened in the sunlight. Moss grew on the cabin roof, making the whole place seem like something from a fairy tale.

From inside the house, a couple of goats wandered out the door, followed by several chickens and a pink pig. A couple of horses rounded the corner, water dripping from their brown muzzles. Granny stood in the doorway, pipe in hand, and waved for the women to come up onto her porch.

"Jest leave the mule to graze. He won't go far."

Polly slid off the mule's back and promptly fell on her butt. "My legs are wobbly from straddling him so long!"

Phoebee slid down and did the same.

"Well, ain't y'all a pair of city slickers."

Granny came into the yard and held a hand out to each. She was surprisingly strong for her size.

"Come sit, I'll get us some sweet tea." She pointed at rockers on the porch. The sun had warmed the old tin roof and it was comfortable beneath.

She gave the two time to gather themselves and waddle up the steps before returning with a gallon jug of dark tea and three pint jars.

"I been keepin' this in the root cellar for y'all. Nice and cool."

Polly reached out a hand. "Happy to meet you, ma'am. How did you know we were comin' today?"

As the old woman folded her wrinkled brown fingers around Polly's, the girl felt a warmth travel up her arm.

"Oh," was all Polly said.

"I guess Omie's family ain't the onliest ones with the *Sight*," Phoebee stated.

Granny poured them each a glass and sat.

"Was a time when most of our folks knew things. Knew the old ways of livin'. The *Sight* weren't so special then." Granny drew on her pipe. "The land showed us ever'thang we needed anyhow. Still does if you pay attention."

Two more horses came around the side of the house from the creek. A small brown donkey followed them. He climbed up the steps and dropped down in front of Granny's chair. She rubbed her bare feet along the creature's flanks and its lips drew back.

"I swear that donkey is smilin'!" Phoebee laughed.

"We both enjoy our daily rub."

"Granny Jones," Polly asked shyly, "How do you tame all these critters?"

"Tame?" The old woman looked amused. "They tamed me, more like. All but the chickens came here on their own. At first, I tried to run them off, but they wasn't havin' it. Specially the horses and this one here."

She used her toes to scratch behind the donkey's long ears.

"People have the same natures as some animals. That animal will be drawn to you like these horses are ta me. They teach me all kinds of things. Keep watch too, make noise if trouble's comin'."

The donkey let out a string of brays.

"Yes, I got some of your nature too, you stubborn thang."

"Are bees my animal, Granny Jones?" Phoebee asked.

"Seem to be. Even if your mamma hadn't got herself stung so bad when she was carryin' you, I 'spect you'd still be a charmer. My daddy was one too."

"He was?"

"You take after him, girl. He was chief of our people until a fever came on him. White man's sickness. Took a bunch of us."

"Did that make you a princess?" Polly exclaimed.

Granny laughed so hard she began coughing. Finally, she answered, "You been at them books too much, Pollywog. Do I *look* like a princess?"

Polly blushed, astonished the woman knew her nickname and fondness for reading. Granny placed a hand on hers. "I'm jest funnin' ya, hon. We didn't use that word, but it was an honor to be a chief's daughter. I had five sisters and four brothers, though. We didn't have any more than anybody else. After Daddy died, I was married to a trapper my brothers met at the tradin' post near here. He needed a wife and I was one less mouth to feed." She tapped out her pipe on the arm of the chair. "He was a good man. Drank like the Irish do, though. Fell off his horse and hit his head on a rock one night. Horse come back here to tell me 'bout it."

"Do I have an animal nature?" Polly asked.

Granny studied the girl for a few minutes, and said, "I cain't rightly tell, darlin'. If'n you do, it'll let you know one day."

Peace settled around them, watching animals come and go. The horses all came into the yard and lay together to soak up the sun's warmth. Soon, goats joined them. The pink pig nosed at the dirt, making a soft hollow for itself and plopped down. Chickens scratched in the loose soil, then tucked themselves up against the pig.

"Well, I never!" Phoebee cried.

Granny Jones removed her pipe from her mouth and nodded. "All creatures get along, given a chance. All but humans. I don't know what the Creator was thinkin' when He made us two legged ones."

"How long have your people been here, Granny?" Polly asked.

The old woman turned to look at her, and said, "*Our* people, young'un. Remember who and where you come from, hear? The blood of the first people runs in y'all's veins, far back as anybody knows, we been here."

Phoebee took this in, then asked. "What happened to the rest of us. Why are you the onliest one still up on the mountain?"

Granny spit off the side of the porch and looked into the distance.

"What ones wasn't caught and took away before the war with them Yankees, was found and forced to fight. Damn White man's war. We had no stake in it, but that didn't matter none."

She scowled and nodded up toward the mountain. "Now they's scratchin' pictures of them confederate generals on our rock's face. Like they's sumthin' to be proud of."

Phoebee attempted to change the mood of the conversation, and said, "I surely would love some of that tobacco you smoke, Granny. Might I get some before we have to head back?"

"You surely can. I'll show you what plants I use, so you can make it when you get home. I got some dried hangin' inside."

Phoebee asked, "Will you help me remember, Polly? I bet Omie will know them."

From the heavy wooden beams, bundles of various herbs hung. The air was scented with so many fragrances, it was hard to distinguish a single source.

Granny Jones reached up and plucked three bundles from their nails. She spread out a dried leaf from each one on the table.

"This 'un here is native tobacco, not the same as that awful stuff white people grow. That'll kill ya. This'll heal ya. Now this'n is called rabbit tobacco. Don't ask me why, I dunno."

Phoebee cried, "Omie told me Emmie used to smoke that when she was young!"

Polly looked shocked. "Aunt Emmie smoked? It smells sweet, Granny."

"You might know this one." Granny unfurled a long, wide fuzzy leaf.

"That's mullein!" Polly looked pleased with herself for recognizing it.

"Tha's right. And lastly, this is red willow."

From out of a leather pouch, came shreds of dried bark.

"If you ain't sure you found the right plants, come back in summer and I'll show you, eh?"

A rain crow called across the meadow from the tree line, and they looked out the door. Sure enough, the sky had clouded up, and a chill wind lifted the leaves.

"Y'all best git," Granny declared. She bundled up a mix of the plants into another pouch. Afterwards, she went to an old wooden trunk at the foot of her bed.

"Take these blankets to keep you warm. Yer gonna need 'em."

Polly gasped. They were beautiful. Hand woven and soft.

Phoebee wrapped hers around her shoulders, amazed by the intricate patterns and colors. "Are you sure? We'll get someone to bring them back to ya later."

"No need. I have plenty. My mamma and her mamma made these. They should go with you."

The two hurried out the door and Phoebee caught Amos' bridle. He sniffed nervously at the rising wind with its scent of snow. From the porch steps, they mounted and looked down into the dark eyes of Granny Jones.

Polly said, "We thank you for everything. For the stories and gifts. I hope we get to see you again, Granny."

"Remember what I told you, granddaughters. You are bones and blood of the first people. That's sumthin' to be proud of."

As Amos began to pass into the trees, Polly looked back and waved goodbye. Granny Jones appeared small in the doorway. Goats and chickens were heading up the steps and into the cabin to escape the chilly wind that had risen.  The pink pig was rising to follow too. This picture was one she would hold close for the remainder of her life, Polly thought. Granny Jones' words sounded in her head.

*Bones and blood of the first people.*

She snuggled closer to her mamma as they began their climb to the bald top of the mountain.

Just above the tree line, hail began to fall in small round pellets. It melted at first, then began to stick, making the path slippery. Amos picked up the pace, anxious to get onto surer footing.

"Easy, boy," Phoebee crooned. "You're all right. We'll be there shortly."

Once inside the woods again, a scattering of hail began to cover the forest floor. There was something magical about it, Polly thought, different from snow.

Ice crystals laced the upper boughs. Once they were descending again, the path was dry and the sky less cumbersome.

There was a distant sound from up above that made Phoebee stiffen. Polly felt it, and asked, "Was that a panther? It sounded like a woman screaming."

"It think so, but it sounded far off."

Amos' ears pricked forward, then back, and he began to trot.

"Let's sing us a song. That'll scare ever'thang off this mountain!"

She began in a strong voice,

*Oh, the cuckoo she's a pretty bird*
*She warbles as she flies*
*She don't never holler cuckoo'*
*Til the fourth day of July*

Polly joined in.

*Gonna build me a log cabin*
*On the mountain so high*
*So that I can see Willie*
*As he goes walkin by*

As smoke from the Winder's chimney became visible against the gray sky, Amos trotted toward the barn, ignoring Phoebee's pull on the reins. Jamie and Kurt ran out to meet them, frowning with concern.

Kurt reached up to help Polly, then Phoebee, down. "We was about to come look for you girls. What were you thinkin', ridin' up there in this weather?"

"It was fine when we left, brother. Hold me up, my legs are plumb numb!"

"Me too!" Polly declared.

Kurt picked up one and Jamie the other, carrying the women over their shoulders and into the house. Phoebee didn't complain this time.

Finley laughed to see his sister and niece come through the door, bottoms up.

"Lordy, you give us a scare!" Welda cried. "Here, let me git you some hot coffee."

The boys plunked them down on kitchen chairs and sat to have a cup of their own.

Granny reached over to stroke the blanket Phoebee was wearing, and asked, "She give you these?"

"Yes ma'am," Polly answered. "Her mamma and grandmamma made them. Said we should have them, since we're kin. We'd have frozen to death without these blankets, the weather changed so quickly."

"Let's get them to drying, I'll fetch you somethin' else."

Welda stretched the heavy wool over chair backs in front of the fireplace.

Granny brought back a couple of quilts to drape over Phoebee and Polly's shoulders.

"Welda and me made these last year," she said with pride. "You might as well take them home with you, too."

The following day, Sarah honked her horn as she came up the drive. Phoebee grabbed her shawl and went out to meet her.

"Come on inside, it's a cold one today."

The family greeted their new friend as she came in, receiving hugs from all.

"Can you sit a spell?" Welda brought over a cup of coffee. "Tell us how things went with your folks."

Sarah accepted the hot drink and took a sip, then sighed.

"My mamma is never going to be happy that I'm not coming back to Virgina. She wants me to get married, live near her, and give her more grandchildren to spoil."

Looking at Phoebee and Polly, she said, "I think she'd settle for me marrying Rusty if it meant I'd go back."

"Who's Rusty?" Jamie asked.

Polly grinned. "Just the handsomest banjo player in the world. Her old beau."

"He was never my beau!" Sarah declared. "Just a friend."

"Not to hear him tell it," Phoebee replied.

"Well, it doesn't matter. It's not happening. I like my life on the farm with you all. I like being a teacher too, which, as Polly and I know, I could not be if I was married."

Polly announced, "Speaking of getting married, did I tell y'all I'm going to be the town librarian after Ezra and I get hitched?"

Congratulations went round and the family promised to come for her wedding in August.

"So, your mamma's settled then, with your brother and his family?" Phoebee asked.

"Yes, and the house has sold. We moved all her things into his home. I'm sure my sister-in-law feels crowded out, but she doesn't complain. Bless her heart."

A chorus of 'Bless her heart' went round and everyone laughed.

The three women soon took their leave of the Winder family, with promises of seeing them again in the summer.

As the auto rolled out the drive and onto the road, Polly said dreamily, "When we get to the hotel, I'm getting a hot bath!"

"Me too!" Phoebee and Sarah cried.

"I ain't felt warm since we got off that mountain yesterday!"

"Ain't, Phoebee?"

"Oh, Lord. I knew I was goin' to have to learn how to talk all over again!"

# Chapter 52

Ezra was pacing in front of the house when the Pierce Arrow pulled into the yard.

Polly hopped out and flung her arms around his neck.

He picked her up, declaring, "I hope you don't never go off like that agin'! I missed you so much."

Sarah looked as if she was about to comment on his grammar, but Phoebee gave her a look.

"Not now, woman! That's love talkin'."

Sarah rolled her eyes, but closed her mouth.

The Silar family came up the hill to welcome them back.

Omie gave each a hug and said, "You must be worn out. Will you come to supper after you have a rest and tell us all about the trip?"

Phoebee sighed and nodded. "We surely will. It's so good to see y'all!"

Grace tugged on Polly's skirts and said, "Me and Georgia Rose made y'all a card!"

In her small hands she held a lovely drawing of the farm; chickens, goats, and as many of the family as could be fitted onto the paper. 'Welcome Home' was printed in colorful letters across the top.

Polly picked the little girl up and declared, "That's the most beautiful thing I've ever seen, you two. Look Ezra, that's you!"

Gracie laughed, "It is not! That's a goat!"

Emmie and Bitsy came to visit the following Sunday.

"I can't believe it!" Bitsy grabbed Polly's hands. "When you marry Ezra, we'll be related, right? Doesn't matter, we're already family. This will just make it official!"

Emmie embraced Polly, holding her close for a long moment. "We are so happy for the two of you." She stepped back, looking into Polly's eyes. "You will let us make your dress, yes?"

"Really?" Polly looked at her mamma. "Did you hear that? Oh, thank you, thank you both so much!"

Omie came out on Phoebee's porch and said, "Are y'all gonna stand out here in the cold all day? Get in here, we have wedding plans to talk about!"

"That's my cue to leave," Ezra said. He picked Polly up and kissed her soundly. Then, he put her down and gave his aunt and cousin a peck on the cheek. "Have fun."

Phoebee handed him a piece of cake wrapped in a napkin before he headed for home.

Once all were settled at the kitchen table with coffee and cake, Emmie asked, "Do you know when and where you'd like to be married? Bitsy and I will help in any way we can."

Polly put her hand on Phoebee's, "We would like to have it right here in the back yard, in Grandmamma Kate's garden. Maybe in the summer when her roses are blooming?"

Omie's eyes filled with tears. "That would have made her so happy, Pollywog. The arch where her Lady Banks are would be a perfect spot. She was so proud of those."

Emmie smiled. "So, June or July? The Mr. Lincolns will be lovely then, as well."

"We're thinkin' August might be better, after the tobacco harvest and all."

As the day passed, the sky turned from pale gray to a bruised color. Emmie looked at Bitsy with concern.

"Maybe we should head back, hon. Looks like a storm coming."

"I suppose we should," Bitsy replied. "I hate to go, though, this has been so exciting!"

Emmie asked, "Why don't you come back to Savannah with us, Polly? We can talk about your wedding dress there."

"Let me go pack a few things."

Phoebee raised her eyebrows as the girl hurried off to her bedroom. "Didn't take much convincin' did she?"

"Would you like to come with us too?"

"Naw, Emmie. I think my girl needs to feel her wings a bit. I know y'all will take good care of her like you did me. Speakin' of, I could wear that dress you made me when I brought Polly to Savannah. Lord, she was just a mite then."

"Aunt Phoebee, that dress is out of style! You can't be seen in that for her wedding!"

"Well, I haven't had reason to wear it since. Seems like a durn shame for it to hang in the closet 'til I'm buried in it!"

"Let me take it with me," Emmie offered. "I'll see if I can rework it into something more fashionable."

"That's me," Phoebee replied. "Fash'nable."

Ezra returned with Georgia Rose and Grace, saying "They ate my cake, Aunt Phoebee!"

Grace shouted, "Yeah, and we want more!"

Georgia Rose chattered on to Bitsy about the wedding. When Polly returned to the kitchen, Emmie asked if she had an idea of what she would like her wedding gown to look like.

"I think it ought to have feathers!" Grace declared. "Mamma has a white tom turkey we could get some from."

Ezra looked at Georgia Rose and winked, "How about some squirrel tails? I hear they got some white squirrels in North Carolina. I could make a special trip, and..."

Emmie stood and offered her arm to Polly. "Let's go to Savannah, shall we?"

Polly accepted and said, "We shall."

Bitsy grinned, then joined them. The three women lifted their chins high as they strode out the door and down the steps. Ezra called out, "Best hope it don't rain or y'all will drown like turkeys!"

# 1939

## JUNE 22

"Mamma, you look tired. Why don't you go back to bed for a while? I'll make breakfast and call you when it's ready."

Phoebee smiled at Polly and shook her head.

"Even if I wanted to, I couldn't sleep. I'm just like the chickens, up with the sun. Don't even need that old rooster to wake me up. Shoot, that bird crows all the day and half the night anyhow. Maybe he needs to be dinner today."

"Well, at least sit and let me bring you some coffee."

Polly returned with her mamma's favorite old chipped mug and set it on the table.

"There, two sugars and lots of cream, just the way you like it."

Phoebee inhaled the strong, rich scent and took a grateful swallow.

"When you reckon Ezra will be able to get back to workin' on the house down there? I don't know why you young'uns think me and Sarah need a new kitchen. Seems like I been cookin' just fine on that old stove all these years."

"Gas is easier to use, Mamma. No more chopping wood and having to get the fire just right to cook. All you have to do is turn the knob and *poof*, ready to go."

"Yeah, *poof* is likely what'll happen to the whole house when I get ahold of that new *range*, as you call it. Silly name."

Polly rolled her eyes. "Stop complaining and just let us do this for you and Sarah! You deserve it. With Sarah gone, this is the perfect time."

Phoebee patted her daughter's hand.

"I don't mean to sound ungrateful, sugar. I just feel in the way here with you and Ezra."

"This used to be your house, Mamma. There's always a place for you here when you need it. We appreciate you and Omie giving it to us when we got married." Polly sighed. "I'm just sorry we haven't been able to fill it with a new generation of Silars."

"Don't you give up, darlin'. Miracles do happen."

Picking up her own coffee cup, Polly took a sip. "Sometimes the library makes me feel like I have dozens of children."

"And they're lucky to have you." Phoebee turned toward the window. "Look, ain't that Ada's boys at the well?"

"Oh Lord!" Polly went out to stop them from pushing back the cover.

Phoebee laughed to herself. "Likely they'd of both climbed down in there. Scallywags."

Shortly, Ada Kate could be heard coming up the road, calling, "Jacob! Cyrus! Where are you? Breakfast is ready."

Omie walked out on her porch, grinning. "Lost the little hellions again?"

"Oh, Mamma, sometimes I wish I could put them back where they came from!"

"You don't mean that," Omie chided.

Ada Kate walked up onto the porch.

"No, I don't. Not after all it took to get them here. They are a challenge though, aren't they? There they are!"

The boys came running down the hill. Polly waved from the old well.

Ada Kate waved back and gave her mamma a sad smile.

"I pray Ezra and Polly can have hellions of their own someday."

"Me too, honey. I keep hoping Grace will come to them with a message from a little one."

"She certainly gave us hope. Maybe that's what you should have named her, Mamma. Hope."

# Chapter 53

## 1931

Omie hummed to herself as she sat at the table with a second cup of coffee. The house was empty, a rare occurance, and she was drinking in the quiet as the sun rose higher in its heaven.

The telephone rang twice and she jumped, then hurried to answer.

"Hey, sister," Emmie greeted before Omie could announce, 'Silar family, Omie speaking.'

"How'd you know I would pick up?"

"You're the only one home this time of day."

Omie laughed. "This dad gum thing still startles me every time."

"I'm just calling to check on Ada Kate. I know she would just say 'I'm fine' if I asked her, but how is she really?"

"Honestly Emmie, everything seems to be going well since the beginning of January. No more nausea and she's stronger. Silly girl thinks it'll jinx things if I check her over again."

Emmie was quiet for a moment, making Omie wonder why she wasn't gladdened by this news.

"Caleb just came in the door, hon. I think he wants to talk to you too."

Omie could hear muffled conversation, as if Emmie had a hand over the receiver.

"Hello," Caleb said warmly. "How are you?"

"Good. I'm good. Is there something going on? Emmie sounded odd."

"I asked her to call you today. I've been doing some research on monozy-gotic, that is to say, identical twins. There's a good chance that the reason Ada Kate is feeling better after having unusual symptoms is because one of the fetuses has died. I know this is hard to hear, Omie, but this is probably for the best. Mother and babies can all be at risk if both fetuses go to full term when one is distressed."

Omie sat down heavily. "Oh no, Caleb. Are you pretty sure this is the case?"

"I'll have to examine her again, of course. I'm pretty certain of what we'll find, though."

"When can you come?"

He replied, "I'll call you as soon as I can clear a day. But very soon, I promise. You might want to prepare Ada and James first."

Emmie's voice came through the phone then, sounding very far away.

"I am so sorry, Omie. Shall I come now? Are you going to tell her today?"

Omie tried to focus. "I need to think about this, Em. I'll let you know."

"All right. Love you."

"You too. Bye."

After she'd hung up, Omie stared at the phone as if it were some strange creature. She put on her coat and walked out into the fields. The grasses crunched beneath her feet. Decomposing leaves from the old live oaks in the cemetery did the same.

*I know death is part of life, Lord. But how do you tell a young mother that she's carrying a dead child in her womb.*

A damp wind drove the cold deeper into her bones, but she didn't care. It was a welcome distraction from the chill in her spirit. Other women she'd ministered to had to carry a child to term that had died, it was not that uncommon. But this was her Ada Kate, her precious daughter, who gave and gave to everyone. Having one of these babies taken from her was hard to reconcile.

Eventually, the cold drove her toward Ada and James house where smoke from the chimney promised warmth.

"Mamma! What are you doing out there? Come in."

Ada took Omie's icy hands between her own and rubbed them until color returned.

James brought a steaming cup of coffee to the table. Omie sat and took a deep drink before removing her coat. Tess climbed into her lap, holding her doll up to be admired.

"Darlin', I just had a call from Caleb and Emmie."

"What?" Ada's brow furrowed. "Are they all right? The children?"

"They're all fine, no worries." Omie wrapped her hands around her mug and took another sip. "He's been doing some studying about twins, and wanted to know how you've been lately."

Ada smiled. "Did you tell him how much better I feel?"

"Yes, I did. Believe it or not, that actually gave him some concern."

James and Ada looked at each other and he asked, "Why would that be a bad thing?"

"He says when there are more extreme symptoms early in the pregnancy, like your nausea and fatigue, it can be a sign that one of the babies is not getting as much blood as the other. The mother's body might let that one die in order for the other to be born healthy. If not, the birth can be dangerous to both babies and the mother."

Ada looked stunned. James tried to take her in his arms, but she pulled away.

"Do you mean one of my babies is already dead? How can God let that happen?"

Omie felt tears running down her cheeks. "Ada, you know these things happen. It's not a punishment."

"Well Mamma, it sure feels like one. And I have done nothing to be punished for! What am I supposed to do?"

"Caleb wants to come check you. He's at his clinic right now trying to clear his appointments. He'll call this evening and I'll let you know."

Omie handed Tess to James. "We don't know for sure yet, Ada. And if it's true, we'll get through this."

Ada got up, went into the bedroom and slammed the door. James covered his eyes with one hand and rubbed Tess' back with the other.

"She's been really testy lately, Mamma Silar. Not herself."

"I understand, James. Let me take this girl home with me while you go to your wife." She put a hand on his shoulder. "Everything will be all right down the road. It'll be hard on both of you for a while, but your love will give you strength to endure the loss."

Omie put Tess' coat on and held her small hand. "Let's go wait for Grace to get home from school, OK? You can draw her a picture and surprise her."

Tess turned to look at her daddy before they went out the door. "Why daddy crying?"

"Sometimes we just need to cry, baby girl. Even boys do."

After supper, Omie asked Grace to take Tess into her room and play. The child asked no questions, just took Tess' little hand in her own small one and led her out of the room.

Omie relayed the news to the rest of the family.

"Caleb should be calling soon to say when he can come check on Ada. She's going to need all our prayers and love to get through this. Probably won't want to talk about the baby, but just be there for her."

Nate stood and placed his hat on his head. "I best go feed the animals."

Omie knew he preferred to be alone with his emotions, and let him go.

Georgia Rose began to cry. "What else can we do, Mamma?"

She put her arms around Georgia's shoulders. "Pray, darlin'. I will let you know if I think of anything."

Ezra sat with his elbows on his knees, head hanging.

"I don't understand how this could happen to Ada. She's the best of us."

"There's no rhyme or reason to life sometimes, son. I wish there were. Would you mind going into town and telling Frank Thomas and Jewel? I don't really want to give them this news on the telephone."

He nodded, understanding that other well-meaning ears might be listening on the party line, and news like this would travel quickly through the community.

"I'll take Polly with me. Want me to send Phoebee and Sarah down here?"

"Yes, please."

The two women hurried down the hill to Omie's house, knowing there was bad news to be told. They took off their coats and hung them up, then sat at the table.

"One of the babies has passed, hasn't it?" Sarah asked softly.

Omie sat and put her head in her hands. She began to sob. Phoebee scooted closer and began rubbing Omie's back.

Sarah reached across the table to take Georgia's hand, and they wept in silence.

When the call came from Savannah, Omie listened and said, "Thank you, Caleb."

She turned to the others. "He's coming tomorrow. He and Emmie. At least we'll know for certain. I need to walk down and tell them."

Georgia Rose walked with her in silence, carrying Tess. James answered their knock and said, "She's still in bed. I'm trying to get her to eat something."

Tess reached out to him and he hugged her close.

"We won't stay," Omie said. "I just wanted to let you know that Caleb will be here by noon tomorrow."

"Thank you," he replied. "Goodnight."

"Goodnight." Omie and Georgia Rose headed home through the chilly darkness.

Early next morning, Emmie and Caleb stopped to pick up Omie, and the three of them rode down the drive to Ada and James house. Tess and James stood in the doorway, motioning them to come in. He nodded toward the bedroom. His eyes were red, with dark circles beneath.

"Hi, little one," Emmie crooned at Tess. "Is that a new dolly?"

She motioned for Omie and Caleb to follow James. "I'll stay here," she whispered.

Ada Kate was sitting up in bed, hair disheveled, a look of resignation about her.

"Hello, my dear," Caleb said softly. He sat on the bed and took her hand. They sat like that for a few moments, Ada looking forlornly into his eyes.

"Let's just see, all right?" he asked. She nodded, then slid down and pushed the quilts back.

Caleb repeated what he'd done before, listening and pausing, then listening again.

When he looked up, Ada saw the truth in his eyes. She began to sob, and Caleb bent down to kiss her forehead, then rose to let Omie cradle her daughter in her arms.

James sat on Ada's other side, stroking her hair as tears ran down his stricken face.

As the bedroom door opened, Emmie took one look at Caleb's face and rose to embrace him. Tess got up from the floor and wrapped her little arms around their legs as well.

He picked the child up and said, "Would you kindly introduce me to your new doll?"

Emmie went into the bedroom and sat beside Omie. All she knew to do was be a witness to their grief, to the heartache this beloved niece and her husband would suffer for some time to come.

As February arrived, Ada was filled with both joy and dread. In Caleb's subsequent visits, he recommended that she come to Savannah for the birth. Complications could arise with the expired fetus and soon it could be too dangerous for her to travel.

When Ada moved into her nineth month, Emmie came to visit one day without Caleb.

"Please, honey. You can all stay with us for as long as you need to, before and after the birth," Emmie assured them. "It will lessen the stress of the situation."

James looked pleadingly into Ada's eyes. She realized then how worried he'd been.

*I've been selfish. This is hard for him and I haven't given enough thought to his feelings.*

She nodded.

As Emmie was leaving, she saw her sister driving up in the buggy with Grace and Georgia at her side.

"Well, hey," Omie called. "I picked the girls up from the bus stop. It's too cold to walk home. Can you come in for a few minutes?"

"Sure," Emmie said, and pulled the car over near the house.

Once inside, Omie asked, "Who would like hot cocoa?"

"Me!" Grace and Georgia shouted.

"Me too!" Emmie echoed.

They all wrapped their hands around the warm mugs. Omie laughed at Grace's chocolate mustache, then made one of her own. Emmie followed suit.

Georgia Rose brought out her sketch pad and began to draw them all as the Three Moustache-teers.

"So, what brings you here?" Omie asked her sister, knowing the visit was really for Ada.

"Caleb feels strongly that Ada Kate should come to Savannah and have the baby. Babies." She said softly. "There could be complications you couldn't deal with Omie, as knowledgeable as you are."

"I know," Omie replied. "It isn't me you need to convince. I've tried to talk to Ada about it, but she's determined to have this birth in her own home."

"Well, she's agreed now."

"Oh, thank goodness. When will she go?"

"Caleb will want to be with us on the drive. The sooner the better, so I told her and James we could come this weekend."

Grace looked from one to the other, then stated, "Mamma, I need to see Ada."

"You do, honey? Why?"

"I have a message for her. Can we go now?"

Emmie looked quizzically at Omie.

"Are you done with your cocoa, Gracie?"

"Yes, Mamma."

"Me too," Georgia added.

Omie raised her eyebrows at Emmie, and the four of them went out the door and got in the car.

Ada Kate answered their knock, looking surprised to see them.

"Grace has something she wants to tell you," Omie said.

James and Tess were drawing paper dolls when they all walked up to the table.

Georgia pointed to his, and remarked, "Those look like monkeys!"

"So," he answered. "I like monkeys."

Grace sat next to Ada Kate as the others took seats around the table.

"I have a message for you, Ada. It's from the baby."

Ada looked startled and stared at her mamma. Omie shook her head.

"He says he couldn't stay this time, but he'll come soon. He wanted his brother to be safe." The girl paused a moment, then spoke again. "He says, please don't be sad."

Ada put her hands over her mouth and gasped. James's face went white.

Grace looked at her mamma to see if she'd done something wrong.

Omie got up and moved to the little girl's side. Squatting down, she wrapped her in a hug. "It's OK, baby. You're such a good sister."

# Chapter 54

In the days following Caleb's pronouncement that one of their babies had passed, James and Ada Kate navigated the waters between grief and comfort. Grief at Caleb's news, comfort from Grace's message. Though for Ada, carrying a child inside her that she had felt move, had grown to love already, and now lost, the comfort was small.

James called his family from the Silar's phone as often as he could. His mamma's arthritis had become too painful for her to travel even as far as the farm anymore.

He was afraid to leave Ada Kate for long, but when supplies ran low, he made a trip to town and stopped in to visit. Seeing the strain on James' face, his mamma motioned him to a chair and asked about the babies. He gave her the sad news that one had died.

"Oh son, I am so sorry to hear that. Ada must be heartbroken. I lost my first child. Many women do, I reckon, but to carry that little one inside you, knowing..."

James began to sob, and she cupped his face between her misshapen hands.

"I'm sorry I can't be there for you both. Please give Ada my love. All of us are keeping her in our prayers. You too."

He took a shuddering breath and tried to regain his composure.

"I know, Mamma."

"Your daddy and brothers are worried for you too. Let us know if there's anything we can do."

He took her hands in his and kissed them. "I will."

They talked then of family news until he became concerned about the time.

"I'd best get back. Give everyone my love, will you? And tell them..."

"Yes. Bless you, honey. Say hello to the Silars for us too."

On the ride back home, he pondered Grace's message again. It was not something he felt he could share with his family. James wasn't so much comforted by it as confused. How could a child never having come into this world reach out to them? Ada Kate seemed to accept this without question. He didn't want to express his doubts though, and cause her to backslide into the torrents of sorrow that had rocked them both of late.

*Maybe Ezra can shed some light. I do believe he sees ghosts, strange as that is.*

He found Ezra in the barnyard knocking ice out of the animal's troughs and water pans.

"Well, hey James. Got cabin fever?"

He got a good look at James' troubled face and set down his hammer.

"Wanna come in the house? Reckon there's some coffee and biscuits left."

"No, Ezra. I got somethin' troubling my mind I'd rather talk about just between us. Maybe you can help me understand."

"Let's sit in the barn at least, get out of this wind."

When both were settled on bales of hay, Ezra quietly waited for James to speak.

"You know, I appreciate little Gracie tellin' us what she did. But...the baby who died, is he a ghost now? How is that possible, when he never was a person?"

Ezra looked out the door of the barn for a few moments, gathering his thoughts.

"I cain't say for certain, James. They's many things we don't know, that's for sure." He sighed and rubbed his hands together for warmth, then stuck them in his pockets. "Could be we're somewheres before we come here. Maybe not like we are now, but spirits floatin' around, lookin' to be born."

James nodded and asked, "Does that mean heaven is a place we come from and go back to?"

"I don't think we're meant to understand it all. Have faith, brother. Gracie is a child. I'm not seein' how anything but good comes from her kind of *Knowin'*." Ezra squeezed James' shoulder and stood. "Reckon I'm done out here. Sure you don't want to come inside and warm up?"

"Thanks, but I think I'll just sit here a minute. I 'preciate you listening."

"Anytime," Ezra said.

James kept himself busy, needing a distraction from worry. Winter was at its peak and there was little that needed doing, so he and Ezra found themselves making fires out in the field, with the excuse of cleaning up piles of brush. Mostly, Ezra wanted to be available for James in any way he could. They would talk about future plans for the farm or sometimes just sit in companionable silence, enjoying the fire's warmth.

Ada appreciated having time alone, knowing she and James each had their own way of dealing with troubles. Omie came each day to fetch Tess, giving Ada some quiet time to think.

Hard as she tried, the young mother failed to find a way to accept this loss. One morning, she just could not get out of bed. James took Tess with him to the fields and let Ada sleep in. A voice pulled her from the deep waters of dreams. She opened her eyes, looking around to see who had been calling her name.

*Ada Kate. You need to get up now.*

She whispered, "Grandmamma?"

Ada had been surrounded all her life by others who could communicate with spirits. This was the first time she experienced the connection though. Secretly, she had felt there was something about herself that was unworthy.

*Listen to me, darlin'. I lost two babies, and I know this is hard. But there's a living child inside you who's lost someone too. You need to think about him, comfort him. He entered the world alongside his brother, and now he's alone. You're all he knows.*

"Oh, Gramma Kate, I miss you so. I don't know what to do."

She could feel warmth all around her now. There was a scent of roses, soft and soothing.

*Yes, child, you do. Ada, you have more than just my name. You have my strength and the strength of all the women who came before you. Get up now. Talk to your son. Let him know you love him, can't wait to hold him. His brother will be along directly. Remember, God's time is not our time.*

Ada cradled her arms around the tiny body inside her and whispered, "I do love you little one. I love you so much."

As Kate's presence began to fade, Ada felt a comfort from more than just her grandmamma's words. It was the knowledge that she was not expected to lay down this grief, but that she would not have to carry it alone.

She rose and made the bed with a determined hand, then walked into the kitchen. Out the window, she saw Ezra and James moving about in the field. There was a sense that they were not alone either. The spirits of the men who had tended this land, her daddy and Mr. Rhymes, seemed to shimmer around them.

One morning, the temperature turned mild, carrying a whisper of spring on the breeze. Omie sat on the back porch steps, face to the sun.

*The air smells like...hope. Is that odd, Lord? I thank you for this gift. I pray my girl receives it too.*

There was a light around Ada Kate recently that had been missing for some time. She'd gained weight and lost the gauntness in her face. Omie had tried to find a balance between helping the couple cope and not being too intrusive. She'd put her faith in the intuition that had always been her trusted companion. Something seemed to be helping, though what, was uncertain.

*Hope and Faith. Are they both sides of the same coin?*

Omie decided to take advantage of this warm spell to air out the house and wash clothes. She stood and brushed off her skirts.

*Maybe I can do some for James and Ada too.*

Ada Kate was standing on her porch with a hand on her belly, looking out in the distance, as if listening to something only she could hear.

"Morning, sweetie. I wondered if you would like for me to put a few of your things in the washpot with ours. The weather is being less ornery today, maybe I can get the laundry done before it rains again."

Ada seemed to come back from some far away place as she smiled gently at her mamma.

"That would be a big help. It's hard to work around this belly. I can't even pick up little missy here anymore. James has had to take on all my chores, including laundry, and he does his best, but..."

"Bless his heart," Omie said with a grin.

Ada laughed, "Bless his heart."

They gathered wash into a basket. Tess contributed her dolly's dress and apron. Omie headed for home where Nate had filled the big iron pot and built a fire under it before heading to town. Looking back, she saw her girl at the window, once again gazing out, a hand over the baby.

Phoebee walked down the hill, carrying a towel-draped parcel. She stopped to help Omie stir the clothes. "Reckon Ada would mind if I bring her a honey cake?"

Omie laughed and said, "Mind? I think she might eat the whole thing before James gets home!"

"She's doin' better then?"

"Phoebee, I think she's turned a corner. Thank the Lord."

"Thank the Lord for sending Grace."

"That's true. It troubled me some for Grace to have this gift so young, but it doesn't seem to trouble her."

"Want me to cut you off a slice before I head down?"

"Don't mind if you do!" Omie replied. "Washing is tiresome work on this old body."

"Old body." Phoebee rolled her eyes. "You can say that when you're shriveled up like Granny Winder. Looks like she sucked on a green persimmon. But you ain't there yet."

Emmie and Caleb's car pulled into the yard just then. As the two opened their doors, Phoebee called, "Well, howdy! What a nice surprise! Y'all are just in time for some honey cake and coffee."

"Smelled it all the way from Savannah!" Caleb declared.

Omie led them to the house, where she put on a fresh pot of coffee.

"What brings y'all out today?"

Emmie sat and replied, "He had a light day at the clinic and the weather is so nice for a change, I suggested we take a ride."

"Then I smelled that cake!" Caleb declared.

Phoebee grinned. "That means you get a extra big slice!"

"I want to check on Ada Kate, as well."

Omie put a mug of coffee in front of him and sat.

"She seems to be doing much better, y'all. There's something passing between her and the baby. Something calming. She doesn't speak of it, and I haven't asked. I'm just thankful."

"I hope they are still willing to come to Savannah to have the baby," Emmie said. "Babies?" She looked at Caleb.

"We won't know what happens until she gives birth." He didn't want to go into details about what might remain of the deceased child.

Phoebee looked a bit green. "I'm goin' to take the rest of this to Ada." She wrapped the remaining cake in the towel and hurried out the door.

Omie raised her eyebrows, watching Phoebee's retreat. "Not a conversation for the dinner table, I guess."

"Shall we walk to Ada's?" Emmie asked. "I feel like I've been closed up inside for months now. What a winter it's been!"

Omie looked at her sister. "Maybe the bugs won't be so bad this year, though. A cold winter is sometimes a farmer's friend."

"True." Emmie looked a little sheepish. "I suppose I forget sometimes how important the weather is for crops."

Ada Kate was waving from the porch for them to come in.

"Seems like a good sign," Caleb remarked.

Everyone took a seat in James and Ada's comfortable little house. A small fire was going in the fireplace, and Tess was sitting on a braided rug with her doll.

"Tess, come sit in my lap and show me your dolly," Emmie said. She turned to the others. "It's been so long since Bitsy was this small."

Caleb had a soft smile on his face, thinking of his daughter. "Maybe you should bring her dolls to Tess."

"I'm not sure she'd let them go," Emmie replied. "She acts like childish things don't matter. But I see her whispering to them sometimes when she doesn't know I'm nearby."

James came through the back door with a smile.

"Hey y'all! What a purty day. Need a break from the big city?"

"We did," Emmie answered.

After catching up on recent events, Caleb brought up the subject of Ada's due date.

"The birth date is only a week away. It's not too soon to come to Savannah and prepare for it, you two. I would prefer to have you there in case this child presents early."

Ada looked at James. "All right, Uncle Caleb."

"We'll give you a couple of days to get ready, then we'll come for you."

Emmie braided Tess' hair and gave her a hug. "We've already got your room ready, with a bed just for Tess." She kissed the girl's soft cheek.

"Do you have a bed for my dolly?"

"I believe Bitsy's dolls would loan her one, don't you think, Caleb?"

"Oh, certainly," he answered. "They are very hospitable dolls."

"Hospital dolls?" Tess looked around as everyone laughed.

# Chapter 55

Bartie hung up the telephone and looked at Shad, worry creasing her face. Emmie had called with news of James and Ada Kate's pending arrival in Savannah. She'd explained the situation and hoped Bartie might come to be with her sister for the birth.

Tears streamed down Bartie's cheeks.

"Mamma has been so angry with me for not going home when Ada needs me. It's been tearing me apart!"

"I know it has, darlin'."

Shad wondered why his mother-in-law couldn't see the depth of damage Bartie's daddy had done. When they'd gotten to know each other well, Bartie confided that she'd truly feared for her life, as the one man she loved and trusted most in the world, beat her. It angered Shad that her own father had stolen a piece of his daughter's innocence and replaced it with a nameless fear that trembled inside her still.

He would have liked to meet this man, to dole out a similar punishment, but Bartie would not want that. Shad walked over and took her in his arms. Lilly hugged her mamma's legs and began to cry as well.

"Why are you crying, baby girl?" Shad asked.

"Oh, honey." Bartie bent down to pick her up. Lilly put her small hands on the sides of her mamma's face.

"I'm alright. I just miss my sister, is all. I think we need to go see her in Savannah soon. Would you like that? You can see your cousin Tess."

She managed a smile and danced Lilly around the small room.

"You're a big girl now, aren't you?"

Lilly nodded.

"Yes, you are!"

Bartie put a hand to Shad's face. "Do you think you can get away too? Would the school let you take a leave?"

"I'll try. With this short notice, I may not be able to find a substitute who teaches jazz piano. Let me ask around."

He picked his daughter up and put her on his back.

She began to giggle. "Horthey!"

Later, when Lilly was asleep, Bartie told Shad the complications surrounding Ada's upcoming delivery.

He pulled her onto his lap. "I can't begin to imagine what she and James have been through. Go right away, you and Lilly. Be waiting for her when she arrives."

"Sure you'll be all fine without us?"

"I'll miss you both, but as you can see, I'm a big boy. Frank Thomas and Jewel will be back in the next few days. He called to say they've finished recording their record in Atlanta. I'll let them know the situation when they stop by."

Shad took them to the train station the following morning. Lilly was bundled up in a red wool coat, holding her doll. Emmie had sent the coat, along with a doll-sized one to match, for Christmas. Bartie carried a small suitcase in one hand and a carpet bag in the other.

"Are you sure you have enough?" Shad asked.

"I can borrow clothes from Emmie. I'd rather Lilly has all that she needs."

He kissed them both as the conductor called everyone to board.

"Let me know how things are, Bartie. I'll come if I can."

As the train pulled away, she blew a kiss to Shad and got Lilly settled in the seat beside her. Occupied with her doll, Lilly was quiet, letting her mamma sink into her thoughts. Looking out the window, Bartie seemed to see her sister's face rather than the frosty countryside. Scenes from their days as young girls, catching snowflakes on their tongues, came to mind.

They'd had a rich childhood on the farm. Much finer than the lives of the Atlanta wealthy could offer, she thought. They'd had freedom. Freedom to roam the fields and woods, freedom to find their place in the natural world around them. She missed that life.

The trip passed in a blur of memories until the whistle blew and a porter announced, "Savannah!"

When their train pulled into the station, Lilly called, "Em!"

On the platform, looking as if she had stepped out of the pages of Vogue magazine, Emmie smiled and waved at them. Thomas stood nearby, ready to collect their things and drive them home.

"Is that all you've brought?" she asked, as Thomas took their suitcase and bag.

"I just wanted to get here. These are mostly Lilly's. I figured I could borrow some dresses from you?"

"Course you can." Emmie stopped walking and turned to look at her niece. "I'm so glad you're here. Come to me, little one."

Lilly reached out and put her arms around Emmie's neck.

Bartie could barely speak the words caught in her throat. "Thank you for calling me. It's been so hard…"

At that, she began to weep. Lilly looked over, concerned.

"Enough of that, let's get you two home to a warm fire and some hot cocoa. Sound good?"

Bartie took a deep breath and wiped her eyes. "It sure does. Right, baby?"

Relieved that all was well, Lilly nodded.

In the back seat of the car, Lilly sat on Emmie's lap with her small face pressed to the window. Bartie asked for more details about Ada's condition, and Emmie caught her up as best she could.

"How are you feeling about seeing your mamma?"

Bartie took a deep breath. "I hope by arriving first I'll have time to get my courage up to face her."

Emmie put a hand on Bartie's arm and said, "Try not to think about anything but Ada Kate. You and my sister will work things out. I'll make sure of it, trust me."

Thomas let them out in front of the Decker house.

"I'll take your bags 'round to the Campbell's, Miss Bartie."

"Thank you, Thomas."

Emmie put a hand on Bartie's as they walked up onto the porch and said, "I wish we had another room for you here, Hon. But you'll be close by. I expect Elizabeth and Daniel will join us shortly for lunch. They're looking forward to seeing you."

"That's fine, Aunt Emmie. I can't wait to hear about their travels in Europe."

Maizie came out of the kitchen and flung her arms around Bartie's neck.

"It's been so long!"

"Too long," Bartie replied. "How are you, Maizie?"

"Busy as a bee, now I have two families to feed again!"

It was obvious she was happy to have the Campbells home.

"Y'all come sit. I have something special for Miss Lilly here."

Lilly held her doll up for inspection.

"Oh, yes! There's something extra special for her, too."

The doorbell rang and Emmie went to welcome the Campbells.

"Something smells wonderful!" Daniel exclaimed.

After hellos and hugs went round, they all sat at the dining room table. Maizie served them a hearty chicken stew with hot cornbread.

"This'll warm y'all up. I swear, I don't think I can wait for spring to show its face. Miss Lilly, I got some blackberry cobbler comin' out of the oven for dessert."

"Do we get some too?" Caleb asked.

"Better ask Miss Lilly, here. It's her cobbler."

Lilly looked up from her doll, who was perched in front of Bitsy's old doll-sized tea set, and nodded.

After the lunch dishes were cleared, the Campbells told captivating tales of their travels.

Bartie shook her head in wonder. "I'm surprised you came back at all!"

Elizabeth smiled. "Well, it's true what they say. There is no place like home."

Eventually, talk came round to Ada's situation.

"Dr. Campbell here has agreed to assist with the delivery," Caleb told them.

The older man nodded. "I'm happy to help. Can't hurt to have two sets of hands at the ready."

Worry creased Bartie's forehead.

"Do you think she and the baby might be in danger?"

Dr. Campbell said, "This is an unusual situation. But rest assured, we'll do everything we can to make sure things go well. The hospital has a ward for newborn care, which is in our favor."

"Also," Caleb announced, "Daniel has pulled some strings and gotten the use of an ambulance to transport Ada to Savannah. We haven't informed the family yet." He grinned. "Thought we'd surprise them."

Thomas had volunteered to drive the ambulance to the farm the next day. Emmie followed in their automobile, figuring Caleb would be inclined to ride with him.

The day was clear, the sky as blue as an indigo bunting. Emmie looked up, feeling her heart swell.

*This must be the color of hope. Surely an omen that all will be well.*

She could not allow herself to think otherwise. Ada Kate was born when Emmie was still a young seamstress at Elizabeth's shop in Savannah. She had been following her dream of a life very different from her sister's, but Omie's children were as dear to her as her own had become. Life without any of them was impossible to imagine.

As they drew nearer to the farm, a small flock of crows settled on Phoebee's barn roof in a raucous cluster. Emmie had never been certain if crows were a good sign or a warning, but she scowled at them just in case.

Thomas rang the ambulance bell as they turned down the driveway to the farm. Nate and Ezra stood outside the barn looking bewildered. Emmie imagined none of them had encountered an ambulance before, fortunately.

Nate shaded his eyes with his hand and muttered, "What in Sam Hill...?"

The men hurried over, shaking their heads as Thomas and Caleb emerged from the strange-looking vehicle, which had pulled up in front of James and Ada's house.

Ada waddled out onto the porch, and Caleb bowed, saying, "Your chariot has arrived, Madame."

James squinted at them. "Looks like a stagecoach."

"I'm not that big, Uncle Caleb!" Ada declared.

"Of course you're not," he replied. "Come look inside. It's one of the new ambulances the hospital has acquired. In the back is a bed and everything needed for emergencies, not that there will be any."

James offered his arm and they stepped off the porch. Thomas opened the rear doors so she could see in.

"It's like a travelin' hospital," Thomas said.

"Yes, that's the point. Many lives are saved now because of these," Caleb told them.

Ada Kate looked at the family all gathered around her.

"Honey," Emmie said, "we only want you to be comfortable. We're not worried."

Meanwhile, Grace had climbed in the driver's seat and rang the bell as she whooped.

"I'm gonna ride up front!"

James loaded their things into the boot of the auto. Omie brought out her bag as well. Georgia Rose placed hers in with the others and Grace plopped another on top.

Polly and Phoebee walked up. "We're packed. Sarah's on the way down with her car in case y'all need more room."

"Is everybody going?" Ada Kate asked in astonishment.

Omie smiled at her and said, "Well, you were sad not to have this little one at home with all the family present. So, everyone decided to go with you."

Ada Kate began to cry, and everyone tried to comfort her at once.

Nate elbowed his way through. "Y'all give her some room, would ya?"

He took her hands in his. "Ezra and me got to stay and tend the farm, darlin', or we'd be there too. You'll be on our minds ever' minute though."

She kissed his cheek and turned to her brother. "I love you both so much!"

Ezra patted her shoulder. "Love you too, sis."

James shook hands with the men, then moved toward the ambulance with Ada.

"Wait!" she cried.

They all looked at her in alarm.

"I have to use the privy one more time."

The mood shifted from one of concern to relieved merriment. When Ada Kate returned, Caleb and James each offered an arm to help her into the back of the ambulance. As she struggled up, Georgia Rose put her hands on Ada's backside and pushed.

"Georgia!"

"Sorry sis, just tryin' to help."

Omie covered her mouth to suppress a giggle, but it did no good. As soon as she started laughing, everyone, including Ada, joined her.

There was only room for James and Caleb to ride in back with Ada, so Omie got in the front seat with Grace, holding Tess on her lap.

Georgia rode in Emmie's car, hoping to talk her aunt into a driving lesson on the way to Savannah.

Sarah's car pulled in behind the roadster. Polly and Phoebee chattered excitedly about being in the city again, and plans for the wedding. Bitsy was working on the wedding gown and asked if they could do a fitting while in Savannah. Ahead of them, the tall roof of the ambulance could be seen, earning stares from folks along the way. When farms and houses came into sight, Thomas allowed Gracie to ring the bell. Startled cows took off across the pastures, chickens ran for cover and coon dogs bayed.

In the back of the ambulance, James held Ada's hand as she rested. Grace's shenanigans made the trip go quickly, so that there was little time to work up a store of worry again.

Thomas pulled up in front of the Decker's house and got out to assist as the men lowered Ada to the street.

Bartie emerged and flew down the steps, laughing and crying as she worked her way around Ada's belly for a hug. The two sisters embraced a long time, sniffling and rocking back and forth.

Omie saw Lilly coming down the steps and swept the child up. "Hey, honey. I'm your grandmamma. Remember me?"

The little girl looked uncertain, but nodded anyway.

"You've grown so much! I hardly recognize you. Who is this here?"

Lilly held her doll up for introductions. "Lolly"

"Lolly and Lilly! That makes perfect sense. Pleased to meet you, ma'am." Omie set her down as Tess came shyly toward them.

"Tess hon, do you remember Lilly?"

Tess smiled around the fingers in her mouth. She held up her own doll for Lilly to see. Emmie helped the little girls up to the porch with their dolls, leaving Omie to face her daughters, who were still holding onto one another.

*They look just like the girls they once were.*

She couldn't hold on to her anger at Bartie and went to embrace them both.

"Hey, Mamma," Bartie said softly.

"Hey," Omie replied.

James walked up to them grinning, and cleared his throat.

"Can I get in on this?"

Bartie laughed and turned to give him a warm hug.

"How are you, James?"

"I'm fine. It's so good to see you again."

Emmie shooed them all inside. "Come in, come in. There's coffee, tea, and cocoa. Bitsy and the boys are waiting to say hello."

Even in winter, Savannah was a wealth of distractions as the days passed. Part of Ada's family stayed with the Deckers and part with the Campbells. Georgia Rose and Grace loved spending time at Emmie's shop, where Bitsy had them sewing doll clothes for Lilly and Tess.

Ada Kate stayed in bed as much as Omie could convince her to. James was obviously a bit lost among all these women, so Danny offered to give him a tour of the city.

"Why, thank you Danny. I never had the chance to visit Savannah, even though my daddy was conductor on a train that passed through here. Always wanted to see it."

Polly haunted the Savannah library, researching what would be required of her to become a librarian. Her enthusiasm impressed the staff, and she was offered an internship in the spring. After walking there with Polly each day, Phoebee returned to take up residence in the kitchen—both at the Campbells and the Deckers. She and Maizie carried on as they worked, cackling at each other's jokes. Often, everyone imagined, much of their humor was about the family.

"James, wake up! My water's broken."

Ada Kate was struggling to rise as he wiped the sleep from his eyes.

"Wait a minute, now! Let me get your mamma."

Omie heard their voices and ran to the room. *I guess a mamma is always listening out for her child in the night.*

She helped James get Ada to the bathroom.

"Sit baby, I'll get you some clean clothes. James, wake Emmie and Caleb."

The Deckers were already up and dressing for the trip to the hospital. When Omie had gotten her daughter changed and led her to the parlor, Ada began apologizing to Emmie for soaking the bedding.

"That is the last thing you need to be thinking about, darling. It's no trouble. How are you feeling?"

"All right, I think. No pains yet."

Caleb came into the room and asked her to recline on the sofa so he could listen to her belly. "The baby's heartbeat is strong. I asked Thomas to get the ambulance, Ada. We'll have you there and settled in no time."

James smiled down at his wife and brushed the hair from her face.

"I look a fright," she said.

"You look beautiful," he replied, and bent to kiss her.

When Thomas arrived, Omie, James and Caleb rode to the hospital with him. Emmie offered to bring the others as soon as they woke.

"The boys can get themselves to school. Call me if things move faster than anticipated, though," she instructed.

"I will," Caleb promised. "I've let Daniel know we're on our way."

Emmie tightened her robe as she watched them fade into the night.

*I know I'm not the most devoted of your flock, Lord. But I'm praying now. Please spare our Ada Kate and her baby boy. She's the best of us all.*

Knowing sleep would be hopeless, she made coffee and settled herself in her comfortable parlor chair. She busied herself with the booties she was knitting for the baby until the lamp was no longer needed. Watching as the sun came shining over the live oaks in Johnson Square, she saw Maizie and Phoebee walking up to the porch.

Maizie opened the door and greeted Emmie. "Mornin'! Just heard the news. Thought we better get some breakfast into this bunch, likely to be a long day. I'll send some biscuits and such with you to the hospital."

Phoebee spoke up, "Maybe I should stay here with the littluns and let y'all go."

Emmie knew the hospital was not a place where Phoebee was comfortable.

"Thank you so much, that would be a great help. I imagine Georgia Rose will want to go, but Grace can stay to help entertain Lilly and Tess. I'll go to the Campbell's to pick up Bartie and the children and drop the younger girls back by here on our way to the hospital. Bitsy is going to mind the shop, but she can come home if you need her."

At the hospital, James could not sit still and his pacing was making Ada Kate irritable.

"Could you please go out to the lobby?" she begged.

"Sorry, hon. I'm just nervous, is all."

Omie smiled at him. "Tell you what, why don't you go out there and greet the others as they arrive. I promise to come get you when the baby starts coming."

Trying not to look too relieved, he nodded and kissed Ada.

After he was out the door, Ada whispered, "Thank you, Mamma."

Her labor began shortly thereafter. Caleb came into the room just as a contraction passed.

"How are you, Ada?" He sat on the edge of her bed.

"I'm starting to feel the pains. Not bad yet."

He looked at his pocket watch.

"It's only been six hours since your water broke. I'm going to make my rounds now, but let me know when they become more frequent. Looks like this little one is ready to come into the world!"

He smiled assuredly as he went out the door.

"Do you think that was a real smile or his doctor's smile?"

"I don't think Caleb would try to fool us if he was concerned. We know too much, and he knows that we do."

As family arrived, they were allowed in to see Ada, two at a time. Bartie stayed in the room though, claiming she was not budging until the doctors threw her out. Mid-afternoon, the door opened and Shad came in. Bartie jumped up and hugged him fiercely. When she stood back to look at him, he brushed the tears from her cheeks.

"Ada Kate, how are you? Mrs. Silar?"

Omie could not help but see the bright lines of love that joined them.

"I'm good, Shad. We're so glad you could come."

"Can I get you all anything?" he asked.

Omie gave him a tired smile. "I would love a cup of coffee, thank you."

"I know how you like it, Mamma. I'll go with him."

When they'd left, Ada smiled. "Thank you for being nice...Unh!" She groaned, then let out a deep breath as the contraction passed.

There was a knock, then Frank Thomas and Jewel stuck their heads into the room.

"Hey sis!"

"Oh my gosh, you two! I can't believe you're here!"

Jewel hugged her closely. "Of course we are!"

Frank Thomas was about to place a kiss on his sister's forehead, when another large contraction hit. As Ada let out a loud cry, he jumped back.

Omie murmured, "Deep breaths, honey. You know what to do. I think it's time."

A nurse came to check Ada's vital signs, then went to inform the doctors.

Shortly after, James returned. Dr. Campbell entered and smiled at everyone. He walked over to the bed and took Ada's hand.

"As soon as Caleb gets here, we'd like to wheel you into the surgery, young lady. Sounds like we're getting close."

He looked around. "I'm afraid that means all of you need to wait here or in the lobby."

When Caleb joined them, he put a hand on Omie's shoulder and said, "I'm sorry, Omie. The hospital won't let you be in the surgery either. Only staff are allowed."

"What?" she cried.

"I'll have a nurse keep you abreast of everything as it happens, I promise."

Bartie took her mamma's hand. "Let's stay in the room. You'll feel closer to her here."

The hours of waiting were torture for Omie, even with reports from the nurses. Not being able to hear or comfort her daughter was tearing her apart. Emmie came in and sat down beside her. Omie closed her eyes and focused, sending all the healing light she could. Elizabeth arrived and joined them.

"You know she's in the best place she could be, Omie."

"I do, Mrs. Campbell—Elizabeth—but I'm not used to being helpless."

"Send her all the love and healing you have in you. That will help. We're all here, doing just that."

Emmie and Elizabeth returned to the lobby, feeling they could be of more use assuring the others that all would be well. Both being doctors' wives, they knew there were no guarantees, but they had faith in Daniel and Caleb's skills.

Bartie stood. "Why don't we go out and stretch our legs a little, Mamma. I want to see if Shad will go check on Lilly. Likely Maizie is pulling her hair out by now, taking care of all the little ones."

Omie reluctantly agreed and groaned as she got up.

"Been sitting so long I'm stiff as a broom! They say you know you're a grownup when you groan every time you get up."

Bartie found her husband standing by a window, looking out at the people coming and going.

"Hey sugar," she said, wrapping her arms around his waist from behind.

"Well, hey yourself." Shad put his arms over hers. "How are you holding up?"

"I'm just ready for this baby to be born and to know Ada's going to be all right."

He turned to face her. "She's going to be just fine, you'll see."

"Shad, do you think we can stay a few days?"

"Course we can," Shad assured her. "I arranged to get some time away. Maybe I should go check on Lilly and come back tomorrow to see the baby. All these folks are likely going to tire Ada out."

Bartie nodded. "When you go to Emmie's, Maizie can take you to the Campbell's and show you our room. I'm sure our baby girl needs her nap. Thank you. Love you."

"I love you too." Shad bent down to kiss Bartie and wriggled his moustache to tickle her.

The doctors and nurse worked with Ada, encouraging her to breathe and push, as she knew to do. When the baby had been crowning for two hours, Daniel listened to the baby's heartbeat between contractions and began to worry. There was a slight weakening, and the mother was beginning to tire also.

"Dr. Decker," Daniel said in a quiet voice.

Caleb nodded, knowing what was coming, but not wanting to alarm his niece. He and Daniel had talked at length about when an intervention might be required.

"Ada."

She turned her head and looked at his face.

"I think for the baby's sake, we may have to do the same procedure I did with Phoebee. It's a surgery called a Cesarean. His heartbeat is slowing down. Will you give us permission to remove him—and the other baby—surgically?"

Ada looked at him for a long moment.

"It's safe?"

"Yes, I've performed this a number of times, now. We both have."

Dr. Campbell nodded.

"All right." She took a deep breath. "All right."

"We're going to administer a drug to put you to sleep during surgery. We'll go let the family know."

While the drug was taking effect, Caleb and Daniel went out into the lobby.

Everyone stood, noting the concern on Caleb's face.

"What is it?" James cried.

"She's fine, the baby's fine." Caleb assured him. "Dr. Campbell and I feel that the delivery is taking too long for the baby's safety. The heartbeat has dropped slightly."

James looked frightened.

"Just slightly, James. Don't be concerned. We want to operate and remove the baby before he and Ada Kate are more stressed." He looked around. "Do any of you remember when I operated to deliver Polly?"

"And I'm here to tell the tale!" Polly announced.

"I've experienced the same situation many times since then," he assured them. "Things will go much more quickly." He put a hand on James and Omie's shoulders. "I'll call you in as soon as we bring them back to the room."

Elizabeth stood and looked into Daniel's eyes, then kissed his cheek.

"She'll be fine," he murmured.

Within the hour, both doctors stepped out with tired smiles to congratulate James on his son's arrival.

"She'll be asleep for some time yet," Caleb said. "James, I suggest for now that just you and Omie go to her. I'll have the baby brought in so you can hold him until she wakes. The nurse is weighing and cleaning him at this moment. Ada would be able to handle other family stepping in later, after she's had a chance to recover a bit."

As James went off to the room to wait, Omie put a hand on Caleb's arm.

"What of the deceased child, Caleb?"

He lowered his voice. "There was not much of the body left. Enough though, that if she chooses, we can swaddle him and bring him to her."

"I believe she will. I'll ask her."

Ada's eyes opened as she felt the baby at her breast fussing. Omie had put him there, knowing the child needed to nurse soon. Ada put a hand on his tiny back, smiling weakly. James put his hand over hers.

"We got a little boy, Ada. A fine one! Look at that hair."

"He looks just like you," she replied.

"Naw! How can you tell what a baby looks like when he's got a little squinched-up face?"

"Mammas see," she replied. "Would you get me some water, James? Thank you, honey."

When he left, she quickly whispered, "What about my other one, Mamma? What did Caleb say?"

"They have him wrapped in a blanket in case you want to see him. But his little body is so wasted, Ada."

"I want to hold him. To say good-bye." She began to cry softly. "Please, Mamma."

"Of course I will, baby girl."

"I don't want James to see him, though. I don't believe he could take it."

Omie wiped away her own tears. "Should I go distract him then? I'll ask the nurse to bring the baby to you."

Once the nurse had agreed to Ada's wishes, Omie went looking for James.

"Oh Gosh, Mamma Silar, I got waylaid by this bunch. I'll go get some water."

"The nurse is taking her some, James. Let's give her a few moments to feed little Jacob alone."

"Jacob!" they all cheered.

Omie quietly slipped back into Ada's room as James was congratulated by everyone.

The tiny form in her daughter's arms lay still against his brother. Caleb stood beside the bed as well.

Ada looked up and asked, "Mamma, will you take the baby home and bury him next to Missy in the old cemetery?"

"Of course I will, honey."

Ada kissed the tiny head and handed the bundle to Caleb, who assured them, "We'll take care of him until you're ready."

He kissed Ada's cheek and left.

Mother and daughter sat quietly until James knocked at the door.

Ada dried her eyes quickly and said, "What are you knockin' for, silly? Come hold your son."

When Ada had rested a bit, she asked James to invite the others in to see this new addition to the family.

Omie laid a hand against her daughter's cheek. "You sure you're up for company?"

"I know they're all waiting, Mamma." Ada kissed Jacob's tiny fingers. "It's time for him to meet his family."

James stepped out of the room with a big grin on his face.

"Y'all can come in now, two at a time."

Georgia Rose grabbed Polly's hand and called over her shoulder, "Y'all have to wait your turn!"

As they entered her room, Ada gave them a tired smile and opened the baby's blanket for them to see.

"Aw, sister, he's so tiny! I love him already. Now I have a niece and a nephew." Georgia counted his toes and fingers. "All there!"

Polly took Ada's hand and squeezed it as tears trickled down her cheeks.

"I've never seen a newborn baby, Ada Kate. What a miracle."

"You'll see plenty of your own one day, Polly."

Ada's words stirred a small sense of unease in Omie's heart. She set it aside to consider later.

Bartie and Emmie were peeking in the door impatiently.

"It's our turn!" Bartie hissed.

Polly pushed a reluctant Georgia out to let the others in.

"Oh, look at our little miracle." Emmie smiled at her sister. "See, I knew these two would be fine."

Ada reached for Bartie's hand and they looked in wordless wonder at Jacob's sleeping face. He twitched and they laughed.

"Wonder what he could be dreaming about?" James said.

Frank Thomas and Jewel came in next.

"Hey," he said softly.

Jewel stood beside him, feeling a sense of intimacy she'd never known as an only child.

"I guess I'm an aunt twice now. Oh, Ada, he's just as sweet as can be."

Frank Thomas laughed, "Yes, you are." He rubbed Jacob's chest and belly softly. "Gotta fatten you up, littlun. Wait 'til you taste your mamma's sausage gravy and biscuits."

"That'll be awhile." Ada smiled up at him.

"Reckon I'll have to eat his share for now," he declared. "Listen, I know it's been a long day. Jewel and I are going to take off before it gets dark. I'll drop her at her grandmamma's and then go tell Daddy and Ezra the good news."

He leaned down to kiss Ada, then Omie. Jewel did as well.

"Love y'all," Ada said.

"Love you too, sis."

While Frank Thomas and Jewel were saying their goodbyes to James, Sarah stepped into Ada's room. She imagined mother and child were exhausted, so she only chose to stay for a few moments.

Staring in wonder at the tiny face they had all prayed to get to see, her throat tightened as she said, "He's so beautiful, Ada."

*I wonder if I'll come to regret not having a family.*

Discarding such thoughts, she offered, "Perhaps I should take this rowdy crew home. Let you all rest. Elizabeth said to tell you she would come tomorrow." She looked at Omie. "I imagine you'll want to stay with Ada and James a few more days?"

"Yes, Sarah, thank you so much."

"Thank you for letting me be a part of your joy. Ada, James. I will see you soon."

"Please thank Maizie and Phoebee for watching Tess, would you?" James asked.

"Of course." Sarah touched the baby's cheek and left.

As Sarah pulled up to the Decker home, Georgia Rose jumped out to be the first to tell Phoebee and Maizie about little Jacob's birth. She declared he was the prettiest baby ever.

As the others followed into the kitchen, they agreed.

"Of course, I've seen very few babies," Sarah admitted.

"Me either," Polly agreed.

Georgia declared, "Well, trust me, he is."

Phoebee rolled her eyes, but said, "I'm sure you're right, little missy." She turned to Sarah. "Reckon we should head on home? Seems ever'body is doin' all right, and I sure would love to sleep in my own bed tonight."

"I'll keep Tess with me until Miss Ada is ready to come home," Maizie offered. Her warm brown skin bore the tracks of tears, and Sarah looked at her with concern.

"Them are tears of happiness, don't worry," Phoebee declared. "She's been leakin' like a sieve all mornin' long."

Maizie took a swat at her friend with a dish towel as Phoebee danced out of the way.

Georgia Rose let Grace draw in her sketchbook on the ride home as the women talked. All were pleasantly tired from the day's excitement. Even Phoebee had a quiet joy about her. As soon as the road to the farm came into sight, Polly perked up, excited to see her Ezra again.

After dropping Jewel at her grandmamma's house, Frank Thomas had headed for the farm to find his daddy and Ezra. They were home at the kitchen table, eating beans and cornbread.

"Hey there," Nate said, "Not much of a supper but they's plenty more if you're hungry. Want some coffee? It's left from the morning, but still tolerable."

Frank Thomas nodded and sat at the table beside his brother.

"Got to beat that wretched swill the hospital serves! Thank you."

Ezra gave him a clap on the shoulder. "What did they name him?"

"Jacob Nathaniel Dillon."

Their daddy paused for a moment. They could see the emotions crossing his face before he turned toward the stove.

"Sounds like a lawyer," Ezra commented.

Frank Thomas replied, "Or a bank robber."

Nate set a mug on the table and looked at them, grinning. "Same thing, ain't it?"

# Chapter 56

Omie had talked things over with Nate about Sarah and Phoebee building a house on the farm. He saw sense in Ezra and Polly inheriting the old family home, and gave his blessing.

Sarah asked him to choose the most suitable spot, wanting him to know she appreciated his generosity and respected his opinions. She and Phoebee walked the property with him, listening to the pros and cons of his various choices.

Omie stayed out of it. Nate needed to feel important in decisions concerning the farm. Growing crops and tending livestock were things the younger men were as capable of doing as he was, but he was still the man of the family. She hoped choosing where to build the new house might give him back some of the self-respect he'd lost in the past.

A small, spring-fed creek bordered the line between the hay field and the pasture. It had looped back on itself, creating a private spot protected from the wind by a copse of cottonwoods and sassafras trees. This west side was shaded from the afternoon sun while the rest was bathed in morning light.

"Oh, Mr. Silar, could this be the place?" Sarah turned in a circle, admiring the view of the pasture as it wandered toward the river and the dappled light pouring through the trees.

"Shur is purty." Phoebee sighed.

The three stood a moment, imagining how well a modest house would fit such a spot.

"As good as any, I reckon," Nate agreed. "Might be we can find a spring close by that creek. Won't take much to get you water."

Sarah and Phoebee clasped hands, cheering, and thanked Nate for all his help.

"I thought I might engage someone in town to design the house for us Nate, and I would appreciate your input when the plans are drawn. Would you mind?"

"Not a'tall, ladies." He tipped his hat. "I'll leave you to discuss things then. I have chores callin' my name."

Phoebee and Sarah saw the lift of his shoulders as he walked away. They knew that not only had they made Nate happy, but Omie would be as well.

Phoebee plopped down beside a patch of daffodils and said, "This here's my room."

Two weeks later, Sarah got out of her auto with a roll of white paper in one hand. She started to take it into Phoebee's house, then turned instead toward the feed lot where Ezra and Nate were slopping hogs.

"Do you gentlemen have a moment to look at the house plans?"

Ezra looked at Nate and Nate grinned back.

"Cain't say I see any gentlemen here, but they's only us and the hogs." Nate set down his bucket. "Give us a few minutes to get cleaned up, Miss Sarah. Else them papers there will smell like a pigsty after we touch 'em."

Sarah went back up the hill and found Phoebee in the barn. "Hurry up and finish milking Daisy! I want to show you something."

Omie stood on her porch with Grace, looking up to see what all the fuss was about. Sarah waved for them to come too. Pretty soon, Polly and Georgia Rose showed up, and Phoebee's table was crowded with people trying to see the plans.

"Why, that's a right nice little house," Nate offered.

"Looks like more porch than house!" Omie exclaimed.

Phoebee nodded. "Just what we want."

The drawings were studied and commented on until Omie announced, "It's time to get supper on, girls. Georgia, get the stove going. Gracie and I will be there directly."

Ezra said, "We got chores to finish too. Sure is excitin' news, Miss Sarah. Aunt Phoebee."

The men turned to leave, but Sarah asked, "Can you recommend any good carpenters to hire? Who built James and Ada's house?"

Nate shook his head. "Me and Ezra and James can build this for y'all. No need to pay somebody. Long as you're not in a hurry."

Omie looked at Ezra, who did not seem as sure.

"I never built a house, Daddy."

"How hard can it be? You and James helped on his, didn't you? If them town boys can do it, we can. Don't y'all worry. After plantin' time we'll get right on it."

Phoebee spoke up, "We would just like to be able to turn this house over to Ezra and Polly when they get hitched."

"Shoot, we'll have it done way before August," Nate assured them.

Once they'd left, Phoebee put a hand on Omie's arm, mimicked, "How hard can it be?"

The women laughed, but not with complete confidence.

# Chapter 57

The time had come to buy tobacco seeds. Seed beds had been burned to kill off brush and put lime into the soil. Late February temperatures fluctuated, but as the earth began to warm, sheets of linen were rolled out beside the beds, ready to protect the emerging plants.

James and Ezra pulled up to the grange. Parked in front was a shiny red Ford truck. Farmers were gathered around it, teasing the Potter brothers as they loaded bags into its bed.

One man called, "Well, heck boys. For a dollar more you could'a got a red un!"

Everyone laughed, including the owners. "We done purty good the last couple years. Thought we could move up into the next century."

"Wagon is more dependable!" someone else declared. "You can grow what ya feed the mules too."

"Maybe so," James ventured, "but I wouldn't mind lettin' a vehicle do some of the work. Bet it's not as temperamental as a mule neither."

"Not so far," the brothers answered and drove off.

On the way back to the farm, Ezra said, "Ya know, between the peanut crop, corn and tobacco, we done all right the last few years too. Got money for seed and a little more. Sure would be easier to get lumber and such for Phoebee and Sarah's house with a truck."

James looked over at Ezra with a smile. "That's true, brother. You thinkin' what I'm thinkin'?"

"Let's talk to Daddy, see if we can convince him of it. Wouldn't that be somethin'!"

Nate came to help unload supplies when they pulled up and saw the grins on the young men's faces.

"Out with it. What'd I miss?"

Ezra described the Potter brothers' fancy new truck.

"Me and James was thinkin' maybe...that is, if'n you agreed, we could go to Savannah and just have a look at them Ford trucks. See how dear they are."

James chimed in, "But not a red one, they likely paid more for that."

Nate made them wait a moment, then replied, "Best talk to your mamma and Phoebee too. Only fair they have a say so."

Ezra raised his eyebrows. "Does that mean you're good with gettin' one?"

Nate grinned back at them. "Don't act too excited, they'll think you're up to somethin', son. The acorn don't fall too far and all that."

"But I don't know how to drive," Omie said. "I tried once with Emmie's car and nearly ran us into a tree!"

"Mamma, there's acres of land without a tree on it where you can practice. I promise we'll teach you."

Omie turned to Phoebee. "What do you think?"

"Ain't no use to try and teach me, I cain't see out the window or reach the pedals." She looked at the men's hopeful faces. "But I can see the sense in it." Looking at Omie, Phoebee said, "Reckon they'll have to take time away from their plantin' to go to Savannah."

"No, no, we'll get all that done first," Nate replied.

James agreed. "Can we do somethin' to help y'all too before we go?"

All three smiled at the women agreeably.

"Let us think on it," Omie replied.

"All right, just let us know!" James hurried out the door with Nate and Ezra on his heels.

Once the men were out of earshot, Phoebee said, "We could have us some fun with this!"

Omie and Phoebee waited a few days before giving their consent, just to see how much the men were willing to do for it. When the garden had been plowed, Phoebee's milk barn mucked out, and fresh hay spread for Dinah, the women took pity on the men.

Omie made one more request, though. "While you're in Savannah, inquire about having electricity installed at the farm, please. We need that as much as a truck."

Ezra suggested giving Caleb a call, to see if he'd come get them so they wouldn't have to bring the wagon back.

Omie turned to Phoebee once the men gone and said, "Do you think Caleb would want to come all the way here just to pick them up? They could use the wagon and not take him away from his work."

Phoebee looked at her friend. "Caleb's a man, ain't he? Big boys goin' to look at big toys. Course, he will."

Caleb was more than willing, and said he would arrange to get away soon. A few days later, he drove to pick up his in-laws. Being on good terms with the owner of the JC Lewis Ford dealership, he hoped to help them get a good deal on a truck. James was already standing in the yard looking for him when Caleb pulled up.

"Hey, Caleb! You need a cup of coffee or somethin' to eat before we go?"

Clearly, the young man was hoping for a no, but his wife must have insisted he offer.

"I'm fine, James. I'll just come say hello to the ladies and we'll be off."

"I'll go git Nate and Ezra then."

Omie hugged her son-in-law when he came into the kitchen and asked the same questions.

"We have some honey cake," Phoebee offered.

Through the window, they saw Nate and Ezra, with James, finish putting tools away and then head toward the Ford.

"I'm afraid those three might poke me with pitchforks if I stay. Raincheck?"

"We made y'all lunch for the road," Omie handed him the wicker basket, covered with a napkin. "Please make sure they can drive that truck before they head home with it. I wish Frank Thomas was going with them."

Caleb laughed. "I think between the three of them, they'll figure it out."

"Don't be too sure of that," Phoebee retorted with a smile.

All day, Omie worked on her resolve to learn how to drive.

Ada Kate said, "Mamma, remember that sayin' you always told us. 'Courage is fear that has said its prayers'."

"My mamma used to say that to me."

Late in the afternoon, as the women were starting to become concerned, Ada looked up from nursing Jacob and said, "What's that?"

Omie opened the door, and they heard strains of *She'll be comin' round the mountain when she comes.*

A shiny black Ford truck was headed up the road with Sarah, Georgia, Grace and James in the back singing at the top of their lungs.

Omie went out with her hands on her hips and a smile on her face. When the vehicle stopped beside her, she reached up to take Grace from Sarah.

"They came to get us at school, Mamma!"

"I see that!"

Sarah stepped down, laughing. Her hair had come undone and was flying in all directions.

"All the other children wanted a ride home too, that's why we're so late. Sorry."

Omie stepped up to the driver's side window where Nate was sitting.

*Here goes nuthin'.*

"Well?" she asked sternly.

Nate turned to look at Ezra and back at her.

"Scoot over!" she instructed, and slid behind the wheel.

"Oh Lordy," Phoebee laughed.

"Ezra, you teach her," Nate insisted. "She might bite my head off."

Georgia laughed as the truck jerked and sputtered down the road. "Don't drive it into the river, Mamma!"

# Chapter 58

"Frank Thomas! Jewel!" Grace had been watching for them all morning, too excited to keep at any one thing for long. Her braid had come partly undone and there were grass stains on her knees and elbows.

"Gracie!" Frank Thomas got out of the car and scooped up his little sister, swinging her in a circle, then setting her on the ground. She wobbled and fell in a heap.

"You drinkin' again?" he kidded, and she begged for more.

"Let's go find Mamma first. You know where she is?"

Grace pointed to Ada and James' house. "Lookin' in on the baby again." She sighed. "I don't know what's so interesting about him. He's like a potato with legs."

"So were you, once," he replied.

Jewel came around the side of the car and took in Grace's state of disarray.

"What in the world have you been up to, young lady?"

"I was watchin' for doodle bugs to come outta their holes. I sang the song and everything, but nothin' happened."

"Song?" Jewel looked to Frank Thomas for clarification.

He sang,

*Doodle Bug Doodle Bug*
*Come out of your hole*

*Your house is on fire*
*And your children will burn*


"That's horrible!" Jewel cried.

"Only, I sing it like this," Grace said.


*Doodle Bug Doodle Bug*
*Come out of your hole*
*I brought you*
*Some honey and biscuits*


"Well, that does have a nicer ring to it," Frank Thomas conceded. "Any honey and biscuits left for me?"

"Nope. Sorry, Brother. Beat ya there!" Grace took off skipping toward Ada's.

"Does that girl ever walk?" Jewel asked.

"Not if she can help it."

"Well, if it ain't my famous brother and sister-in-law!"

James stuck out a hand and shook with Frank Thomas. He kissed Jewel on the cheek and stepped aside to let them in the house.

"Hey, Darlins. Just in time for dinner." Omie came to get a kiss from both. "Want to hold your nephew?"

Jacob looked at them with a drooling grin, took his fingers from his mouth, and reached for Jewel. She tried not to shrink away, but quickly said to Frank Thomas, "Why don't you take him, Hon? I need to powder my nose."

She made a quick beeline out the back door, heading for the outhouse.

Grace stared at her retreating figure. "Why is she going outside to put powder in her nose?"

Ada Kate said, "It's just a saying ladies use sometimes when they need to potty, Gracie."

The girl shrugged and went back to picking at a scab on her knee.

"How's Atlanta treatin' y'all?" Ezra asked. "Still makin' music with Shad?"

"Mostly, yeah," Frank Thomas replied. "We go when we can. Jewel's grandmamma isn't doin' as well as she used to, so we stay in New Abercorn some of the time."

Omie raised an eyebrow and looked at him sternly.

"I know, Mamma, we want to get by and see you more. There's just so much goin' on. When we're not playin', we're practicin' and writin' new songs."

"How's it pay?" James asked.

"There's not as much money to be made at dance halls with prohibition on, but we get by. It was a real piece of luck to have a music scout hear us. There's lots of folks with radio shows looking for talent. We're hopin' to get a contract from that record he made of my song, if it does well. He likes Jewel's songs too."

Just then, Jewel came back inside. "I write the sad songs, he writes the dance tunes. Plenty of call for both, they say."

Grace stood, walked over to study Jewel's face for powder, then skipped out the door.

"What's Daddy doin?" Frank Thomas asked. "We saw him stompin' around in the pasture lookin' like a hornet about to sting somethin'."

Omie sighed. "He volunteered himself and these boys to build the new house for Sarah and Phoebee. It hasn't gone as well as he'd hoped."

"Has he ever built a house?"

Ezra answered, "When did that ever stop him? Once he gets it in his head to do somethin' he's like a dog with a bone. It's supposed to be built before me and Polly get married so we can have Grandma Kate's old house."

Frank Thomas shrugged. "What's the problem?"

"He cain't figure out how to lay the corner stones so they're squared up, and he don't want any advice from me or James."

"He'll get there," Omie assured them.

"Mamma," Ada Kate said. "It's almost the end of June! The wedding's in August!"

"I know."

Jewel spoke up, "After we eat, let's go say hello to Ezra's future bride and mother-in-law, shall we?"

Frank Thomas looked at his brother. "What are you supposed to call your mother-in-law after you're married? Aunt Mamma Phoebee?"

"I hadn't thought about that," Ezra replied.


After a hefty helping of banana pudding, James stood and patted his belly.

"Reckon we better get back to work. That corn ain't goin' ta harvest itself."

Ezra looked at his brother. "Want to take a walk out to see if Daddy's made any progress?"

Frank Thomas rolled his eyes. "No, but I will. Meet you in a few minutes, Jewel."

Nate looked up when he heard his sons talking. They approached the house site and Ezra asked, "Made any progress?"

"Not since you asked me an hour ago." He wiped his face and looked at Frank Thomas.

"Hey, Son."

"Daddy."

"I don't suppose you come to help?"

"Sorry, me and Jewel are headed back to Atlanta. I wish you luck with the house, though."

"Figures," Nate muttered.

"What's that supposed to mean?"

"What it means, Son, is ever since you got the notion you're a Grand Ole Opry star, you done let ever'body down. You don't come to see your mamma. You ain't around when we need help." Nate waved a dismissive hand in Frank Thomas' direction and stomped off.

"Still the same old sumbitch as ever." Frank Thomas glared at the retreating back of his daddy.

"He don't mean it, brother. He's just frustrated."

James came out to them and asked, "Why's he so mad?"

Ezra shook his head. "He's mad at hisself 'cause he don't know what to do."

"Well, I helped build my brother Bill's house and learned how to lay out the foundation. I just don't want Mr. Silar gettin' upset with me for tellin' him how."

"Can we do it now and pretend he fixed it?" Ezra grinned.

Frank Thomas spat in disgust. "You two can treat him like a baby, but I'm not having any part of it." He started walking toward Phoebee's.

Ezra called out, "Wouldn't want you to get mud on them fancy shoes, anyhow."


The house began to take shape slowly. Between harvesting and drying the tobacco, getting a second field of corn planted and all the daily chores on the farm, there was little time left for building. The men worked on it every evening, but by now, July was almost over. The inside, as well as the porches, had yet to be finished.

Omie approached Nate one day as he was cleaning the hoes and rakes.

"Nate, I don't want to push you, but I think we need to hire some help to get the house done before the wedding."

He looked up, exasperated. "I am doin' my best, Omie. Me and the boys will get it done. We don't need any help."

"Why are you being so stubborn? There's nothing wrong with asking for a hand."

"You don't think I know what I'm doin', do you?" he shouted. "So why don't you just go find somebody who does?"

She saw his exasperation in the fiery lights around him.

"Nate, it's not that..."

"Fine!" He threw down the hoe in his hand. "Maybe Caleb's brother can come down from the big city and do it for you!"

"Oh, please! Not that again." She stomped her foot and hurried back to the house.

Nate saddled up one of the mules. His curses could be heard all the way up to where Phoebee sat on her porch. When he had ridden to the river road, she walked down the hill and found her friend slinging pots and pans around as if they had offended her somehow.

"Omie!"

"What?"

"I have an idea."

When Nate didn't show up at the table for breakfast, Ezra asked, "Is Daddy ailin'?"

Omie told him about his daddy's hissy fit.

"We can't afford that nonsense right now, Mamma! There's too much to do. I'm goin' to look for him."

James saw Ezra saddling up the mule and went to see what the matter was. When he learned Nate had run off again, he asked, "Want me to help?"

"I know where he's likely to be," Ezra replied. "I'll be back directly."

Ezra followed along the river, checking his daddy's favorite fishing and drinking spots. He found the mule tied to a tree branch about halfway to New Abercorn. Ezra slid off his own mule, then tied it to the same tree.

"Daddy!"

Nate was seated on a log below with his head in his hands, looking like he'd spent a cold night there. Ezra walked down and saw the whiskey jar sitting on the sand. Disgustedly, he bent to pick it up, only to discover the jar was full.

Nate sighed and dropped his hands to his knees.

"Daddy, why are you here? We got a house to finish!"

"I know, son. I just been feelin' like a fool for thinkin' I could build it. Your mamma thinks so too."

Ezra sat beside him. "She does not. I promise you. It's just that time's getting' short, is all."

Nate picked up the jar of whiskey and threw it in the river.

"Here ya go, Big Jack." He stared at the water a moment. "At least I had the sense not to go down that road again after I bought it. I hope she can appreciate that."

"She will. And I do too. But we need to get back and finish."

Nate turned his face away.

"Look here, Daddy. I ain't ever asked anything of you. But I'm askin' now."

A few moments passed by, the silence broken by a bullfrog that had decided to serenade them. Nate wiped a hand across his face, and said, "A'right, son." He stood up stiffly and followed Ezra up the bank.

When the two men were near the house site, they saw Phoebee and Sarah standing there. Expecting to be chastised, Nate got slowly down from the mule with his head bowed.

"Oh Lordy, y'all! I'm so glad to see you." Phoebee walked up to Nate. "I have a favor to ask, and I hope it's not too much trouble."

Ezra and Nate looked at each other.

"What is it, Phoebee?" Nate asked. "Everything ok?"

"It's my brothers," she said. "Mamma called and said they were determined to come build this house for me and Sarah. When I told her y'all had mostly got it done, she said they'd be awful disappointed."

"Well, maybe they should..." he began.

"No, Nate. You don't understand. All them boys know how to build is log houses. We don't want that!"

"No," Sarah nodded in agreement.

"They might be dumb as a bag of hammers when it comes to buildin' a real house like this, but they're strong. They'd work hard if you'd just tell them what to do. Please say yes!"

Nate took off his hat and scratched his head. "You sure they'd be ok with that?"

"If Mamma tells them to, they will. They're good boys."

"What do you think, Ezra?"

"Why not?"

As they turned to get back on the mules, Phoebee gave Ezra a quick wink. A smile spread across his face, and he tipped his hat to the women.

Two days later, a truck came down the road honking like a flock of mad geese. Welda and Granny were riding in the cab with Phoebee's oldest brother Kurt. In the back, Jamie and Finley were standing up, beating on the roof as they whooped and hollered.

Polly and Phoebee ran down the steps to meet them.

Jamie jumped down and swung Phoebee around. "So, this is where you been hidin' from us all these years!"

"Dang it! You found me."

Ezra and Nate came from the fields to see what the ruckus was.

Granny and Welda hopped out of the truck and hollered 'Howdy' to all, then took off, declaring, "We gotta go to the privy!"

Introductions were made among the menfolk, then they wandered down to look at the house. The women gathered inside Phoebee and Sarah's for a visit.

"Thank you so much for comin', Mamma, Granny."

"Oh, Honey. Those boys was fit to be tied when they learnt you needed help. They'd a come sooner if they'd known."

Omie placed a hand on Welda's arm. "My husband was bound and determined to do this on his own with our boy and James. He's never built a house, but wouldn't take advice from anybody. 'Specially me."

"Men." Welda shook her head. "Prideful. Stubborn as mules."

Granny cackled. "Why the Lord made women so smart! Can't take the whip to 'em, so we have to outfox 'em. Make ever'thing seem like their idea."

Sarah nodded. "You taught Phoebee well!"

Soon, both trucks were headed to the mill for lumber and nails. Ezra stuck his head in the door first to ask if there was anything the ladies needed from town.

"Five-pound box of ten-dollar bills?" Granny quipped.

"Don't I wish!" he replied.

By the time the men returned, tables were set up in Phoebee and Sarah's yard, and a hearty dinner was ready for them. Baked beans, ham, potato salad and biscuits sat beside freshly sliced tomatoes and cucumbers soaked in vinegar. Three buttermilk pies waited on a side table with pitchers of sweet tea.

They fell on it like a pack of wolves, Phoebee's hefty brothers especially.

"Didn't Mamma and Granny feed you boys on the trip?" Phoebee asked.

"Cold chicken and cornbread don't fill a fella like this does!" Kurt declared. He turned to his mamma. "Not that it wadn't good."

"I hear ya, boy. These women have taught our Phoebee how to cook!"

Phoebee blushed at the praise. "Sarah and Polly helped too."

Finley raised his glass. "Well, whoever done it, we're mighty proud to be eatin' it. Pass them pies around, sister."

When every crumb had been eaten, the men climbed in the trucks and headed for the new house site. Hammers rang out until the sun had nearly set.

Nate showed up at the door, worn out but looking very pleased with himself.

"Hey there, Ladies."

"Y'all gettin' hungry again?" Welda asked.

"Yes ma'am. Those sons of yours learn real fast. I only had to show them what to do once and they was good."

To keep from rolling her eyes, Omie turned back to the stove. "Supper will be ready shortly. Tell the boys to wash up, would you?"

He hurried back out the door and headed down the hillside.

All the women had a hand in cooking up a feast for the men. Omie made fried porkchops, a favorite of her menfolk. She'd picked fresh collard greens and butterbeans from the garden, seasoning them with a liberal dose of bacon fat. Granny and Welda contributed fried okra along with a big bowl of chicken and dumplings. Ada's biscuits and cornbread accompanied everything, served with fresh butter and sorghum syrup.

Phoebee had baked two of her honey cakes for dessert. Georgia Rose and Grace had gone blueberry picking that morning and Sarah taught them to make crusts for pies.

Tired, hungry men gathered around the tables in the soft twilight. Omie lit lanterns and placed them near enough to give light, but not close enough to draw insects.

Ezra said grace, thanking the Lord for these kind folks who were soon to be family. And for the work they had been able to get done that day. When he had finished, the Winder men clapped him on the back.

"Feels like we're all family already," Phoebee remarked.

"I'll toast to that!" Nate said, winking at Omie. "Even if it is with tea."

Sure enough, by the end of the next day, the inside walls covered in beadboard. Windows Sarah ordered were brought from the mill and set in place. A door was hung that had glass set into the top half, so the women could look out on the fields, even in winter.

Last, a large cast-iron cookstove had to be picked up from the store in New Abercorn. It took all of the brothers plus James and Ezra to carry the thing.

"Ladies, unless the floor caves in or the roof falls down, I don't ever want to pick that thang up again!" Finley panted.

After supper that evening, Ezra brought out his fiddle and Omie brought her banjo to the porch. Kurt had his guitar, and music soon filled the air. It turned out that the Winder boys had good voices and harmonized well together.

"Been singin' all their lives," Welda told Omie. "I reckon they got it all from their daddy, I cain't carry a tune in a bucket."

Granny spat into a can. "Me neither."

"We'll be able to play on Sarah and Phoebee's porch tomorrow evenin'," Kurt said. "Have four sides to choose from!"

A flurry of noise began at daybreak as the men began the work of building porches and steps. After a quick dinner, they got back to it, trying to finish up before dark. Finally, Ezra came to Omie's house where the women had gathered to make supper.

"Y'all c'mon and see what we got done! It's hard to believe."

Everyone gathered to admire the new house in all its glory. Nate put a hand on Ezra and James' shoulders. "We done kilt a bear, boys, as my mamma would say. Nice work."

"We owe you so much," Sarah said, with tears in her eyes.

Phoebee turned to her brothers. "Y'all are the best. I don't deserve you after I run off like I did."

Kurt picked her up and swung her around.

"Now we know where you are, you cain't hide from us no more."

"Put me down! Just 'cause I'm small don't mean I cain't whip your tail!"

"I reckon we can finish the rest ourselves," Ezra remarked. "Shouldn't take more than a day."

"I 'spose we'll be off in the mornin', then," Welda said. "I'm itchin' to see them grandbabies."

Granny nodded in agreement. "Bet their mammas will be glad to see us too."

# Chapter 59

Polly twirled around in front of the shop's mirrors.

Emmie and Bitsy stood with their arms around each other's waists, beaming.

"You'll be a beautiful bride, Polly. Even if I did make the dress myself!" Bitsy went over to straighten the lace veil.

"Not completely by yourself!" Emmie objected.

Knowing that it would be hot outdoors in Kate's garden, the gown was designed with short, lace sleeves. During the ceremony, gloves would give a more formal touch, but could be removed afterwards.

Emmie had embroidered seed pearls on the silk sash and bodice, The rest was a soft cascade of lace, snug at the waist and full below. With Polly's diminutive figure, she looked like one of Bitsy's porcelain dolls.

"Do you like the cap and veil, Polly? It sits well among your curls."

"I love everything. The dress, the veil, the gloves. I feel like a fairy princess!"

They realized Phoebee had not said a word.

"Mamma?"

She sat with a hand over her mouth, tears pouring from her eyes.

"Are you ok?" Polly hurried over to put an arm around her mamma's slight shoulders.

"I just can't believe you're mine! I'm so proud of you, Pollywog."

"Don't make me start crying, too. I don't want to get my dress wet."

"You're next," Emmie said, taking Phoebee's hand. "The mother of the bride must shine as well."

"I'm too old and tarnished to shine."

"Nonsense."

There was little of Phoebee's dress from twenty years ago in the new one. Just enough so Emmie could make good on her promise to use it. Phoebee had not gained an ounce in all that time, despite her love of honey cake.

This dress was of a soft linen in pale blue. Ribbons of a deeper shade were woven into the bodice with a sash to match. Emmie made a shrug from the jacket of Phoebee's old dress and garnished it with the same ribbons.

"We need to get the final touches done on these, my dears," Emmie said, "so I can get you home. I imagine there's a lot to do in the next four days before the big event!"

Early Thursday morning, Sarah took Phoebee and Polly into New Abercorn to buy a few more decorations for the wedding. All were feeling antsy, ready for Saturday to get there.

Omie took this time to wander in the backyard of her old home, enjoying memories. Her mamma's flowers were still beautiful, not as much as when Kate's hands tended them, but a feast of color all the same. The wedding would be lovely here. An arch of pink climbing roses defined the center of the garden, flanked by her beloved Mr. Lincolns. Pathways wound through perennial flowers grown from seeds ordered by mail. Omie remembered her mamma and Mrs. O'Dell pouring through the pages of the Burpee catalogue when it came to the store. It was the one luxury Kate allowed herself.

Around the corner of the house, sunlight filtered through the leaves of the old live oak above the well. Omie sat on the bench at its edge, enjoying a respite from the heat. After a few moments, she stood to slide back the cover, remembering all she'd seen in the deep, cool water. Even now, something shimmered at its edges. A child's face took form. Then two. Boys. She could see them laughing and playing beneath this same oak. Were they from another time? A promise for the future?

The images faded and Omie was left to wonder about the nature of time. Memories and visions seemed sometimes to come from the same place. Sliding the cover back over the opening, she stood there a bit longer, intending to head home.

Instead, she went back to the garden and picked a bouquet of flowers. She stopped at the barn to find a jar and filled it with water and the bouquet. Carrying them down to the shadowy edge of the old cemetery, Omie placed the jar next to Missy's grave, arranging the flowers tidily. A small mound at its side marked where Ada's little one had been buried.

Nate had built a tiny box at her request, promising to keep this between them, as Ada asked. She had taken a shovel to the cemetery herself, and laid the miniature casket in the ground beside Missy. A sense of peace had enveloped her then, as it did now.

The sound of automobile horns disturbed her revery. At the house, a pickup truck and two cars came to a stop.

*The Winders!*

"Hey there!" Welda shouted as Omie came up the hill. "Thought you might could use some help gettin' ready fer the weddin'. Brought the whole dang family, but don't you worry where to put us. We got big canvas tents and beddin', we'll be just fine. Brought vittles with us too."

Omie was speechless, as Phoebee's brothers, their wives and children poured out of the vehicles. She was so flustered, she forgot their names as soon as they were offered. Nate, James and Ezra came to greet all the Winders. They joined the men in setting up tents near the new house, and in no time, vehicles were moved and the families settled.

Fortunately, Phoebee and Sarah's privy had been dug and built a couple of days before. Nate had also finished piping water up from the well he'd dug.

Once again, a car horn sounded as Sarah drove up with Phoebee and Polly. The Winders considered Sarah one of their own now, and all came up to greet them.

"I reckon it's begun," Phoebee said. "No turnin' back now, Pollywog."

Ezra came to scoop his fiancé into his arms and swing her around.

Phoebee let out an exasperated huff. "What is it about men wantin' to swing us around like a feedsack?"

"Nobody wants to swing me around," Omie retorted.

"Count yourself lucky. I'm gonna part with my breakfast on the next one who does it to me."

After dinner, the women shooed the men out of the house and got a look at Polly's bridal gown. None had ever seen anything as fancy, they said. Sarah made Phoebee bring out her dress too, and exclamations of appreciation went round the room again.

Welda hugged Polly, then put her hands on either side of Phoebee's face.

"This is the next best thing to having a weddin' gown of your own, darlin'. I'm just sorry that Ephram didn't see to it you did."

For once, Phoebee didn't have smart comeback.

"Thank you, Mamma."

"While the fellas is out doin' who knows what, let's hear about this weddin'!"

Omie motioned for them all to follow her into the back yard.

Little needed to be done in Kate's garden. The Winder women were impressed by all that had gone into making this small backyard paradise.

Polly stood under the bower of pink roses. "Ezra and I chose not to have anyone stand with us, since the arch is just big enough for us and the minister. We wanted a simple wedding anyway."

"You are goin' to be the most beautiful bride ever!" Granny told her, and the rest agreed.

"Thank y'all. The minister will come at noon on Saturday. We got our papers from the courthouse. I think everything's ready, except for the food after. We were hoping you could help with that."

"Did you have somethin' in mind?" Welda asked.

Polly looked at her mamma and Omie, then at the other women gathered around her.

"We'd be happy with anything you make. Thank you all so much for being here with us." Polly began to sniffle and was swept up into the arms of her new-found family.

"No possum, though!" Phoebee declared.

The following day, Omie took Phoebee and Welda to town in the truck, showing off her new driving skills. Phoebee wasn't sure they would make it there before the wedding at the speed Omie was going, but said nothing.

They bought the supplies needed, and Mrs. O'Dell threw in two smoked hams, just to be sure there was plenty of food.

"I'll see you all tomorrow!" she called, as Omie slowly backed up.

The wedding cake would be baked that afternoon by the chef at The Marshall House in Savannah, a gift from the Campbells. Thomas promised it would ride up front with him the next morning, and he'd guard it with his life.

All that remained was to wait. To Polly, it seemed like an eternity.

Ezra had gotten a fair share of ribbing from his future uncles. Finley was the only one of Phoebee's brothers who hadn't yet married, and he took the most pleasure in teasing Polly's beau.

"I would tell ya to run, Ezra, but you're home. Looks like she's caught you."

"And why would I want to run, Finley? What do you know about married life anyhow?"

"Just look at my brothers. Wives and young'uns tellin' 'em what to do. Me, I come and go as I please. I'm a free man!"

"Free to live with your mamma still."

Finley grinned. "I reckon you got a point. Seems like Polly's a good girl. She probl'y won't take a fryin' pan to ya like them Stone Mountain women."


The evening before the wedding, Finley and his brothers cornered Ezra in the barn. They were joined by James and Nate. Behind them came Frank Thomas with several jars of corn liquor.

Ezra looked around and said, "Now y'all, I cain't get drunk tonight. Polly would skin me alive if I showed up at our weddin' hungover."

The Winder brothers looked at each other.

Kurt put a hand on Ezra's shoulder and said, "It's family tradition, young feller."

"Looks like you don't have a choice!" Frank Thomas declared.

"A'right. Just a couple sips, though."

Toasts and stories began. Laughter rang out from the barn, louder and louder as the evening wore on. Omie stood on the porch with her arms crossed and announced, "Looks like we're on our own for supper, ladies."

Polly jumped up from the table and joined her.

"Is Ezra out there?"

"Who do you think this party is for?" Omie put an arm around Polly and said, "Don't fret about it, darlin'. He'll survive. This is one time to let men be the heathens they are."

"But..."

Phoebee, Granny and Welda stood in the doorway listening to the revelry.

"They's hard workin' men, honey. Need to raise a little hell now an' then."

"Granny's right. In the mornin' we'll feed 'em up good and keep the coffee comin'. They'll be right as rain by the weddin'." Welda waved them back into the kitchen. "Let's not waste these viddles, they're gettin' cold. Come tell us more about tomorrow, Pollywog."

The women finished eating and did as much preparation for the next day as they could. They left biscuits and ham on the stove for the men if they came in hungry.

There were still rowdy noises coming from the barn, but James had made his exit early on, claiming it was leave then or be locked out all night. They all doubted this was true, but the baby's cry could be heard all the way up at the barn. A sleep deprived mamma was not to be trifled with.

The two older Winder brothers stumbled back to their wives, leaving Finley to match the Silar men dram for dram.

Polly and Phoebee were walking back home when a shadow separated itself from the old oak by the well.

"Polly."

She stopped and looked around. Ezra came into the lamplight with a sheepish look on his face.

Phoebee said, "I'll see you inside, darlin'." She took the lantern and left, giving the two some privacy.

"Ezra, I can't believe you're out there getting drunk the night before our wedding!"

"I didn't start this, Polly. You got to believe me. Mostly, I just pretend to take a swig when they hand me the jar. I hate that stuff."

He wrapped his arms around her, and though she could faintly smell alcohol, he didn't seem drunk. They stood together as the moon wove its way through the old branches.

Finally, he declared, "I gotta get back or they'll come lookin' for me. I told them I had to go do my business." As he let her go and headed for the barn, he called back, "I cain't wait to marry you, Pollywog."

She smiled and replied softly, "Me too, Ezra Silar."

Early in the morning, Omie looked out toward her mamma's old house. Something about that time of day, when it was bathed in soft light, brought back sweet memories of her life there. She thought she could see Kate wandering among the roses, then realized it was the slight form of Polly.

Omie prepared a cup of sweet, milky coffee and made her way up the hill.

"Just the way you like it, hon."

Polly smiled gratefully and took the mug. They sat on one of the dozen or so benches the Winder brothers had scrapped together in place of chairs for the ceremony.

"Sleep any?"

"Barely. I'm too excited to care about sleep. Did you ever think this day would come, Aunt Omie? Seems like a dream sometimes."

They sipped their coffee and sat in comfortable silence watching the sky turn from pale blue to azure. "Never doubted it for a minute, my girl. You and Ezra were born so close together. In the same room, in fact. Almost like twins from the beginning."

She stroked Polly's long brown hair. "Did you?"

"I wasn't sure what to do about being able to teach. It's what I've always wanted, but I hated having to choose between the classroom and Ezra. I think God had a hand in delivering Sarah to us. I'm just as happy to be a librarian so I can be a wife, and that's all due to her."

"Did I hear my name? Whatever it was, I didn't do it!"

Sarah carried out a cup of her own and sat beside them. She gave Polly a hug and kissed her cheek.

"I was just saying how this wedding is possible because of you."

"You would have found a way. The two of you are peas in a pod, as they say."

"Well, I appreciate all you've done for us, Aunt Sarah. I hope you know that."

After a few moments, Sarah turned to Polly with tears in her eyes.

"I've chosen a different life. I don't expect I'll have children, and you are the closest thing I'll ever know to a daughter. I feel blessed to have you, honey."

"Are y'all out here cryin?"

The screen door slammed, and Phoebee made her way down the steps, wrapped in her robe.

"I swear, this is the cryin'est bunch lately. You'd think we were buryin' somebody."

"Oh hush." Omie laughed and gave her friend a hug.

"Don't slosh yer coffee on me!" Phoebee scolded as she stepped back, but they could all see the pleasure on her face. "Let's just get them two married off so's I can move into the new house!"

Phoebee took Omie's coffee and drank a big gulp, but it didn't hide the moistness shining in her eyes.

Soon, the smell of bacon and biscuits filled the air. Nate, Frank Thomas, Ezra and Finley stumbled out of the barn, squinting in the sunlight. Finley headed for his folks camp, and the other men made their way to the house.

No one said a word, just handed them cups of coffee and went back to preparing breakfast. Ezra pretended to be as hungover as his daddy and brother.

"Here." Omie glared with mock seriousness. She set a platter of hot biscuits in front of them and they fell on it like badgers.

Georgia Rose started giggling. Omie and Gracie couldn't help but join in.

Nate looked up with syrup on his chin. "You ain't mad?"

"We knew y'all would have to get up to some nonsense with Ezra last night."

He and the boys looked relieved.

Omie looked at each one in turn. "You'll pay for it later."

Frank Thomas grinned and nodded. "Pass them biscuits, would ya Daddy?"

Folks began to arrive around ten o'clock. The Campbells carefully helped Thomas and Maizie carry the cake inside. Everyone breathed a sigh of relief when it was set on the table.

Granny whistled. "Would ya look at thet? Them roses look real!"

"Oh my," Polly breathed out. "I've never seen anything so grand!" She put a hand on Thomas' arm. "Thank you for being so careful with it."

Thomas removed his hat. "My honor, Miz Polly."

The Campbells each gave her a hug and a kiss on the cheek.

"It's our pleasure to help you celebrate this day," Elizabeth said warmly.

The men were gathered at Kate's old house, soon to be the newlyweds' home, and Daniel went to join them.

Omie's kitchen smelled of fried chicken and ham, vegetables harvested from the Winder women's gardens, cracklin' cornbread and Granny's specialty, hominy.

Though the wedding cake was to be the main event, a selection of favorite pies and cobblers were on display, as well.

In Omie's room, the bride and her dressmakers were busy getting things in order. Polly's hair was styled on her head in a way that left soft waves close to her face beneath the cap and veil. Phoebee watched for a bit, then declared she was jumpy as a frog in a skillet, and needed air.

"Why are *you* nervous. Mamma?"

"Don't know, honey. Just am."

As the gown was being buttoned up the back, Omie came into the room.

"Oh, Polly," she cried. Looking at her sister and niece, she declared, "You two have outdone yourselves. She should be pictured in a fashion magazine!"

Sarah stuck her head in the door. "Good thing I have my new camera ready for photographs!"

The Winder brothers tried to entice Ezra into having a little whiskey, to 'get rid of the jitters'.

"If I have any 'jitters' it's because y'all got me so drunk last night. I'm just fine, thank you very much."

They clapped him on the back and went out to find a private place for a little pre-wedding celebration.

"How can they keep drinkin'?" Ezra asked his daddy and Frank Thomas.

"Sometimes a little 'Hair of the Dog' is needed to cure a hangover," Caleb said.

The other men looked at him like he just spoke gibberish.

"Well, I did have a life before Emmie. And two younger brothers to help sober up way too often."

He thought he saw some newfound respect in Nate's eyes.

"A'right, y'all get out so I can put this monkey suit on," Ezra said.

When he was alone in the room, Ezra looked at his image in Polly's mirror.

*Am I good enough for this woman? Just 'cause we've known each other our whole lives don't mean I'm right for her.*

A scent of roses came to him. The sweet voice of his grandmamma whispered, "You were made for each other, my darlin' boy. Never doubt it."

He took a deep breath, wiped his eyes, and began to dress.

Jewel arrived with Mrs. O'Dell and a change of clothes for Frank Thomas. He held her close and murmured, "What would I ever do without you?"

"Let's hope you never have to know," she replied with a kiss.

The front benches were decorated with bows to show where family would sit. Other folks began to fill the benches behind. Some of Polly's students and their parents were in attendance, as well as friends who'd watched Polly and Ezra grow up together. Some of Aunt Julia's kin, Alberta and her family came, bringing offerings of food.

The minister walked into the garden with a bible in his hand and a large smile on his face. He greeted everyone as he passed by, many of them his parishioners. When he turned to face the house, he talked about memories of Kate and Frank, how they had grown up together.

"This old house has held a lot of love. It pleases me no end to think of more generations filling it."

Phoebee walked down the aisle on the arm of the eldest Winder brother, Kurt, who seated her, then returned inside to escort the bride. Granny and Welda were escorted by the other brothers. Omie followed with Nate, taking their places in the front as well.

Once all the family were seated, Frank Thomas went to stand by the porch steps with his guitar in hand. Jewel stood beside him, and they began to sing, *It Had to be You,* then, *Dream a Little Dream of Me.*

Ezra walked out, looking very uncomfortable to be the center of attention. He took his place beneath the rose arbor and focused on the door where his bride-to-be would soon emerge.

There were whispers behind the screen, and Frank Thomas began the first notes of *Here Comes the Bride.*

Everyone rose as Emmie and Bitsy stepped out to hold the screen door open. Kurt emerged first, helping the bride through the door. He offered his arm, and Polly stood by his side a moment, taking in the scene. Without her glasses, things were a bit fuzzy. This had the effect of blending all the blooms into a watercolor scene. She focused on Ezra's face, and nodded she was ready.

Voices exclaimed *what a beautiful bride* as Polly passed. Georgia Rose followed behind, keeping the veil from getting caught in the roses.

It was all Ezra could do to keep from bursting with joy as she stepped up beside him.

What Polly could see clearly was the love on his face as he took her hand. The minister's words seemed far away as they gazed at one another. When vows were called for, Grace walked up carrying a small embroidered pillow topped with a nest of ribbons, in which the rings lay.

No one tried to hold back tears as these two young people said their promises and Ezra bent to kiss his bride. Cheers rang out when the minister pronounced them man and wife.

Hugs and handshakes were given as the bride and groom made their way back up the path. Sarah set the camera up on a tripod in front of the arch for pictures once the couple had mingled with the crowd for a bit.

Omie and Welda finally managed to corral all the Winders to pose for Sarah. The Silar family was next, and then variations of the two groups.

Under the old oak, tables made from sawhorses and boards had been set up and covered with snowy white cloths. The women had carried what seemed an endless stream of food from wagons and autos, and up from Omie's kitchen, until there was no room left for another bowl or platter.

As the merriment went on, Omie took a few moments to step over to the well and look back at the scene. Family and friends sharing joy, celebrating each other's good fortune. As had always been done. She could *See* the faint lights of loved ones who'd passed, moving among the living. Kate, Frank, Aunt Julia. Others who must have belonged to the Winders, too.

Emmie waved at her sister from the doorway and Omie went to help bring out the wedding cake.

Maizie shook her head as she cautiously eyed the ornate, many-tiered cake on a side table.

"How we gonna get that thing out the door and down them steps? There's no place to put it, neither."

Omie considered the situation for a moment and replied, "I guess we'll just have to take the table too."

Maizie stepped to the back door and called, "Thomas, git in here!"

The three women and Thomas each took a corner, easing out the door, then carefully making their way down the steps.

Adults and children clapped with excitement as Ezra and Polly walked over, hand in hand.

Polly looked at Emmie and said, "It's just too beautiful to cut!"

"No more beautiful than you are, my dear. Let me help."

Once the first piece was removed and shared between the bride and groom, she and Omie passed slices around.

"Can you believe this day has come?" Omie slipped an arm around her sister's waist. Emmie laid her head on Omie's shoulder.

"I'm as happy for them as if they were my own."

"Won't be long before you'll be watching Bitsy walk down the aisle."

"Oh, Omie!" Emmie looked as if the thought had never occurred to her. "I am not ready for that!"

Polly called for all the single women to gather so she could toss her bouquet. As it flew through the air, the oldest of Kurt's daughter leapt up and caught it.

Phoebee and Sarah walked up to Omie, commenting on the sudden absence of the men in the family. Looking around, they saw Jewel whispering something in Ezra's ear. He came to stand beside his bride and they thanked everyone for coming.

Lines were formed and rice tossed as the couple headed toward the barn where the truck was waiting to carry them to Tybee Island. It was surrounded by grinning men. So many cans were attached to the bumper, it looked as if a grocery truck had lost its load. *Just Hitched* and various epitaphs to Ezra's freedom were scrawled on the windows.

Ezra and Polly ran past the truck. No one had seen Jewel sneak in front of her car and crank it. She stood up and stepped aside as the couple jumped in. Polly leaned out and waved goodbye as they drove away, leaving the women laughing and the men staring after in disbelief.

Omie noticed Ada Kate standing among the crowd, waving, with one hand resting on her belly. Omie closed her eyes and said a prayer of thanks.

"Mamma!" Grace was tugging at Omie's skirt. "I have a message for Phoebee and Tadpole from a man. He says he's sorry."

"Thank you, baby, I'll tell them later."

Grace ran off to play with the other children again.

She shook her head.

*Even in death you can't get it right, Ephram. She's Pollywog, not Tadpole. Sorry, today is not a day for digging up the past, but a day of planting seeds for the future.*

A large shadow passed overhead. Omie looked up to see a great blue heron flying toward the river. She closed her eyes and waited to feel a sense of the *Sight.* Her mamma had told her that herons sometimes carried messages from the beyond.

*Please, only good news.*

A loud *Grok!* Sounded nearby and she opened her eyes to see another heron, the first one's mate, she supposed. They headed toward a tall cypress on the river bank.

*Sometimes a bird is just a bird. May you find an abundance of fish and frogs.*

Her heart soared with them. She turned and walked back toward the people she loved, wrapped in the perfect rightness of this day.

# About the author

*In memory of our Little Liza Jane*

Rebecca Holbrook grew up steeped in the rich culture of the south. Her mother's people were some of the first settlers around Savannah, Georgia. Their stories, passed down through generations, inspired her first book, Omie's Well, which won the 2024 Nancy Pearl Award for Literary Fiction. Its sequel, The Deer Stone, was published in 2026. She has been a banjo player, songwriter, poet and storyteller for many years. Rebecca moved from Tennessee to the Pacific Northwest with her husband and editor, Gary. She spends her time hiking, writing, making music and finding joy in life.

www.ingramcontent.com/pod-product-compliance
Lightning Source LLC
Chambersburg PA
CBHW070302310726
48976CB00005B/1542